# Bloodfire and the Legend of Paradox Pond

## a novel

## Rosemarie Sheperd

D1520639

*Bloodfire and the Legend of Paradox Pond* is a work of fiction. Names, characters, businesses, places, events and incidents are either products of the author's imagination or used in a purely fictitious manner. Any resemblance to actual persons, living or dead, or actual events is purely coincidental.

I dedicate this humble accomplishment to Michael, David, and Sally, my three greatest accomplishments.

To Michael, the first to strongly encourage me to put *Bloodfire* online.

To David, my mentor and colleague in writing, for his priceless counsel, guidance and encouragement and for teaching me how drama works.

To Sally, for her honesty and creative insight. Without her innovation and technical assistance *Bloodfire* would never have seen the light of day.

To Joe, my husband and my best friend, for his deep love and support, for his tireless encouragement and feedback and for his constant faith in me.

# Chapter 1

**Port St. John, New York**
**Morgan Matthias**
**May 22, 2008**

A chill spring breeze passed through her kitchen window. It tousled the curtains, ruffled the fronds of a hanging fern and brushed against Morgan Matthias, making her shiver. As she leaned over the sink and closed the window she heard papers rustling behind her, as though closing the window had shut the breeze in rather than shutting it out.

Morgan closed her eyes and smiled. The paper *rustler* had to be Chuck. He'd missed her enough to cut his trip short. He knew she loved surprises as much as he loved reading *The Times*. He must've spotted *The Times* on the counter between the phone and a brand new camera still in its blister package. Buying the camera and *The Times* on impulse today had seemed like the right thing to do, except for one thing.

Morgan Matthias rarely acted on impulse.

She opened her eyes and turned quickly. As the smile slipped from her face into the empty room, she not only saw the newspaper *rustle,* she watched its pages leaf forward, back, and forward again. Stopping abruptly, *The Times* shifted toward her, prompting her to read.

Shaken, Morgan kept her distance and shook her head emphatically, confirming that whatever she thought she saw happen—most definitely had not happened. Stress manifested itself in many ways–so she'd been told. To say she was stressed was an understatement, but who wasn't these days? Unless her stress was telekinetic she must've opened the paper, promptly forgetting she'd opened the paper. No big deal, really. People did mundane things, forgetting they did them all the time. Didn't they call it muscle memory or acting on auto pilot?

*But she saw the pages turn by themselves from a few steps away with her own eyes.*

Morgan swallowed hard. Okay. So she shut the window after the breeze had rustled the papers. Her rationale was flimsy, but it seemed to silence the voice in her head.

Ignoring an uneasy feeling worming through her, Morgan slid onto a stool, leaned on the counter and frowned at *The Times,* and said, "Houses for Sale?"

Under a color photo the size of a cell phone the caption read: On a hill overlooking Mirror Lake and Lake Placid reigns this Stately Queen Anne, a real painted lady and belle of the ball in her day. Interested? Call Placid Properties at 518-555-7963 for an appointment.

Spellbound, Morgan took in the house. Trimmed in lemon-pie yellow and raspberry cream, the Stately Queen Anne was a decadent pastry, and she was a starving, Dickensian waif with her forehead pressed hard against a bakery shop window.

Gazing at the house, she smelled freshly cut grass and felt the buttery sun warming her face. As a gentle breeze combed through her hair, her stress melted into a calm she hadn't known since before her father had died. Her lips curved into a slow smile at a riot of blood-red tulips that bloomed on both sides of the delectable house's porch steps.

Running her finger along the roof past the gable, she stopped on the tower and frowned, wondering why its window and the second floor bedroom window beneath it were white while the rest of the windows were black. Shrugging it off as a misprint, she pulled a pen from a holder next to the phone. Heart pounding, she grasped the ruby red pendant she always wore and circled the number.

Morgan dropped the pen. What in God's name was she doing? If she thought she could actually buy that house she wasn't stressed, she was in deep psychological trouble. No surprise there. Teaching by day and dealing with her senile, abusive mother at night was doable while Chuck was at home. But he went to Australia on business so often lately she felt overwhelmed and abandoned—a lethal cocktail that had her on the brink of emotional collapse. She suddenly realized if she didn't take action soon, she really would have a breakdown.

Change. That's what she needed.

Change was good. And a change in her life was long overdue.

A soothing residue from the old Victorian lingered, and Morgan smiled at the ad. If the house was as fantastic as the Placid Properties' caption said, why not make that change now? On one hand the timing was perfect but on the other? The calm she'd felt just looking at the photo had trumped any and all trepidations. She'd give the world to feel it again.

Her mind made up, Morgan ran jittery fingers down the links of a silver chain to the ruby pendant hanging around her neck. As a little girl she'd believed the pendant was her good luck charm. It was only paste and glass, but wearing the heart shaped stone in its sparkling setting close to her own heart had always calmed her and made her feel safe.

She fondled the ruby-red stone in the center. Squeezing the pendant, she frowned at an irony that had always puzzled her. The pendant used to belong to her mother, a person with whom she'd never felt calm or safe. In retrospect, it seemed that the pendant was the only thing that Mother had ever loved. Mother knew Morgan loved it too. One day when Morgan was very young, Mother had taken the pendant from her own neck and clasped it around Morgan's. It was a perfectly sweet and mother-like thing to do, except—

Mother hated her.

So why would she give Morgan such a cherished possession? Morgan sighed, let go of her past and the pendant and studied the ad. Even though Chuck and she loved winter sports and had toyed for years with the idea of settling in Lake Placid, she couldn't consider any house without running it by him first, unless this was the real deal or she fell head over heels at first sight. But she wasn't the type, and when was the price ever right?

Morgan looked at the digital camera near *The Times*, still in its blister packing. Why in the world had she bought it? The receipt was in her purse. While deciding whether to return it, she sized up her kitchen, wondering how it compared with the Stately Queen Anne's.

Wooden cabinets gobbled up most of the wall, leaving eighteen suffocating inches between cabinets and countertops. The remaining walls were papered with red, green and gold fruits and flowers, a sorry attempt at still life that might've brightened the kitchen once, but years of boiling and frying had dulled it to a stew of colors she couldn't identify, colors that dwarfed light and space despite a large picture window.

The dining and living rooms housed an eclectic mix of nondescript furniture and forgettable knickknacks. Mother's bedroom, along with hers and Chuck's, had heavy-legged beds and mahogany dressers with deep, dust filled, wound-like grooves.

Suddenly, Morgan realized that her mother's dreary house was a metaphor for her life. A call to Placid Properties could change that, if for once in her life, she had the guts to let it.

She checked her wristwatch against a clock over the kitchen window. It was three in the afternoon, and despite the bright sun and blue skies the kitchen was dark and oppressive.

That did it.

She grabbed her pendant and looked at the circled number. Her eye wandered toward the phone and back to the photo. She bit her lip, grabbed the phone and stopped in mid-air. She held her breath, stared at the ceiling and listened. Mother was upstairs asleep. It was now or never. She checked the ad again and dialed quickly.

The phone rang. Morgan paced. She stopped and frowned. Her feet ached. She kicked off her black high-heels, wiggled her toes and let out a sigh of relief. Teaching five English classes a day, five days a week for thirty years at Port St. John High, she should know by now to wear shoes that made sense. The phone clicked.

"Placid Properties, Maggie Duran speaking."

"Ms. Duran, my name is Morgan Matthias and—"

"Could you hold for a moment, please, Ms. Matthias?" The phone clicked again.

Morgan hunched over the counter, leaned on her forearm and reread the ad. A Victorian on a hill in a bowl of mountains, overlooking Lake Placid and Mirror Lake sounded too good to be true, *ergo* it probably was. The ad said call for a price. Morgan smirked. A blind fish could see that hook. The realtor would reel her in and spring an insane price. But right now she realized she was desperate enough to agree to any price.

"Ms. Matthias?"

Morgan straightened up. "Ms. Duran?"

"Sorry for the delay. I'm the only one manning the phones today. I'll be a while longer. I can return your call if—"

"No." Morgan interrupted. She ran shaky fingers through her hair. "I mean, um, it's okay. I'll hang on. Thanks."

"Okay then." Maggie Duran clicked off.

Upstairs bedsprings suddenly creaked. Morgan winced. She clutched her pendant, froze and stared at the kitchen ceiling. A muffled voice groaned. One heavy foot fell. A second was followed by the familiar thump of her mother's rubber-tipped cane. With every footfall that rattled the ceiling light, Morgan's heart pounded harder.

Mother was gaining weight as quickly as she was losing her mind. Standing five-five and weighing two-fifty and counting, Mother had become impossible for Morgan to handle alone. The doctors suspected senility due to old age complicated by a series of mini-strokes. With her numbers out of sight, Mother had passed hazardous on the radar a hundred pounds ago. That was another mystery. Mother had been obese ever since Morgan could remember, but Daddy claimed that Mother had been a knockout when they met. And when she flashed her flint-blue eyes, men didn't stand a chance. Neither had her sweet, loving father, and by the time he realized what he'd signed on for, it was too late.

Dr. Mendoza said there was an opening at the best assisted living facility in Port St. John but she had to act fast. Morgan glanced at the Pine Bush Acres brochure she'd left on a small Formica table in the breakfast nook in front of the picture window facing their modest back yard. Mother had been uncooperative and irascible as usual. Convincing her to move by Sunday of Memorial Day Weekend had taken some doing. Not one to mince words, Dr. Mendoza made his prescription clear. Lose weight or die. Living in a home where caregivers made Mother stick to a diet could save her life. Mother reluctantly agreed and then reneged the next day. The papers had been signed and money had changed hands. There was no going back, a fact that did little to ease Morgan's conscience. On his deathbed Daddy had made her promise not to abandon Mother. No matter how neurotic and miserable a bitch Mother had been, Morgan kept the promise. Thirty years ago after they'd married, Chuck and she had moved into Mother's house. Lately, if she mentioned Chuck, Mother would fly into a rage and scream, "Stop pretending that Chuck and you are married!"

Morgan glanced at the ad with a pounding heart. After all these years, would Chuck and she actually have a place of their own? Her father's face loomed in her mind. She hoped he understood that she wasn't breaking her promise. She just couldn't keep it any longer.

When Daddy's face dissolved into Mother's, Morgan knew she would never buy a house of her own anywhere. The longed-for change, so close moments ago, was fading like the wallpaper. She couldn't fight Mother on this alone. She needed Chuck. Why did she read that damned ad? What made her buy the camera or pick up the phone? This was all wrong, a horrid mistake—

"Ms. Matthias?"

The ceiling groaned and Morgan looked up. Her heart raced. She closed her eyes and squeezed her pendant.

"Yes, Ms. Duran."

"Call me Maggie, please. I'm sorry for the delay."

"I'm calling about the Victorian." Morgan said, praying the house had sold and praying it hadn't.

"My God, you should've told me that right away."

"Have you taken poetic license or is it as lovely as you say?"

"Lovelier." Maggie laughed. "But I'm biased. Why not come by this weekend and have a look?"

"I'll need a price." Morgan closed her eyes, squeezed the pendant harder and frowned. Did Maggie just blow out a breath?

"Two hundred thousand."

Stunned, Morgan opened her eyes. The money that she and Chuck had saved by living with Mother would make a decent down payment. She knew nothing of mortgage rates, but to make ends meet, she could tutor and Chuck could treat extra patients.

This was her chance. Should she take it?

The upstairs toilet flushed.

Morgan darted an anxious glance at the ceiling. With Mother living at Pine Bush Acres, why would she need to move at all?

"Hello?" Maggie said.

"I'm here but I - I'm not sure. My husband's out of town. I probably should wait until--

*On the kitchen counter the digital camera whirred on.*

Losing focus, Morgan stared without seeing.

*A haze clouded the lens. The clouded lens zoomed out, straining blindly against the blister packing.*

"Ms. Matthias? Are you still there?"

Morgan shook her head and blinked. She smiled and let go of her pendant. "Yes," she laughed softly. "And a bit flabbergasted at the price. Call me Morgan, please," she said, smiling.

"Morgan, the price is only the beginning. Trust me. I know this is Memorial Day weekend, but what do you say?"

"I say I'd be crazy to pass it up."

"Terrific."

Morgan could almost hear Maggie smile.

Damn. She'd made arrangements to move Mother into Pine Bush Acres on Saturday and Sunday. Morgan fondled her pendant.

"We have to meet on Monday, Memorial Day itself."

"No problem. By the way, where are you coming from?"

"Port St. John." Morgan answered.

"Do you know how to get to Lake Placid?"

"Who doesn't?" Morgan said, smiling so broadly her cheeks ached. "How about one o'clock?"

Maggie laughed. "That works for me. We're on Marcy and Main. See you then."

# Chapter 2

## Morgan

Morgan clicked *end*, put the phone on the counter and listened to Mother descend step-by-gargantuan step until her cane thumped on the floor at the base of the stairs. As Mother made her way through the dining room, bumping table and chairs, the floor moaned under her weight, and china and glassware danced on the breakfront shelves.

Eyeing the ad, Morgan bit her lip. Deciding to keep the Lake Placid house a secret until after the Pine Bush Acres move would not be an easy task. Morgan was not a good liar.

Morbidly obese, Lucy filled the doorway. Cane first, she stepped into the kitchen. The floor groaned and Morgan sighed. Lucy had burst the seams of decent, off-the-rack clothing decades ago. Respecting her father's wishes, Morgan had hired a seamstress to tailor-make several outfits. The stylish, but wrinkled black slacks and white man-tailored blouse Lucy wore now had been one of several.

Morgan grasped the pendant. "Did you have a nice nap, Mother?"

"How can I when I know it's the last nap I'll take under my own roof?" Lucy wore her usual pained expression.

Morgan chose not to react. "Your blouse and pants look like a road map. Did you sleep in them?"

"I did."

Lucy raised a pudgy hand and smoothed her wrinkled blouse. Her chunky fingers probed her mammoth breasts and found her glasses. They hung on a croaky around her neck. She perched them on her nose and blinked accusingly at Morgan.

"No thanks to my daughter who stays after school helping strangers' brats instead of coming home to do a wash so her mother can have a clean nightgown."

Morgan ignored the bait. Mother was into her eighty-eight-going-on-terrible-two routine. In other people, being irrational was a curable habit. In Mother it was a birth defect. Heart thumping, Morgan told herself she was a sensible, mature, intelligent woman who must stop feeling prepubescent every time Mother walked into the room.

Lucy ran her chunky fingers through short, severely parted gray hair. She shuffled past Morgan in fluffy beige slippers and squeezed her voluminous self into a vinyl-cushioned booth in the breakfast nook. She sniffed with disdain at the Pine Bush pamphlets on the table and turned her back to the picture window. Her fingers coiled like bloated slugs around the handle. She tapped her cane on the floor, jiggling the flesh that hung from her arm. She squinted at Morgan, and said, "Your phone conversation woke me up. You don't have any friends, so who the hell were you talking to?"

Morgan averted her eyes. "Tea?" she asked, skirting the question. She grabbed a kettle from the stove, walked to the sink and filled it.

Lucy's frown puckered the flesh between her eyebrows into meaty creases. "Tea? Yes." She shivered. "Didn't you turn the heat up?"

"This morning for two hours. It's almost June, Mother. Heating season is mostly over. You know gas and oil prices went crazy ever since that hurricane Katrina. The whole country is still economizing," she rambled on uncomfortably, wondering how many issues she'd have to skirt before the weekend was over and Mother was safely tucked away in Pine Bush Acres. "It's a great day. I thought we'd let the sun—"

Lucy banged her cane on the floor, cutting Morgan off.

"Well, you thought wrong." Her pugnacious tone made her voice grate like fork tines on slate. "Heating season's never over for an old woman." She squinted at the kitchen clock above the sink. "Forget the tea. It's almost dinnertime. What are we eating?"

"Dr. Mendoza said—"

"Mendoza? Don't mention that traitorous bastard to me."

Determined to stay calm, Morgan set the kettle on the stove. "You need to eat light." She opened the refrigerator. "I've got chicken soup and a garden salad."

"You can shove your chicken soup, garden salad and these," she raised her tree-trunk of an arm and swept the Pine Bush pamphlets off the table, "where the sun don't shine."

Morgan's calm wavered. She closed the fridge and looked down at the storm of pamphlets on the floor. "How did my father marry a vulgar woman like you? You and he weren't just polar opposites you were antithetical."

"Speak English." Lucy slid one beefy, overlapping cheek at a time off the vinyl cushion. Grunting, she got to her feet and jutted her jaw in Morgan's direction. "And who the hell are you calling vulgar?"

Morgan stifled a gasp. Lucy was dangerously close to the counter.

Morgan glanced at *The Times*, cursing herself for leaving it in plain sight. She darted her gaze to her mother. Desperate to keep her moving past the ad, Morgan kept talking.

"You've been humiliating me since I was little. Actually, Mother, vulgar doesn't cut it. You must've come from a place where creatures ate their young to control the birth rate!"

As Lucy squinted harder, Morgan clenched her fist and realized her hand was empty. She was so focused on getting her mother past the ad she had actually taken a stand without needing to clutch her pendant. Chuck always said she didn't need a charm to fight Lucy. The power was in her. She just had to tap it. He was right, and it felt so good it made her smile.

Lucy took another step. "Wipe that smirk off your face." Her lip quivered. "You're talking to your mother. The woman who raised you after your father dropped dead and made her a helpless widow."

Morgan scoffed, eyeing *The Times.* One more step.

"You? Helpless? You're about as helpless as a pit bull." On a roll, she continued. "My father was a saint to put up with you. If he were here, things would have turned out differently."

Lucy stopped walking and Morgan held her breath.

"You bet your sweet little ass. He never would've let you team up with Mendoza to throw me out of my house like yesterday's garbage." Lucy pounded the paper. The camera jumped. She glanced down and frowned at the circled ad.

"What's this?"

"What's what?" Morgan said, keeping her tone neutral.

"Don't play dumb." Her finger followed the column back to *Houses for Sale.* "This."

Morgan fingered her pendant. "It's a house for sale."

"Tell me something I don't know." Lucy glared at her.

"In Lake Placid." So much for skirting issues.

Lucy's flint-blue eyes widened. Her mouth sagged and she swallowed as if her throat hurt. Not the reaction Morgan expected. "Where?" Lucy said.

"Lake Placid."

Morgan frowned. To survive childhood she had become adept at reading her mother. Mother and fear was an oxymoron. She'd bet Lucy Quick had never feared anything in her life. Morgan glanced at *The Times*. Afraid of what? An ad in a paper?

The fear clearly forgotten, Lucy smirked. "I see. You put me away, sell my house and use my money to buy a house in, in," Lucy scowled at the ad and shivered. "Did you turn up the heat?"

The doctors said Mother would deteriorate quickly. Long periods of lucidity would alternate with bouts of encroaching senility until the latter enveloped the former. But they didn't know Mother. In Morgan's opinion, Mother had a way to go before being counted out. But fear? That was a new wrinkle.

Lucy stared at the ad. "Where are you going?"

"To see a Victorian that looks too good to pass up."

"Victorian? You're doing this to punish me, aren't you?"

"Punish you?" Morgan frowned, puzzled, and then shrugged it off.

Rather than lie, she dug hard for truthful nuggets. If she talked about retiring before moving her mother into Pine Bush, Mother might feel abandoned. But the desperation she felt right now might make her look stressed enough to pull off an explanation Mother might believe.

"I'm not doing this *to* you I'm doing it *for* me. I'm exhausted. Burned out. I need to recuperate from the school year. A trip to Placid would help. If Chuck were here he'd—"

"Damn you! Stop with this pretend marriage to Chuck! I've listened to your insane fantasy for years. I'm sick and tired of it. Do you hear me?"

Morgan bristled. Chuck may be a sore subject for mother, but he was her husband. "Dr. Mendoza was right, you are senile!"

"Turn up the heat. I'm freezing my ass off."

Senile? Morgan thought, heading for the thermostat in the dining room. Daddy and Mendoza should hear Mother now. Morgan heard Lucy mimic her from the kitchen.

"'I'm exhausted. Burned out. I need to recuperate.' Well that's dandy. And what about me? Do I stay locked up all alone until we're ready to go?"

*We?* "You won't be alone at Pine Bush, Mother." Morgan walked into the kitchen. "You'll have an aide twenty-four, seven."

Lucy banged her cane, adding dents to the already badly pockmarked linoleum. "Aides are strangers ... strangers don't count." She smoothed her hair in short, angry strokes. "If I had my way you'd have gone straight to work. Your father insisted you go to college where children learn at their parents' expense in more ways than one. If I had my - you'd - work - your father – sent- college where," Lucy's voice trailed off. She raised her eyes, and stared as if the rest of her thoughts were written on the ceiling.

# Chapter 3

**Lake Placid, N.Y.**
**Harlan Wainright**
**May 23**

Harlan Wainright held a red mug of hot black coffee under his nose. Steam rose in fragrant ribbons promising flavor decaf never delivered. Ass-deep in the worst slump to hit housing in eighty years, Harlan closed his eyes and sipped, scalding his lips.

"Damn it to hell!"

He set the mug down on his desk, hard. Coffee sloshed over the rim, streaking the white *Placid Properties'* logo with brown tears. He grimaced and hit the intercom. "Hutch!"

Gloria Hutchins, his secretary and loyal friend of twenty-five years, answered cheerfully. "Good morning, Mr. Wainright."

Harlan licked his burning lips and winced. "Get me some paper towels and bring me the Welcome files." He frowned at the coffee. "And Hutch."

"Sir?" She sounded unruffled.

"Brew me some *real* goddamn coffee."

"Roger on the files, Mr. Wainright, but you know what your doctor says about you and caffeine."

Harlan grunted, clicked off and frowned at the red mug. The mug's hairline cracks had turned the white *Placid Properties* logo and contact information into prophetic fragments. Who would've thought that this mug, a cheap promotional stunt, would symbolize the cracking of the empire Harlan Wainright had spent the last forty years busting his balls to build? He toyed with tossing the mug in the can, and then changed his mind.

He stared at his desk. Under coffee-stained contracts, the *New York Times* and the *North Country Tribune* a regional rag, was a leather-bound month-at-a-glance planner. Pushing the clutter aside, he set the mug on Memorial Day. He gazed at a Waterford Crystal ashtray with feathered etchings and a matching whiskey tumbler. Symbols of yesterday's vices, today they held red matchbooks and business cards with the same white contact info as the prophetic mug.

Against a paneled wall stood a bookcase stacked with North Country area maps, *Time, Newsweek, The Economist, Adirondack Life,* and the most perused, *Sports Illustrated.* The wall above the bookcase, a rogues' gallery of photos, showed a younger, leaner Harlan with serious blue eyes and chiseled features being honored by mayors, councilmen and sundry who smiled, knowing goddamned well that Harlan Wainright had never achieved anything according to Hoyle. Harlan's smile implied they could take what they knew straight to hell.

His MBA from the University at Albany and his New York State Realtor's license, the two gems in his mosaic of achievements of which he was the most proud, hung in the center. Harlan lifted his mug, frowned at the decaf and sipped.

Gloria Hutchins knocked softly, opened his office door and approached his desk with paper towels, two thick manila folders labeled "Welcome" and a carafe with an orange collar.

A slender, handsome woman with sharp blue eyes, Hutch wore her grayish blond hair the same way she had the day he'd hired her, parted in the middle and neatly fastened at the back of her neck. She handed him the paper towels and topped off his mug. He finished wiping his fingers and threw the towels into a waste basket under his desk. He looked up and frowned, ignoring the coffee. Hutch met his frown with hers.

"Mr. Wainright, are you okay?" She handed him the files.

The folders felt cool and silky under his touch. He managed a grin. "Just tired, that's all."

Hutch leaned over and put her free hand on his. Her hand felt comforting. He always thought it a shame she'd never married. She would've made one helluva wife.

"Mr. Wainright?" she said. He raised his eyes and looked into hers. She pulled her hand away, awkwardly. "You look pale."

"I'm fine, Hutch, thanks." He sounded unconvincing. He stared at his naked hand. It looked old and defenseless.

A splinter of pain pierced his heart, and he tried to remember. Had he taken the small vial of Nitro from his nightstand this morning? He suppressed the urge to grope his breast pocket. A bead of sweat pearled above his lip. He kept his eyes unreadable, willing the pain to subside. Only his doctor knew about these little events, and that's the way it would stay. For now.

"Hutch?" He shifted the papers on his desk, keeping his voice businesslike despite the pain. "Is Maggie in yet?"

"No." Hutch stared at him, frowning.

Knowing her frown had nothing to do with his question, he looked away. "How about Kevin?"

"He was here. But a guy who saw our sign on the Essex Café came in. Kevin took the file and walked down there with him."

"That's my boy," Harlan said, taking a shallow breath. He managed a crooked grin. "Zeroing in like a heat-seeking missile." He tapped the Welcome files. "I want to see Maggie the minute she gets in. And Hutch?"

"Yes, Mr. Wainright?"

"Get the door on your way out." He waved, dismissing her.

Harlan patted his chest, felt the vial, reached into his breast pocket and pulled it out along with a white linen handkerchief. He uncapped the vial and stared at the pills, assessing his pain level. Maybe the pain was indigestion, but he'd pop one just to be safe. He mopped the sweat from his lips and capped the vial. He slipped the vial and handkerchief into his side jacket pocket and breathed a sigh of relief.

He opened a file drawer on his right, reached under a pile of leases behind "Z" and pulled out a box of Cuban cigars. He put the Welcome files on his desk, set the cigar box beside them and lifted the lid. Taped on the inside cover was a Polaroid shot of the only woman he'd ever loved.

In the photo Lilly Duran stood on a sandy wedge of Mirror Lake beach, smiling at him with lips he could still taste. The wind had parted her hair, exposing a luscious shoulder. Her dress, a blizzard of violets on turquoise chiffon, fell in sheer folds over breasts and thighs sweeter and more velvet than any flower God ever created. He'd taken the photo on Mirror Lake opposite Cobble Hill Road, a secluded spot surrounding an English Tudor. He'd built the house as a wedding present for Lilly. He still lived in it alone.

Harlan loosened his tie and reached in the box. He'd promised himself that legal or not he'd always have Cuban cigars. He thought he'd always have Lilly too. He bit the tip off, jammed the cigar between his teeth, grabbed a matchbook, pulled a match and struck it.

The flame danced in his breath. At that moment he'd give all he owned to light the goddamned cigar. He cursed his doctors and blew the flame out before it burned his fingers. He tossed the cigar in the box and picked up his coffee. The mug left a black ring on Memorial Day. He hoped it wasn't an omen. He'd had enough bad luck over the years to fill ten lifetimes.

He sipped and grimaced. The coffee was cold. He put the mug aside and caressed Lilly's picture. He glared at the Welcome files, hating the day he'd first laid eyes on the Stately Queen Anne and remembering the reasons why he could never walk away.

The early seventies had brought rumblings about Lake Placid hosting the 1980 Winter Olympics. Smelling a huge return, Harlan had quietly mortgaged himself into the twenty-first century, grabbing key properties. The Welcome place had been one of them.

Steeped in Lake Placid realty since the sixties, Harlan knew that Jared Welcome, a wealthy Lake Placid merchant, had built the Victorian as a wedding present for his bride. Five years after moving in, both Welcomes had mysteriously frozen to death in the bedroom below the tower. Believing the house was haunted or worse yet-cursed had tanked its appeal. The few times he'd managed to sell it, the house had not remained sold.

As a pragmatist, Harlan believed the failure to sell the Welcome house had more to do with what the Victorian would cost to restore than any haunted-house bullshit. As a businessman he knew out-of-town buyers would kill for a Stately Queen Anne on a hill in the Adirondacks, overlooking Mirror Lake and Lake Placid, within walking distance of the village.

Curses and haunting aside, what better or safer investment could he make than a house on ground high enough to evade the infamous hundred-year-flood, due to hit any year now?

Rumors had scared the competition shitless, so Harlan had acquired the house quickly, given it a facelift and put it on the market. He'd covered all bases. Waiting was the hard part.

The Olympics had been in full swing. To his surprise few properties sold. The Welcome house had not been among them. He'd barely turned a profit. Between taxes and upkeep he had to do something drastic or the ink on his ledgers would be redder than his goddamned mug.

One night Harlan dreamt he was standing alone in the dark Welcome tower, buck naked, when something cold and wet *caressed* him. With every hair on his ass standing at attention, he sucked in a strangled breath and woke in an icy sweat.

The next morning he'd ordered his staff to find a buyer for that goddamned house. To prove he meant business, he said he'd not only hold a cut-rate mortgage, he would personally triple the selling agent's commission—with two provisos. The buyer must be subject to his approval—no questions asked—and the house had to *stay* sold, adding, if he'd had that incentive as a rookie, he'd have sold every house in the Love Canal despite its toxic bowels.

In 1983 against her will, Lilly had shown the Welcome house to the Connellys, a couple from Florida, and their thirteen-year-old son, Tommy. Jenna, the wife, had loved the house, but as the new chef at the Bradford House, her husband Tom, would not earn enough to afford it.

That night Harlan dreamt he was naked in the mist in the tower, but this time the cold, wet thing had wrapped itself around him so tightly, he'd stopped breathing. He woke choking and gasping for air. The next day after making an arm-twisting phone call, the Connellys qualified and bought the house. And Harlan's nightmares had stopped.

One month after the Connellys had moved in, Jenna found Tommy frozen to death in the same bedroom where the Welcomes had met the same fate. The news spread faster than wildfire, scaring the bejesus out of everyone, even Harlan.

That night the police found Lilly in her nightgown, wandering Midlakes Road, dazed and blaming herself for Tommy's death. She claimed she had seen an apparition in the tower the first time she'd showed the Connellys the house. Lilly believed if she had fully disclosed, they never would've bought the house and Tommy would be alive. She got hysterical, insisting the apparition or something in that house had killed Tommy. Her doctor prescribed a rest at High Peaks Sanitarium.

To this day Harlan swore to himself that Tom Connelly had been the right buyer, God help him, the buyer the house *wanted.* If Lilly found out Harlan had strong-armed Jack Bradford into paying Connelly enough to afford the house, she'd blame him for Tommy's death, and he'd lose her forever. After the kid died, Harlan's nightmares had returned with a vengeance, along with an obsession to find the right buyer.

His office wavered before his eyes. His face felt doughy and sweaty. A fist of anxiety grabbed his heart. His mouth twisting in pain, he held his breath. He reached into his side pocket. The vial of Nitro slipped through his trembling fingers to the floor and rolled under his desk. The fist squeezed his heart tighter. He slid off his chair onto all fours and clutched the vial. His back pressed against the desk drawers, he panted and snapped the cover. He dumped the tiny white pills into his hand, stuck one under his tongue and leaned his head back, sweating harder. His spasm on the wane, he pulled the handkerchief from his pocket and swabbed his forehead and lips. Taking quick, shallow breaths, he put the remaining pills in the vial and capped it. He closed his eyes and breathed slowly. He got to his knees, clutched the seat and knelt. He grabbed the corner of his desk, lifted himself into his chair and laid his head on the desk.

The Connelly kid's death had dredged up ancient Welcome history, attracting thrill-seeking horror freaks to the village like sharks to a bloody carcass. That house had been bleeding him out. The roof had sagged, the paint was chipped and fading and the front porch needed shoring up. But the Olympics fiasco had left him overextended. He had to stop the repairs and put the house back on the market as it was. Before he did that he needed to know everything the authorities knew about the Connelly kid's death. He'd summoned Police Chief Oberdon, a rogue on his office gallery wall, and asked him point blank.

"Are there any leads? And tell me something the North Country Tribune is not already reporting for Chrissakes!"

"We're withholding information that only the perpetrator could know." The chief had said, stretching his neck as if his collar were two sizes too small.

Harlan leaned forward. "Which is?"

Oberdon rubbed his lips. "Harlan, you know I can't—"

"Damn it!" Harlan had slammed his fist on the desk.

"This is confidential, Harlan. If you tell anyone—"

"Do you take me for a fool? I've got a fortune riding on that house."

Oberdon sighed. "The kid was frozen so badly his arms and legs snapped like dead branches from a dead tree. Blood, bone and flesh hit the floor, shattering on contact like ancient Chinese pottery and littering the room like confetti."

Thirty years later there was no new evidence, but Oberdon's words still stopped the blood in Harlan's veins. Imagine the hype if the press had had *all* the facts.

With sales finally on a slow but steady rise, Harlan had given his contractors the green light to get the Welcome place ready. That was a year ago. Now those pain-in-the-ass economists predicted housing would bleed out by the end of the fiscal year.

His chest tightened. Harlan touched Lilly's photo. He closed his eyes and waited for the iron fist squeezing his chest to let go. If things had been different, he and Lilly would be celebrating their twentieth anniversary. Harlan hit the intercom.

"Maggie's not in yet, sir," Hutch said, as if predicting the question.

"Why the hell not? It's almost time to call it a day."

"She's at the high school with Natalie's vice principal."

Harlan closed his eyes. "If Maggie's niece doesn't stop sucking the life out of her—"

"Sir? Maggie just walked in."

Harlan closed the lid and put the cigar box in the drawer.

"Send her in immediately."

# Chapter 4

**Lake Placid**
**Maggie Duran**

"Maggie, Mr. Wainright wants you in his office yesterday."

"I know, Hutch." Maggie closed the door behind her and walked through a grouping of overstuffed burgundy leather chairs. She dropped her plum bag and matching gloves on a coffee table piled with magazines. She slipped off her teal spring coat and hung it on a rack against the right wall. "Any calls?"

Hutch held up a bright pink *While You Were Out* slip. Maggie brushed the lint from her lilac cashmere sweater and pinstriped black pants and glanced at the slip. She picked up her bag and gloves, put them on her desk and read the message.

"A Morgan Matthias from Port St. John called at nine about the Welcome place," Hutch said, sorting the mail on her desk.

"Hmmm." Maggie frowned. "She called yesterday while I was here alone and made an appointment. I hope she's not canceling."

Maggie looked at Harlan's office door. It was closed. Her watch said 11:30. She loosened a thick knot of hair at the back of her neck, shook it free, and then retied it.

"Ms. Matthias left her number." Hutch said, frowning at a neon-orange flyer, advertising a Gypsy Bazaar coming to Lake Placid on Saturday, July twelfth. "She's moving her mother into a nursing home." Hutch ripped the flyer in half and tossed it into her waste basket. "She said she'd call back later."

Maggie narrowed her eyes and motioned at Kevin's desk. "Does he know about this?" She waved the pink paper in the air.

"No. He's showing the Essex Cafe. Ms. Matthias called right after he left."

"Good." Maggie knew damned well that Harlan planned on using Kevin to squeeze her harder about selling.

"Do me a favor will you, Hutch? Can you keep this," she held up the pink slip, "between you and me for now? Please?"

"Sure thing, Maggie."

"Thanks." Maggie flexed her fingers and rubbed her hands together. On the counter at the rear of the office was a BUNN coffee maker with two carafes. Both were half full. Maggie filled a PPI mug with regular and walked past Hutch's desk to the reception area. "I'll be with Harlan. If Ms. Matthias calls, interrupt us no matter what. Please."

"You bet." Hutch winked and Maggie smiled.

She knocked, opening Harlan's door. "You wanted to see me?"

"Come in," Harlan said, folding his hands on the desk.

She set her mug on his desk and pulled up a chair.

"Well." He leaned back in his chair. "You look stunning as always. Cashmere sweater." He sniffed the air emphatically. "Do I smell Chanel number five?"

Maggie chuckled and shook her head. You had to hand it to him. "Smells great, doesn't it?" She sipped her coffee.

"At ninety-five bucks per quarter ounce, it better."

Maggie put her mug down. "Okay, Harlan. I'm sure you didn't call me in here to talk about my sweater and perfume."

"Indirectly perhaps."

"Really?" She arched her brows in mock surprise. "How so?"

He tapped the Welcome files. "You've got to sell a lot of houses to stay in Cashmere and Chanel. Speaking of which, how's your niece?"

Maggie ignored the barb. Her younger sister, Marcy, and brother-in-law, Mark Sawyer had died in a car crash three years ago, leaving Natalie, thirteen at the time, living with Mom. Her mother needed help, so Maggie had moved back home.

"Nat's got a case of senioritis. She'll graduate soon."

"That's what keeps me awake nights. Too bad," he grumbled.

"Too bad?" Maggie said, thinking, here we go again.

"Too bad the school didn't find Natalie precocious enough to skip two grades. That way she'd already be in college."

Maggie rolled her eyes. Harlan stood up, walked to the front and sat on the corner of his desk. "She's in school full time and she's got you on overload. What will happen when she's on summer vacation?"

"God, Harlan. Please, not now." Maggie picked up her mug.

"If not now, when? I'm serious. I hope that kid's college is prepaid. That way, come September you're home free. If not—"

"I get it, Harlan." She put the mug down.

"You used to get it, Maggie. But now I'm not so sure."

"She's my niece, my dead sister's kid. What am I supposed to do?

Toss her out on her underage ass?"

Harlan grabbed the Welcome files and dropped them in her lap. "Sell this goddamn house or—"

Maggie pictured Kevin and shook her head. "Or the son you always wanted will inherit the kingdom?"

"Something like that." He leaned forward. "You used to be smooth as steel. Kickass. One hell of an operator."

"Used to be? If it weren't for me you—"

"Ancient history." He held up *The New York Times*. "Your new ad wouldn't attract a fly to honey! What are you going to do about it?" He threw the paper down on the desk.

A phone rang and Maggie heard Hutch greet Morgan Matthias.

The intercom buzzed. "It's for Maggie, Mr. Wainright. It's a Ms. Matthias about the Welcome place."

Maggie smiled. "I think Hutch just answered your question."

# Chapter 5

**Maggie**

Maggie Duran hung up smiling. Morgan Matthias was serious. She'd called to reconfirm the price. The deal should be a slam-dunk, her smile waned, provided that damned house wasn't "possessed" like her mother and a few crazy locals believed. It had a spooky past, but the only one possessed was Mom—possessed with guilt over Tommy's death. Maggie closed her eyes.

"Morning, ladies."

Maggie opened her eyes as Kevin Delaney walked through the door with a cardboard tray of assorted sweet rolls.

"Compliments of the Essex Café." He set the tray down on Hutch's desk and pulled out a check. "A binder from the new owner," he said, waving it in the air.

Hutch clapped and laughed. "Congrats, Kevin."

"Thanks, Hutch. Is the boss man in?"

"Care for a breath mint before you enter the hallowed chambers?" Maggie said, annoyed. Hutch's twinkling eyes showed she was enjoying Kevin's moment as much as he was. Either that or Hutch had the hots for Kevin like every other cockeyed female in Essex County, including Natalie, her niece. Why? That was the trillion-dollar question. He may be good looking, if you liked the insipid-jerk type. Maggie pointed a pencil at the check in Kevin's hand. "I'd like to give you some sage advice."

Kevin raised his eyebrows. "As we studs say in poker," he smiled, "I check to the power."

Maggie dropped the pencil on her desk, "Yogi Berra recycled is all I can muster. 'It ain't over till it's over.'"

Kevin sniffed the air, "I smell sour grapes." He picked up the tray and stuck it under Maggie's nose. "Danish?"

Hutch giggled. Maggie stared at him coldly. Kevin Delaney was the most self-centered, egotistical bastard she'd ever laid eyes on. Worse than Harlan or Steve Rivers, an ex-lover, she had lost in a battle over the Welcome place years ago.

Kevin's smugness irked her. Harlan constantly played them against one another. God knows what he'd promised Kevin, who was hungry enough to metaphorically slit her throat to get whatever Harlan was dangling in front of him.

"Whoa, sunshine." Kevin smiled, flashing his dimples.

*Sunshine?* "You mistake me for someone who's not immune.*"*

Pouting, Kevin said, "A simple no, thanks, I'm watching my waistline would be kinder."

Hutch burst out laughing. Maggie shot her a look. Hutch lowered her head, pulled out a tissue and wiped her eyes and mouth, stifling more laughter. Maggie straightened up ready to cut him down, when Natalie pushed through the office door.

"Hey, guys." Nat slipped off a navy blue hoodie.

"Hey, yourself." Kevin smiled.

She blushed, looking at Kevin as if he was the only one in the room. She was sleek in her tight blue jeans. The light wool red sweater matched the red in the plaid flannel lining of her turned up collar and cuffs. Nat dropped by the office a lot since Kevin had signed on, Maggie noticed. Doe-eyed and breathless, Nat flashed her dark almond eyes and smiled slowly. This syndrome broke out whenever she was exposed to Kevin. It made Maggie anxious.

Nat plopped her knapsack on the floor and draped herself on an oversized chair. She ran her slender fingers through long silky hair, picked up a magazine and leafed through it, acting like the adorable high school senior she could be, instead of the insufferable brat that would do her grandmother in if Maggie failed to keep her under wraps.

"Nat, you are hot in red," Kevin said.

Maggie scoffed. If he kept that up, she'd have to sop Nat up from the chair with a giant sponge.

"Thanks," Nat said, hiding her face behind the magazine.

Jesus. Maggie could practically hear Nat's heart beating. She looked at Kevin. Thank God he was twenty-five. At sixteen Nat was jailbait. The havoc a thing between Kevin and Nat could wreak ran Maggie's imagination ragged. But wasn't Kevin hanging out with Kellie Williams, the other waitress at the White Birch Inn?

"Hey, Nat," Maggie frowned. "Why aren't you at work?"

"I stopped by to tell you." She smiled at Kevin and put the magazine on the table. "Tomorrow's senior skip day. So, if Mr. Hornsby calls and says I'm absent, you'll know why."

Maggie was up and out of her seat. "Senior *what* day?"

"Now, sunshine," Kevin teased. "You can't be so old you don't remember senior skip day." He smiled, glancing at Hutch.

Hutch wore a neutral expression. Wise move, Maggie thought. The friction between Maggie and Nat was no laughing matter.

Kevin shrugged Hutch off and looked at Natalie. "Sounds like a blast," he said. His lips curved into an easy smile.

"Yeah," Natalie said. Her smile lingered a little too long.

Nat had dropped her news like a bomb. Instead of causing a scene and embarrassing herself in front of Kevin and Hutch, Maggie gambled that Nat would cooperate. "Can you get your stuff and step outside with me for a minute, please?" Maggie said, in a soft, non-threatening tone.

"Sure." Natalie shrugged, scooping up her knapsack.

Bingo, Maggie thought, relieved.

Natalie smiled at Kevin and Hutch. "Later."

Out on the street, Maggie grabbed Nat's arm. "Are you nuts?"

"Lighten up, *Aunt* Maggie." Natalie jerked her arm away.

"Lighten up? Your vice principal summons me. I leave my job and risk getting fired because you've disrupted or cut class or whatever. Taking your illustrious rap sheet into consideration, do you honestly think I'm going to give you permission to cut school on this," she waved her arm, "this senior skip day?"

Natalie jutted her chin at Maggie. "I didn't ask your permission. It was just a heads up. As long as Harlan is hot for Gran, you'll never get smoked, and you know it."

Maggie couldn't believe Natalie was in tune with the dance going on between Harlan and Mom. "I'm skipping school tomorrow, and you can't stop me."

As Nat turned her back and walked away, Maggie heard the phone ring inside. She watched Nat saunter down Main Street free as you please. "We'll see about that, you little—"

Kevin stepped outside onto the sidewalk. "There's a Morgan Matthias on the line for you."

*Again?* Now Maggie was worried.

Kevin looked down the street. "I can take the call if you have to go after—" He nodded in Natalie's direction.

*"No!"* It came out so sharply Maggie winced inside. Surprise at her strong response showed on Kevin's face. "I mean thanks." She squeezed his arm, "but no thanks." He looked at her hand and frowned harder. Touching him was like flashing a neon sign. She let go. *Damn!* "I mean I'll take the call now and deal with Nat later," Maggie said. Kevin

shrugged and stepped inside.

A neon-green flyer taped to the office window caught Maggie's eye. It advertised a Gypsy Bazaar on Saturday, July twelfth. Remembering Harlan's tirade that Gypsies were bad for business, Maggie tore it from the glass, crumpled it in her hand and followed Kevin inside. She tossed the flyer in the can and picked up the phone on her desk. "Maggie Duran."

Kevin's desk was in front of hers. He pretended to leaf through files, but she'd bet her life he was listening.

"Hi, Maggie. Sorry to bother you," Morgan was saying.

"No worries. What can I do for you?" she said, careful not to call Morgan by name. It might stick in Kevin's pea brain, and she'd be damned if she'd let him sell the Welcome house out from under her.

"Instead of meeting on Monday of Memorial Day Weekend, I'd like to meet on Sunday. After moving my mother to the home that weekend, returning on Monday might be a bit much. I'll stay over Sunday night and then head home on Monday."

"Sounds like a plan."

"Great. See you at one on Sunday."

The phone clicked off in Maggie's ear.

# Chapter 6

**Pine Bush Acres**
**Lucy Quick**

Lucy opened her eyes, started yawning, and stopped abruptly. She moved her head from left to right and grunted herself up on her elbows. She ignored the creaking bedsprings, took in the strange room and figured it out. She died, and Morgan had laid her out in some cut-rate funeral parlor. The floral bedspread and matching curtains, the rosette-strewn rug, two molded plastic chairs were all done in pink and mauve. The window faced a large lawn bordered by balsam pines.

To her right the mahogany chest of drawers and the mirror hanging above it were hers. She eased herself up higher and grunting harder, she reached over her shoulder. The familiar feel of the carved headboard confirmed this was her bed. The nightstand and the brass lamp with the nicked base and beige shade still in its cellophane wrapper, just-the-way-she-liked-it thank you very much, were hers too. So was the digital clock. But the large brown envelope leaning against the lamp did not belong to her.

Reaching for the envelope, Lucy looked down and noticed the pale blue cross-stitch on the white flannel nightgown she wore. She put the envelope on her lap and ran her fingers down an extra-long placket with six buttons. The pin-tuck detailing did it! This nightgown must be a cast-off from a convent. What the hell was the matter with these people, making her sleep in a goddamn nun's nightie? She'd show them, she thought, plucking the buttons off one by one.

Where the hell was she anyway? She stopped plucking and looked at the envelope on her lap. The black print said Pine Bush. Son of a bitch. Morgan actually grew a pair and did it.

Lucy tore the envelope open and fanned the papers on her lap like a giant hand of poker.

An admission application, a brochure with a picture of her goddamn room, a financial disclosure, a medical evaluation, an order *not* to resuscitate, and last but not least burial arrangements! Why that little— she ripped the forms in half and threw them on the floor. Satisfied, she leaned back. She'd lie here and wait to see what happens. She wouldn't even fix her pillow to make herself more comfortable in case there were hidden cameras. Lucy shivered. Why the hell was it so cold in here? Didn't Morgan pay them enough to turn up the heat?

Her eyes crawled around the ceilings and walls, looking for cameras. She wasn't a born-yesterday goddamned fool. "Go ahead, you bastards," she muttered. "Make the first move. Lucy Quick won't give you a goddamned thing. You've got no idea who in the hell you're dealing with, but you'll find out. And damned soon too!" She stuck her chin out. "Yeah. You've got no idea who in the ... but you'll—"

The rest of her words lay in an unspoken pile on her tongue. Suddenly, Lucy was scared. Was she repeating herself like Morgan kept saying she did? No. Morgan was never the sharpest tool in the box even with a college degree.

Determined to get the hell out of here yesterday, Lucy folded plump arms over her ample belly. Being determined felt good, but waiting for *them* to make the first move made her hungry. If she didn't eat now, she'd get a head-mashing migraine that would lay her up for hours. Her stomach growled. She bunched the sheets in her fists. I'm hungry goddamn it. Hungrygoddamnithungrygoddamnit.

"I sacrificed my life for your daughter, Benny. Do you hear me, you miserable bastard wherever you are?" she whispered, nervously scanning the ceilings and walls. "And what do I get? Evicted. Locked away like somebody's crazy old mother-in-law."

In the old days children took care of their parents. Surely Lucy had cared for her mother. She frowned, trying to remember. Bored, she yawned, dismissing it. That was then and this is now.

 Life had gone along just fine until Morgan went to college and met Chuck Matthias. His name still tasted vile on Lucy's tongue. Morgan was naïve and weak, and he was a smart–ass psychiatrist. Schooled in the tricks of his snake-oil trade, Chuck Matthias had turned Morgan against her own mother.

"Well, things don't always work out as planned, do they, *Doctor* Matthias? I fixed your Aussie ass good, didn't I? How did that saying go? "It ain't over till the fat lady sings?"

Lucy chuckled at the irony. Wit and humor! What a surprise to experience both at a time when she thought life had no longer held either. Her laughter subsided, taking her hunger with it. Lucy sniffled and wiped her eyes with the back of her hand.

Benny. Morgan. Chuck. Their names stuck in her throat. Benny

Quick had a talent for doing things wrong. Dropping dead at the wrong time in her life had been his crowning glory. If he'd died before pre-paying Morgan's college, Morgan never would've left home and she never would've met Chuck.

Lucy lay in her bed thinking about the biggest mistakes she'd made in her life. Thank God there had only been two. She'd made the second biggest mistake the first time she got pregnant. Thank God for the suckers that took that kid off her hands. But as long as she lived, Lucy would never forgive herself for the biggest mistake of all.

Marrying Benny Quick.

# Chapter 7

**New York City**
**Lucy**
**1957**

It was Post World War II. The economy was booming. There were plenty of jobs, but war had created a shortage of men. Lucy E. Hadley had landed an entry level job in Midtown Manhattan for American Oil. Armed with ambition and aggression, Lucy had become Executive Assistant to the Vice President of Real Estate. Damn near impossible for women to achieve in the forties and fifties, shortage of men notwithstanding.

A quick study and willing to work harder than her male counterparts, Lucy had gained a well-earned nod from the men "upstairs". Eager to advance, she surveyed the corporate flow chart. She had ambition, but did she still have the ammunition? One night she stood naked in front of her full-length bedroom mirror and took inventory. Medium height. Chestnut brown hair. Cool flint-blue eyes. She smoothed her hands over her breasts, belly and thighs and stepped closer to the mirror. Man, did she still have it! But she was thirty-seven. Crows feet and laugh lines began mapping secondary routes to her nose and mouth. Men still found her sexy, but she had to act while the acting was good.

Lucy had two options: Marry or climb the corporate ladder.

Marriage was great for men. That's why the bastards invented it, but for women marriage was a losing proposition. And who needed it? She had everything married women had, and she usually got it from their husbands. Sizing up the goods, she decided on option two. She'd start with Paul Jacobsen. She'd helped him, and now it was time for him to return the favor.

Her back to the mirror, Lucy glanced over her shoulder at her pear-shaped ass, the one luscious fruit she knew Paul could never resist. She pivoted, scooped a firm breast in each hand, aimed them at the mirror and winked at her reflection.

The corporate ladder it was.

The next day while the grunts were out to lunch, Lucy made her move. She lured Paul into the copy room. He was into her hot and heavy, when the door opened. In walked Helen Flanders, a brown-nosing, stiff-as-a-corset, holier-than-thou, suck up. Helen's eyes swelled to three times their normal size. She dropped her sheaf of price lists and ran out like the devil himself was in hot pursuit.

Paul swore and pushed Lucy aside. He stumbled into his shirt and pants and did up his fly. He ran his hands through his hair, straightened his tie and checked the hall. The coast must've been clear. Without so much as a nod, he bailed.

Lucy fastened her bra and slithered into her slip. She hoisted her panties, garter and hose. To avoid the fools who worked during lunch, she'd pull it together in the powder room. She grabbed her dress, heels and bag and opened the door. The coast was clear. She made the break. Her make-up smeared, her hair tousled and her ample breasts straining against a flimsy bra that barely contained them and a flimsier slip, Lucy crept into the hallway. Dress and heels in hand, she hugged a wall that went on forever, reached the powder room, glanced up and saw Benny Quick, standing by the elevators, mouth open, getting an eyeful.

Benny Quick who had walked in six months ago with impeccable references, degrees up the yin yang and got hired before the ink had dried on his application. To make matters worse the brass had plunked his boring ass two desks behind her. For several skin-crawling seconds their eyes locked.

The next morning Lucy got off the elevator, rounded the corner and heard the typists, jaw-boning at the cooler. Lucy was an embarrassment the brass could no longer afford, no matter how well she did what she did. And everyone knew what that was. Lucy fumed. Jacobsen's ass was as deep in it as hers, but nobody mentioned *him*. Jacobsen, the man, would escape the fire, but Lucy, the woman, would go down in flames.

Like hell she would.

Helen catching Paul and Lucy in the act in the copy room had spread more quickly than the Spanish flu. The men who'd stood in line drooling all over their Brooks Brothers suits to help Lucy yesterday, would avoid her like the clap today. Her past would close in on her, fast. Lucy considered the only option left. Marriage.

Husbands did not grow on trees. She needed her job until she found one. Lucy dug into her bag of tricks and extracted her last, but most powerful tool: Blackmail. A few strategically placed whispers and all the married men would be tripping over each other, helping themselves help her out of their lives.

Part A of her problem was solved. She would keep her job, temporarily. Lucy pondered Part B. The husband.

One day while passing Benny Quick's desk with an ass load of files in her arms, Lucy tripped. He rushed to her side and Lucy scoffed. He certainly was quick—no pun intended—and intelligent. He had a stellar reputation, a dazzling future with the company, and if you could believe those twits in the powder room, he was available. His wife had died a year ago. He had a three or four-year-old kid. His late wife, Martha, an English teacher, had named their daughter Morgan for Morgan le Fay, King Arthur's half-sister. Jesus. Did people like these really exist?

Lucy was not mother material, but she could handle one kid. And if she married Benny, there would be only one kid, and it would *not* be hers. She was pregnant once a long time ago and once had been enough. Anyway, marriage might be a kick. It came with a meal ticket, and she'd be the boss. The more she tried on marrying Benny, the better it fit. He wasn't bad looking and he was definitely interested. She'd bet he hadn't been laid since his wife died. And she had been right.

Poor Benny Quick never stood a chance. Lucy's plan was as old as Adam, the snake, little Eva, and that juicy, red apple: Lucy chased him until he caught her. After they had sex he actually thanked her for screwing him. Gratitude for sex? Now there was a concept.

Her career was in the toilet, but she had the upper hand. He proposed. She said yes with one proviso. She'd quit work and stay home with Morgan. Benny was so delighted he tripped over himself all the way to City Hall to pick up the license.

Benny and Lucy eloped. The next day she marched into work, handed in her letter of resignation, the contents of which had spread through the office faster than poison oak in a nudist colony. Basically it read that she was a mother now, and a mother's place was in the home with her daughter.

Lucy moved into Benny's Manhattan apartment and found three-and-a-half-year-old Morgan exactly as she should be: dull, quiet and easily frightened.

During their alone time, Lucy taught Morgan the rules. A closed bedroom door meant Lucy was napping and did not want to be disturbed. Lucy closed the door. Thinking it was a game Morgan had toddled over and opened it. Lucy tied Morgan to a kitchen chair and went back to bed. When Morgan cried, Lucy stormed in, rummaged through drawers for tape and covered Morgan's mouth. One hour later

Lucy tiptoed into the kitchen and found Morgan asleep in her chair, her cheeks streaked with tears and her nose caked with snot.

Whenever the phone rang, if Morgan was not quiet, Lucy would lock her in the small, dark bedroom closet. If Morgan ate or drank anywhere but the kitchen table, Lucy slapped her hands, chucked the food, and Morgan went down for a nap, hungry. Any toys lying around after playtime got taken away. Every day Lucy warned Morgan to never tell daddy about their alone time. Every night Benny came home to his loving wife and his favorite food. After dinner he bathed Morgan, read her a story and tucked her into bed. Morgan got quieter, paler and thinner but the sequins in Benny's eyes kept him from seeing.

With Morgan and Benny whipped into shape, the high point of her day was the banal chatter of Central Park mothers. Lucy longed for the corporate life. She missed her job, her freedom, the men and the booze she'd forsaken to marry Benny. Depressed and bored to tears, she picked up the phone and called Paul. She listened to Jacobsen's fancy, reformed-husband footwork. After he'd talked himself into a corner, she offered the standard deal:

Good times. No strings.

Life would have been perfect again except for Morgan. What if the sniveling brat woke up while Paul and she were—? Lucy ransacked the medicine cabinet. By the time Paul arrived, Morgan had already finished a glass of warm milk that Lucy had laced with sleeping powder.

And so it went for six of the hottest months in her life, until the day Benny had decided to knock off work early...

Benny had gotten an accounting job with a small leather shop in Port St. John, a tacky little town on the Mohawk River in upstate New York. The thought of moving anywhere north of Westchester County drove Lucy insane. She lay on the couch screaming hell would breed snowmen before she'd leave New York.

Suddenly, meek, mild, milk-toast Benny rose up like a tidal wave. He dared her to stay in New York. After he sent an open letter to *The New York Times,* she'd be lucky to get a job cleaning subway toilets. After all was said and done, Lucy had one fear: Morgan. If the imp tattled about her alone time with dearest Mommy, Benny would kill Lucy.

One night the solution to her problem came in a dream.

Lucy owned a pendant. The diamonds and ruby were paste and glass. She couldn't remember exactly why she had always loved that worthless piece of junk.

Most importantly, Morgan had loved it too.

One day while Benny was making moving arrangements, Lucy sat Morgan down. Her pasted-on smile masked her fury. She'd lost everything, and now she would lose her pendant.

She took the pendant from her neck and slipped it around Morgan's. Then she said that if Morgan ever told her father about their alone time in New York, she would take the pendant away, and that would be the first of a very long list of very bad things that would happen. Morgan had kept their secret.

The Quicks had moved to Port St. John where Benny worked, Morgan went to school and Lucy did time in a dark, dreary house, in a darker, drearier climate. Thanks to them she would rot in upstate New York for the rest of her life. Insomnia plagued her until she discovered the path to a good night's sleep.

She vowed to spend her time dismantling Benny and Morgan, piece by emotional piece for the rest of her natural life.

# Chapter 8

**Morgan**
**May 25**

Morgan drove her tan Buick Regal through the slow heavy traffic of Lake Placid village. She scanned the village and realized she'd left the camera at home on the counter, unopened. Between moving Mother into Pine Bush and leaving for Placid, the camera had been the last thing on her mind. No big deal. She would just have to describe the house to Chuck in detail.

The day was clear, chilly and forty-five. She passed Town Hall on the corner of Main and Mirror Lake Drive at 12:40. Twenty minutes to go before meeting with Maggie Duran.

Around the bend from Lake Placid High School was the Olympic Center and Convention Hall where the U.S. had slammed Russia in hockey at the 1980 Olympics, shocking the world.

Chuck and she had been watching the game from home when he choked on his beer over the U.S. win. She smiled at the memory wishing to God he was here. By marrying a psychiatrist, she knew what she'd signed on for. She would see the Victorian, alone. Chuck trusted her judgment, and he'd be home soon. Across from the Olympic Center was the White Birch Inn. Her memory of the U.S. win was a good omen. She would register, meet Maggie Duran, see the house and then head home tomorrow.

Home. The word, a source of warmth and comfort to others, made Morgan cringe. Home was synonymous with a mother that had denigrated her for as long as she could remember. She wondered how Mother liked being the helpless, confused one now. Morgan should gloat, but as Daddy would say, for better or worse, Lucy was her mother. Even though Lucy was selfish, egotistical and the root cause of all her own problems, Morgan refused to reap joy from so bitter a harvest. Enough! This trip was supposed to be fun. She pushed Mother out of her mind and took in Main Street.

The village was crammed with sweet shops, restaurants, boutiques and hotels. Tourists streamed through crawling traffic like fish past rocks in a brook. Morgan noticed the Placid Properties sign on her left near Ben & Jerry's. Who could miss those creamy white letters on that crimson red background? Oddly enough, the colors lifted her spirits, confirming that coming here had been the right thing to do. She parked in front of Ben & Jerry's.

"Okay, Maggie Duran, let's have a look at this house."

Morgan noticed a neon-yellow flyer taped to the glass office door. It advertised a Gypsy Bazaar on July twelfth. She peeked in. A stunning blond in her late thirties sat at the second desk on the left, smiling and talking on the phone. Her hair was thick, parted to the side and fell to her shoulders. Her smooth bronze skin would turn an enviable golden brown under the summer sun. Morgan knocked. The blond smiled and waved.

She walked in on the usual office fare. Three overstuffed burgundy chairs. A table littered with magazines. A coat rack. Morgan opted to leave her jacket and purse on a chair. She brushed the lint from her jeans and turtleneck sweater, toyed with her pendant and looked around.

On the counter at the rear of the office was a BUNN coffee maker with two carafes. One had an orange collar. Morgan smelled hazelnut crème. A cup of that now would do just fine.

The woman stood, looking tall and slender in a fringed eggplant jacket with pink stitching and wide lapels, a pale raspberry blouse and eggplant slacks. She covered the phone with slender fingers and perfectly manicured nails.

"Help yourself to some coffee if you like," she said, as if reading Morgan's mind. Her eyes were aquamarine. Her nameplate said Maggie Duran.

"Thanks." Morgan smiled. Wouldn't it be great if all her wishes came true as easily?

She walked past Maggie Duran to the coffee maker, picked up a mug with the same colors and logo as the sign out front. She walked her coffee back to the oversized chairs and sat.

The person on the phone Maggie was speaking to must've said something funny, because Maggie threw her head back, parted her raspberry lips and laughed, exposing straight white teeth. Maggie combed gleaming nails through her hair. When she tucked an errant strand behind her ear Morgan noticed chandelier earrings in eggplant and pink. No doubt about it. Maggie Duran was a fashionista, Morgan thought, sipping her coffee. Her tone of voice implying the conversation was over, Maggie hung up.

"Hi. You must be Morgan. Who else would be here on a beautiful Memorial Day weekend but you and me?" She laughed and walked toward Morgan, extending her hand. "I'm Maggie Duran. It's good to meet you at last."

Morgan put the mug on the table and shook Maggie's hand.

Maggie spied her pendant. "What a beautiful amulet."

"Thanks. My mother gave it to me when I was little."

"It looks real."

"If only."

"I apologize for the phone call," Maggie said. "That was my mom. For two women who live in the same house, you'd think we'd be sick of talking to one another."

"Don't apologize. I think it's great. Makes me a little jealous to tell you the truth."

"Oh God." Maggie turned serious. "You did mention your mom moved into a home this weekend. I'm sorry. That was indelicate."

"Not to worry." Morgan was annoyed with herself for slipping. "Things were never good between my mother and me." She waved it off. "Now. Tell me about this wonderful house."

Maggie patted Morgan's hand and smiled. "One look, as they say, is worth a thousand words. Where are you parked?"

"Right outside," Morgan said. She sighed, picturing her brand new camera at home in Port St. John.

"Leave yours. We'll take mine. It's the green Lexus out front. I'll scoop up my purse, briefcase and key and meet you outside."

# Chapter 9

## Morgan and Maggie

Despite Maggie's easing her Lexus curbside on Midlakes Road for maximum affect, seeing the Queen Anne left Morgan thunderstruck. If only she hadn't forgotten the camera.

Morgan fondled her pendant. Eyes fixed on the house she ran her fingers along the car door's creamy leather to a small hard nub, pressed, and the window slid noiselessly out of sight.

A pale blue sky and a generous wedge of mountain served the raspberry cream Victorian on a green square of closely cropped lawn that smelled like someone had just finished mowing.

A tower trimmed in persimmon and shingled in milk chocolate brown was perched on the edge of the roof like a giant inverted ice cream cone. A reverse gable to the left of the tower had four windows and three large decorative orange ovals in each of the gable's angles.

"Well?" Maggie said, breaking the spell.

"I'm speechless." Morgan moved her fingers over the leather terrain of the car door and groped for the handle.

"Speechless. Well, that's a first class endorsement." Maggie's voice indicated a smile. "My ad met your expectations?"

"Exceeded them." Morgan said, grasping the door handle.

"Great!" Maggie got out of the car, opened the back door, picked up her briefcase and purse. "Let's have a closer look." She closed the door and crossed in front of the Lexus.

Morgan got out of the car and joined Maggie who touched her arm softly, and they both stopped walking. Maggie opened her briefcase and grabbed a file marked "Welcome."

"That's one chunk o' house to handle alone."

Morgan bristled at the innuendo but feared hurting the deal. "That's a good reason to marry well. My husband's a doctor, a psychiatrist. He's in Australia on business right now."

"Australia." Maggie raised her eyebrows and smiled. "Impressive." She snapped her briefcase closed and held the Welcome file in her hand. "May I ask how you met?"

"University at Albany. I was getting my B. A. in English, Secondary Ed and Chuck was doing post grad work in an exchange program Albany had with the University in Melbourne."

Maggie smiled. "Cool. I bet your kids love that story."

Morgan's smile faded. "No kids."

"Oh God." Maggie duh-tapped her head with the file.

Morgan waved her hand. "No need to apologize. God knows we tried, but I guess it just wasn't meant to be."

"I'm really sorry."

"Thanks. I've made peace with it."

Morgan gazed at the house and sighed. "I've seen scores of Victorians over the years, but this one?" She paused and smiled. "At first I credited the gestalt to the perfect sunny day, a cool, gentle breeze, birds chirping, but I think this house would look magnificent on a nasty day in November."

Maggie laughed. "I'm pleased you like it."

"When I teach literature, I always encourage my students to look at the context in which Victorian fiction like Bronte's *Jane Eyre* was written. Politics, books, customs of the day are important, but when kids compare and contrast Victorian houses with their own, they connect the past to the present in a relevant way. The kids moan and groan." A tiny smile played at Morgan's lips. "But you'd be surprised at the conversation a little enrichment can generate."

"Very creative," Maggie said, sincerely, Morgan thought.

"My parents taught Social Studies." Maggie stared at the house. "They wanted me to be a teacher. If I'd had a teacher like you, another realtor might be showing this house today."

"Thanks," Morgan said. "How did you get into the real estate business? Your dad?"

Maggie shook her head and smiled awkwardly. "My parents got married right out of college. A few years later my dad left for Vietnam. JFK had sent advisors. Dad was support personnel. Mom taught, but without dad's help she couldn't make it. So she got her license. Dad got wounded watching others get killed. He came home physically and emotionally shattered and unable to work. Mom continued to work two jobs even after Marcy and I were born. My dad died when I was ten and Marcy was nine." Maggie got quiet.

"I'm sorry." Morgan closed her mind to the hole her father's death had left in her heart.

"Yeah. Me too. But that was a long time ago." Maggie set the briefcase down on the grass, bracketed it between her ankles and opened the Welcome file. "My ad described this Stately Queen Anne as a real 'painted lady' and 'belle of the ball in her day,'" she said, "but I've got a little personal information you might share with your students as part of your human interest angle."

"Terrific." Morgan glanced at the file.

Maggie shuffled through the papers then read while Morgan studied the house. "Jared Welcome, the original owner and a successful Lake Placid merchant, built the Victorian in 1919 as a wedding gift for Elspeth, his beautiful bride."

Morgan placed herself in Elspeth's turn-of-the-century shoes. "Can you imagine a young bride getting this house on her wedding night? It's so romantic, don't you think?"

Not on your life, Maggie thought, but smiled to appease Morgan. She picked up her briefcase, slipped the file in and snapped it shut, when movement lured her gaze to the tower.

A small, pale figure stood in the window.

Maggie froze. Morgan's voice faded out. Birds stopped chirping. Breeze stopped blowing. Nothing moved. Not a blade of grass or a leaf.

Maggie could not see eyes but the weight of a cold, penetrating gaze chilled her like a November drizzle. Suddenly, a familiar memory belched itself up like something she'd eaten long ago but had never fully digested.

The night Tommy Connelly died the police had found Mom wandering Midlakes Road in her nightgown, rambling on about an evil presence in the house. The police had called the EMTs who'd sedated Mom and took her to the hospital. The doctors referred Mom to High Peaks Sanitarium for evaluation. After being released, Mom had confessed that if she'd kept insisting that the apparition she saw in the tower had killed Tommy, her doctors would've locked her in a padded cell.

Morgan's voice faded in. "Did you know that contrary to popular belief those vivid colors were not chosen whimsically?"

"What? No, um, I didn't." Maggie whispered, her gaze riveted to the tower.

At times Maggie still cried herself to sleep wishing to God she'd believed Mom, but she and her kid sister, Marcy, had been in Mom's car that day, and they never saw a thing.

Maggie clutched her briefcase and stared at the pale figure in the tower window. Tension, like steel fingers, pressed her temples. Her head drummed: Mom had been telling the truth.

Morgan touched her, sounding concerned. "Are you okay?"

"Fine." The steel fingers pressed harder, crushing her skull. Maggie looked away from the tower and faced Morgan. She swallowed her nausea and feigned interest.

"So there's really a method to all this color madness?"

"Bold, brash colors serve a very specific purpose for Victorians," Morgan said, pointing to the tower.

Maggie looked and drew in a sharp breath. The figure was gone. She should feel relieved. Instead she wanted to vomit. Her tongue was dry. Her mouth felt like cotton. "I didn't know that either," she heard herself say.

"I'm glad," Morgan said, "because now it's my turn to give you some tasty Victorian tidbits to share with your clients." Morgan touched her shoulder. "Maggie?"

"Sorry." Maggie swallowed. *Get a damn grip.* "I'm fine." She cleared her throat. "And I really could use new stuff."

Morgan smiled. "Victorian homes are huge by design. Selecting their colors is not just a matter of taste. It's the artisan's way of harnessing size and bringing it under control."

"Interesting." Maggie's mind scrambled for a rational explanation. She probably imagined the apparition. She'd been hearing Mom's story since she was an impressionable, brainless teen. The reference brought Natalie's face into sharp focus.

"It is interesting," Morgan said. "Window sashes and casements need to be dark to make the house seem smaller."

"Really?" Her lips formed a shaky smile. What was her problem? Of course she'd imagined the apparition. Add sun and clouds to the power of suggestion and presto! Shadow tag.

The steel fingers loosened their vise-like grip. Her temples stopped pounding. "Sounds like a colorful sleight of hand." Maggie was giddy with relief that she'd imagined it all.

"That's a great way to put it." Morgan said.

Her illusion folded up and filed neatly away, Maggie slowly walked toward the house. Morgan followed. They climbed the steps and stood at the front door. Maggie opened her purse and pulled out the house key, wondering, for the first time what the key might unlock besides the front door.

Clear-headed and confident, Maggie wiped her feet on the welcome mat and smiled broadly. "Did you say you taught your students about Victorian furnishings as well?"

Morgan wiped her feet on the welcome mat and smiled broadly. "You have a good memory."

"In that case," Maggie said, unlocking the house, "if the outside blew you away, wait till you walk through this door.

# Chapter 10

## Kevin Delaney

Kevin walked into the White Birch Inn hoping to see Natalie before meeting Harlan for lunch. Kellie, a waitress he dated, was scheduled to work the dinner shift. After verifying Nat was on for lunch and dinner, he asked the hostess to seat him in Nat's section. The hostess grabbed a menu. He followed her to a small corner table near the dining room fireplace.

"You lucked out. Kellie's on dinner tonight," she frowned. "Or maybe it wasn't luck at all." Her frown melted into a smirk.

Her nametag said *Bridget*. Kellie talked about her all the time. Damn! Time for damage control. "Look," he squinted at her nametag, "Bridget. I know what you're thinking, but—"

"Relax, sweetie." Bridget handed him the menu. "Your secret's safe with me."

Kevin watched her walk away, knowing she'd smoke him the minute she went on break. Kellie hated Nat. She said Nat was a spoiled brat whose real estate family threw the WBI so much business she'd never get fired. He'd taken a risk coming here, but he had to see Nat now without raising Maggie's or Harlan's suspicions. Kevin found out that Maggie was actively showing the Welcome place. To beat her at her own game, he needed inside information. He closed the menu and eyed the kitchen door.

Nat was hot for him, which cranked the heat under Maggie's ass. Maybe under Harlan's too. But Kevin had to be cool. Nat was sixteen. Jailbait. Even though he was not interested in Nat in that way, one dumb move and Maggie could put him away.

Kevin's head ached. He closed his eyes and pinched the bridge of his nose, frowning. Silverware clanking on dishes and cups clattering on saucers still grated on his nerves. After busting his butt through college serving jerks, he swore he'd never hear those sounds from the wrong side of a table again. Kevin opened his eyes and instead of a dining room, he saw a stockyard of animals in various stages of feeding. Some scowled, waiting to be seated. Some scowled, waiting to be served. Some ate and smiled, while others craned their necks, looking annoyed, trying to catch their server's eye.

Natalie glided through the swinging door with a tray of sandwiches, salads and soups that had to weigh more than she did. She jockeyed the tray and a stand past several tables, opened the stand and set the tray down as the kitchen door stuttered closed. Kevin grinned. Nat was strong and moved fast. A smile frozen on her face, she set the last sandwich down, when a fat, gray-haired woman behind her reached up and tapped her shoulder. Nat turned. The woman pointed a pudgy finger at a logjam of French fries on her plate, like she wanted ketchup. Nat smiled, but her eyes flashed annoyance. Something only he, as an ex-server, would notice.

He looked at the woman, thinking. Go ahead, Big Mama. Slap more fructose corn syrup on the fat. He looked at the thin, bald guy sitting beside her. Hope you've got good insurance, dude. XXL caskets don't come cheap.

Nat checked her pad and frowned. She slipped it into an oversized pocket, lifted the tray and worked her way back through the maze of tables. She nudged the kitchen door open with her hip, and the kitchen swallowed her whole.

Kevin looked at his watch. He had to snag her before Harlan came in. As soon as the thought crossed his mind, the kitchen door opened, belched up Nat in a flavored breath with another stacked tray, ketchup and all. She passed Big Mama's table and dropped it off. She made her way to a table near his, opened the stand, set down the tray and saw him.

She frowned then smiled. Sinking her teeth into her lip, she looked like a girl in a Rockwell painting. Kevin pulled out the stops. Shooting for max affect, he smiled, deepening his sexy, to-die-for-so-he'd-been-told, dimples. Nat turned away before the glow in her cheeks went from healthy to embarrassing. Kevin picked up the menu, thinking, this could be fun.

He peeked over the menu and watched Nat take the plates from the tray. Her hands shook so badly a wave of soup in one bowl dripped over the edge onto the saucer. The customer looked at his soup. "Oh for Chrissakes!" he said, all indignant, like the jerk he was. Kevin watched him lift the bowl and put the white linen napkin between it and the plate.

Blushing, Natalie stammered. "Enjoy your meal."

"I need another napkin," the soup jerk said. "Uh, if that's not too much trouble." And the other jerks smirked.

"Right away, sir," she said.

Kevin heard the tremor in her voice. He closed the menu and watched her move around the tables in his direction. Good. Let the jerkoff wait for his napkin.

Their eyes met and the world went into slow-mo. Natalie made her way toward him, her hips and breasts in a rhythmic sway under those sexless black threads. She looked down and reached into her pocket for her pad and pencil. Her black hair fanned out in front of her face like a curtain of Chinese silk. She lifted her head, turned and every strand sailed seamlessly into place. She held her pencil to her pad and smiled. She stood so close he could feel her heat.

"Can I help you, *sir*?"

Her voice changed the speed from slow to normal, and Kevin blinked. "Baby, you help me just by standing there."

Her jaws dropped. She lowered her arms. Her guard followed and for the first time, Kevin *saw the real Natalie*, young and vulnerable enough for him to rethink his motives. Where did that come from? He fumed behind the menu. He had to go through with his plan. To survive, he needed intel on Maggie. By wanting to hook up, Natalie was setting herself up for the fall.

But she was just a kid.

Getting what he needed and then cutting her loose before she fell too hard was the best he could do. "Actually," he closed the menu, "I'm waiting for Harlan."

"Oh. Something to drink while you wait?" She kept her eyes on her pad, sneaking a peek when she thought he wasn't looking.

"Double Goose and tonic." She was small and chic. Dark eyes. Thick lashes. She was the bomb. Too bad she wasn't older. "Anybody ever tell you, that you're as hot in that apron as you were in your red sweater that day at the office?"

Her color deepened. "Thanks," she smiled, and stuck the pad in her pocket. "I'll get the Grey Goose right away."

Kevin watched her walk away and then checked his watch again. 1:30. Good thing Harlan was late. He drummed his fingers on the table and rearranged the napkin and silverware. He looked up. Nat came toward him with his drink and a cocktail napkin on a little tray. Traffic at the bar must be light. She set the Goose and tonic down. "Anything else?"

The Goose was smooth going down and warmed him. "Yes," he whispered, "but I don't know how to say it."

Her eyes widened. She leaned over. He smelled her perfume. *Dream* from the Gap. It smelled like roses and soap. He hesitated then leaned back. "Never mind. It's nothing."

"Kevin," she whispered. "You can tell me anything."

He smiled, feigning surprise and humility. "Really?"

"Really," she breathed, leaning closer.

His stomach was empty. Feeling the Goose, he sniffed past the *Dream* and caught her *real* perfume. He cleared his throat. "Every time I see you I get this, vibe. I know you get it too."

Natalie stared at him, speechless, for once. He glanced at the hostess stand. Harlan stood next to Bridget. Kevin talked fast. Natalie blushed. Her defenses were down, but Goose on an empty stomach jammed a guy's conscience.

"I have to see you. Alone." He looked at Harlan again, then back at Nat. "For lunch, or coffee. It has to be away from Placid," he said quickly. "If Harlan or Maggie found out—"

She gaped at him like a giddy teen. *Duh!* He reached for the napkin and swabbed his lips. Bridget picked up a menu and pointed in their direction. Kevin put the napkin down. Harlan and Bridget were closing in. He looked at Nat who stared at him like she was on ex or coke.

"Look, Nat, think it over. If you're interested, give me your cell and I'll call you. If not—"

"Well, Kevin, my boy." Harlan offered Kevin his hand.

Kevin stood and took it. "Thanks for meeting me. Sit. Please."

"Don't mind if I do," he said. Bridget put Harlan's menu down and winked at Kevin.

"Natalie." Harlan grumbled, without looking at her.

Kevin glanced at Nat who still had her eyes on him. Had Harlan noticed? Harlan opened the menu. Engrossed, he frowned. Maybe not. Kevin guessed Harlan was gruff because he was pissed at Nat for throwing his golden girl off her game. Feeling buzzed, Kevin stifled a smile while Harlan studied his choices.

"Tell you what, Nat." Kevin wanted to kick himself for hanging his career on a teenager. "How about giving Harlan and me a few minutes? In the meantime how about another one of these?" He held up the glass, jiggling the ice cubes.

"Sure," she smiled. "Hi, Uncle Harlan."

Kevin rolled his eyes at her delayed reaction to Harlan's greeting.

Natalie frowned. "A few minutes to look over the ... Oh. Sure. Gotcha."

Praying he hadn't made the biggest mistake of his life, Kevin buried his face in the menu. Nothing registered.

"Well, my boy," Harlan said, closing his menu, "at my age there's only one choice. A garden salad with pear infused balsamic vinegar. So, order a steak and enjoy it while you can."

Kevin laughed, closed the menu and laid it on the table.

"Now tell me, what's so urgent that you had to pull me away from a Memorial Weekend cookout at Lilly's?"

"Well, Sir, it's about Maggie and the Welcome place."

Harlan perked up. His eyes glittered with interest.

"When you hired me two years ago you promised me a major commission and a share in the business if I sold the house."

"And made the sale stick, my boy. A crucial component."

Kevin cleared his throat. "Right."

"I remember," Harlan said. "But the last time I checked, my name was still on the deed. Ah. Here comes Natalie with your drink. Natalie, my dear. You're looking lovely. I am hungry, but on second thought, I'll just have a glass of mineral water. I'm due back at Lilly's for dinner."

Why was the old bastard suddenly being cool with Nat? Kevin raised the glass and sipped. This time the Goose didn't burn. He looked at Nat. "I'll have the Reuben." He gave her the menu.

"Sure thing, Kevin." Natalie smiled.

Maybe it was her broad slow smile, or the way she said his name that made Harlan look from Nat to him, deliberately. Harlan handed her his menu. She took both and left.

"I thought we had an understanding," Kevin said, wondering if Nat had just tanked his career.

"Had? Hell, my boy, we still do." Harlan laughed, leaned over and patted Kevin's arm.

The Goose had numbed Kevin's tongue. "I thought the Welcome place was mine," he said, hoping he'd heard his voice slur in his head.

"Yours? I don't understand."

He fidgeted with his glass. "You said—"

"I said there would be a substantial reward for whoever sold it. That includes Maggie. I also said in essence that my money's on you." His eyes bore into Kevin's. "And I hate to lose." Suddenly, he smiled. "Ah, here comes Natalie with my mineral water. She's as efficient as she is lovely."

Natalie put the mineral water in front of Harlan. He had a curious look in his eye. Nat might as well be flashing a neon sign. Normally bitchy with everyone else Nat was a pussycat now.

"Thanks, Nat," Kevin said. "Can you check on that Reuben?"

"Sure," she said to his relief she slipped away.

"Now, where were we?" Harlan said.

"You were telling me you don't like to lose."

"I don't think I will," Harlan's eyes were on Natalie.

"Meaning?" Kevin's head was swimming. He picked up the Goose, changed his mind and put it down.

"Just what I said." Harlan sipped his mineral water.

"You know that Maggie's showing the house right now." Kevin swirled the ice cubes.

"I know everything that goes on in my office." Harlan set his water down. "So Maggie showed the house. That doesn't mean it's a wrap. Get yourself out there. Find out what's shaking."

Kevin stared. Had the old man read his mind? Harlan smiled.

"You can't expect info from me." Harlan raised his eyebrows, feigning dismay. "It wouldn't be fair to Maggie to play favorites. She's been more like a daughter than a loyal employee." Harlan's smile widened, irking Kevin.

Harlan glanced at his watch. "I promised Lilly I'd be back soon."

Kevin signaled for the check. "My treat, Kevin."

"No, sir, let me," Kevin smiled. "After all, I asked you to join me."

"Very well." Harlan smiled and returned his credit card to his wallet.

Natalie approached with the Reuben. Kevin drained his glass. Natalie took Kevin's credit card and had it back before Kevin could take his first bite. She handed him a black check folder. Kevin opened the folder, and a small piece of paper slipped out of a compartment.

Harlan frowned. "Now what have we here?"

"Just a receipt," Nat said, shifting awkwardly.

Kevin saw Natalie's cell number and winced. Busted. Again.

Harlan grinned and patted Kevin on the back. "When I hired you, I knew I'd picked a winner."

# Chapter 11

## Morgan

Morgan's room at The White Birch Inn was standard fare. Red plaid curtains and matching spread. A small table and two chairs by a window overlooking the parking lot. Two winter landscapes and a TV bolted to the wall and dresser opposite a double bed.

Morgan yawned and stretched. She tossed her overnight bag and jacket on the bed. She took her purse into the bathroom and laid it on the counter beside the sink. She washed and dried her face and hands and looked in the mirror.

She wore her thick dark hair in a stacked bob. The sides angled toward her chin. The wind on Midlakes Road had tumbled and spiked it, exposing some gray. She grabbed a brush from her purse and brushed her hair forward. It settled around her face with the right pouf. She patted errant wisps into place. She plucked a makeup case from her purse, reapplied and assessed.

Her eyes were large and dark in the soft light. Her skin had retained a youthful healthy glow. She had a delicate nose and a broad smile. Chuck said she was beautiful. Most said attractive. She saw herself as somewhere in between. Living near the Adirondacks, she loved to bike, snowshoe and ski. Good healthy habits because she loved to eat. But the glow in her cheeks had more to do with the Queen Anne than her health.

Morgan remembered standing on the welcome mat. When Maggie turned the key and they stepped inside, Morgan's eyes had seared every magnificent detail into her brain.

The door opened onto hardwood floors framing a deep-piled moss green area rug. On their left in the living room an overstuffed Prince of Wales sofa, two matching armchairs, a mahogany marble-topped coffee table and matching end tables were grouped around a Victorian fireplace. The hearth was a fine cast mantle register fitted with ash guard and tile cheeks. The andirons, fine-finished Black Dog Grate with brass mounts, were stacked with logs ready to be fired up. A beveled plate framed a Dresden Mirror that hung above the mantle.

The lamps on the end tables had fringed shades with bases of porcelain ladies in ruffled gowns holding tiny fans in their dainty fingers. They stared at her with sparkling black eyes and shiny smiles on their tiny red lips. The walls were papered in earth tones that complemented the autumn flowers embroidered on the upholstery and drapery. Crown molding and trim were stained in the same dark shade as the bookcase lining the far wall. Its shelves held the classics bound in leather. Morgan had pulled *Canterbury Tales* from the shelf. Its exotic mustiness still lingered in her nostrils. The spine looked worn but felt straight under her fingertips.

Next to that wall a T staircase and four steps led to a landing and four additional steps that descended into the kitchen. To the right of the landing were stairs to the second floor.

The chandelier in the dining room, Late Victorian Gas-Style, was finished in lacquered polished brass. It had five gas shades over candelabra-base bulbs. The glass was tinted rose and etched with a floral design. The chandelier hung above a mahogany table and six chairs that stood on an Oriental rug. The walls above the wainscoting were pale, harvest gold. The area between the dark chair rail and baseboard was papered in magenta. The buffet stood against the left wall. A breakfront to her right stood between two oversized windows. Muted-green, gauzy curtains with scalloped hems were embroidered with the same swirling vines as the living room drapes and upholstery.

Entering the kitchen from the dining room, Morgan had gazed at the cherry wood cabinets and the tin ceiling with tiny rosettes etched at the center of each ceiling square.

Upstairs there were three bedrooms with full baths and tubs perched on four paws. Its shower curtains hung from brass rings. Each room had a Victorian fireplace with mantle mirror and lamps resembling those in the living room. In the bedroom at the end of the hall was a door. Behind that door were stairs to the tower.

On their climb to the tower, Maggie had mentioned a legendary hundred-year flood due any day, if you believed the old-timers. She laughingly reassured Morgan if the phantom flood struck the house would be high and dry—a selling point with traction.

Transfixed, Morgan had gazed at the view of both lakes from the tower window. She closed her eyes and saw every detail.

On the right, Mirror Lake fused heaven to earth in a seamless glimmer of sky, mountains and village. To her left, mountains descended to cobblestone beaches with granite-toothed shores where the lake hugged Moose and Buck Islands in two arms of placid water. A swath of shoreline wended its way toward the curve of a cliff with a barefaced, dramatic drop-off.

Morgan opened her eyes and put the brush down on the hotel's bathroom sink. There were two minor oddities. If every other detail hadn't been so perfect, she wouldn't have noticed.

The first had occurred in the tower. Morgan remembered shivering, as if something had blown a breath of cold through the hollows of her spine. She'd rubbed her arms.

"Something wrong?" Maggie had asked.

"Did you feel that chill? It gave me goosebumps."

"Sorry," Maggie had said, quite wide-eyed come to think of it. "I didn't feel a thing."

Then Maggie averted her eyes, quickly consulted her file and said, "I almost forgot. You haven't seen the cellar."

"What's this?" Morgan had said, five minutes later, pointing to scratches on the bottom corner of the cellar door.

"Jinx." Maggie had blown out a breath.

"Pardon?" Morgan frowned.

"Mom's Golden Retriever. We live close by. I used to walk Jinx here to check on the house until she started this scratching thing." Maggie knelt and ran her hand over the scratches. "It got so bad I had to stop taking her with me." Then Maggie had gotten to her feet and clapped the dust off her slacks. "It's no big deal. Harlan will fix it. I promise."

Morgan stared at herself in the bathroom mirror and shook it off. She smiled at the possibility that Chuck and she might actually retire in that spectacular house. A miracle in itself and an event she vowed not to jeopardize by questioning the powers that be. Yet, she couldn't help wondering why someone else hadn't snapped this house up by now. And who actually *owned* it?

Maggie said that Jared Welcome had built the house for his wife in 1919. But while some of the furnishings were authentic, others had been hand-crafted and the rest were high-end retail. All in all, it must've cost a fortune. Maggie said they went with the house. Even with a burst housing bubble, the price was steep for her and Chuck, but a steal, considering. If it seemed too good to be true—

Her stomach growled and Morgan checked her wristwatch. No wonder she was paranoid. It was six, and she was running on empty. She grabbed her purse and jacket and headed out.

The rustic Adirondack dining room at the White Birch Inn was dimly lit, enhancing the décor. Morgan looked at the paneled walls, fireplace and the antlered deer head mounted above the mantle. There was a bearskin rug on the floor in front of the hearth. The tables had white cloths. White vases held red tapered candles.

The hostess picked up a menu and smiled. "Table for one?"

"Please." A shawl of cold evening air draped Morgan's shoulders. She shivered. "Can I sit near the fireplace?"

"Sure." The hostess smiled warmly. "This way please."

Morgan followed the hostess through a crowded dining room. She slipped into her seat, and the hostess handed her the menu. Someone will be with you in a few minutes."

"Thanks."

As Morgan opened the menu, she heard a server approach, looked up and smiled.

"Hi. I'm Natalie." She was petite and pretty with large almond-shaped eyes and long black hair. She smiled and poured water from a pitcher into a glass. "I'll be your server tonight. Can I get you something from the bar?"

Normally Morgan would've declined, but seeing the Queen Anne today and dining in the firelight tonight, she felt like celebrating. "Why not? I'm checked in for the night, so make my Manhattan a double. Straight up."

"Yes Ma'am." Natalie scribbled, smiling. She stuck the pad in her apron pocket and fixed the place setting.

"Our special tonight is Manhattan clam chowder, Atlantic salmon encrusted with sesame seeds, garden asparagus, rolls, butter and rice pilaf. I'll leave the menu and get your drink." Natalie smiled and left.

With salmon on special, there was no contest. Morgan closed the menu and looked around. Couples and families with children streamed in. As the hostess sat them, Natalie wove her way through with a Manhattan on a small cocktail tray. She put the Manhattan on the table in front of Morgan and eyed Morgan's pendant. "That's a beautiful necklace."

"Thanks." Morgan sipped her drink and coughed. "Wow. Potent." She took another sip. "But good," she giggled. "Thanks."

"You're welcome."

While Natalie reached into her apron pocket for her pad, Morgan pictured every precious detail of her house, which looked as good as her drink tasted. She should've given Maggie a binder before someone else beat her to it. She took another swallow and made up her mind. She'd give Maggie a check on her way out of town. Morgan frowned, wondering why Chuck hadn't called since before Memorial Day Weekend. Feeling light-headed and carefree, she let the thought go. Was she feeling the drink? Already?

Pad and pen poised, Natalie said, "Here on vacation?"

"Actually, I'm here to buy a house," she said.

"Really?" Natalie's eyes were the color of dark chocolate.

"Yes." Tingly spokes spread from Morgan's core outward.

"Hey, great."

"I'll have the salmon." Morgan gave her the menu, finished her drink and held up the empty glass. "Bring me another?"

Natalie took the menu and glass. "Right away," she smiled.

Morgan watched Natalie serpentine her way around dining room tables. Feeling deliciously numb, she glanced around the room and saw a dad cutting his little boy's steak, while the mom kissed their little girl's nose. Morgan smiled, sadly. She loved kids and regretted not having any. She sighed, spotting Natalie. True to her word, the kid was gone and back in record time.

"I was born here and my family, that is my aunt, is a realtor." Natalie set the drink and a fresh napkin in front of Morgan. "Gran was a realtor too before she retired. So I know every house for sale in town. Do you remember the address?"

"Burned in my memory," Morgan giggled. "It's the red, raspberry dream at thirteen fifty-six Midlakes Road."

Natalie froze as if someone had pressed *pause* on a remote. Morgan was buzzed, but not enough to miss the same strange look in Natalie's eyes that Maggie had in her eyes while showing the house. "Why the look?"

"What?" Natalie's eyes widened. "Um, I should check on your order." She backed away.

Morgan took another sip and frowned. The whiskey was going down too easily. Was she reading more into a look than there was?

So Natalie's grandmother and aunt were realtors. Hmmm. Is Maggie her aunt? Considering what Maggie said about her family earlier, it fit. Their coloring was different. Except for that look in their eyes, they bore no resemblance to each other.

Swirling the glass in her hand, she mulled over their odd vibes toward the house. She lifted the glass to her lips as a tiny red flag waved a warning. Morgan ignored it, drained the glass and set it down. After tiptoeing around the mother from hell and lonely for the husband who always seemed to be out of town, she deserved that house. She dabbed her lips with the napkin. Guilt plagued her more than usual lately. She hated it. With Mother fighting the move into Pine Bush and the battle she would have to wage if Chuck and she decided to move—

"Ma'am?"

Startled, Morgan watched Natalie set the encrusted salmon on the table. Suddenly feeling woozy, the sight and smell turned Morgan's stomach.

"Would you like another drink?" Natalie held the tray between her arm and her hip.

"No. Thanks," Morgan said, sorry she'd gulped two doubles on an empty stomach.

"Well, enjoy your dinner then." Natalie began walking away.

"Natalie?"

Natalie stopped and turned. "Yes?"

Morgan's tongue felt slow and thick. She pressed her lips between her teeth then forced them to form words. "When I described the house on Midlakes your eyes had this look—"

Clearly ill at ease, Natalie switched the tray to her other hip. "I didn't recognize the description or the address."

The hell you didn't. Shifting in her seat, Morgan felt the whiskey slosh in her stomach. "Your aunt, the realtor. What's her name?" She struggled hard not to slur her words.

Natalie picked up the empty glass. "Why?"

"Just curious."

Natalie stiffened. "Maggie Duran. Will that be all, Ma'am?"

Morgan nodded. Natalie slipped away, leaving Morgan to cram her imagination back into its cage. Trouble was it no longer fit. She looked at the fish, stifled a gag and signaled for the check.

The night air seemed to calm Morgan's stomach for the moment but it did nothing for her head. She was cold, and had to pee. She stumbled toward her room and stood at the door, rummaging through her purse. Comb. Car keys. Planner. Tissues. Wallet! Thank God.

She extracted the plastic key card and slipped it into the lock. Green light flashing, she made her way through the door and hit the switch. She dropped her purse on the bed, headed for the bathroom, sank to her knees, hugged the bowl and vomited.

She got to her feet, stood at the sink and brushed her teeth. Skipping the rest of her nightly routine, she found the bed and slipped between the sheets.

Morgan closed her eyes. The room spun like a centrifuge, breaking her head and stomach into dozens of pieces. She inched to the edge of the bed, planted her feet on the floor, and the room stopped spinning. She fell back on the bed. Her eyelids clanged shut, echoing through the vastness between her ears.

Swallowing Morgan whole, sleep spit her up—

*...under a barren moon and scatter of vacant stars.*

*Cradled in two strong arms, she stares over a barefaced cliff. Dropped over the edge, she falls fast and hits water so dark and cold the impact slams air from her lungs. Wracked with spasms, she sinks fast. Wrists and ankles bound, she holds her breath. Her calves and thighs twitch. She struggles to free her wrists which are tied behind her. The rope cuts off her circulation.*

Morgan woke up, choking. The scene collapsed around her. Did she just dream that someone had tried to kill her?

Shaken, she kicked the blankets back and closed her eyes. The images may have dissolved, but their imprint remained. The jaw of a barefaced cliff jutted into a lake. Moonlit waves lapped at its chin. A tuft of pine forest lined a small clearing at the top.

Morgan opened her eyes. She had seen Mirror Lake and Lake Placid yesterday from the Queen Anne's tower window. Maggie had called the cliff Pulpit Rock. The base of Pulpit Rock jutted into Lake Placid.

Her head ached. She squeezed her eyes shut, hugged her knees to her chest and winced as a bubble of whiskey burned her throat.

Her wrists and ankles on fire, she groped around in the dark and found the lamp on her nightstand. She clicked the switch, squinted against the light and drew in a sharp breath.

A bracelet of welts circled her wrists and ankles. As a teacher and mandated reporter, she'd seen pictures of rope burns in child abuse classes. She shivered and closed her eyes. She breathed in, opened her eyes and gasped. The rope burns were fading as quickly as the dream that had spawned them.

Her head pulsed like a strobe light. Swearing off demon rum, she slid between the sheets and pulled them tight under her chin. She drifted off. As the lakeshore and cliffs wavered behind her eyes, she wondered, had the burns really been there, or had she dreamed them?

# Chapter 12

## Natalie

Natalie's shift was finally over. She pushed through the swinging doors, balancing a tray of dirty dishes. Working lunch *and* dinner was happening a lot lately. Why didn't they hire more people instead of burning out loyal staff?

Exhausted, she plunked the tray down on the dirty dish table and stacked her dishes next to the pre-wash sink where Zach, the dishwasher, stood and rinsed. Sam, the cook, wiped the ranges with industrial cleaner. Acrid fumes hung in the stagnant air making her want to puke. Sam looked up and smiled. His eyes explored her, stopping in places that made her squirm. He polished his way toward her.

"Ugh." The sound slipped out. Scared he'd catch on, she quickly added, "I'm sick of cleaning up after other people."

"Yeah." His eyes seemed to glow at the sound of her voice.

It was ten o'clock. Closing time. Except for Kellie Williams, the snot who was breaking the dining room down, the rest of the wait staff had clocked out. Kellie hung out with Kevin. The thought of them getting it on drove Natalie wild. Kellie had Nat by three years, old enough to date Kevin, but not for long. Wait till Kellie found out that Kevin had asked for her number.

Nat dreamed of painful ways to let Kellie know. Totally into Kevin, Nat had begged God to make him call. Suddenly, she realized this was the twenty-first century. She could call him, but she needed a good reason, one that would really turn him on.

The smell of industrial cleaner got stronger. Sam was close. Shuddering, she sidestepped and picked up an empty tray. "Got one more table to clear." She glanced at Zach on her way out. He gave her the creeps too.

Kellie was setting up for tomorrow's breakfast shift near the table where Natalie had served Kevin lunch. Natalie gazed at the table and heard, "Baby, you help me just by standing there." Her heart pumped tingles down to her toes. She was in love.

As she cleared the last table, embers sparked in the hearth, reminding her of the woman who'd sat near the fireplace earlier. Aunt Maggie had shown her the Welcome house.

If Natalie heard Maggie say once that Kevin wanted to impress Harlan so badly, he'd hock his soul to sell that house, she'd heard it a hundred times. Maggie had chuckled and called Kevin a total nimrod for actually believing that selling the Welcome place would lock up his future with Harlan.

That was it. She'd call Kevin and tell him about the woman and the Welcome place. She closed her eyes. God, what a tool she was. Kevin and Maggie worked together. He must know about that woman already. Nat opened her eyes and thought hard.

The woman said she was staying at the WBI. Maybe she'd be in for breakfast tomorrow. Just thinking about working the early shift made her back ache. True, she'd acted all weird when the woman had mentioned Midlakes Road, but she'd just play it off like it was that time of the month or something.

Nat went to the hostess stand to check the schedule. Kellie had breakfast. Nat had to suck up to the skank to make her switch. Kellie hated her guts. The feeling was mutual. Betting that Kellie hated working Memorial Day more, she sidled over.

"Kellie?" *Whore.* "I see you're working breakfast tomorrow."

Kellie tossed dirty silverware onto an empty tray. "So?"

Natalie breathed deeply. "So, how about switching? I'm going to college in September and I need the money."

Kellie picked up the tray and glanced at her sideways. "You? Need money?" she scoffed. "Right."

"Forget it." Nat walked away, calling Kellie's bluff.

"Hold it." Nat heard Kellie slam the tray down on the table, making the silverware jump. "Knock yourself out."

Her back to Kellie, Natalie smiled and sighed, "Thanks," in a bored voice and walked away. She scooped up her stack proudly.

On her way to the kitchen she realized that spying for Kevin meant betraying her flesh and blood. Feeling lower than pond scum, she stopped at a table by the swinging door, put her tray down and sank into a chair.

Maggie was always on her about everything. Leaving for college meant leaving Gran, Kevin and Jinx, their dog, but if getting away from Maggie was worth it, why did she feel like a traitor over the Welcome house? That freaking house had split Gran and Uncle Harlan up and put Gran in the loony bin. People still said that house was haunted. She glanced at Kevin's table, remembered his eyes and teasing smile and rationalized. That woman already knew Nat was Maggie's niece. Talking about Maggie would be a logical way to dig. What harm could it do? Maggie was a pro and could sell Kevin inside out any day of the week.

Her conscience eased, Natalie pushed her way into the kitchen and bumped into Sam. She put the tray down. "Where's Zach?" If he was on break, that meant she and Sam were alone.

"Left early." Sam smiled and the soles of her feet froze.

*That coke-snorting jerkoff!* "That's the third time this week!" She looked at the dirty dishes. "We have to pick up his crap too. No wonder we're always short-handed."

"Hey, Nat. Can I ask you something?"

Wary, she hesitated. "Sure." Had he heard one word she said? Funny. She never noticed how wolfish his eyes looked.

"Ever wonder why I never married?"

*What?* The question made her flesh crawl more than he did.

"Excuse me?" She sounded sarcastic, but he grossed her out. She had to leave now or she'd lose it. She turned her back, unloaded the tray and started rinsing the dishes. "Don't mind me. I'm wiped," she said, praying he'd change the subject.

"Tried it a few times, but it didn't work," he said.

Her eyes got so big she couldn't frown.

He moved closer. "Getting married I mean." His sweat mixed with the smell of his greasy hair and the cleaner.

Cringing, she rinsed the dish in her hand. She needed to bolt, but she couldn't get fired now. This job had morphed into a special connection to Kevin and besides, Maggie would ground her for the rest of her natural life. She had to steer Sam in a different direction. She read somewhere that surprise was the best defense. She slipped her apron off and wiped her hands with it.

"Mind if I leave early tonight? I just switched shifts with Kellie. I'm working breakfast, and I'm beat."

His mouth dropped and he hesitated. "Well I—"

"Thanks." She gave him the broadest smile she could muster.

"Sure, kid. You look like you need a break."

Now Kellie had to help Sam clean up. She'd be pissed, but she could sleep in tomorrow. As Natalie grabbed her jacket from a hook by the staff entrance, a delicious image of Kellie and Sam alone swam into view. Nat giggled and slipped out the door.

# Chapter 13

**Morgan**
**May 26**

Feeling the timid May sun on her face, Morgan stirred, turned on her side, moaned and pried her eyes open. She sat up and groaned. Her head felt as if it was caught in an iron vise. She gazed at the bedspread and matching curtains and remembered. She was in a hotel in Lake Placid. She leaned toward the nightstand and felt her brain bump against her skull. She turned the clock toward her. 7:00 a.m. She remembered the salmon and felt her face turn pea green.

The dream suddenly flashed through her mind. She understood dreaming about a lake. The house she had fallen in love with stood on a hill between two gorgeous lakes. The granite cliff seemed familiar, but upstate New York was filled with them. She'd probably seen a few on her way up. But, Morgan Matthias drown? Not in this lifetime. She was a strong swimmer, Olympic material, her high school coach had said. She would never end up in a lake with her hands tied behind her back—unless, Morgan shuddered, someone tried to kill her. That thought came from a dream fueled by two doubles on the empty stomach of a woman who rarely drank. Remembering the numbing-cold dream, she shivered and rubbed her arms. One thing was certain. That dream had not taken place in July.

She pictured the painted lady in her Gothic garb and knew she was hooked. She had to call Maggie and leave a binder. She swung her legs over the bed, got up fast and sank back down. She cupped her head in her hands. If she couldn't make a simple call, how would she drive home today? She could do breakfast at the hotel restaurant, but the thought of food made her stomach contract. She plunked her feet on the floor and moved around. Feeling a tad better, she pulled out her cell phone and Maggie's card and dialed.

Morgan peeked through the glass Placid Properties' door at Maggie, who sat at her desk in a magenta velveteen jacket and matching cami, sifting through papers. Wow, could that woman dress. Painfully aware of her plain white scoop-neck sweater and faded blue jeans, Morgan knocked softly.

Maggie looked up and smiled. She pushed a shock of thick blond hair behind her right ear, exposing a gold hoop earring and waved Morgan in. Morgan opened the door and smelled coffee.

"Morning. Have a seat. I'll get you a hot mug of coffee."

Morgan sat as Maggie made good on her word.

"Cream and sugar?"

"Black thanks." Morgan hoped her stomach was too busy groping for homeostasis to perceive what was coming its way.

"You look a little blurred around the borders." Maggie set the steaming PPI mug down.

Morgan closed her eyes and sipped slowly. The coffee was hot, strong, and felt surprisingly good going down. "Dinner last night turned out to be liquid. Manhattans."

"Ouch." Maggie said, shifting the papers on her desk into a neat pile. "Been there a few times. Sure you're up to this?"

"Yes. In fact," she put the mug down, opened her purse and pulled out a check. "I'm not leaving town without giving you this. I wrote it out this morning."

Maggie took the check. Her smile seemed less than exuberant. Morgan frowned at something she saw in Maggie's eyes.

"This gives us a month to get serious," Maggie said, distractedly.

"I am serious. Do you want me to sign a contract?"

"Not necessary." Maggie seemed anxious. "Not yet, I mean."

Maggie ran her finger along Morgan's check. Her signals seemed mixed and confusing. The house of her dreams seemed to be slipping away. She had to say something.

"May I ask who owns the house?" Morgan blurted. Suddenly, realizing that knowing who owned it was vital.

Maggie picked up a pencil and tapped it on her desk. She dropped it and looked at Morgan. "My boss, Harlan Wainright."

"Your boss?" Morgan straightened up. "Isn't that unusual?"

"Not really. Being in the biz, we come across deals every day. Some are too good to pass up."

"I suppose," Morgan said. Maybe this Harlan Wainright was just eccentric. "I'll definitely need that month," she said, brightening. "I've got review classes, finals and Regents exams." She rummaged through her purse for her cell, feeling excited despite Maggie's conflicting signals. She flipped it open and checked her organizer. "Let's see.

Graduation's the twenty-first. I'll need the rest of June to prepare things at home." She looked at Maggie. "I'd like to be in for the summer."

Maggie looked concerned. "Morgan, there is one other thing."

*I knew it!* "I've never bought a house." Morgan talked fast, afraid to hear what that one thing was. "Do I apply for the mortgage?" She looked at Maggie. "Your boss isn't changing his mind about selling, is he?" She clutched her purse.

"No." Maggie smiled. "The Welcome place has been his special project for years. He's, shall we say, emotionally involved."

"I'm afraid you lost me."

"He insists on screening the clients who want that house."

"Screening? When? Why didn't you tell me before? I can't stay today, and I can't come back until after school closes." She let go of her purse and fondled her pendant.

"Relax. That's fine as a matter of fact."

"Why will I be interviewed?" She squeezed the pendant.

"No bank. Harlan will hold the mortgage."

Surprised, Morgan let go of the pendant and lifted the mug to her lips. Her hand shook.

"Don't worry, please." Maggie said, and Morgan put the cup down. "Maybe *interview* was a poor choice of words. Background and credit check are more like it." Maggie touched Morgan's hand softly. "A necessity especially in today's market."

Morgan grabbed her pendant. "What if I don't qualify?"

"You've been a teacher for years. Your husband is a psychiatrist. Even if you were single, I don't see a problem. And neither will Harlan. Trust me."

*Right.*

"Now that we've squared that away," Maggie smiled, "Will I meet Dr. Matthias at the closing?"

Morgan dropped the pendant. "I forgot all about him," she whispered.

"Stuff happens." Maggie said smiling but clearly puzzled.

"Chuck will be here, but if he gets called away again I'll be here alone. Speaking of screenings and closings," she looked at her cell calendar. "I can't get here until July first."

Maggie marked the date on her desk planner. "Sounds perfect. If you meet with Harlan July third, you could move in on the fourth. How's that for a memorable date?"

"Terrific." Morgan smiled. She was drained, hung over and should head home. Home made her think of Mother. The tide of anxiety the Manhattans had helped to ebb for two days, started to rise. She pictured the house, slipped the cell into her purse and touched her pendant.

"Could I see the house again before I leave? I'll follow you there in my car."

Morgan and Maggie stood on the lawn and faced the house. "I'm sure you'll agree that you can't do anything to improve the interior," Maggie was saying. "Think of yourself as an artist and the lawn as your blank canvas. With your Victorian expertise, the grounds could be your signature work."

Morgan nodded on cue. The Gothic turret, the reverse gable, the small center windows and orange ovals were so exquisite she got lost in their intricate detail.

As she feasted her eyes on the sugar cone tower, clouds crept over the sun. Shadows grew long. She frowned. A white haze was obscuring the windows in the tower and the bedroom beneath it. A chilled finger grazed her cheek, raising the hair on her back of her neck. She shivered and tightened her jacket around her. She frowned harder, and two wires crossed in her mind, fusing the smells of newsprint and freshly cut grass.

The PPI ad swam into view, and Morgan suddenly realized that the day she'd first seen the ad she hadn't imagined a thing. But if there had been no whited-out misprint in those windows, what had the ad photo captured?

Yesterday, all the windows were black, weren't they?

The haze in the tower began swirling, and Morgan gasped. Clearly, the haze was not on the window, it was *inside* the tower. It thickened into a figure. Slight. Like that of a child or perhaps a female. Fear surged through her veins like current through an electric grid.

Stripped of its former charm, her Victorian cottage suddenly smacked of *Hansel and Gretel*. And every three-year-old knew that behind gingerbread walls lurked a wicked witch.

Morgan looked at Maggie who was looking at the tower and bedroom but seemed not to see it. "Maggie?"

Maggie turned. "Over there you could plant—" Maggie's voice trailed off. "God, you look so pale." She sounded concerned.

Morgan smiled weakly. "Still a little spacey, I guess."

Was that it? "Manhattans pack quite a wallop."

"I'm sorry," Maggie said.

· "Don't be. It's my own fault." Morgan said distractedly. "Guess the coffee didn't work as well as I'd hoped."

"You need food. How about some breakfast? My treat."

"I'm not hungry. Thanks." Scared, Morgan shivered. How could she extract herself without looking like a crazy idiot?

"Okay then," Maggie held up the key. "Shall we go inside?"

"No! I mean—" God, Maggie must think she was certifiable.

Morgan didn't know what rattled her more, the look on Maggie's face or fear of stepping inside that house. Five minutes ago she would've grabbed the key, skipped the welcome mat and rushed inside herself.

But now she wanted her binder back. She needed Chuck's input before money changed hands. After all, what wife gives a realtor a binder without her husband's input?

She squeezed her pendant until the stones bit into her hand. She looked at the house. Being here was worse than crazy. It was all wrong. But how could she call the deal off when she wanted the house so badly. Morgan held her breath and closed her eyes. Please, God. Let nothing be in the tower. Not a thing. Nothing.

Morgan opened her eyes and exhaled slowly. Clouds crawled away from the sun. Shadows vanished. All the windows were dark, including the tower and bedroom.

"Morgan?"

Morgan jumped as if awakened from a nightmare.

"No offense, but you look like hell. Don't drive home today. Call in sick and stay another night."

Stunned, Morgan kept staring at the tower and bedroom windows. "It – it's just that I thought I—"

"Saw something?" Maggie said, touching Morgan's arm.

She seemed to look ill at ease, and Morgan wondered why.

"Morgan, please. If you're not going to stay the night, have a good meal before you leave. You're hung over, dehydrated and starving. No wonder you're seeing things. "

"Seeing things?"

Morgan ran a dry tongue over drier lips. Wanting Maggie to be right more than she'd ever wanted anything, she closed her eyes, tipped her chin to the sun and let it warm her face. She opened her eyes, looked at the house.

Seeing things made perfect sense. When she'd looked at the ad at home, she'd been under incredible stress. Today she was hung over and dehydrated. Suddenly she smiled. The painted lady had become the house of her dreams again. Credit checks, hazy windows and interviews melted away along with her doubts about buying the house.

"Morgan?"

"I'm fine, better than fine." Morgan actually giggled. "I'm starving, and I will get something to eat, I promise." She looked at her watch. "I've really got to get going."

"But, won't your husband want to see the house first?"

"He'll love it, just like I do." She shook Maggie's hand. "Call me to firm up the interview and closing dates."

Digging through her purse Morgan found her key. She hurried to her car, leaving Maggie on the front lawn looking confused.

# Chapter 14

## Lucy

Lucy sat in her bed in a pink granny nightgown. Did they have one of these fashion-less statements for every color in the goddamn rainbow for Chrissakes? She looked around this interment-chapel of a room where Morgan had conspired with Doctor Mendoza and *them* to stash her. Where the hell has Morgan been anyway? She's probably too busy sticking a *For Sale* sign on the lawn to show her guilty face.

"Is that what I get after sacrificing my life for Benny Quick's ingrate of a daughter?"

Lucy propped herself up on her elbows and her mattress let out its familiar, painful groan. She moved her pudgy fingers across the bedspread in short brisk strokes. She'd show Morgan and Doctor Mendoza. Her strokes got brisker. The dust motes took flight and chased each other through a shaft of sunlight. Wouldn't *they* shit silver dollars when she just upped and walked out of this *mauve*-so-leum? She grinned at her sharp wit. Who cared if Morgan and Mendoza believed Lucy Quick was losing it? But, before getting out of the place, she had to lift her gargantuan ass out of bed. Her grin faded. After squeezing it into that Munchkin chair in the corner, then what?

Lucy lay back. Disgusted, she gazed out the window and saw a large grassy field and a wall of whispering pines. Might as well be a prison yard and a barbed wire fence. Her stomach rumbled. It was late and she was hungry. If she didn't eat soon, she would get a migraine. Dinner ended at seven but the dining room was so cold she'd refused to eat there. At 6:55 the attendant quietly stuck a tray under her nose.

"What the hell's the matter with you?" She balled her fist. "I should report you for scaring an old woman half—" The aroma of roast pork, mashed potatoes and gravy wafted up to her nostrils. She stared down her nose, disgusted at the size. The portions looked like a sample plate from the Price Chopper.

"Daughter back yet, Ma'am?" the clown-of-an-attendant asked.

"Back?" Her mouth sagged and dropped.

"Yes, Ma'am," the clown said.

"Back from where?" Brown slop from her lips spattered the sheets and the front of her nightgown.

"Lake Placid. I helped her move you in Friday and Saturday. Said she was going to look at a house. Seemed pretty excited."

Lake Placid. Lucy remembered. She slammed her mind and mouth shut against the clown, shivered, put her fork down and rubbed her arms. Has the world gone crazy? Why the hell don't they turn off the A/C? She swallowed and glared. The clown mumbled something, shook his head and slipped out the door.

A fly-like buzz ran through her brain and stopped behind her eyes. She stared at her food and frowned. Where did he say Morgan was? Lucy scanned the room. Where the hell did that damned attendant go? Young ones today had no respect. They left without saying good-bye. Lucy opened a packet of sugar, poured it into her coffee and stirred, clanking the spoon against the side of the cup. She frowned hard and remembered. Lake Placid.

Convinced her memory was better than ever, Lucy smiled and picked up her fork. She grimaced and stabbed a piece of meat. She used the meat to scoop up some mashed potatoes. Before the food touched her lips, she stared blankly.

Everything became crystal clear. Morgan planned to sell the house and move to Lake Placid, while Lucy rotted away in this place for the rest of her life.

Suddenly, something happened that hadn't happened in years.

Lucy lost her appetite.

# Chapter 15

**Maggie**
**May 27**

Maggie had tossed and turned the night away to images of her mother, the apparition and Morgan Matthias parading through her mind. Yawning, she glanced at her digital clock. It read 4:00 a.m. She sat up, reached for the lamp on her nightstand and propped her pillow between her back and the headboard. She pressed her eyes with the heels of her hands and sighed. Harlan had scheduled a staff meeting first thing today. If she didn't get some sleep, he'd game her and win before she poured her coffee. Maggie sensed that a good night's sleep was not in the tea leaves tonight for two reasons: Guilt and confusion.

If Maggie ever weakened and told Mom that she had seen the apparition in the tower, Mom would be all over Harlan to yank the house from the market. Fat chance he'd do it even for Mom. Harlan had been hell-bent on selling that damned house to his phantom "right" buyer for as long as Maggie could remember. For another, if Harlan found out about the apparition, the chance of Kevin finding out would increase exponentially. She knew that Kevin would give his next three commissions to sell the Welcome house out from under her. The question is would he be gutsy enough to sabotage her deal with Morgan, and then what? She raked her fingers through her hair—her eyes widened—and then buy the house himself? She scoffed. Even Kevin wouldn't be fool enough to take that gamble.

It was 2008. Real estate had one foot in the grave. If Harlan found out that Kevin had purposely tanked Maggie's deal, he'd bury Kevin along with it. Whatever Maggie saw or thought she saw had psyched her out enough to dredge up bad memories.

The Welcomes and Tommy Connelly had frozen to death in that house in the bedroom under the tower. Details had never been made public. To this day the mystery remained unsolved, and the house never stayed sold. Maggie should know. She'd spent years trying to sell it and so had Mom. Maggie sensed that Morgan had seen something in the tower on Memorial Day that had freaked her out enough to almost call off the deal. Her eyes glistened.

"Mom saw an apparition and Tommy died. I saw an apparition. Does that mean Morgan will die? Is that it?"

She looked at the clock, groaned, slid under the covers and closed her eyes, trying to sleep, but her conscience pricked like a bed of uneven nails. She had to tell Mom everything. After the hell Mom had gone through with that house, she deserved full disclosure. Morgan deserved full disclosure too, *before* her interview with Harlan, which was set for July third. With a little bit of luck, Harlan might not approve the loan, but if he did, would Morgan die?

She reached under her nightstand for her purse and grabbed Morgan's check. She propped it between the lamp and phone and stared at it. What if she was wrong? What if a game of tag between shadows and sunlight had played tricks on her eyes, prompting her to see something that had not really been there? What if, besides being hung over, Morgan had been distracted by some unrelated event, like putting her mom in a home? Maggie knew if she raised any suspicions, warranted or otherwise, she would lose the deal and her job. And, how could she risk telling Mom anything based on what she *thought* she saw?

Maggie struck an uneasy deal with God. She would wait on telling Mom. After what had happened all those years ago, what difference would a few more weeks make? She wouldn't tell Morgan anything yet either, under one condition: If Morgan moved into that house and so much as blinked the wrong way, she would tell Mom and Morgan everything. And Harlan could go screw himself.

But, what if Mom had been right all these years, and she really had seen something in the tower? Maggie sighed. No use trying to sleep. She might as well shower.

She forced herself out of bed. The hardwood floor was smooth and cool under her feet. She made her way to the closet and wiggled her toes into a pair of terrycloth slippers. They swam on her feet. Frowning, she padded into the bathroom, flipped the light switch and looked down. The slippers belonged to Steve. She wore them just like old times, except for two things. She was still in her nightgown, and she was home alone.

Maggie leaned over the clamshell pedestal sink and stared at her reflection in the mirror. She'd seen Steve's byline occasionally, so she knew he was still a staff writer for the *North Country Tribune*. Ironically, it was Steve's curiosity about the Welcome House that had brought them together. She remembered as if it had happened yesterday.

It was 1993. Steve was a twenty-three-year old rookie. Maggie was twenty-three and had just started working for Harlan. While on another assignment, Steve had stumbled upon the Welcome story. He found out that thirteen-year-old Tommy Connelly had frozen to death just like the Welcomes had sixty years earlier. Like a dog with a bone, Steve dug. By the time he walked into her office that day, he'd already known that her mother had sold the house to the Connellys and that Harlan had held the mortgage and that was fine, he supposed, except for one thing: In the pool of Lake Placid realtors, why would a barracuda like Wainright hold a mortgage at a rate with little or no return?

Maggie would never forget the day Steve had walked through the office. He was sexy with confidence that bordered on arrogance. He had a fine nose, deep dark eyes and an appetizing mouth. Her fingers still flexed with the feel of his thick, coarse hair. That night over dinner he'd tried to interview her, but their attraction kept distracting them. Barely able to contain the heat, they'd skipped dinner and went straight for dessert at his place, that night and every night thereafter.

Maggie had gotten lost in Steve Rivers so hard and fast the memory still gave her vertigo. Young, in love and totally unaware of the consequences that dredging up the past would have on her Mom or any future sale of the house, she'd given Steve everything. She even told him that Harlan had bought the Welcome house back after Tommy had died.

For the next three years Steve and Maggie had gotten into each other hot and heavy enough to start looking at rings. There was, however, one little fly in the wedding soup: Steve's obsession with the Welcome/Connelly mysteries. The Welcome case was older and colder than the Arctic Circle, but the authorities hadn't come up with any new leads on the Connelly case for a decade. This had irritated Steve's obsession badly enough to spark an idea.

September of 1993 would be the tenth anniversary Tommy's death. Steve had planned on running the Welcome/Connelly mysteries every five years on the anniversary of Tommy Connelly's death, featuring the newest developments or repackaging the old.

When Harlan found out that Evan Burke, Steve's editor, had jumped at the idea, he swore that Steve had never loved her, and that after Steve had worked her for all she was worth, he would kick her to the curb. Harlan had chipped away, creating doubt. One day he'd dared her to force Steve to choose between her or his idea. He wagered his business that she would lose.

Maggie took the bait and Harlan had won. Steve's story hit the stands and had blown the *North Country Tribune's* readership and Harlan Wainright out of the water.

Harlan had been livid. He called her a traitor. He accused her of putting her mother at risk for another breakdown and of undermining Placid Properties, the one constant that had kept filet mignon in her stomach and designer clothes on her back. Apparently Mom was a hell of a lot stronger than anyone had realized, and as far as keeping herself in choice meats and high-end fashion, the blip on Maggie's sales had yet to flat-line.

Steve's obsession with the Welcome house mystery had been cut from the same alluring cloth as the Lizzie Borden axe murders and the death of Marilyn Monroe. The public's love of the lurid was Steve's golden goose. How could her love compete?

Maggie closed her eyes, wondering if and when the pain and humiliation of that episode would ever fade. She scooped up Steve's slippers and pressed them against her cheek. The terry cloth drank in the nickel-sized tears seeping through her lashes.

Suddenly, a flood of noise that Nat and her friends called music sluiced through the hall past Maggie's door, signaling that Nat's alarm had gone off.

Maggie opened her eyes and wiped what remained of her tears away. She dropped the slippers and looked in the mirror. Twisting her hair into a topknot, she pulled until the subtle lines around her eyes and mouth vanished. She stared at herself wondering idly if she could still turn Steve on.

She shook out her hair and slipped out of her nightgown. It puddled at her ankles in a warm heap. She grabbed her sonic toothbrush, ran it under the water and squeezed a pearl of toothpaste on the bristles. As she pressed the green button, angled the vibrating brush and moved it across her teeth, her gaze wandered to a birthmark in the valley between her breasts. She was the only one in her family that had it. Whenever she asked why, Mom changed the subject. The mark was strawberry red, the size of a dime, and shaped like a crescent moon. The thought it might turn to cancer scared her. The doctor said to call if she noticed a change. But then she'd get dressed and forget about it until she had gotten undressed again. She squinted. Were her eyes playing tricks? Or had something changed?

Deciding the former, Maggie rinsed her mouth, ran the brush under water and stuck it in its stand. She moved the clear shower curtain aside, adjusted the water and stepped in. Her back to the nozzle, she closed her eyes, bowed her head and swept her hair up.

Pinpricks of hot water pelted her shoulders and neck and ran down the curve of her back, buttocks and thighs. She picked up a gold and white striped cloth and a bar of green tea and cucumber soap and held them under the water. She rubbed the lathered cloth between her breasts, over the birthmark and closed her eyes. She remembered how Steve had pressed her against the tile in his shower. She felt him wrap her hair around his fist, bend her head back, kiss her neck, her breasts and birthmark before making love. Maggie closed her eyes and leaned her forehead against the tile. That was fourteen years ago. Why did her body react as if it had happened last night?

The night Maggie learned Steve had gotten married her pain was so bad she'd stayed drunk. Mom was frantic. Harlan had called her a damned fool and threatened to cut her loose. She'd hated him for it, but if he'd followed through, God knows where she'd be today. She dated some guys after Steve but it never worked.

Maggie soaped herself up, rinsed off and reached for the shampoo. She lathered her hair, remembering the day she got word Steve had divorced. In her perfect world Steve had divorced because he still loved her. That day she traded Absolut for club over ice with a twist. He never called, of course, but by then she'd accepted they were over. The few times she'd spotted him, she ducked out of sight. She liked being clean and sober.

Maggie rinsed off. She had to get moving. Couldn't be late for Harlan's urgent meeting. What the hell was he up to now? She stepped out of the tub, grabbed a soft, white and gold Turkish towel from the towel bar and rubbed her hair. She dried her shoulders and arms and made up her mind. She'd stick to her decision and tell Mom later. Right now she was more concerned about Morgan. "But, she's got a husband to protect her. That's more than I have."

*Tommy Connelly had parents to protect him and he's dead.*

Maggie wrapped the towel around her and closed it over her breasts. She took a washcloth from the vanity cabinet drawer, wiped an oval of steam from the glass and gasped.

Lillian stood behind her. She yelped and then turned and faced her mother.

"Mom! You almost scared me into the middle of next week."

Lillian stuck Morgan's check in her face, pointing to where Morgan had written "Welcome House" and said, "Who the hell is Morgan Matthias, and how can you sell her that house?"

# Chapter 16

**Natalie**

Natalie stepped out of the shower, grabbed a red towel from the bar, wrapped it around her and opened the bathroom door. Tongues of cool air rushed in and licked steam from the mirror. Hearing the muffled ring of her cell, she dropped the towel and ran across her bedroom rug, leaving a trail of wet footprints. The cell rang again. Madeline Hudnut, her best friend, was the only one who dared call this early. She rifled through a hillock of sheets and blankets.

"Damn you, Maddy, I'm late. This better be good or I swear I'll—"

The cell rang a third time. Where was it anyway? One more ring and the call would get kicked to voicemail. Natalie dropped on all fours and peered under the bed. She spotted her purse and pulled it out and turned it upside down, spilling her wallet, makeup, keys, and the cell on the floor. She pressed *call*. "Hello?"

"Hello yourself, squirt."

*Kevin?*

Her heart leaped to her throat. She had given Kevin her number at the WBI, but when he didn't call, she figured he was teasing her like always.

"Hey. You there?"

Oh my God it's him! Natalie plopped on her rump and stretched her legs out in front of her. A dark veil of hair fell past her shoulders. Drops of water meandered haphazardly down her shoulders and over the curve of her breasts. One bubbled around her nipple, and Natalie drew in a breath.

"Hello?"

"Kevin," she whispered, swallowing and licking her lips.

"In the flesh. Well, more or less." He chuckled, teasing.

Natalie closed her eyes. Her calves, thighs and butt were turning to liquid. Pretty soon there'd be nothing left but a stain on her bedroom rug to prove she'd even existed.

*Say something, stupid!* She opened her eyes. "Kevin?"

"Right again," he laughed, and Natalie shivered.

*OhGodohGod.* "Hey," she laughed. Is that the best you can do, dork, say *hey* then laugh like some clown on a *Hee Haw* rerun?

Kevin cleared his throat. "Did I wake you?"

Natalie searched for her voice. "No! I mean—" Way to go, nimrod! Natalie closed her eyes. She couldn't bear watching her whole body blush. She tried to sound cool. "Of course not."

"Listen, squirt," he breathed, "I need to see you."

His voice made her humid and chilly all at once. She swallowed, barely drawing a breath. This had to be a dream. A hottie like Kevin could have any girl, but he called her!

"Nat?"

"Yes?" Great. He probably thought she wasn't listening. God, she was such a nerd.

"Ever since lunch at the WBI, I can't get you out of my mind."

Natalie opened her eyes and squeezed her cell nearly dropping his call. If this were a dream, she'd rather die than wake up.

"Could we meet? After school, that is."

Her entire room faded to black. Kevin, her universe, stood before her. His lips curved in that Kevin-smile. His blue eyes mocked like always.

"Truth is, Nat," he paused, "I want to see you." His honeyed words dripped from her cell. "Do you want it too?"

Did she want it too? A soft moan escaped her.

"Nat?"

"What? I mean I'd love to!" Okay. Don't go melting all over him like teenage ice cream in August. Goose bumps skittered along her spine to her hairline, making her scalp tingle.

"Okay then. What time does school let out?"

"School?" Yeah. School. You heard the man. Answer him, dip wad, before he hangs up! "I'm out by three."

"Turn your cell on at two fifty-five, and I'll call you."

Kevin hung up and Natalie stared at the phone like she'd never seen one before. She hit *end*, got to her feet and froze.

"What should I *wear?*"

Verging on panic, she scraped her fingers through damp hair, threw her cell on the bed and noticed the clock on her bureau said 6:30. She had ten minutes to decide.

Her closet was a warehouse of clothes. She dug through slacks, skirts, and jeans. She had to wear something sexy, something that made her look older but not too old. She didn't want to red-flag Gran, Maggie, or Vice Principal Hornsby, the old horn. Maddy and Carla told her that Hornsby pulled her out of class because she turned him on. She said they were nuts, but now that Kevin had called maybe they knew something she didn't.

"Oh my God Kevin." She stopped ripping through her clothes and closed her eyes. Suddenly, she was acutely aware of every twist her tongue made to say his name. KE spread her tongue across her mouth, making its sides press against her back teeth. VI sunk her teeth softly into her bottom lip. N forced the tip of her tongue to come to a point and rest behind two front teeth. Lacing her fingers, she rested her palms on top of her head.

"Eight-and-a-half torturous hours to go." She hated school on a normal day. How would she get through it today? Now the clock said 6:45. Make that eight hours, fifteen minutes.

Having read that skirts turned men on, Nat reached for her crushed cotton tiered skirt with a hot terracotta and cocoa Aztec print, and her terracotta tank top. The one with beads sprinkled across the front like granules of brown sugar. The top was cut low and stretched tight across her breasts. If Gran didn't catch that, Maggie would. Damn. She spotted her new blue denim jacket. That ought to cover her *motives* she thought, giggling. She pulled the skirt and top from their hangers and hugged them against her body. She twirled around and around then stopped and looked in the mirror that hung on the wall over a dresser cluttered with bath and body lotions and two jewelry boxes dripping with earrings and bracelets.

Her eyes glistened. She licked her trembling lips. "Do you believe that Kevin Delaney, the most gorgeous hunk of flesh this side of Hollywood, wants to see *you*!"

She jumped up and down.

"Oh God." She stopped. "Undies." She tugged at her dresser drawer, rattling bottles and jewelry. Leafing through scant satin and scantier lace, she pulled out burnt orange bikini panties and a burnt orange lace bra. She held them against her top and skirt. Not a perfect match, but after spending two weeks dodging Sam at the WBI to earn the money to buy these babies, she'd pull the match off. A fellow clotheshorse, Maggie would understand her fashion choice, but Gran would split a gut. She held the bra across her breasts and smiled. "Well little bra and panties, you'll just have to be mine and Victoria's secret." She hugged herself. "When Maddy finds out, she'll *freak!*"

Natalie looked at the clock. She was running late. She could *not* give Hornsby a reason to get on her. Not today. Not with hers and Kevin's, oh my God, *date* going on.

She pictured Maddy's face when she heard the news. That reminded her. Makeup. Frantically scanning the room she saw her makeup case on the floor where she'd dumped it. She scooped it up. Clothes and makeup in hand, she hit the bathroom. If she pulled herself together fast, she could bum a ride with Maggie.

Natalie looked at herself in the mirror and gave a varsity cheer. "You're dynamite. You're dynamite. You're tick tick tick tick tick tick tick tick—boom. Dynamite. Boom. Boom. Dynamite!"

She giggled, lifted her hair and sprayed some *Heaven* behind her ears and across the back of her neck and then stuck the perfume bottle into her purse. She stepped into black leather sandals and grabbed her knapsack. Praying Maggie was still home, Natalie opened her door, walked toward Maggie's room and froze.

"You heard me, Maggie," Gran said, sounding very unhappy.

"Who the hell is Morgan Matthias, and how can you of all people sell her that house?"

Gran never swore, and by the tremor in her voice, Gran meant the Welcome place. Nat held her breath and inched closer.

Sensing peripheral movement, Natalie glanced toward the staircase. Oh God! Jinx, their Golden Retriever, had climbed the steps probably looking for Gran. "Shoo, Jinxy. Gran'll be down in a second," she whispered. "Go. Go," she said, shooing Jinx toward the steps. Jinx raised her ears and cocked her head. "*Please,* girl."

Jinx hesitated then lowered her head dejectedly. She sniffed the rug, turned and headed for the steps. Nat held her breath until Jinx was safely down the steps. She exhaled her relief and set her knapsack and purse on the floor. She flattened her spine against the wall, leaned her head back, closed her eyes and listened intently.

"Please, Mom." Maggie kept her voice low and neutral. "I'll explain later," she said, squeezing the towel tightly around her. "Harlan's wired about something. He scheduled a staff meeting first thing." Maggie rushed past Lillian into her bedroom. Maggie's feelings got mixed again and made her uneasy.

"I don't give a damn about Harlan's meeting," Lillian said, "Damn it, Maggie. How can you do this?"

"Do what?"

Lillian followed Maggie out of the bathroom. "This!" She waved the check in the air.

"It's my job, Mom," Maggie said over her shoulder.

"Your job." A rare sarcastic laugh escaped Lillian's lips. "Dear God. I can't believe what I'm hearing. You've been working with Harlan for so long, you're becoming just like him."

Fighting to keep from spilling her guts, Maggie watched her mother blink back tears. There was a time she'd have sold her soul to hear someone compare her to Harlan. But today the comparison stung like a nest of hornets.

Lillian looked at Maggie. "Fine. Let me spell it out for you. If this woman moves into that house," her lower lip trembled, "She'll die just like Tommy did. I know it."

Maggie hugged Lillian. "That's not true." Her voice lacked conviction. Like cheap veneer, it covered her feelings badly.

"Something in that house killed Tommy Connelly the same way it killed Jared and Elspeth Welcome."

Maggie pictured the tower and the apparition. If it was her imagination, how could she see it so clearly? Maggie closed her eyes and gave Lillian one last squeeze.

"Sorry, Mom. I'm late, and I've got to go." When would that house stop ripping her family apart? She kissed Lillian's hair and let her go.

"Have you heard anything I said?" Lillian grabbed Maggie and spun her around. Maggie's towel peeled like skin from a ripe fruit. She stared at the birthmark between Maggie's breasts.

Maggie followed Lillian's gaze. "Has my birthmark changed?"

"No," Lillian said, shaking her head. "There's no change."

"Why are you staring then?"

"I haven't seen it in so long I forgot it was there."

"Then I shouldn't worry?" She searched her mother's eyes.

"There's no change, Maggie." Check in hand, Lillian sat on Maggie's bed. "When did Harlan do it?" Lillian said.

"What?" Maggie wondered when her mother had started to age.

"Put that house back on the market."

"The ad's been in The Times since the middle of May."

"Damn him," Lillian bunched Maggie's sheets in her hand. "He was here for a cookout Sunday. He never mentioned—"

"He knows how you feel." Grateful Harlan was on the hot seat, Maggie opened her closet door.

Frowning at a wall of slacks, blouses and sweaters, she wedged her right arm in the middle. "He busted his tough old rump worming his way back into your heart. Do you honestly think," she grunted, pushed hard and parted the wall. She pulled a white tailored blouse, a long sleeved berry red cashmere sweater, and a pair of chocolate brown corduroy slacks from their hangers and faced Lillian, "he'd risk losing you again?"

Lillian stared past Maggie into the closet and waved her arm. Maggie sighed. The imminent subject was a sore one and always surfaced at the worst possible time.

"The closet, bursting its seams with so many skirts and blouses you can't even close the door. The brand new Lexus. The husband and children you don't have."

"Mom, please," Maggie said. Steve's face flashed through her mind. "Don't do this." She folded her clothes over her arm, refusing to think about losing Steve twice in one day.

"Your obsession with making that almighty sale, especially the Welcome place, cost you that young man you loved so much didn't it? The reporter. What was his name?"

"You have a short memory, Mom. Steve Rivers dredged up a story that knocked us all on our asses. You *do* remember how Harlan hated him for those anniversary feature stories. Besides, if Steve and I were meant to be, nothing could have split us up. That was the glue you used to hold me together, if I recall."

"I tried to shield you from Harlan's business." She put the check on the bed and shivered.

Maggie sat beside Lillian and grabbed her mother's hands. "Don't slip away from Nat and me again, please, Mom."

Tears ran down Lillian's cheeks. She wiped them away with her hand. "Don't sell that house. Burn it to the ground!"

"If I don't sell it, someone else will."

"Like Kevin Delaney."

"Yes. Then Harlan will toss me out the door."

"Never!" She said it with such conviction, if Maggie didn't know Harlan better than she knew herself, the reassurance would have put her totally at ease.

"Maybe he won't do it while he loves you, Mom, but some day that won't be enough to save me."

"I'd give my life to convince you that something evil in that house wants people dead." Lillian sniffled.

Maggie grabbed Lillian's hands. "Listen. Nothing will happen to you, Morgan Matthias or me. I promise. I've got something I need to tell you." Maggie sighed. So much for deciding not to mention the tower. Maggie closed her bedroom door.

Outside in the hall, Nat made a fist and pounded the air. Sidestepping every creak in the floorboards under the carpet, Nat moved closer to Maggie's room, held the doorframe to steady herself, pressed her ear to the door and listened hard.

Maggie's voice was a smooth low hum and tooled along just like her Lexus. But Gran's was high and screechy like skill saws through plywood in Tech Class. She read Gran clearly.

"When did this happen?" Gran sounded perturbed.

Maggie mumbled in clusters of words. Natalie squeezed her eyes shut, trying to pull the clusters apart. But before she could grasp meaning, the word families split into letters whose orphaned sounds made as much sense as alphabet soup.

"Why did you wait so long to tell me?" Gran sounded meltdown-angry. "Come with me to the police, Maggie, before Morgan Matthias buys the house." Gran's voice broke. She started to cry. "If we tell them together, they'll finally believe me."

Come with me to the *police?* Natalie moved from the door.

Morgan Matthias was the woman who got drunk at the WBI and never touched her salmon. The one who never showed up the day Nat had taken the early shift for Kellie. Nat was still pissed over that one. But Morgan Matthias had actually done her a favor. The scoop Natalie was looking for that day had not yet materialized. Maggie sounded as if she was trying to calm Gran down. Natalie pressed her forehead against the cool hardwood door, trying to hear what Maggie was saying. She pictured Kevin, opened her eyes and looked at her watch. God! If she didn't get to school soon, she'd be late and get detention.

Suddenly, the door opened. Natalie quickly raised her fist, knuckles up, pretending she was about to knock.

"Nat? Why are you still here?""

In her bra and panties, Maggie looked *hot*. Nat pictured Maggie working with Kevin and wanted to scratch her eyes out.

"Morning, Gran," Nat said, ignoring Maggie. She sauntered in and kissed Lillian's cheek. She saw Maggie shake her head.

"Good morning, Natalie."

Gran smiled, patting Nat's head like she was still in kindergarten. When would that stop? It was so embarrassing.

"I'll be down in the kitchen," Gran said.

Her eyes were teary. It looked like Maggie's little talk had jacked Gran right off her heels. Nat watched Gran walk down the stairs and noticed how her robe hung on her body like a coat on a wooden clothes tree.

"Nat?"

"Huh?" Nat said, facing Maggie.

"I said," Maggie folded her arms, "why are you still here?"

"Oh. I was late getting ready this morning and missed the bus. Could you drop me off at school, please, Maggie?"

Maggie sighed and rubbed her forehead as if she were getting a headache. "Give me a few minutes to get myself together, okay?"

"Sure thing," Natalie said. She scooped her knapsack and purse up from the floor. "I'll catch you downstairs."

Sitting across the table from Gran, Nat poured milk over her Frosted Flakes and bananas and scooped up a spoonful. The cheery kitchen with its cocoa counters, red cabinets, white chairs and red and cocoa cushions was her favorite room. White shelves on the slate wall held cocoa and red pottery pieces and dishes. Maggie might be a royal pain but she sure had great taste. Jinx sidled up to Nat's chair.

"Jinxy. There's a good girl." Nat held out her hand and Jinx sniffed her palm with a cold nose.

Gran usually asked her about school, asked if she had a boyfriend, stuff like that. But this morning Gran was quiet, and it gave Nat time to think. Taking another spoonful, Natalie replayed what she'd overheard before Maggie had closed the door.

She knew Maggie had been into some guy, but she didn't know the Welcome place was the reason she'd lost him. And no one had ever given him a name until now. Steve Rivers. A reporter for the *North Country Tribune*. Interesting. Nor did she realize how paranoid Maggie was. Jeez. Kevin had a job of his own. He wasn't after hers. Nat stopped chewing. Was he? Did he take her number to use her for what he could get on Maggie? "He wouldn't."

"Did you say something, dear?" Lillian stopped eating. Nat watched Jinx nuzzle Gran's thigh. Gran laughed and petted her.

"No, Gran. Just thinking out loud I guess."

Kevin was on Maggie's hot seat, and Nat knew what that was like. She clocked so much time there her butt had permanent burns. Natalie watched Gran eat her cereal. She looked so pretty when her face wasn't all stitched up with worry. She could see why Uncle Harlan still had the hots for her. Natalie tilted her bowl and ladled the last of the milk, a few soggy flakes, and the last half moon of banana into her mouth. She glanced out the doorway. The hall was clear. Maggie must still be upstairs getting dressed.

"Why were you and Maggie talking with the door closed?"

"Because we didn't want you to hear what we were saying?"

Maggie stepped out of the little bath off the kitchen and Nat scowled. Maggie grabbed her leather briefcase from the counter, laid it on the table and snapped it open. She stuck a check in the accordion pleated file on the inside cover.

"Let's go, toots." Maggie looked at Nat. "Bye, Mom."

Maggie kissed Gran on the cheek. Gran didn't say a word. She didn't even smile. She's pissed at you, *Aunt* Maggie. Natalie wiped the milky smirk from her lips with a red cloth napkin.

"Bye, Gran." Natalie kissed her cheek.

"Goodbye, dear. Have a good day," Lillian smiled.

Natalie picked up her purse and knapsack and trundled after Maggie.

"Natalie? Are you coming straight home from school today?"

*Thanks a heap, Gran.* "Um, no, Gran." *Think of something. Quick!* "Actually, I'm going to Maddy's. To study."

Maggie raised an eyebrow.

*Study? Idiot!*

"We've got final exams at the end of this month." Her date with Kevin evaporating, she wanted to cry.

"I'm glad you asked, Gran, or I would've forgotten to tell you. Bye," she smiled, playing it off like a pro, for now.

Slipping past Maggie, Nat ran out the door. She had to get to school fast. She needed an alibi. What if Maddy was sick or had a doctor's appointment? Nat climbed into Maggie's Lexus. She threw her knapsack and purse in the front well and folded her arms across her chest to keep from shivering. She didn't care where Maddy was or what Maggie or Gran did if they found out she'd lied. She was going to be with Kevin today no matter what.

# Chapter 17

## Maggie

"Hey, Maggie." Hutch sighed at the huge stack of mail on her desk. "Morning."

Maggie dropped her purse and briefcase on the coffee table, walked to the coat rack and grabbed a hanger, wondering what Nat was up to. When Maggie let Nat off at school she'd seemed more distant than usual. Maggie slipped her jacket onto a hanger. Why did Nat always get so angry when all Maggie had ever wanted to do was love and guide her?

"Maybe it's a good thing Steve and I never made it. Maybe I'm not mother material," she mumbled, hanging her jacket up.

"Did you say something?" Hutch said, sorting the mail.

Maggie scooped up her purse and briefcase from the coffee table. "Had a lousy night's sleep. You know how that is."

"Still basking in the glow of your profitable weekend?"

"You bet," Maggie smiled and winked. "Unloading the Welcome house and its gruesome past, what's not to love about that?" Maggie's smile faded. The thought of Morgan buying that house still rattled her. She changed the subject. "Any messages?"

"They're on your desk," Hutch said, tossing the junk mail.

"Thanks." Maggie dropped her purse on her desk and checked her messages against her planner. No cancellations on local appointments. Harlan's scrawl overlapped the squares of days, noting a few walk-in appointments for June and July. The scent of fresh coffee wafting through the air, Maggie headed to the rear of the office, filled a PPI mug, took a sip and then carried it back to her desk. She glanced past Hutch's desk at Harlan's closed door. "He in?"

"He is." Hutch frowned at the neon-yellow flyer advertising a Gypsy bazaar on Saturday, July twelfth.

"Can I get a heads up on this morning's urgent meeting?"

"Sorry." Hutch ripped up the flyer and dropped it into her waste paper basket. "He called me at home to make sure I'd be here, but he didn't elaborate."

"Called *you* at home?" Maggie put her mug down. "Why?"

"Beats me." Hutch shrugged.

"Good morning, ladies." Kevin smiled, walking in the door.

Hutch looked up from the mail and smiled. "Hey, Kevin."

Maggie sighed. Large doses of Kevin Delaney this early in the morning could wreck a girl's makeup. Maggie looked him over sideways. Powder blue tee. Tan sports jacket. Loafers and no socks? He needed a shave and a haircut. Did his barber die?

"Little scruffy around the edges today, are we?" Maggie ruffled papers, pretending to look for something.

Kevin scratched the stubble on his chin. "Not really. Last night I watched TV Land. Remember Miami Vice?" he said, smiling. "I thought I'd shoot for the Don Johnson look."

"Really? Well, you're getting Yassir Arafat."

Hutch burst out laughing. The intercom buzzed on cue. Fighting for self-control Hutch picked up the phone. "They're here." She looked at Maggie and Kevin. Hutch grabbed her pen, pad and the stack of pertinent mail. "Right away, sir."

Maggie picked up a pad, pen, her briefcase and mug. Kevin grabbed a tablet and a pencil. He poured a mug of coffee and then followed Maggie and Hutch into Harlan's office.

"Well, I'm glad to see we're all in on time."

Maggie heard "for a change" between the lines.

Harlan folded his hands on his desk, and they pulled their chairs up. Hutch put the mail on his desk and opened her pad. Kevin and Maggie sipped their coffee and put their mugs on his desk. Maggie glanced at Harlan, then at the pictures on his wall. She noticed his aging had marked time for a while, but the youthful worsted wool sports coat and slacks he wore this morning were ill-fitting as if he'd lost weight and height. The blue shirt and butter and navy tie exaggerated the shadows under his eyes, turning his skin a shade paler. He looked vulnerable, a word she'd never have used in the same sentence with his name—until now. Suddenly, she was worried about him.

"Okay. First things first." Harlan sipped his coffee, grimaced and glanced at the mail. "Things went well with Ms. Matthias over the weekend?" He put the mug on his desk.

"To put it mildly."

Maggie hid her reservations about Morgan and the house, and smiled brightly especially at Kevin. She snapped open her briefcase, retrieved Morgan's check and put it on Harlan's desk.

Harlan licked his lips like the big bad wolf, savoring Little Red Riding Hood's Grandma's mortgage. "Very good work, my dear."

Maggie beamed, wanting to kick herself. Why did a pat on the head from Harlan still have such a dramatic affect?

"Let's not get ahead of ourselves. We'll have to see if Ms. Matthias passes stage two. The interview. Even so, she still could fly the proverbial coop. Keeping her in that house, now that would be the real coup. I suppose I made a pun, of sorts."

Leave it to Harlan to give with the right, and bitch-slap with the left. Maggie felt Kevin smirk. Screw him. She grabbed her mug and sipped.

"So, why the urgent meeting?" Kevin grinned.

"Patience," Harlan said. "Learn to savor life's precious moments. Considering the human life span, there are so few."

To Maggie's glee Kevin cleared his throat and shifted uncomfortably in his seat.

"Pardon?" Maggie said, giving him her ear, expectantly, fighting hard not to smile.

"Okay, people. I've got some news," Harlan said. His staff straightened up. "I had lunch with Evan Burke last Friday."

Burke was the Editor of the *North Country Tribune* and Steve's boss. At first he'd kept Steve on a tight leash. Maggie remembered how Steve had complained. But Steve liked and respected Evan. After her heartache had subsided, she read Steve's column from time to time. His style had improved. Apparently, Evan's mentoring had paid off.

"Burke announced he's retiring from the paper this year."

Maggie, Kevin, and Hutch glanced at each other, puzzled.

Harlan smiled sardonically. "As you know, Burke and I haven't always been on the same side of the fence to put it mildly. But as a respected member of the Fourth Estate, he was gracious enough to give me a heads up on an upcoming and potentially nasty situation." Harlan cleared his throat. He seemed worried, Maggie thought.

"I don't know if you're aware, but this September will be the twenty-fifth anniversary of Tommy Connelly's death."

Harlan stared hard at Maggie, as if giving his words time to sink in. Maggie knew time had passed, but twenty-five years?

"Burke warned me that Rivers is gearing up for *a special* edition." He smiled crookedly at Maggie. "I don't suppose you have any influence with that cheeky little bastard."

"Influence?" Kevin looked at her. "You know Steve Rivers?"

"Know him?" Harlan said. "They were Siamese twins, joined at the genitals for over five years."

Maggie felt the heat rise in her face. How could she have felt sorry for him? She looked at his pale face and wished him a heart attack. "Excuse me," she said, cleared her throat and got to her feet. "I need more coffee."

"Sit down, Maggie." She glared at him, frozen where she stood. "*Now!*" Harlan banged his fist on his desk.

Hutch flinched. Kevin sat tight-lipped and speechless. Maggie's emotions were raw. Harlan's salt-encrusted words stung. She lowered herself into her seat. If she shed one tear in front of Kevin and Hutch, she thought, widening her eyes to accommodate the ones forming, she'd pick up his crystal ashtray and bash his fucking brains out.

"I'm sorry for being indelicate, Maggie."

She glanced sideways at Kevin and Hutch. Avoiding her eyes, Kevin was stone-faced. Eyes downcast Hutch scribbled on her pad.

"I did it to make a point. If Rivers makes half the splash Burke thinks, I don't know what'll scare Ms. Matthias off first, his anniversary story or the house itself. "We've got to find a way to stop Rivers." He stared at Maggie again.

Maggie felt her red-hot face get hotter and redder, but refused to look away. She took a deep breath and cleared her throat. "What's that got to do with me?"

"Everything, my dear," he smiled. "You're the most potent weapon in our arsenal. Our own sexy, gorgeous neutron bomb."

Maggie's lips got thin and white with anger. Her eyes clouded. She curled her fingers around the arms of the chair, whitening her knuckles and pushed herself up

"You outrageous, hypocritical bastard!" She banged her fist on his desk and knocked her mug over. Liquid fingers splayed across Harlan's blotter, turning it dark green. "The minute Steve walked into my life you did everything in your power to break us up. You accused me of putting him before my mother, you, and your almighty empire. For all I know you even paid that slut he married to seduce him. And now because it suits your purposes, you want me back in his bed? To do what? Stop the press? Well if I couldn't accomplish that when we were 'joined at the genitals' as you so graphically put it, why do you think I can do it now?"

Maggie turned and walked out of his office.

"Get back here!" Harlan snarled. "This meeting isn't over."

He'd gone too far this time. She walked out the front door, forgetting her purse, her keys and her briefcase.

# Chapter 18

## Natalie

Natalie noticed that Madeline Hudnut's astonished dark eyes hadn't blinked once since she'd grabbed her in homeroom and began her incredible story, starting with lunch at the WBI.

Clearly devouring the tasty teaser, Maddy had dogged Natalie for more. Tickled, Nat served detail after scrumptious detail like a seven-course, gourmet meal. Maddy had appeared to savor each course like a starving, homeless waif. In eighth period study hall Nat served dessert:

Her date with Kevin at three.

It was 2:45. The PA came on. While Vice Principal Hornsby made announcements no one listened to, Nat turned on her cell.

"Oh my God, Nat." Maddy ran her fingers through her long straight brown hair, looking dreamy eyed. "You are sooo lucky."

The dismissal bell rang and Natalie rushed Maddy out of the classroom. "I swear that clock never moved today. Come on."

Maddy followed Nat into the lav. She watched Nat squirt soap in her palms and run the water. "I've got to wash the stink of school off my hands, besides," she dried her hands, "I want to show you this." Natalie took off her blue denim jacket and lifted her terracotta tank top.

"Oh my God, Nat." Maddy gaped at Nat's uplifted cleavage in her burnt-orange lace bra.

Giggling, Nat lowered her tank top, lifted her skirt and bared her legs, revealing matching bikini panties.

Maddy sucked in her breath. "Did you wear that because you and Kevin might—?"

Natalie let her skirt fall. "With a man like Kevin, a girl's gotta be prepared." She fished through her purse for a brush.

"But," Maddy frowned. "We made a pact, remember? We had to be in love with a guy who loved us before we—"

Natalie pulled out a pink brush with stiff black bristles and faced Maddy. "I remember," she said, trying not to sound annoyed, but Maddy was getting to her. Her jaw set tight, Natalie stared into the mirror and brushed her hair, hard.

"And what about condoms, Nat, what if—"

"God, Maddy. I'm sorry I told you." Maddy recoiled as if Nat had slapped her. Her eyes glistened. "I'm sorry," Nat said. "I'm psyched and nervous and you're not helping."

Nat pulled away and started brushing her hair again. Why was Maddy acting like a poop? Carla had warned Natalie that Maddy was jealous of her. Nat didn't believe it at first, but now? She checked her wristwatch. 2:58. *Yikes!*

"Look, Maddy, I—" Nat's cell rang. The girls froze. It rang again and Nat fished through her purse and pulled it out. "Hello?" Pause. "Oh hi, Kevin."

Nat and Maddy did deep knee bends with excitement.

"Looking Glass Lodge parking lot at three-twenty? You bet." Nat closed the cover. "Wish me luck." She hugged Maddy and started out the door. Suddenly, she stopped and turned. "Oh. I told Gran and Maggie I'd be at your house studying this afternoon."

Maddy's mouth dropped.

"Cover for me this once, and I'll owe you forever."

Kevin sat in the Looking Glass Lodge parking lot in his '08 fire-engine red Acura convertible glancing at BMWs, and SUVs, pissed off at the privileged pricks that owned them. If it weren't for a friend at Placid Acura who told him the car had been traded in because the shade of red didn't match Ms. Privileged Prick's nail polish, he'd still be tooling around in his old Neon. He made the Acura's payments all right, but even with the trade in, the down payment had cleaned him out. It was all about the ching. If you played the game, you had to play the role. A few hefty commissions and he'd be back on top.

He grabbed the *North Country Tribune* from the back seat and pictured the fire in Maggie's eyes this morning when she told the old bastard off and then stormed out. Kevin had ordered lunch in to watch the final act, but Maggie never showed. Blew her appointments off. When the old man asked Hutch to cancel Maggie's afternoon due to a family emergency, Kevin knew Harlan had been worried. He should be. Maggie was a pro. She had never trashed her clients for any reason— until today.

Kevin put the paper in the passenger seat. He'd stopped envying Maggie's family connection. If Harlan cut Lillian's daughter to shreds, what would he do to the rest of his staff?

So, Maggie and Steve Rivers were joined at the genitals. What a way to put it. He'd never forget Maggie's face when Harlan lobbed that one over the net. She looked so betrayed he'd actually felt sorry for her.

Kevin smiled. So the ice queen had genitals. Could've fooled him. The first time he saw Maggie he thought, man, she was some piece of sterling silver. Vintage, but tight and mighty fine with aquamarine eyes, spun gold hair, legs that didn't quit, and a bodacious butt he'd vowed to do more with than feast his eyes.

Kevin slunk down in his car seat, remembering the hot August day she had walked into the office in this little pink and beige number with those off the shoulder peasant sleeves and pink capri pants. She was almost completely tan, except for strap marks, two narrow roads, that looped south over her hills and through her valleys, turning him on. He remembered needing to pull his chair close to his desk until she left. He hadn't thought about Maggie that way for—Kevin looked at his bulging crotch. He rolled his eyes, worried. Nat could be here any—

"Hey," Nat said, smiling. "You decided to put the top down!"

"Hey yourself." Kevin grabbed the paper and stuck it on his lap. "Climb in." He brushed the leather seat off. "Don't want you to get newsprint all over that skirt. Burnt orange?"

Natalie opened the door and slid in. She lifted her skirt, baring her leg and slid her sweet butt onto the seat. When she threw her purse and knapsack in the back, her denim jacket opened, exposing her tight burnt orange tank top. Her nipples were pencil-eraser hard and poked through her top. Kevin centered the paper on his lap. Man, these Duran women drove him nuts. Dressed in that top and skirt, with her black hair, black eyes and those mink lashes, Natalie looked like an Indian princess. She may look like a woman, but he knew she was just a kid. All he wanted was information. Now, if Maggie were sitting next to him—

"Yes, it's burnt orange," she said, looking impressed. "I didn't think guys noticed the color of women's skirts."

Kevin looked her in the eye. "I'm not just any guy." He smiled, giving up both dimples.

Eyes wide, Nat gave a slow smile and he started the car. He pressed a button and the top rose.

"What are you doing?"

"We can't tool around in the open. We can't be in town. I told you at the WBI that Harlan and Maggie can't know about us."

She nodded. "Where are we going?"

Kevin eased out of the parking lot. "How about Whiteface Ski Center for hot chocolate?"

"Right." Suddenly, Nat looked worried.

Kevin idled across from the Looking Glass Café, waiting for an opening and glanced at her. "Listen, I don't ever want you doing anything that makes you uncomfortable."

"It's not that. It's just that I told Gran and Maggie I'm studying with my friend, Maddy Hudnut at her house after school today. We've got finals in a few weeks."

"Sounds like a great cover."

Yeah. Except that I don't have to study. I mostly get it the first time. School bores me. That's why I get into trouble."

*Great!* "Look, don't worry. Maybe they'll believe it because they *want* to. Take it from one who knows."

"I guess."

Natalie reached for her purse, looking distracted. Traffic thinned and Kevin put the pedal to the metal.

Maggie had been at the Looking Glass Cafe at a table near the window, sucking back Absolut on the rocks since she'd left the office this morning. She may be crocked, but the red convertible at the corner got her attention. She squinted. She'd know that sneaky bastard's car anywhere. Natalie was with him. She recognized Nat's denim jacket.

She stood up, stumbled closer to the window, but stayed in the shadows. She couldn't risk Natalie spotting her, but she needn't have worried. Nat looked too wrapped up in Kevin who looked too wrapped up in himself to notice. Kevin and Natalie. Thank God she was presently anesthetized. She eased herself into her seat, put her elbows on the table, rested her head in her palms, and worked her way back through her alcoholic haze to this morning, when little *gnat* said she'd be at Maddy's studying. She'd planned to call Shirley Hudnut as soon as the meeting had ended. That was before Harlan blindsided her. Talk about best-laid plans. She hoped the mice were having better luck.

How could Harlan talk to her like that in front of Kevin and Hutch? Maggie swilled her Absolut and shuddered. He knew what Steve had meant to her and how their breakup had destroyed her. Mom always said Harlan never gave a damn about anything but himself and the business. She should march right back and quit, but if Harlan was there she might kill him.

Maggie signaled for the check. She felt her lap for her purse and frowned. She fumbled under the table, wondering if somebody had stolen it. Except for the server no one had come near her table. She felt panic rising, and then she remembered her purse was in the office where she'd left it this morning. Maggie pressed her fingers against her aching temples. Her bill could probably match the cost of the Olympic Hockey Rink.

Her server came by. "Will that be all, ma'am?" she smiled.

"Oh God. This is embarrassing." Maggie pushed her hair behind her ears. Her voice slurred. Her cheeks were numb but she felt the heat rising. "I left my purse in the office and —"

"I've got it," a guy said.

Maggie exhaled, relieved. "I'll pay you back," she smiled and stood. Weaving like a stalk of wheat in a windy field, she turned toward his voice.

"Thank—"

Her legs gave way. She collapsed into her seat like a rag doll and watched him sign.

"Steve." The whisper amplified, filling her head.

"Maggie."

Did she hear concern in his voice?

"Don't say a word," he said.

Little did he know she couldn't speak if her life had depended on it. Stunned didn't cover it.

As small as Lake Placid was Steve and she rarely crossed paths. At first when it hurt to breathe, not crossing paths had been a blessing, but as time healed and she heard he'd divorced, she started looking for him, around every corner, in every doorway. The *North Country Tribune* was based in Plattsburgh where he lived. She had no solid reason to go there, except to check out some listings and that happened very infrequently. He looked fit. Trim. Sexy. She looked rumpled, stale. She pictured her blotchy eyes and red nose. She must look like—"

"You look like you need a cup of coffee." Steve held out his hand. She stared at it, blinking. "I'd like to buy you one. If you'll let me."

Maggie's eyes watered. You can't do this again and survive, she thought, but she nodded and swallowed. She took Steve's hand without looking up. It felt warm. Strong. Achingly familiar. She felt like an alcoholic, swearing she'd only have one. A teardrop worked its way through her lashes and slowly rolled down her cheek. She closed her eyes and got to her feet.

*You're nuts. You know where his loyalties lie. You leave with him now and you're sealing your fate.*

Maggie and Steve walked out of the Looking Glass Café together.

# Chapter 19

## Maggie

The morning sun on her face, Maggie frowned, moaned and tried to open her eyes, but her lashes felt stitched together.

"Morning."

She heard his voice. Was she still dreaming? She smelled coffee, pried her lids apart and rubbed her protesting lashes. He stood by the bed with a tray in his hands.

"Orange juice. Toast buttered lightly and coffee. Black, just the way you like it," he smiled.

It wasn't a dream. But what was he doing here in her— She looked around, confused. It wasn't her place, and she'd never forget his bed.

She raised herself up and frowned. The Absolut she'd banged back had turned her brain cells to jelly. "Oh God," she groaned.

"Don't try to sit up, Maggie."

"I'm okay." She refused to say his name or look in his eyes until she knew exactly why she was here. She put her palms flat on the mattress and raised herself up. The blankets and sheets fell away, and she was relieved to see she had her clothes on.

Steve set the tray in front of her. "Try to eat something."

"Thanks," she averted her eyes. "But I don't think I can."

She sneaked a peek at him when he turned and went to the closet. He looked clean and pressed in Docker khakis and short-sleeved red plaid shirt. His shoulders were broad. His back tapered to a narrow waist.

She looked at herself in a mirror that hung on the wall opposite his bed. Her head was a haystack of hair and her eyes were smudged with mascara. Trying to wipe it away would only make it worse. She watched him pull a terrycloth robe from a hook in the closet. It was blue like his slippers, the ones in her bedroom closet. He laid the robe at the foot of the bed.

"Maybe you'll feel more like eating after a hot shower." He looked at his watch. "I'm late for work. But you're welcome to—"

"Why did you bring me here?"

"You needed help."

"You think?"

She handed him the tray, threw off the covers, swung her legs over the bed and stood. A wave of nausea buckled her knees. He set the tray on the bed and grabbed her. She waved him away. "Where's my purse?"

"At your office. That's why I got the tab at the Looking Glass last night." Steve scooped the tray up. "Remember?"

Right. She left her purse at the office along with her car keys, which meant she was stuck here in Plattsburgh with him. She plopped on the bed, fighting back tears, dizziness and the episode in Harlan's office that had launched her into oblivion.

*I don't suppose you have any influence with that cheeky little bastard. Kevin was surprised ... You know Steve Rivers? ... They were ... joined at the genitals for over five years.*

Steve crossed the room and set the tray on his dresser. She closed her eyes and breathed in. His scent in the sheets filled her nostrils. Her heart hammered. Wrestling it under control, she opened her eyes. Steve stood near her. She swallowed and cleared her throat. "Why not tell me the real reason I'm here?"

"I did."

Steve was tan, like he'd been vacationing somewhere sunny and warm. How easily she could get lost in his deep, dark eyes. She hated how he could still reach in and grab her after all these years.

"Try again." She stood up and teetered. She felt hundreds of hairline cracks web her skull. He caught her in his arms, making her heartbeat erratic. She pressed her palms against his chest. "Please let me go." She struggled to push him away, but her heart joined forces with his.

He kissed her. Completely off guard, she went limp.

He walked her backwards and pressed her against the wall. He ran his fingers through her hair, took her face in his hands and looked into her eyes. He ran his hands along her sides from her breasts to her hips and up again, while brushing her lips with his. Her addicted heart throbbed, aching for him to kiss her again, hating herself for wanting him more now than ever. He smiled like he'd read her mind and pressed his lips to hers.

*Rivers is gearing up for a very special edition.*

She twisted around, broke his hold and walked to the bathroom. She couldn't do this again. She ran the cold water, cupped her hands and doused his kiss from her lips. Her heart raced. Steve stood behind her.

"I've missed you."

She grabbed a hand towel and faced him. "Funny how things

coincide." She smirked at his puzzled look. "Don't pretend you don't know what I'm talking about." She wrapped her hands in the towel to keep them from shaking.

"I don't."

"Does the twenty-fifth anniversary of Tommy Connelly's death ring a bell?"

Steve left the bathroom, went to his dresser, flipped his cell open and dialed. Maggie stood in the doorway, arms folded, watching. "Hey. I might have a twenty-four hour bug." He paused. "I'll be here if Evan needs me. If not, I'll see you on Monday." He paused again. "Thanks." He laughed and flipped his cell.

"You didn't have to do that for me."

"I didn't."

"I appreciate the rescue, but I need a ride home, please."

"Not until you shower, have something to eat and we talk."

After he'd kissed her like that? "I don't think so."

"I do."

"There's nothing to talk about. Everything's—"

"Neat. Simple. And wrong."

"You haven't denied my accusation."

"You wouldn't believe me if I had."

"You got that right." Maggie went into the bathroom and ran the water. He took the terrycloth robe from the bed and followed.

"There's a new toothbrush in the left hand drawer of the cabinet. I'll freshen your breakfast while you shower." She knew that tone of voice. "Here," he said, and she took the robe from him. "Drop your clothes outside the door. I'll send your sweater and slacks to be cleaned and pressed, and I'll throw the rest in the wash."

Except for Steve's terrycloth robe, Maggie was naked and hungrier than she realized. He set a plate of eggs and bacon in front of her and joined her at the breakfast bar. She gazed out the patio doors, beyond the commons to Lake Champlain. She popped the last piece of toast into her mouth, finished her coffee and looked around.

Judging from the condo, he'd done well for himself. On the first floor there was a living room, kitchen/family room combination and half bath. The family room had a hickory fireplace on a brick wall. The way the wind whipped off Lake Champlain in winter he'd need it. The chimney and hearth were tiled in terra cotta. The furniture was masculine. Brown leather and wood with simple lines. He'd mentioned that upstairs there were two bedrooms and a bath.

Their conversation was stilted at first, becoming less so as the morning progressed. Two topics remained. The Connelly anniversary piece and Steve's ex-wife.

He grabbed the carafe from its warming plate. "More coffee?"

She nodded. He topped her cup off, replaced the carafe and sat. She sipped and looked through the doors at the lake. She felt his eyes take her in. It excited and scared her.

"When will my clothes be ready?" She put her cup down.

"Not until Monday."

"What?"

"The cleaners quit early today, and they are closed on Sundays."

She became acutely aware of her nakedness under his robe.

*Siamese twins, joined at the genitals for over five years.*

Her eyes brimmed. She slumped in the chair. Her face burned with anger and shame. Right now she hated him as much if not more than she hated Harlan.

"Maggie, I'm sorry."

Steve must have assumed she was upset about her sweater and pants. He touched her hand, and she jumped as if hit by a thunderbolt. She couldn't speak.

"You're a six, right? I'll run out to the store and—"

She found her voice. "I'm not upset about my clothes." She left Harlan's office wanting revenge; well, this was her chance. "I had a run-in with Harlan yesterday." She told him what'd happened verbatim. "I can't believe he humiliated me like that in front of Kevin and Hutch."

Steve's eyes glittered. "Believe it. He's a real piece of work, Maggie." He got to his feet, took his cup to the sink and dumped his coffee and mumbled, "You have no idea."

Was she imagining things, or was he overreacting?

Steve pressed his palms on either side of the counter and bowed his head. "Damn him," he whispered, pounding the counter.

She drew the robe tightly around her. Was he upset for her or did he have his own agenda? He sat across the counter from her and took her hands.

"I need to say something I should've said a long time ago."

"Right." She stiffened and pulled her hands away.

He grabbed her hands "You've got to listen."

"Why should I?"

He looked into her eyes. "Because I love you."

Stunned, she jerked her hands away and got to her feet. "You're worse than Harlan ever was." Tears ran down her cheeks. "He was right. You'll do anything for that story." She ran through the living room, up the steps and headed for the laundry room. She'd get to Placid if she had to hitchhike naked.

Steve took the steps two at a time. He grabbed her from behind and held her to him.

"Leave me alone! Haven't you hurt me enough?"

He locked her in his arms and whispered into her hair. "I never got over you."

"Really?" she sobbed. "You mean getting married didn't work? Because it sure fooled me."

"That was my second mistake. I married her because she looked like you. It didn't work because she wasn't you."

"Liar," she struggled. "Let go of me."

He turned her around, cupped her face in his hands and forced her to look into his eyes. "Not until you hear me out."

Exhausted, scared and confused she stopped fighting. Her head felt swollen to three times its normal size. He took her hand, led her downstairs and sat her in front of the fireplace.

"I didn't bring you here for an update on the Welcome stuff, Maggie, I swear."

She smirked. Did he really expect her to believe that?

"I heard you'd stopped drinking. When I saw you at the Looking Glass Café alone and drunk, I didn't know what to think."

Keeping tabs was he? Damn him. *He would not get to her.*

"If getting married was your second mistake, what was your first?"

"I was young and ambitious. I wanted to make a name for myself, but one month after we fought and you left, I realized I'd made the biggest mistake of my life."

A tear fell. She wiped it away. "Are you gearing up for number twenty-five or not?"

"Guilty—"

"Then we have nothing to talk about."

"—with an explanation."

She laughed, closed her eyes. Another tear fell.

"Harlan's been blackmailing me for years, Maggie."

Her grin faded. She opened her eyes and stared.

"After we broke up I stopped by the office late one night, wanting to see if you and I could compromise. Harlan was there. He said he was glad I'd stopped in." Steve tightened his jaw. "When I was a junior in college our fraternity had a party one night, this girl was the last to leave. The guys were drunk. Things got out of hand. She accused us of rape."

She sniffled. "You didn't—"

"Of course not."

"Why didn't you tell me?" She wiped the tears from her cheek.

"I was terrified I'd lose you. When we went to trial, DNA testing had already had judicial notice." Maggie frowned and he said, "Meaning the justice system recognized it as strong enough to stand on its own as evidence in a court of law. We were acquitted; the girl was underage. The judge sealed the records—"

"Sealed? Then how did—"

"Harlan found out about the trial and paid someone off for a copy of the records. He pulled them out of his desk, waved them in my face and said if I tried getting back with you, I'd never work in the North Country or anywhere else again."

"But you were innocent."

"I was young, inexperienced and accused of rape, Maggie. I believed most people would avoid me like the HIV."

"Why would Harlan stop at threatening you to stay away from me? Why not get you fired and kill the story for good?"

"Evan told me Harlan had threatened to sue if the paper kept printing the stories." Steve locked his gaze with hers and inched closer. "Harlan's a powerful man, Maggie." He ran his finger along her cheek. "But not powerful enough to take on the press." He moved a lock of hair from her eyes. Her breath caught. "With readership up, Evan laughed him off the phone."

Her heart blocked her throat. She looked into his eyes and forced her words past it. "Even after Harlan told Evan about the rape charges?"

"Evan never mentioned the trial or charges." He stroked her cheek with his thumb. "In time I realized that Harlan never told Evan but I lived in fear he would—until now."

Every inch of her craved to believe him. She swallowed hard. "Harlan would never leave an enemy's jugular intact."

"I stopped counting the nights I lost sleep over that one."

His lips brushed her cheek. Thunder filled her ears. Lightning skittered across her flesh.

"But I think I finally know why," he said. "You."

"Me?" Her head screamed run, but flames devoured her heart. "But

Harlan blamed you," her words stumbled over trembling lips, "for ruining the sale of his house and his business"

"I may have dried up his local market." He loosened her terrycloth tie, "but think, Maggie. Harlan's a survivor."

Her robe fell away, exposing her breasts. She shivered.

"He regrouped and targeted buyers from out of town." She watched his eyes devour her nipples, her naked breasts. He moaned. His hunger infected her compromised heart.

"The paper runs my story every five years." He leaned forward. The tip of his tongue flicking her earlobe, Maggie dropped her head back and shuddered. "I doubt his new buyers knew my stories existed." Laying her down, he kissed her neck, stopping her heart. "Even so, they'd need to dig through the North Country Tribune's morgue to find them." He ran his hands down the curve of her breasts. "What are the odds of that happening?"

Desire stirred in her toes—

"Harlan never told Evan about me because of you, Maggie."

--and worked its fevered way up. "I still don't understand," she said, fighting to swim ahead of the wave.

"Ironically, Harlan and I agreed on one point. You were more important to us than some ridiculous ghost stories." His tongue, wet and familiar, teased her nipples. The wave gaining, Maggie groaned. "You were his moneymaker." Her heart slammed against his. "His golden girl, but you were crazy in love with me."

Steve slipped out of his pants—

"Harlan knew something I didn't—until it was too late. If he'd exposed me back then, he would've lost you."

-and inside her.

"He couldn't stop the press, but he could do the next best thing. You were my pipeline to new information. Cut the flow and my stories died."

High voltage currents shot through her flesh to the throbbing nugget between her legs.

"Harlan was dead wrong about one thing."

A wave of desire sucking her under, Maggie whimpered.

"My stories never scared Harlan's buyers away." Steve plunged himself deep inside her. "The Welcome house did."

And Maggie screamed, exploding around him.

# Chapter 20

**Lake Placid**
**Morgan**
**July 4**

Morgan devoured the last of an ice cream twist. She licked the residue from her lips, dabbed her mouth and deposited the napkin in a large garbage can by the curb. It was dusk. Soon the Olympic Center would become fireworks central. Pegged to her side was a canvas tote. In it were a light wool blanket, her purse and a cotton sweater.

Main Street was a river of tourists. Laughter, excitement and murmurs of anticipation rippled through the rising tide of people. On her way to claim a piece of grassy shore on Midlakes and Mirror Lake Drive Morgan breathed exotic, spicy air seasoned and stirred whenever a café door opened. She passed the Lake Placid Library, suddenly realizing she was the proud owner of an incredible house with her own astonishing library!

She'd brimmed with excitement explaining to Chuck how they'd lucked out. Super-psyched, he'd wanted to ride up with her and check the house out like she knew he would. Looking back, she could've kicked herself for leaving the camera on her kitchen counter at home a second time, but she'd been swamped with end of school year obligations, and as luck would have it, Chuck had gotten called away, again. Morgan shrugged it off. Nothing would spoil tonight. Chuck had her number and their new address. He'd be here soon enough.

She closed on the house alone, as usual. But thanks to Maggie's boss, Harlan Wainright, everything had come together without a ripple. Mr. Wainright, who'd insisted she call him Harlan, had even arranged to have the interview and closing on July third just as Maggie had promised.

The interview was an experience, that's for sure. Wainright was nice enough she supposed, so why did she feel something lurking under the polish and cordiality? He must've sensed her unease, because he took her hand, said she looked familiar and asked if they'd met before. When she said she thought not, he'd smiled politely and handed her the contract. After a few simple questions he gave her three keys, one each for the front and back doors. The third, a skeleton key, unlocked a door in the bedroom; behind it were the stairs to the gothic tower.

The sleep she'd lost over that dreaded interview! Morgan shook her head. She was no banker, but in today's market holding a mortgage in so cavalier a manner would be risky. The house had been exquisitely furnished, a miracle in itself. And now that she'd moved in, one task remained: Telling Mother.

Mother was behaving more irascibly than usual. Her mind faded in and out like a bad cable connection. What kind of a daughter abandoned her mother in a home and then moved to Lake Placid? That's the message Mother kept sending. No matter what rationale Morgan used, she was guilty as charged. She looked up. Her mood and the sky were in a dead heat to a dark finish. Her money was on her mood.

Mother aside, life was good. This coming school year would be her last. Chuck and she had discussed it. She never thought she'd want to retire, but violence in schools across the country made her uneasy. The district had offered a good buy out. It was time.

She passed the Bradford House, a magnificent Victorian country inn and historic landmark next to the Looking Glass Café. She wanted a peek, but it was getting dark. She wanted a good spot by the lake. She decided to dine at the inn tomorrow night.

Morgan's blanket was but one square in a folksy quilt that cloaked a shore where lovers held hands and kids chased each other with sparklers. Dads spread blankets and opened coolers while Moms handed out soda, iced tea and cookies.

Framed by blue-gray clouds the lake and sky were glassy and seamless. The village draped the shore like a jeweled necklace. Darkness suddenly exploded in pinwheels of cascading brilliance. The lake mirrored dots and dashes that sequined the velvet sky to melodious oooohs and aaaahs. She missed Chuck. Next year they would watch it together.

Morgan pulled her sweater out of her canvas bag and draped it around her shoulders. It must be hotter than hell in Port St. John. She pictured Mother, fighting with staff to turn off the A/C, while she sat here, by a lake, needing a sweater. Her guilt crouched on all fours like a cat waiting to pounce. She pushed it away determined to enjoy the show, but two claw-footed questions scratched their way through. Mother hated being cold, but lately she'd been acting as if being cold terrified her. It didn't make sense. Morgan shivered and tightened the sweater around her.

The fireworks ended. Parents scooped up coolers and kids. Morgan folded her blanket into her canvas bag and walked with the crowd, chatting amiably about fireworks, the weather and how September was only eight weeks away.

Morgan waved goodnight, crossed Mirror Lake Drive and headed up Midlakes Road. There were only a few streetlights in front of the houses along the way, but they were not necessary tonight. Not with that hunk of honeydew moon in the sky.

She was almost to John Brown Road, when the moon ducked behind the clouds. She looked up the hill at her house and frowned. She must have forgotten to leave her porch light on. Her house faced a wooded lot. Even with her street lamp lit, her block seemed unusually dark. She made her way up the sidewalk toward her house mindful that if she tripped and twisted an ankle, she could spend the summer on crutches.

The curtain of clouds parted as if on cue. The moon took back the night, and Morgan noticed that of her three corner streetlamps only one was lit. The other two, ensconced in separate housings, were darker than graveyard dirt. In the daylight, the lamps seemed close to the house. Fearing they would light up the bedroom under the tower and interfere with her sleep, Morgan had chosen to sleep in the master bedroom.

Didn't computerized power grids pick up malfunctioning lights? Either way, the two broken lights must be fixed soon. The moon wouldn't light her way every night. She'd speak to Maggie Duran or Harlan Wainright first thing in the morning.

# Chapter 21

**Kevin**
**July 5**

Kevin sat in the office at his desk all morning, shuffling papers, wondering how he could ditch Nat without Maggie finding out. He'd met with Nat a few times since picking her up after school that day. Aside from Lillian being pissed at Maggie for selling the house, and Maggie closing her bedroom door before Nat could hear the one little piece of dynamite information, Nat's intel had not changed. However, Nat had said something he couldn't let go. Lillian had begged Maggie to call the police, saying the police would believe her now. Did Maggie actually back up Lillian's ghost story?

Kevin had thought long and hard about paying Ms. Matthias a visit, but without the missing piece of Maggie's story he still had the same haunted house B-movie crap he'd never bought to begin with. And, scaring Ms. Matthias out of the deal would definitely cost him his job.

Since Maggie had closed the Welcome deal, the old man treated her like the prodigal daughter, and Morgan Matthias had moved in before Kevin had gotten a chance to meet her. As far as Natalie was concerned, Kevin believed he'd unleashed a monster. She was hot. And she was falling in love with him. In addition to texting the hell out of him, she stopped at the office so many times on the pretext of seeing Maggie he'd been forced to switch most of his appointments to dis her. When school let out, she'd be a fixture. Kevin gathered the papers on his desk into a pile and pushed them aside.

"For God's sake, Delaney." Kevin jumped and turned around. "What's got you so fidgety and bummed?" Maggie reached for her purse, and pulled out her Blackberry. The phone rang. Her attention diverted, she glanced at Hutch.

"Placid Properties," Hutch smiled. "It's for you, Kevin. It's Kellie."

"Thanks, Hutch." He picked up the phone as Maggie shot him a look. "Hey, baby, what's happening?"

Kevin had to hook up with Kellie on the days Nat worked. He had Nat on a tight leash, for now. He never thought he'd hear himself say it, but thank God she was jailbait—a great excuse to keep her out of his bed. And thank God she'd skipped a grade in school. When she turned legal in September she'd be away at college and he'd be free.

"Hey, Kevin. Are we still on for tonight?" By the sound of her voice Kevin was certain Kellie did not have a clue.

"Hold on." He flipped his cell open to his organizer and checked. Nat had the dinner shift. "How about I scoop you up at home for an early dinner, babe, somewhere away from here?"

Kevin hung up. He watched Maggie transfer notations from her desk planner to her Blackberry. There were so many leaks in his boat, every time the phone rang—

Hutch answered and then covered the mouthpiece. She looked at Maggie. "It's Haskins about the property on Stevens Road."

Maggie picked up the phone. "Maggie Duran. Now?" Maggie checked her wristwatch. "It's eleven-thirty. I'm free for an hour or so. Sure. No trouble at all. See you in ten."

The phone rang. Hutch answered,. "Placid Properties. I'm sorry. Mr. Wainright hasn't come in yet. Yes," Hutch said, scribbling a name. "He'll return your call as soon as he does."

Maggie swung her purse over her shoulder and smiled at Kevin. "I think you can reach Harlan at Mom's, just in case you need him, that is," she said, smugly.

Bet she thought it would irk the hell out of him, but this time she was wrong. She pushed her chair under her desk and started for the door. She stopped at his desk and tilted her head like Jinx, her Golden Retriever. He almost laughed out loud.

"Look at the face on this poor boy, will you, Hutch?" Her voice all syrup and sympathy, she shook her head. "He looks like," she tapped her lip with her finger. "Like he's suffering from acute erectile dysfunction."

Hutch burst out laughing. Kevin flushed and glared at Maggie. He felt like shouting, why don't you ask your niece about that? Maggie leaned over conspiratorially. She put her cheek next to his then whispered loud enough for Hutch to hear.

"Celery."

"Celery?" he foolishly asked.

"A stud like you hasn't heard? One whiff and you're stiff."

Maggie raised her hand, twiddled her fingers in a ta-ta wave and sauntered out the door. Kevin picked up his pen and threw it on his desk, pissed. Hutch pulled a tissue from the box on her desk and wiped the tears of laughter from her eyes.

"You two ought to take your act on the road. I swear to God. I'd forego my salary and work here just for the laughs."

Kevin watched Maggie climb into her Lexus. Damn, she bugged him. She'd looked so tired and distracted before the knock-down- drag-out with the old man he thought she'd be gone for good. But a few days later she showed up focused, energized, and considering the lousy market, she was selling houses quicker than Agway sold woodstoves in January, which had the old man beaming like a stadium floodlight.

Well, he had to trip her breaker. Soon. Kevin remembered what Harlan said and smiled. Selling the Welcome place was one thing, but getting the sale to stick was another. His mind revved like a turbo jet. This new and improved Maggie didn't calculate. Why the change? He needed to know.

Natalie had mentioned that Maggie and Rivers used to be an item after Harlan had dropped the A-bomb. It was old news, so Kevin had ignored it. Maybe he'd been too hasty. Maybe he wasn't done with Natalie yet. He pulled out his cell about to check her work schedule, when the door opened.

"Well, good morning, Morgan," Hutch said.

"Hutch," she said, smiling.

*Morgan?* As in Matthias? Kevin looked up.

Man, what a great smile. She stood about five-five and weighed maybe one twenty. Her hair was thick, dusted with gray and fell to her jaw on an angle. A classic cut. She was vintage, early fifties maybe, but looked mighty fine. He noticed a trinket on a chain around her neck. Ruby and diamonds. Dude, if those stones were real!

Hutch said, "I don't believe you two have met. Morgan Matthias, this is Kevin Delaney. Our other agent."

Kevin flipped his cell closed and dropped it on his desk. He got to his feet and extended his hand. Morgan switched her purse to her left hand and gave him her right.

"I'm happy to meet you, Mr. Delaney."

Her hand was warm, her fingers long and tapered. With those large dark eyes and broad smile she was exotic and alluring.

"The pleasure is mine, Ms. Matthias. Call me Kevin, please."

"Is something wrong, Morgan?" Hutch looked worried.

Considering that house's track record, Kevin was wondering the same thing.

"Not at all. I have a question for Maggie or Harlan."

Hutch looked at her watch. "Harlan's not in and Maggie left

minutes ago. She should be back within the hour. Gosh, speaking of which." Hutch stood up and took her purse from a drawer in her desk. "Sorry for being rude, but I've got to run. I'm late for a dentist appointment."

Kevin was all over it. "Go ahead. I can help Ms. Matthias."

"Thanks, Kevin," she said, stepping out from behind her desk. "See you guys later."

Hutch hurried out the door. Kevin pointed to a chair beside his desk and Morgan sat.

"Nothing's wrong, I hope," he smiled.

"Gosh no. I still can't believe my great luck."

Damn, Kevin thought, keeping his expression neutral.

"But there is one thing," she said.

Kevin grabbed a pencil and pad.

"After the fireworks, I walked up Midlakes and saw that two of the three lights on my corner street light were out."

"Strange."

"That's what I thought. I must insist the lights be fixed right away. It's dark and dangerous. I don't want anyone getting hurt, and I certainly don't want to get sued."

"I don't blame you."

"Could Maggie or Harlan make a call, or give me a name?"

Kevin scribbled. "I'll see they get the message."

After bidding Ms. Matthias good day, Kevin rewrote the note embellishing her concerns and put it on Harlan's desk.

Maggie was the first to return. She glanced at Hutch's empty chair and frowned. He pressed his lips tight to keep from smiling.

"Any calls, Junior?"

"Nope." Technically he was telling the truth. It was hard to keep a straight face.

"Where's Hutch?"

"She had an—"

Harlan came through the door, looking dour.

"Did you and Mom have a nice lunch?" Maggie said.

He grunted. "I'll be in my office."

Maggie shrugged, turned her back to Kevin and sifted through the mail on her desk. Apparently, the intel Nat had given was accurate. Judging from the grim set of Harlan's jaw, Lillian was still mad at him and Maggie for selling the house and whatever else Maggie had told her mother behind closed doors that day. That was another thing that still didn't fit. Maggie showed no signs of being upset. Normally, if she and Lillian were at odds, Maggie would be lower than a snake in the weeds.

"Hey, guys." Hutch came through the door carrying a can of Coke and a white lunch bag with Essex Café printed on the front.

"Gosh, it got warm out there." She plunked the bag on her desk, slipped into her chair and pulled out a tuna fish sandwich. She put the sandwich on the flattened bag, popped the soda, sipped and looked at Kevin. "What did Morgan want?" She took a bite of her sandwich.

"Morgan?" Maggie pivoted. "Matthias?" She glared at him.

"Is there anyone else?" he smiled.

"You said no one called." She took a step. "You—"

"Calm down. She didn't call. She came in person." Geez. Talk about overreacting. Flaring nostrils and all.

"Everybody!" Harlan yelled. "Get the hell in here, now!"

Hutch swallowed and dabbed her lips with a tissue from a box on her desk. She grabbed her pen and pad. Maggie and Kevin stopped arguing and hot-heeled it into Harlan's office.

Harlan waved the note, glaring at Maggie. "What is this?

She took the note, mouthed the words and seemed relieved, puzzling Kevin further. "While I was showing Mr. Haskins the piece on Stevens Road," she glanced at Kevin, "boy wonder spoke to Morgan and wrote the note. Why don't you ask him?"

Harlan ignored her. "Hutch, did Municipal ever fix those street lamps on the corner of Midlakes and John Brown Road?"

The old man knew damned well those lights hadn't been fixed. So why was he pretending to be bent out of shape?

"I don't know. I guess not." Hutch opened her pad.

"Get on it."

"I tried once before, but they said—"

"I don't give a damn what they said. Morgan Matthias is the first solid buyer we've had on that house since the Connellys. I don't want two broken streetlights taking us down."

Hutch lowered her head and scribbled on her pad. Maggie turned to leave.

"Maggie!" She stopped and faced him. "I want you to follow up, if you have to go up there, stick your finger in the socket and electrify those goddamned lights yourself!"

Kevin watched Maggie shrug and give Harlan an icy smile as if she knew something the old man didn't.

# Chapter 22

## Morgan

Morgan followed the hostess through the lobby of the Bradford House, Victorian Inn and historic landmark. The carpet, a delicate pink and white diamond pattern, ran the stairs between the oak wainscoting and horizontal balustrades to the second floor. A nineteenth century double cut ruby-on-white lamp with a brass bottom crowned the newel post.

The living room walls were white with pink embossing. In the far corner to the right of a grand piano, gold cornices framed two oversize windows dressed in white sheers and dusty rose drapes that fell in soft folds to a pale gray carpet. The mantle held a gold framed baroque mirror, gold candelabras, and a Celtic crystal vase filled with pink roses.

People sitting in leather sofas, armed chairs and rockers laughed and conversed softly. Dusty rose chairs were grouped around a glass-topped octagonal table where a milk glass vase held a small bouquet of pink roses. There were paintings in gold frames, end tables and Victorian lamps, wall sconces and a crystal chandelier.

"May I?" Morgan nodded toward a room across the hall.

"Certainly." The hostess smiled.

Morgan stepped into a library with winged chairs, velvet covered sofas and cherry wood reading and writing tables. Plant-filled, ceiling-to-floor windows faced manicured, tree-shaded gardens. There was a large mirror above a cherry wood mantle. People read books or leafed through books on sculpture, art, architecture and sundry.

The hostess led Morgan through blond French doors into the crowded dining room. She slid into her chair. Morgan took the menu, but opted to gaze around.

"What do you think?" The hostess said.

"I'm afraid I haven't finished processing."

The hostess smiled. "Happens to everyone the first time." She nodded toward a petite blond. "Grace will be your server,"

Morgan smiled at her server. After careful deliberation she ordered the soup sampler, New York strip steak with chef's butter, whipped potatoes and a house salad.

"Something to drink?" her server asked.

"Lemon water over ice, please," she said, remembering the disastrous outcome the last time she'd dined in Lake Placid.

She handed her server the menu and gazed at the dining room again. Parquet floors met walls papered in robin's egg blue. The pedestal, buffet and dining tables were covered with white on pink cloths and set with crystal, china and silver. Oak chairs upholstered in pink and white candy stripes sat under oak tables. Pink and white candles stood on metal tiers in a hearth in the fireplace. Their tiny flames glowed, enriching the ambience, if that were possible.

"Good evening," he said. He smiled and held out his hand. "I'm Jack Bradford. Welcome to the Bradford House."

Jack Bradford, about seventy-five, was tall with thick gray hair. Mischievous eyes and a robust smile made him seem younger.

"Thank you, Mr. Bradford. I'm delighted to be here. She took his hand. It was strong, warm, and pleasantly rough.

"Call me Jack, please."

"I'm Morgan Matthias."

"A pleasure, Morgan. Are you vacationing here?" He placed his free hand on hers and squeezed gently.

"Actually, I'm your neighbor. I just bought a house."

"Really? Wonderful. Where?"

"On Midlakes Road. The old Welcome place."

His smile faded. This reaction to her house puzzled and annoyed her. "Something wrong?" she said, strongly.

He frowned, looking guilty. "Of course not. Congratulations. Enjoy your meal." His smile seemed forced. He let her hand go. "Will you excuse me?"

"No." She refused to let him run away without explaining.

"I beg your pardon?" He looked genuinely surprised.

"Sorry to be rude." She took the pink and white linen napkin from her plate and spread it on her lap. "But I need to know why my house freaks out half of Lake Placid." The server returned with her ice water. "Thanks," Morgan said, trying to smile and took a sip.

Jack hesitated. She thought he'd leave, but to her surprise he pulled a chair out and sat.

"What the hell," he sighed. "I don't owe Wainright a thing." He looked directly into her eyes. "As a matter of fact, I hate his guts."

Surprised, Morgan set her lemon water glass on the table. "How did you know it was Harlan who—"

Jack waved his hand politely. "Long story."

"I'm in no hurry."

Her server arrived with a steaming tray, featuring three tasting portions of homemade soups. She sniffed the French onion and lobster bisque and dipped her spoon in the cream of tomato.

Jack studied her with clear, sharp eyes. "So, you want to know about your house from me," he smiled, clearly savoring the moment.

"Instead of Maggie or Harlan." Morgan returned his smile. "Point taken."

"Under one condition." He folded his hands on the table. "I start with Julia, his late wife and my kid sister."

Morgan put her spoon down and waited.

"Wainright got to Lake Placid in sixty-one with his real estate license in one hand and a load of *chutzpah* in the other.

"Julia, a petite, dark-eyed blond of twenty-two fell for Wainright forty-seven years ago the minute he walked through that door." Jack stared wistfully into the distance. "I knew he never loved her. I believe that deep down, Julia knew it too. He was an ambitious, arrogant upstart, and he was broke. Julia owned half this restaurant so he married her. Oddly enough the marriage seemed to be working, until Lillian Duran walked into his office two years later, needing a job."

"Duran? As in Maggie?" Morgan picked up her spoon.

"Her mother." A shadow eclipsed his eyes and deepened the lines in his face. "Harlan fell hard and Julia drank harder.

"In the late seventies Harlan needed capital to bankroll some big real estate deal involving the Olympics. He forced me to buy Julia out." He squeezed his hands together. "On March fifteenth, nineteen eighty-four they had a knock-down-drag out. I'd bet the inn they fought about Lillian. Harlan walked out. Julia got drunker and climbed behind the wheel." He lowered his eyes. "She was forty-five." His voice cracked. He leaned on his elbows and pressed his thumbs to his eyes.

"I'm so sorry." Morgan reached out and touched him.

"Julia's money helped that bastard and all the Durans get fat and rich." He scoffed. "But they'll never be happy."

Morgan followed his lead. "Why?" She finished her soup.

"Did they bother to mention the Connellys to you?" He stared at her. This time his eyes glittered, making her uneasy. She reached for her pendant. "I didn't think so." He shook his head and got to his feet.

Morgan swallowed. "Who are the Connellys?"

"I don't want to scare you."

She grasped the pendant harder. "Not knowing scares me more." She picked up her glass of lemon water. Her hand shook. Her server appeared and removed the soup sampler.

"Please, Jack. If the Connellys owned my house and something bad happened I have a right—"

He nodded, sat and looked into her eyes. "Did they tell you anything about the house?"

"That Jared Welcome had built it for his new wife in 1919."

He shook his head. "Five years later the Welcomes froze to death in the bedroom under the tower. No one knows how or why."

She squeezed her pendant. "*Froze* to death? In my house? Is that even possible? If I'd known that, maybe I wouldn't—"

"Exactly. No one within miles of Lake Placid would touch that house. So Harlan tapped the unsuspecting at large—like you. In August of nineteen eighty three, Lillian showed your house to the Connellys from Florida and their thirteen-year-old son, Tommy. They came here because I advertised in The Times for a chef." Jack sighed. Thomas J. Connelly qualified.

"Regardless of my personal feelings toward that bum, that's something I'll have to live with for the rest of my life. "Julia told me that Harlan was so obsessed with selling that house to the right buyer he even decided to hold the mortgage."

"My God," Morgan gasped, "Did he think I was the right buyer? What does that even mean?" she said, more to herself than to Jack. "God. He's holding my mortgage. It was so easy to get."

"I'm not surprised. When Harlan found out the Connellys wanted your house, he paid me a visit. He said we were in a mutually beneficial position. I needed a chef—he needed to sell the house. Apparently, the Connellys were broke. Harlan was obsessed all right. He promised to sell at a loss if I paid Tom enough to cover his mortgage and taxes. I threw him out. Julia begged me to help, believing he would love her if I did.

"Tom was a talented chef. He was also a drunk. Within two weeks he was hitting the bar heavy. I think he abused his wife. She came to see him, wearing his prints on her arm."

"Dear God," Morgan said, thoroughly chilled.

"Right," Jack snorted. "Thanks to Tom we were either low on bourbon or out of it. You get the picture."

"He lost his job and the house," she said.

"Something more precious than that, I'm afraid. Twenty-five years ago young Tommy froze to death in the bedroom under the tower like the Welcomes. Both cases are open."

"But that's not possible."

The hazed over windows in the tower and bedroom suddenly flashed before her eyes. She hadn't been seeing things. The haze in the tower had morphed into an apparition. Her server put the New York strip steak in front of her. The meat sizzled and the smell, normally mouthwatering, was forcing her throat closed.

"Sorry." She shook her head. "I'm not--"

"It's all right." Jack looked at the server. "Take it back please, Grace, and bring us some coffee. Thanks." He looked at Morgan, "Unless you'd prefer something stronger."

"Coffee's fine," she smiled weakly, "thanks." Her eyes met Jack's. She breathed in slowly then spoke. "Were there," she swallowed the lump in her throat, "other buyers?"

"After the Connellys, a few out-of-towners, but no one else froze to death if that's what you mean. Maybe they got scared off before something happened."

Her heart pounded. What in God's name was she mixed up in?

Grace brought two cups of coffee. Morgan added cream and stirred. Jack took his black. He sipped, put his cup down and frowned, probably wondering if he'd scared her. He had.

"What scared them off?" She laughed nervously, blinking back tears. "Murky apparitions? Hazy ghosts?"

"Maybe. Wainright never shared the specifics."

Jack refused her Visa, but took her hand. "If you need me, call me. I'm always here."


Morgan walked halfway up Midlakes to the last of the working streetlights and leaned on the lamppost. She gazed past the glow to the dark streetlights in front of her house, confused. In retrospect she realized the mortgage rate Harlan had given her for that house wouldn't yield a respectable profit. As far as she knew Maggie's commission was less than modest. Why had she, Morgan Matthias, been the only one who seemed to profit?

Morgan liked Jack Bradford. He seemed forthcoming, but he hated Harlan. Did he want her to hate Harlan, too? She closed her eyes. Everything in her screamed, cut and run, but she'd spent Chuck's and her hard-earned money on a house, blindly.

If the situation were reversed she'd be furious with Chuck. She opened her eyes and clenched her fists. Damn. Why was Chuck never around when she needed him? At the time Maggie had seemed sincere and Harlan seemed generous and accommodating, but after hearing Jack's story, she believed that they'd tricked her.

She looked past the streetlight up the hill, realizing they didn't sell her that house, they gave it to her! Angry and confused, Morgan walked home determined to find out why.

# Chapter 23

## Morgan

Morgan stared at the Stately Queen Anne. Three people had died in the bedroom under the tower and no one knew why. Is that how the house eliminated the "wrong" buyers by freezing them to death? Was she the wrong buyer too? Suddenly, renting a room at the White Birch Inn seemed very appealing. Morgan sighed. For how long? And then what?

She stood at the front door and dug through her purse for her keys. There were no such things as ghosts, no matter what Jack Bradford said. She grabbed the keys and made a fist to steady her shaky hand. Scolding herself for not leaving the porch light on, she flexed her fingers and ran them over the cold metal lock. She felt the keyhole, slid the key in, wiped her shoes on the welcome mat and opened the door. She peered and squinted, forcing her eyes to adjust.

Tables, lamps, chairs and porcelain ladies in long ruffled gowns loomed uneven and lumpy under a blanket of darkness. She pictured the sneer on their glassy red lips and felt their dead eyes, watching and waiting. Fear skittered up her spine and lodged at the base of her skull. Failing to dislodge it, she reached to her right, flipped the light switch and looked at her watch. It was only a little past nine, but she was scared and exhausted and needed to sleep. Tea always calmed her. She dropped the keys into her purse, headed for the kitchen. She brewed tea and took the steaming mug and her purse upstairs.

The master bedroom, main bath and a guestroom were down the hall on her left. The bedroom under the tower was down the hall to her right where, according to Jack, the Welcomes and Tommy Connelly had frozen to death. She pictured Harlan and scowled. She'd deal with him in the morning. Right now she had to face the bedroom under the tower to prove there was no murky, beckoning ghost. Her hand shook. Tea sloshed over the rim.

Angry, she leaned against the wall and her shoulder touched a light switch. She flicked it, licked the tea from her hand and sipped, trying to image the bedroom under the tower.

If memory served, it had been as tastefully decorated as the rest of the house. The woodwork, walls and area rug were done in rich earth tones. In it were a bookcase, night table, Victorian lamp, chest of drawers, queen-sized bed and a fireplace.

In the living room and the other bedrooms the fireplaces and logs in the hearths were set up and ready. She had imagined sitting with Chuck by a cozy fire, sipping a cup of hot cocoa, watching a blizzard pelt the windows, and now she almost smiled.

Unlike the other bedrooms the one under the tower contained two doors opposite the windows. Behind one was a closet. Behind the other were stairs to the tower and perhaps to the room in the gable? She set the cup on a small table against the wall and headed for the bedroom. She took a deep breath and cracked the door.

A narrow wedge of light fanned into the room from the hallway. She splayed her fingers across the door, opened it wider, switched on the light, looked the room over and held her breath. Swallowing hard, she tried the interior door to her left. The closet was empty. The door to her right was locked.

Grateful for a stay of execution, she exhaled a sigh. The relief was short lived. During the interview Harlan had given her a skeleton key. He said it opened the door to the tower stairwell. She fished through her purse, found it, held her breath and tried. What do you know? Harlan had told the truth. Anxious, she slipped the key on the ring and put the keys in her purse.

The stairwell was dark and the air tasted stale and moldy. Where was the light switch? Convincing herself she had nothing to fear, Morgan climbed, counting each creaking step out loud until she was on the landing. Her eyes widening, she walked into the tower. She ran her hands over the walls on either side, located a switch and threw it.

The tower was empty. Morgan smiled.

She shivered suddenly, as if caught in a blast of a cold air. Her smile faded. She rubbed her hands over her arms, backed out and hit the light. She descended the tower stairs, rationalizing that no matter the renovation, old houses were drafty. She closed the bedroom door, making a note to caulk those tower windows. She grabbed her tea from the hall table, tossed her purse on the bed. Her tea was cold. She set the cup on the bathroom sink.

After brushing her teeth, she put the teacup and purse on the dresser, pulled out a nightgown and changed. She turned down the bed. The pendant hung loosely between her breasts. She usually took it off. Tonight she sensed she should leave it on.

She slipped between the sheets, looked over her toes at the fireplace across the room. She imagined lying in Chuck's arms, watching a fire while a gentle snowfall dusted their world. She lay on her side and gazed out the window. Folding her thoughts up, she tucked them away. Her eyelids were heavy with sleep. Shortly after they slammed shut, her breathing slowed.

Perspiration beading above her lip, Morgan stirred. Easing her arms out of the covers, she lay on her back. She exhaled a sigh, turned toward the wall, sniffed and frowned. Through gauzy sleep Morgan heard crackling. She forced her eyes open and peered through a web of lashes. A ghostly orange glow danced on the wall behind her lamp and nightstand.

"Fire!" She gasped at the hearth, kicked at the covers and scooted back. Knees to chest, she pressed her back into the headboard.

Fire raged. The hearth's flaming tongues scorched the floor, frazzled and melted the rug. The hot, acrid stench stung her eyes. The hearth belched and smoke filled the room. Morgan rolled off the bed coughing and gagging. She hit the floor narrowly missing a ball of flame that burst through a wall of smoke. Flames engulfed her lamp and nightstand.

Like an army of hellish Pacmen, flaming balls ate a path to her bed, gobbled her bedclothes and began feasting on her mattress. Her skin and scalp *burned!* Every breath she took seared her lungs. Sweat plastered her hair to her head. Her nightgown clung to her body. She tried to crawl toward the door, but her knees and hands felt hermetically sealed to the floor. Tears streamed down her cheeks. She was going to die. She sank to the floor and closed her eyes. Terrified, she grabbed her pendant, squeezed - and frowned.

The room felt cool. Her skin felt dry. She opened her eyes. Stunned, she let her pendant go. Her room was completely intact, as if the fire had never happened.

Morgan shivered hard, not giving a damn that she and her nightgown were bone dry. That every stick of furniture and stitch of fabric was unscathed or that the logs were neatly piled in the hearth - unburned. What just happened was not a nightmare or a hallucination. It was real.

This was an old house with a checkered past and a long list of buyers. Whatever just happened here and now must've happened to others. Harlan and Maggie owed her answers. She'd get them before leaving town to visit Mother, but she couldn't rush in and confront them.

She needed a good night's sleep and a plan.

She looked around and shivered. She couldn't sleep here, not tonight for sure and maybe not ever again. She pulled a blanket from her bed, heard footsteps and stopped. Her heart pounding, she turned in their direction.

A dark, shadowy figure *whooshed* past the doorway. Morgan dropped the blanket. Shaking, she inched toward the hall and peeked out. The dark figure entered the bedroom under the tower. Terrified, she clutched her pendant and crept along the walls to the bedroom. She stood on the threshold and stared into the room.

Its back to her, the dark figure stood at the doorway to the tower. Its chalk-white hand reached for the door. Vibrating with fear, Morgan cleared her throat and found her voice.

"Wh-who are you?

The figure turned slowly. Under a shock of thick, black hair was the face of a young, teenage boy, very pale and very dead. His dead eyes shining like nuggets of unburned coal, the boy turned away -

"No! Wait," Morgan begged.

--and passed *through* the closed door.

Morgan ran across the room and grabbed the knob, screamed and pulled her hand away. Stunned, she blew on her hand and stared at the frozen knob. She waited, seconds, and tried again, but the door would not budge. She pounded, sweating and breathing hard.

The drop in temperature was sudden and dramatic. Morgan shivered, rubbed her arms and saw her breath. Teeth chattering, she backed away from the door into the warm hallway. On trembling legs, she stumbled back to her bedroom, grabbed her cell from the nightstand and dialed.

"I know it's late but you said to call if I needed you."

Jack and Morgan sat at the Bradford House bar. Their glasses were empty. Jack signaled the barkeep who took a bottle of Maker's Mark from the shelf behind him. He chucked ice in their glasses and poured. The ice cracked.

"Thanks, Bill." Jack banged his back. Morgan sipped hers. "Leave the bottle, will you?"

Bill nodded, reached for a rag and polished his way to the far end of the bar.

"I can tell you don't believe me, Jack," Morgan said, "but the fire. The boy. The bone-chilling cold in that bedroom all happened exactly as

I said. "The boy I saw was Tommy Connelly." She knew she was rambling but she couldn't help it. "You've got to admit it makes a weird kind of sense." Morgan clasped her hands on the bar until her knuckles were white.

Jack shook his head, filled his glass, sighed and then pushed it away. He covered her hands with his. "For the record I believe you."

She relaxed under the warmth of his hands and his words.

"I don't know if it helps, but you're not the first buyer with stories about that house."

"That boy was Tommy, Jack. I feel it in my guts." She slid off her stool, grabbed her purse, stared blankly and frowned.

"You know, Jack, seeing Tommy got me thinking." She looked directly into Jack's eyes. "Why didn't his mother and father freeze to death? Why was it just him?"

Jack's eyes widened. "That's a damned good question." He sighed and shook his head.

Terrified to sleep in her bedroom, Morgan took her nightgown, blanket and pillow downstairs. She spread the blanket out on the Prince of Wales sofa and turned all the lights on.

She burrowed in and braced for a long sleepless night, but she was asleep before her head hit the pillow. She frowned and moaned. Her moan turning into a whimper, she found herself …

*…Under a barren moon and scatter of vacant stars.*

*Cradled in two strong arms, she stares over a barefaced cliff. Dropped over the edge, she falls fast and hits water so dark and cold the impact slams air from her lungs. Wracked with spasms she sinks fast. Wrists and ankles bound, she holds her breath. Her calves and thighs twitch. She struggles to free her wrists which are tied behind her. The rope cuts off her circulation. She can't feel her fingers. Her lungs are on fire. Seconds before blacking out she kicks hard and makes her way up.*

*Her pulse throbs in her throat. Fireworks burst behind her eyes. She breaks the surface, tips her face to the sky and gulps down the frosty night.*

Morgan awoke teeth chattering, remembering she had seen the lakeshore and cliffs from her tower. They were the same ones she'd dreamt about after her White-Birch-Inn liquid dinner. Maggie had called the bluff Pulpit Rock.

Her wrists and ankles burning, she sat up and reached for the lamp on her nightstand. She felt the back of the couch and remembered. She was downstairs in the living room. She swung her legs over the side, slid down the sofa toward the end table near the fireplace, reached under the fringed shade and found the switch above the dainty porcelain lady. She gasped as the burning welts on her wrists and ankles began fading.

Trembling, she pulled the blanket around her and dug her toes into the deep-piled rug. She stared at the fireplace, mirror, leather-bound books, her love-at-first-sight buttons this house had pushed. Terrified, she wrapped the blanket tighter around her and sank into the cushion.

The unsolved deaths, the dreams, the fire, the boy had her wanting to fly out that front door and never look back. The dream freaked her out most, because it made the least sense. Why would she dream she'd been dropped off the cliff into the lake with her hands tied behind her back? Did the dream foreshadow her death? Oh sweet Jesus. Or did the fire?

Morgan considered her options. Staying in the house may risk her life but leaving would cost her the investment and maybe Chuck as well. Was the enemy of her enemy her friend? Jack Bradford was in her corner. He was cavalry enough until Chuck got here. She pulled the blanket to her chin, closed her eyes and pictured Harlan and Maggie. She would pay them a visit before going home to see Mother.

Compared to the house on Midlakes Road, home was looking pretty good. If she weren't so scared and bone weary she'd burst into peals of unstoppable laughter

Forming a plan on how to deal with Maggie and Harlan, Morgan fell into a dreamless sleep.

# Chapter 24

## Chuck

Chuck was thankful his flight had arrived at Albany International Airport on time. Exhausted, he made his way from the baggage claim to the Avis counter near the terminal exit. He stared at the blurred car rental form, forcing his eyes to focus.

He should take a room near the airport and start out in the morning, but too psyched to sleep, Chuck handed his Master Card over. The clerk ran it and asked if he wanted a map or a GPS. The route to Port St. John indelibly etched in his memory, Chuck politely declined both. Taking the keys to the Impala, he mumbled thanks and headed for the exit.

On his way out Chuck noticed the difference between the airport now and the last time he'd been here. Aside from information centers and tightened security measures, there were designer restaurants and coffee bars, food concessions, business and conference centers. They even had interfaith prayer rooms. The last time he'd arrived, thirty years ago, Morgan had been here to meet him. It seemed like yesterday.

Chuck pictured Lucy. He had only known her briefly, but well enough to realize that knowledge of his delicate situation at that time would have been deadly in her hands. In retrospect, he believed he had sorely underestimated her. As the exit door slid open, he stepped into the hot, muggy air and vowed that if Lucy was responsible for what had happened between Morgan and him all those years ago, he would make her pay.

The Impala was parked across from the main entrance under clear skies. He stowed his bags in the trunk and started the car. It was 10 a.m. The external temperature readout said seventy-five. He adjusted the A/C and pulled out of the parking lot. He took the Thruway West. Exiting an hour later, he was amazed at how built up Port St. John had become.

Replacing the country highway was a strip mall with a Super 8, a Holiday Inn, a shopping center, a movie theater, car dealerships, restaurants, drug stores, banks and video rentals.

The closer he got to Morgan's house, the harder his heart pounded.

He wiped the sweat from his brow and turned up the A/C. He turned right on Erie Canal Blvd. Her driveway was up the hill on the left. He parked across the street and looked around.

How many times had he dreamt of this moment? He climbed out of the car and slowly made his way to the house. His heart paused. What if she lived somewhere else, *with her husband and children?* He pushed the thought from his mind. If she pursued the career she'd started years ago, she'd be a high school English teacher. She might be on holiday for the summer.

Her block was quiet. In stark contrast to the others, Morgan's house had deteriorated. The paint was faded or chipped. The mortar between the red and gray flagstones that led to the front steps was missing or cracked. It looked like two women with very little money still lived here. He needed to believe that. The thought simultaneously relieved and unsettled him.

He walked down the driveway and peered through the windows. No sign of life. It was humid and 30C, about 90F. None of the windows appeared to be open. He remembered Morgan saying they never had A/C because Lucy hated the cold.

He wiped the sweat from his brow wondering if any of the old neighbors still lived here. Needing to know about Morgan and Lucy, he returned to the sidewalk and looked up and down the street. It too was deserted. In the house across the street Chuck saw someone peer at him from a glass panel beside the front door. He crossed and knocked. A tall, thin, elderly man with thick gray hair and piercing blue eyes opened the door a crack.

"G'day, mate. Don't mean to intrude, but I used to know the lady, who lived across the street with her mum," he said, nervously. "Do they still live there and if not, where are they?" Chuck felt for his wallet. "I'm an old friend. I have some identification."

The old man squinted. "Put that away. I know who you are. Ain't lost that Aussie accent." He gave Chuck a big toothy grin.

"I guess not. Right about now I couldn't be more grateful."

"I remember you. I remember Morgan was crazy about you too."

Chuck smiled. "Your name, mate?" Chuck offered his hand. "Your memory puts mine to shame."

The gentleman took it. "Arthur L. Parker."

"Mr. Parker! Of course! Can you tell me where they are?"

Is she married, Mr. Parker? I'm too much of a coward to ask.

"Memorial Day weekend, Morgan put Lucy in Pine Bush Acres, a home for women five blocks that way," he pointed, "west of here."

*Morgan* took her mother to a home? *Alone*? As in single?

"Thanks, Mr. Parker."

"Name's Art. Don't mention it. Yep, she moved her mother right on out of here. Shoulda done it a long time ago. It would've saved the neighborhood years of trouble."

You're right about that, Mr. Parker, Chuck thought.

"As for where Morgan is, dunno. She teaches English, at the high school, but school's out. She might be on vacation. The wife said that back in June, Morgan mentioned something about buying a house in Lake Placid."

Chuck grinned. Parker said *she* might be out of town. Relieved, Chuck shook Parker's hand. "Thank you, sir." Ecstatic, he hurried to the Impala. Mr. Parker may have answered his dreaded question before he'd been forced to ask it.

By the time Chuck got to Pine Bush Acres, he was certain Lucy had destroyed his relationship with Morgan. And by Christ he'd find out how she did it— if he didn't kill her first.

After checking with reception, Chuck stood outside Lucy's room. The door was slightly ajar. He peeked in unprepared for what he saw. He recalled Lucy had been short and heavy, but now she was obese. He knocked before entering.

Lucy looked up. Her eyes, once narrowed and lethal, had lost their glitter. She frowned, looking confused. He moved toward her bed.

"How did you do it?"

Her flint-blue eyes met his with slow, icy recognition.

"What? No prelude like, my, Lucy, time has been kind to you. Leave our manners in the land down under, did we?"

"How? Goddamn you!" He clenched his hands into fists.

"What does it matter? The point is I did."

Chuck groaned. Lucy grinned. His eyes blazed while hers remained as cold as steel.

"Did you think you could just walk in, steal my meal ticket and leave me to die alone?"

His assessment had been off. Her memory was fine, and her venom was deadlier than he remembered. She lowered her eyes and picked at the cross-stitch on her nightgown with pudgy fingers.

"I knew men like you who claimed to love wives or girlfriends then betrayed them every chance they got." She picked threads from her blanket then looked at him directly. "You, *Doctor* Matthias, brought Morgan to the edge." She shrugged. "I merely pushed her over."

Chuck flexed his hands. "Tell me now!"

Lucy salivated with joy. She knew someday he'd be back, demanding to know all, yet she still couldn't make up her mind what to tell him. On one hand he was an arrogant bastard who deserved to die broken-hearted and ignorant. On the other, now that he stood here choking on guilt and anger, perhaps telling him the whole truth would be the more satisfying choice. Well, maybe not the *whole* truth. She'd keep Morgan's sick little fantasy about being his wife a secret. How she wished she could be there when that piece of insane shit hit his balls.

Chuck was at her mercy again, and they both knew it. Controlling a man was good for the soul. Controlling Chuck Matthias was positively rejuvenating. The pleasure of seeing him writhe in agony made her juices flow. When was the last time she'd indulged herself so? Watching him, she grinned. Her heart was beating strong and hard. Her razor sharp instincts debrided layers of sludge from her mind. A skilled predator, she positioned herself and struck.

"At the end of the spring semester, when Morgan said she wanted to stay at the university to start graduate school, I knew something was off, because before that we'd had a big fight. She was so furious with me she announced that as soon as school was out you were going to marry her and *tike* her to *Ostrailia.*" Her fleshy jowls quivered. "Now I ask you," she fluttered her eyelids in grotesque sexual parody, "if she were going to Australia, why enroll in graduate school?" Lucy watched his eyes widen and his jaw tighten. The poor boy could hardly speak. She suppressed a smile.

"She came home three weeks after school ended, deeply depressed. She said she was tired and needed to sleep. A few days later your letter arrived, stamped with an old date. The university address had been crossed off and ours penciled in. Some Good Samaritan went to a lot of trouble to make sure Morgan got it." Lucy chuckled. "Downright poetic."

She laughed hard and her bedsprings screeched. Tears crisscrossed her cheeks. She reached for a tissue from her nightstand. She dabbed her eyes, wiped her nose and her laughter subsided. She cleared her throat, looked at him and almost burst out laughing, again. Mute with astonishment? The look suited him well.

"Anyway, I intercepted your precious letter."

Chuck stiffened. Ignoring him, she raised her eyes. Cloaked in mock holiness, she quoted him as accurately as if the white ceiling were the page upon which his letter had been written.

"So touching how you, 'understood her devastation', and, oh - oh yes, and 'even though there was a child to consider', you 'intended to carry out your responsibility and be a part of its life,' that you, 'loved her and wanted to marry her and nothing could change that'. I'd say you got that wrong, *Doctor* Matthias."

"So, you never gave her the letter?" Chuck clenched his jaw.

"Of course I gave her the letter. Why wouldn't I?" The fool looked surprised. "For a smart-ass psychiatrist, typing the letter was really dumb. You know why?" she asked, thrilled at outsmarting him, "because a typewritten document can be retyped.

"I edited the part that said you intended to marry her. And the place where you planned to meet when you returned? Where was it again?" She furrowed her brow as if she'd forgotten. She snapped her finger. "The table in the university library where you first met." She clasped her hands as if in prayer. "How romantic." She glanced at him sideways. "Did you ever show up?" He didn't answer. "Good thing," she sneered, locking eyes with him, "because I edited that little piece out completely."

He looked stunned. "You son of a bitch!"

She laughed and clapped her hands harder.

"You were my greatest ally," she paused. "You see, *Chuck,*" her cold eyes shone with the cunning of a wolf, "getting your Aussie girlfriend Barbara pregnant was a stroke of genius. It was the one thing I couldn't have done without you."

He stepped toward her. He was very close, but he didn't scare her. She could still read that Aussie bastard like a cheap novel. She fluttered her eyelids and smiled. Despite everything, she always found him quite attractive. She saw tears brim in his eyes. She watched him clench and unclench his fists. She sensed him wanting to tighten his fingers around her throat and squeeze until she turned purple. Why? Because in crushing hindsight he knew she was right. He had been her greatest ally.

"Years ago I called and you said Morgan had a breakdown."

"You destroyed her. I said I had to send her away."

"You can't expect me to believe you did that to help her."

"Help may be an exaggeration. I was fed up with intercepting your calls and letters. I had to get rid of you."

"Where's Morgan now?"

Lucy couldn't remember, but if she kept Chuck in town till Morgan got back, she would see the fireworks first hand.

Then again, if she told him that Morgan went to - Lake? Goddamn! Lake? He'd rush up there. The poor darlings will pass like two ships in the night. When he realized he'd missed her again, he might have a heart attack. A fitting end.

Placid! She'd tell him the truth. He'll never believe her. "She's in Lake Placid, buying a house. She'll be back today."

Chuck slammed the door behind him. She didn't expect a thank you, but after telling him the truth, the least he could have done was say goodbye.

# Chapter 25

## Morgan and Maggie

Morgan parked her car in front of Main Street Wine and Liquor across from Placid Properties and glanced at the overcast skies. It was 8:30. Placid Properties opened at 9:00.

She scanned the street from her parking space. Maggie's Lexus was parked in front of the office. The fire-engine-red Acura convertible parked behind the Lexus looked like a car the young realtor, Kevin, would drive. If so, they were both inside. She remembered that Harlan drove a burgundy Escalade. It wasn't there. She hoped he would be in shortly. She wanted them all there. Even Hutch. She almost called for an appointment but opted to surprise them instead.

She tilted the rearview mirror. Makeup looked good. She smoothed her hair. She wore striped green knee length shorts. The pendant hung in the V of her white sleeveless blouse.

Looking calmer and more collected than she felt, Morgan glanced at the clock on her dashboard. 8:35. She drummed her fingers on the wheel, thinking about her conversations with Jack Bradford. She clasped her hands in her lap, fuming over the details Maggie and Harlan had conveniently omitted from their sales pitch. Her own experience proved that Bradford had told the truth. Morgan caught herself rubbing her wrists. She shook her head and checked. Neither her wrists nor her ankles had burn marks. The rational part of her insisted that there was an explanation for everything. Her irrational side said her house was haunted.

Haunted. God, the word scared her.

She was angry, duped and afraid, but she couldn't barge into the real estate office and go off on them. She had to remember that the main thing was not to lose sight of the main thing. She was a teacher who earned her living writing objectives. This morning she had framed one, and she intended to use it. She took a calming breath. It was 8:45. As she tightened her fingers around the wheel and waited, her eye caught a neon-green poster taped outside the liquor store window. It advertised a Gypsy Bazaar on Saturday, July twelfth.

Maggie sat at her desk, perusing contracts, trying to keep from running back to Plattsburgh and jumping into Steve's bed. They'd been together since the night he'd rescued her from the Looking Glass Café weeks ago. How had she made it without him? She could spend the rest of her life filling herself with him and still crave more. Her heart beat at his command. Yet, she loved and distrusted him more now than ever.

The paradox scared her to death. She pushed the contracts aside, propped her elbows on her desk, rested her chin in her upturned hands and gazed around the office. Steve couldn't lie about something as horrendous as being accused of rape. Harlan, however, was treacherous enough to use that information to get what he wanted, not giving a damn if he destroyed Steve and anyone else in the process, including her. Yet, in effect, hadn't Steve done the same thing? She pressed her eyelids with her fingers, wrecking her eye shadow.

Steve knew about her mom's breakdown and stay at High Peaks and how his stories might affect her. But he took the chance and wrote them to get back at Harlan anyway, sacrificing their love in the process. The question is would he do it again?

Harlan and Steve were more alike than she realized. She never felt happier or more miserable. Eyes closed, Maggie rubbed her temples. Love shouldn't feel like waiting for an axe to fall. She pictured Harlan and opened her eyes. Now that she and Steve were together, she could be Harlan's worst nightmare. She remembered the pale figure in the tower window and smiled. Steve didn't know it yet, but his anniversary stories were about to go nuclear. Her instincts told her to keep their affair secret. Steve had agreed.

Kevin's desk was in front of hers. She stared at his back. Her greatest fear, besides taking another chance on Steve, had materialized. Kevin and Nat had formed an unholy alliance. They didn't know she knew, and even though she'd decided to keep it that way for now, she tried several times to warn Natalie indirectly that Kevin, like Harlan, would stop at nothing to get what he wanted. That included using her, if she let him.

Kevin came in pale and green around the edges, like he was hung over. And the weekend hadn't begun yet. Pity, she smirked.

She glanced beyond Kevin out the window. Harlan had parked his SUV in front of her Lexus. She was sandwiched between him and Kevin. She smirked at how the order of their parked cars clearly demonstrated their indelible rank. She was about to light that little fire under his ass, when the phone rang. Hutch was away from her desk. Maggie sighed and answered,

"Placid Properties, Maggie Duran speaking." Hutch came out of the restroom. Maggie smiled and gestured she had the call.

"Harlan forgot his briefcase here this morning," Lillian said in Maggie's ear.

Every time Harlan visited Mom, Maggie cringed. Even though Mom had vowed not to, she was too close to telling him that Maggie had seen the figure in the tower.

"He just pulled in now, Mom."

"I'll drop it off shortly on my way to the vet with Jinx," Mom said, the phone clicked in Maggie's ear.

Harlan came through the door and nodded at Kevin, but stopped at her desk, smiled and bowed ceremoniously. "Good morning, Maggie."

Kevin swiveled around. Maggie met his scowl with an impish smile. After Harlan's infamous meeting, she'd called Mom from Steve's to say she'd be out of town for a while and if Mom wanted to know why, to ask Harlan. Apparently, Mom had, and Harlan had lied, she guessed. Scared shitless she'd tell Mom the truth, Harlan had been a pussycat ever since. Maggie returned to work happy instead of morose. She knew Harlan wondered why. She had to be careful he didn't find out about Steve. She was about to mention the briefcase, but Morgan Matthias walked in behind him.

"Morgan." Harlan smiled warmly, extending his hand. "You look lovely and cool on what promises to be a hot day."

Morgan scowled at him. "I need to speak to you now."

His smile disappeared slowly. Morgan caught a glimmer of something in his eye. Was he worried? He should be.

"Very well. Shall we step into my office?"

"Not without them." She meant Kevin and Maggie. "And Hutch."

"Hutch must man the office and phones," Harlan smiled, unruffled. "So we won't be interrupted, of course."

"Of course." Morgan conceded the trivial point.

Kevin and Maggie were out of their seats and in Harlan's office before he was. Harlan passed them and sat at his desk as Kevin and Maggie pulled up three chairs.

"There you go." Kevin offered one to Morgan.

Morgan thanked him and looked from Maggie to Harlan.

"Why did I have to learn all about the house from Jack Bradford?"

she blurted. So much for not rushing in like a fool.

"I don't understand," Harlan said.

"The hell you don't." Morgan grasped her pendant.

"Why not enlighten me?" he said, looking cool and unflustered.

"How about Tommy Connelly freezing to death like Jared and Elspeth Welcome had in the bedroom under the tower?"

Harlan cleared his throat. "Rumors."

"Oh really?" Morgan leaned forward in her seat. "Then why are both cases open? And why did your local market dry up so badly you had to go out of town to scare up new buyers?"

"You can't believe anything Bradford says about me, my dear. I used to be married to Julia, his sister. He hates me and will use any opportunity to discredit me. It's a long story."

"I know. He told me. He also confirmed what Maggie had said in May. You were so obsessed with selling to the right buyer you decided to hold the mortgage." Morgan watched Harlan shoot Maggie a look. "Tell me, Harlan, am I the right buyer? Is that why you practically *gave* me a fully appointed house?"

"You got the house because you qualified."

Right. He kept his voice and demeanor calm despite her accusations. "Something happened in that house on Memorial Day Weekend," she said.

Maggie moved to the edge of her seat, and Kevin, who hadn't moved since getting Morgan a chair did the same.

"I saw an apparition or something in the tower the second time I went back to the house with you, Maggie, on Memorial Day." She still couldn't read Harlan or Kevin, but Maggie seemed jumpier and more worried than she had been on that day. "You saw it the day before, didn't you?"

Maggie lowered her eyes. The heat of success rising in her cheeks, Morgan said, "Since I moved into that house strange things have been happening. One night I dreamt someone had bound my wrists and ankles and dropped me off a cliff into a lake where I drowned. I woke up in a panic and with rope burns on my ankles and wrists."

Maggie and Harlan exchanged nervous glances.

"Last night I woke up to a fire devouring my room. And then all of a sudden it was gone, like it never happened."

Morgan gauged their reactions. From what she could deduce, the incidents did not appear to surprise them, but her detailed descriptions of them did. Puzzled, but rather than appear completely unhinged she decided to keep Tommy Connelly's apparition to herself for now.

"Well?" She started to speak, but Harlan cut her off.

"Did Bradford say anything else?" he said, taking her in a different direction.

"Yes." Annoyed, she kept her eyes on his. "That the few buyers subsequent to the Connellys got scared off before anything bad happened to them." She squeezed the pendant in her hand. "My house is haunted. Is that why you lied to me?"

Kevin stared.

Maggie's eyes moistened. "Morgan—"

Harlan opened his mouth. Morgan held up her hand. "Please. No more lies. Allow me. The bottom line is either I stay in the house and risk my life, or abandon it and lose my investment and maybe my husband. Does that about sum it up?"

Harlan's mouth and eyes were cold, as if chiseled in stone.

"I see." Morgan held the pendant firmly in her hand. "Well, I don't intend to do either." She glanced at Kevin. "Nor will I let any of you get away with this."

Kevin never blinked. Morgan stood. As if on cue, Kevin, Maggie and Harlan rose and stood at attention.

"Tomorrow I'm going to Port St. John to see my mother. When I get back I want answers. And one more thing." She looked directly at Harlan. "I want the two broken streetlamps in front of my house fixed by next week. Are we clear?"

"Crystal."

Morgan walked out of Harlan's office and closed the door behind her, practically bumping into an attractive, older woman outside Harlan's office door. She had a Golden Retriever on a leash. Judging by her expression, she'd heard every word.

The dog wagged its tail and looked up with soulful eyes. Surprised it was so friendly Morgan smiled, petted the dog's head and looked at the woman, "boy or girl?"

"Girl." The woman smiled, nervously. "We call her Jinx."

"Hey." Morgan scratched Jinx's neck. Jinx licked her hand.

"She likes you," the woman said and Morgan laughed. The woman held out her hand. "I'm Lillian Duran."

Lillian Duran. From Jack Bradford's story. And Jinx was the dog that had scratched her cellar door. Morgan extended her hand. "Morgan Matthias."

By the look on her face, Lillian clearly knew who Morgan was.

Perfectly logical, considering, Lillian was Maggie's mother.

"Nice to meet you, Morgan." Lillian smiled.

"Likewise." Morgan returned the smile. She let go of Lillian's hand and stroked Jinx. "Bye, girl."

Morgan stopped at Hutch's desk. She opened her purse and pulled out a spare key.

"Would you do me a favor, Hutch? My husband Chuck is due any day now. He knows Placid Properties is my real estate agent." She held out the key. "If he shows up while I'm out of town, could you please give him this and point him in the right direction?"

"Will do," Hutch smiled.

"Thanks." Morgan nodded goodbye to Hutch.

Morgan crossed the street, approached her car and frowned at her windshield. Under the wiper was a neon-pink flyer advertising a Gypsy Bazaar on Saturday July twelfth. She pulled it out, stuffed it into her purse and drove off.

# Chapter 26

## Harlan and Maggie

Harlan leaned his head back, laughed out loud and smacked a palm on his desk. "Boys and girls, I haven't felt this alive in years!" His eyes glistened. "Morgan Matthias deserves a standing O. One hell of a woman. Her husband's a lucky man. I do believe I've finally found the right buyer. What do you think?"

Maggie and Kevin stared at him, dumbfounded. Lillian walked through Harlan's door with Jinx's leash and her purse in one hand and Harlan's briefcase in the other.

"Lilly, darling. Join us for coffee to celebrate. "Kevin," Harlan continued, "get Lilly a cup of regular coffee with cream and sugar. Maggie, I want you to get," Harlan frowned, "what's his name, the Municipal Electric Department Superintendent on the phone and tell him to get his men to Midlakes Road and repair those goddamned lights."

"Kevin, Maggie, stay where you are!" Lillian glared at Harlan. "You know the lights won't work. If you don't get Morgan Matthias back in here and tell her the whole truth, I will."

"Lilly, evidently you didn't hear the entire conversation." Harlan smiled at Kevin and Maggie to enlist their support.

They stared at him blankly. He'd deal with their disloyalty later. "Thanks to Bradford, Morgan knows all and has decided to stay in the house in spite of it," Harlan said, smiling.

"I heard every word and it didn't sound like that to me." She slammed his briefcase on his desk and glared at him. "Damn you, Harlan. You heard her. Among other things, she saw a figure in the window too. She asked if the house was haunted. Doesn't that shake your foundations a little?"

"The weather over Memorial Day weekend was magnificent. The sun merely caught the windows at an odd angle and—"

"What killed the Welcomes and why? Do you know how many times I've asked myself that since Tommy died? Whatever killed them had killed Tommy too. I feel it like I feel my own pulse. They were all singled out. Why?"

"For God's sake, Lilly. How could the Welcomes and Tommy be 'singled out' when they died decades apart?"

"Tommy froze to death in September in his bed in that house like the Welcomes did. Can you tell me how that happened? Because the police still have no earthly explanation."

"God, I don't know, Lilly."

Harlan was telling the truth. He remembered in his dream, standing alone in the tower, butt naked and vulnerable as a newborn, locked in a cold, inhuman embrace. Sweat from his armpits tickled down his back and sides.

"Why can't you believe there is no rational explanation?" she said.

Harlan already believed it. He loosened his tie. Suddenly, he was exhausted.

"I know the police are hiding something, Harlan." She looked closely at him. "And I'll bet you know what it is."

*The kid was frozen so badly his arms and legs snapped from his torso like dead branches from a tree trunk. Blood, bone and flesh hit the floor, shattering on contact like some ancient Chinese pottery and littered the room like confetti.*

Pain, like a scorpion, moved through his chest, its pincers nipped at his heart. The Nitro was in his pocket. He had to get to the bathroom. If word leaked about his heart, friends and foes alike would view him as weak and move in for the kill.

"There's something evil in that house," Lillian said.

Harlan felt his skin go clammy.

"I got out lucky, Harlan. It only gave me a nervous breakdown. The Welcomes and Tommy died, and Morgan Matthias will die too if you don't—"

"Please, Lilly." He stood up and clutched his heart. His facial features chalk white and twisted, he collapsed.

*"Harlan!"* Lilly screamed.

"Kevin!" Maggie yelled. "Call nine-one-one! *Now!*" Kevin stood as still and mute as a statue. "Damn you, Delaney, move!"

Eyes on Harlan, Kevin picked up the desk phone and dialed.

"Mom, help me unbutton his shirt." Lillian froze. "Mom! What's the matter with you?"

Maggie was no EMT, but in the movies if a doctor suspected a heart attack, he always loosened the victim's clothing. Harlan wore a white short-sleeved shirt. He didn't wear undershirts in summer. It was July.

Maggie ripped his shirt open and froze.

The birthmark on his chest was strawberry red, the size of a dime, and shaped like a crescent moon.

Identical to hers.

Maggie's heart thundered. She jerked her head up and stared at her mother. The question burned in her eyes.

*Is Harlan my father?*

Lillian's tears spilled, and Maggie had the answer.

Maggie stared at her *father's* birthmark. Countless implications, few of them good, struck like poisonous fangs. Her head throbbed with questions. She was almost forty. When the hell was her mother going to tell her that Bob Duran was not her real father? Was her kid sister Marcy, Bob's or Harlan's? Had either man known the truth?

If Harlan knew she was his daughter, he never would've humiliated her in front of Kevin and Hutch at that meeting. Or would he? Her eyes stung. She looked at her mother, through shimmering tears that refused to spill. She planned to slip into Steve's bed tonight, and after mind-bending sex, thrill him with every one of Morgan's revelations and accusations. But this, she looked down, her gaze riveted to his birthmark, had changed everything. Or had it?

"Maggie." Kevin said, stopping her mind from rocketing into space. "The EMTs are here."

Dazed, Maggie watched a man and woman wearing bright blue gloves enter the office carrying a canvas bag marked EMT, a clipboard and what she assumed was a defibrillator.

The woman knelt beside Harlan and identified herself as an EMT with the Village Volunteer Fire Department. She questioned Harlan, evaluated his situation and gave the findings to her partner. "As soon as the ambulance arrives, they'll take him to the hospital."

"Ambulance?" Lillian raised a trembling hand to her pale lips. "Aren't you - I thought the ambulance was already here."

"Sorry for the misunderstanding, Ma'am," the EMT said. "We're the Village Volunteer Fire Department. We're closer, so we help with initial assessment and treatment." She looked at Harlan. "In the meanwhile," she grabbed a pen from the clipboard and started asking him a series of questions when the ambulance arrived. The EMTs lifted him onto the stretcher, covered him and kept the oxygen the first EMT had administered intact.

Following them out, Maggie and the others watched the ambulance crew lift Harlan's stretcher into the ambulance. The driver jumped into the front seat of the ambulance. "Any blood relatives here?" said the paramedic with Harlan.

"I am," Maggie said, looking at her mother and then at Kevin. Lillian sobbed. Kevin shot Maggie a stunned, confused look, reflecting her feelings precisely.

"Relationship?"

"Daughter," Maggie said her voice barely audible.

"Okay, Miss. Meet us at the Medical Center in Lake Placid."

Not knowing how to feel, Maggie instinctively took her mother's arm. Before heading out, she looked at Kevin.

"Go ahead," Kevin said, barely hiding his shock, she thought. "Hutch and I will close up and join you later."

"Thanks," she said, relieved and surprised she meant it.

# Chapter 27

**Kevin**

"It's okay, sweetheart," Kevin said, holding an inconsolable Hutch in his arms. "They don't come any tougher than Harlan. He'll be chewing us out again in no time."

"I don't know, Kevin." Hutch shook her head against his chest. He looked so vulnerable." Hutch's legs started to buckle.

Kevin eased her into Harlan's chair. "Sit here and rest while I start canceling Maggie's and my appointments."

He sat at Maggie's desk and held his head to keep it from spinning off his shoulders. Maggie was Harlan's daughter? How did that get by him? Dude, he must be getting old.

He closed his eyes, trying to sort it out. If Natalie knew Maggie was Harlan's daughter she'd have told him. By the look on Maggie's face when she opened Harlan's shirt, Maggie definitely hadn't known either. Kevin sat back and grinned, because the mystery wasn't so mysterious. The players and the setting were different, but the plot was soap-opera central. Married woman has affair and gets knocked up, but did the biological father know Maggie was his daughter?

Kevin viewed the facts. Maggie's stepdad was dead. Harlan and Lillian weren't teenagers. If Harlan knew, why would he keep it a secret? The more Kevin thought about it, the more it seemed that Harlan was clueless as well. Kevin smirked. Lillian almost got away with it, but Harlan's heart attack had fried her and everyone she'd lied to.

Maggie was Harlan's daughter. In the New World order, where did that leave him? Kevin canceled Maggie's calendar and was about to start on his when his cell rang.

"Kevin?" she said in his ear, "About last night—"

"Look, Kellie. Something happened and we're closing early."

"You're lying. You're meeting that little whore!"

Kevin sighed. If life kept coming at him like this, he'd be in the hospital with Harlan by daybreak. Last night after having sex with Kellie, by the time he got back from taking a leak, Kellie had gone postal. She'd opened his phone and showed him a text from Nat. He'd spent all night telling her he was after information only. This morning she still didn't believe him.

"The old man just had a heart attack. The EMTs are on their way to the hospital with him right now."

"That ought to make you happy."

Kevin was exhausted. Suddenly, he didn't feel like taking her crap. "Believe what you want. And have a nice life while you're at it." He hung up. Did he just, as his mom used to say, 'cut off his nose to spite his face'? It seemed to fit.

Speaking of Natalie, he flipped open his cell and dialed.

"Hey, baby. Miss me?" Natalie breathed in his ear. She must've seen his number on her caller ID.

"Where are you?" Kevin said.

"Home. Why?"

"You need to get to the office right away."

After swearing she could drive, Hutch had left for the hospital. Natalie and Kevin were in Harlan's office. The blinds were drawn. The *closed* sign was in the window

Natalie leaned against him. "Oh my God, Kevin," she sobbed.

"It's okay, baby." He held her close and stroked her hair.

"Is Gran okay?"

"Yeah." He wanted to tell her about her new grandpa, but he did not want to end up on the wrong side of the boss's *daughter.*

"Kevin?"

Natalie looked into his eyes. Damn she was gorgeous, and she always smelled so good. She reached around his neck, pressed her body to his. Kissing him full on the mouth, she moaned and moved against him, coaxing the throb in his groin.

His lips on hers, he ran his hands over her silky shorts, cupped her little butt and pressed her against him. A freight train rushed through his head. If he didn't slam on the brakes—

He pulled her arms from his neck. Her head fell back. Eyes half closed, she licked her parted lips, slipped her arms over his shoulders and locked her hands around his neck.

"Please." She breathed the moist, husky word against his neck, sending a jolt through his spine to his groin. His head pounded. "Please."

Appointments had been cancelled. Phones were off. They were alone. It would be so easy to sit her on his lap and just—Kevin shuddered and closed his eyes. He pulled her hands apart, loosening her grip and squeezed.

"What's the matter with you?" he scolded.

Natalie blushed. Way to blame the victim. His conscience was growing like a malignant tumor. What was that all about anyway?

"Harlan might be dead. Your grandmother just had the stuffing scared out of her. Maggie's trying to hold it together and you're coming onto me?" he said, praying he sounded convincing.

"Sorry. I just—" her voice trailed off.

She was driving him crazy. It took everything to pry her out of his arms. "Let's get to the hospital right away. Agreed?" She nodded. Kevin locked the door behind them, trying real hard not to think about what might happen next time.

# Chapter 28

**Morgan**

Morgan sat in her car in her driveway. Her body was exhausted, but her mind was on overload and kept replaying her go around with Harlan and Maggie.

She put the car into park, pulled the key and tossed it into her purse. She climbed out and slammed the car door. Fast and furious, her steps gobbled up the front lawn and porch. She opened the mailbox beside her door. There were flyers from Hannaford, The Price Chopper and coupons from the GAP and LL Bean. She left the flyers in the box. No bills yet. Thank goodness for little favors. She would be leaving for Port St. John in the morning. She'd see to all other mail that had been delivered when she got back.

She pulled the house key from her purse and wiped her feet on the welcome mat. She let herself in and headed for her bedroom. She planned to leave early.

After packing, she lay on her bed, closed her eyes and fell asleep, frowning and moaning.

*... shadowy figure whooshed past ... stood at the doorway to the tower ... chalk-white hand reached for the door. The figure turned slowly ... the face of a teenage boy, very pale and very dead ...* passed through *the closed door.*

Morgan woke to the wild beat of her heart and a mouth as dry as sawdust. She headed across the hall to the bathroom, ran the tap and snagged a cup from a plastic dispenser. Her shaky hand filled it. She drank, filled it again, crushed the cup, lobbed it into a waste basket and wandered back to her bed.

Clutching her pendant, she gazed at the shadowy terrain of her room then looked out the window. When she had lain down it was light. Now it was dark, but instead of feeling rested, she was still exhausted and scared enough to junk everything and get out. But she knew she couldn't. As soon as Chuck got here, they would face whatever was going on together.

Morgan blew out a breath, praying she wasn't making a mistake.

She let the pendant go and looked at the fireplace and the brass mounts in the hearth stacked with logs. She buried her face in her hands, thanking God the hearth hadn't burst into flames.

*Crackling.*

Her shoulders and arms *burned!* She lowered her hands. Facing a wall of thick gray smoke, she gasped in a lungful, coughed it out and inadvertently sucked in more. Her eyes and throat stung. Her nose ran. The fire raged. She had to get out, but the smoke was so thick she couldn't. Balls of flame burst through the smoke, hit the wall behind her and fell on her bed. Her pillow burst into flame, igniting the sheets and mattress. She had to move. Now!

She'd read that the purest air in a burning room was near the floor. She slid off the bed. The scorched mess that once was the rug seared her feet. Through mind-melting pain, she smelled flesh burning. Howling like something inhuman, she pulled her legs back. Sobbing, she grabbed her pendant and closed her eyes.

The room felt cool. Her pain stopped. She opened her eyes. There was no trace of fire.

Dumbfounded, she let the pendant slip from her hand. She sat on her bed and sobbed. She sniffled and wiped her eyes. She stared at the hearth, realizing that the instant she grabbed her pendant, the room had reverted to normal. Again. Did that mean that the fire, her pendant and her dreams were connected?

In both "fires" she clearly had not been harmed.

She suddenly wondered what if the house wasn't trying to harm her? What if the house or whatever possessed it wanted to *communicate* with her? She ran across the hall, flipped on the bathroom light and stared in the mirror.

"Why would this house or whatever was in it want to communicate with you? What if you're wrong?"

Suddenly, she knew she was right. On one hand she thanked God she was packed and ready to go. The quicker she got home to Port St. John, the sooner she'd get back. On the other hand …

She lifted the pendant and chain over her head, dropped it in a coil on the edge of the sink, turned, on the faucets and adjusted the water.

Events with shaky connections swirled in her mind. She stripped and stepped into the shower. How quickly things change, she thought, grabbing the soap. Yesterday, she was so scared she couldn't wait to get out of town. Today she was twice as scared, but would give the world to stay.

222222222222

# Chapter 29

**Lucy and Morgan**

After a breakfast of oatmeal and prunes, Lucy moved to a blue, wing-backed chair in the Pine Bush Acres living room and waited for her ingrate of a daughter to visit.

Bored, she twiddled her thumbs, took in the room and winced. The sight of it soured her stomach. The white ceilings must be twenty feet high. The rug was dark green and the walls were done in a mauve and white floral print. There was a gas fireplace on her right. A large gold-framed mirror hung above the mantle. The breakfronts and shelves along the walls held books, magazines and little doodads made by the senile citizens in residence. Those who were not snoring and catching flies with drool were gaping at CNN.

A frail white-haired senile citizen wearing baggy gray sweats and too much lipstick, clutched the arms of her chair with twisted fingers, raised her ass and fell back twice before getting to her feet. Pushing her walker, she maneuvered her bones across the rug and sank into an empty chair beside an attendant reading a book.

"Would you please find Days of Our Lives?" Her false teeth clicked like a dial, cranking her volume with every word.

Days of Our fucking Lives? Christ. Lucy shifted forward in her chair and locked her fingers around the handlebars of a metal walker that barely bridged her enormous knees. She glared at a small white plastic basket with *Lucy* printed in black magic marker tied to her walker. She groaned her way to the edge of her chair. A plump, gum-snapping, bleached-blond attendant with hoop earrings and orthopedic shoes held out a hand. "Need some help, honey?"

*Don't call me honey, you damned fool.*

Lucy smiled sweetly. "I'll do it myself." And goddamn it she would, if it killed her.

Lucy grunted, raised her massive hulk and lumbered over the dark green rug through the living room door. A slow-moving barge on the Erie Canal, she made her way through the hall, stood at her bedroom door and sighed. Her bed and bureau didn't belong here anymore than she did. This charade had to stop. She wanted out of this fucking place before she really went fucking nuts.

Failing to squeeze into a vinyl chair, she sat on the bed and gazed out her window. She couldn't remember the last time she saw Morgan. There must be a list of visitors. She'd ask one of those fool attendants. Lucy rubbed her arms. Speaking of fool attendants, she needed one to turn up the heat. It was always so cold in this place. Didn't Morgan pay them enough to turn up the heat? Did she just say that? Damn, she was hungry. They should've served breakfast already. What the hell's wrong with these people! She'd ring for something to eat, but first she must think. If only she could remember what it was she needed to think about. Where *was* Morgan? She called home day and night but Morgan never answered. Being defiant was so unlike her.

Lucy was losing her grip on Morgan just like she had years ago, when Chuck Matthias came into their lives. Memory be damned. She'd never forget how he stood in her house, big and imposing like he owned the place. And Morgan hung on his every Australian word, like he was Crocodile Dundee. They couldn't fool Lucy. They were sleeping together. She saw it in Morgan's eyes then, just as she'd seen it now. A fly of a thought buzzed in her brain. She puckered her dried lips. Was Chuck back, or had she dreamt it? If she asked an attendant, would she get a black mark under "memory"? Maybe Morgan and that doctor, Men—what's his name—were right and she was getting senile. The thought unnerved her. Lucy forgot her hunger. She lay on the bed, stared at the ceiling and fell asleep.

Morgan pulled into the crowded Pine Bush Acres parking lot before dropping her bags off at home. She turned off the motor and looked at the building and the pines bordering the lawn. Had she really moved Mother in here a few short weeks ago? So much had happened since, it felt like years. She dreaded going in. Mother, whom she hadn't called in over a week, would be furious.

Morgan leaned back for a minute and rubbed her palm over the cool tan leather of the passenger seat. Weeks ago, before all the really crazy stuff started happening, Chuck had called. She told him she'd bought the house. Her enthusiasm had infected him. He promised that as soon as he landed he'd drive to Lake Placid.

She'd give anything for Chuck to be there, waiting. But not out of fear. Oddly enough, after theorizing the house or something in it was trying to communicate with her, none of its antics scared her – as much. She missed Chuck like crazy. Owning a haunted house put her in serious need of his dispassionate perspective. And her house was haunted. Of that she had no doubt.

Maggie had said that Harlan was so obsessed with selling to the right buyer he even decided to hold the mortgage. Since connecting her pendant to the fire, one thing was for sure.

She, Morgan Matthias, was the right buyer.

She had to get back to Lake Placid, but not without seeing Mother. Whatever wanted her attention would be there, waiting.

The answers she wanted from Harlan and Maggie had better be waiting too.

# Chapter 30

## Lucy and Morgan

Lucy woke up abruptly and soaked in sweat. Had Chuck really been here, or had she dreamed it? She had to ask Morgan. Goddamn it all to hell. Getting old stunk. If you couldn't count on yourself, whom the hell could you count on?

Morgan had carried on this ridiculous fantasy about Chuck as if it was real. If Lucy hadn't played a major role in destroying them years ago, she'd actually believe Morgan had a husband. Morgan's sick act was so convincing it unnerved her, and Lucy was not easily unnerved.

Lucy heard, "Hello, Mother," and twisted around.

Morgan smiled at Lucy from the doorway.

"Christ on a crutch. You scared the living shit out of me. So, you remembered you had a mother and decided to grace her with your presence."

Lucy watched Morgan approach her through narrowed eyes. She looked good. The vintage rose dress heightened the blush on her cheeks. Was Chuck at the root of her healthy glow? Lucy grabbed a tissue from her nightstand and swabbed her brow. Morgan leaned over, kissed Lucy's clammy forehead and frowned.

"Are you all right, Mother?"

"Why shouldn't I be?"

"You're soaked through." Morgan fluffed Lucy's pillow.

"It's July, remember?" Lucy shook her head. "And I'm the one doing time for being senile." She wiped her wet forehead, rolled the soggy tissue into a ball and threw it on her nightstand. "If you really cared, you'd take me to—" she paused, "when will I see this place of yours? I need a vacation too."

"Mother, you know what the doctor said."

"Don't give me that horse poopy. You pack my stuff up and take me home, or I'll—"

Lucy spied the pendant, and her flint-blue eyes glittered. She grabbed the chain and yanked the pendant from Morgan's neck.

Morgan grabbed Lucy's hand. "Let it go, Mother."

Lucy tightened her grip. "It's mine. I never gave it to you for keeps. I want it back. Now!"

Suddenly, Lucy let out a howl. She flung the pendant across the room. Tears streamed down her cheeks as she gasped at a heart-shaped welt the pendant had burned on her palm.

*"Ice!"* she cried.

Frozen, Morgan stared at the angry red welt.

Lucy's eyes pooled with tears. "Ice. Over there. Hurry!"

Morgan plucked an ice cube from a pink plastic bucket on Lucy's dresser. Lucy pressed the cube against the burn.

"Where the hell did you have that thing?" Lucy switched the melting cube to the good hand and blew on the burn, while Morgan stared at the pendant. "Stop looking at it and answer me."

"I don't have an answer, Mother." Morgan stared at the pendant as if she'd never seen it before, Lucy thought.

"Bull." Just try and distract me from my real mission! "So, is Chuck enjoying the house?"

Morgan dropped the pendant. Her eyes widened.

Despite her burn Lucy smiled. "What's the matter?" The deliciously stunned look on Morgan's face! Lucy bit her lip to keep from laughing.

"How am I supposed to react?" Morgan said.

"Don't I have a right to ask a simple question without you making a Federal case out of it?" *Goddamn.* Her hand *hurt!*

"Of course. But you've never accepted Chuck as my husband. In fact, you act like he doesn't exist. It hurts my feelings and I know it hurts his feelings too."

Jesus, Mary and Joseph. Lucy almost brought her hands together and raised her eyes in prayer. I'm not the one who dreamed this marriage up. And what did it matter anyway? Suppose Chuck had been here? Suppose he and Morgan meet and he tells all? It's ancient history, and it won't change a thing.

"It's a shame when a widowed woman's daughter abandons her for a house in—" What was the name of that town?

"Lake Placid." Morgan said, wearing the same confused expression Benny wore, Lucy thought. Suddenly, for the first time in years Lucy saw the naked truth in her daughter's eyes. Morgan was going to sell the house, take the money, move to Lake Placid with Chuck and leave her to rot in this place forever.

Mother's lips quivered. Her face seemed to collapse in on itself. She bunched the sheets and pulled them up to her chin.

"What are you doing, Mother?"

Lucy's eyes looked strange. Just like they had in May, the first time Morgan had mentioned Lake Placid.

"What do you mean? Can't you see I'm cold?"

"A minute ago you were soaked in sweat." Morgan put her palm on Lucy's forehead. "Has Dr. Mendoza been in to see you?"

"I don't need him." She pushed Morgan's hand away.

"You're cool, but—"

Out of nowhere Lucy asked, "Have you been home yet?"

"What?" Would Mother ever cease astounding her?

"Go home! You've been gone," she grimaced as if it hurt her to swallow, "a long time. The lawn needs mowing."

"I was going to take care of that tomorrow."

"Go home and do it now."

Lucy folded her arms, tightened her jaw and stared straight ahead. Morgan knew that look. The subject was closed.

Morgan parked her car in her driveway. When Mother yanked the chain, she broke a link. The clasp was intact, and Morgan fastened it to the next link. She cradled the pendant in her hand, thinking. If she told Chuck her pendant had left a welt on Mother's hand like blessed metal on Dracula, he'd commit her. But that's exactly what had happened.

She traced the ruby and heart shaped setting of diamonds with her forefinger. For years it hung around her neck sort of, *dormant*—the word unnerved her—until today. What was it about the pendant that affected her mother and her so?

After giving Morgan the pendant decades ago Mother had never mentioned it again. Speaking of the unmentioned, for years mother had treated Chuck as if he'd been invisible. Why acknowledge him today?

She let the pendant go and drummed her fingers on the steering wheel. Ever since answering Maggie's ad, Morgan's life had taken a weird turn. Why would Lake Placid unnerve Mother, when to Morgan's knowledge Mother had never been there? Mother demanding to come home was a predictable response. All her life she'd been domineering and independent. Now she was stuck in a home, and her mind was disintegrating. In May Dr. Mendoza and Director Creutz had told Morgan there would be a period of adjustment. But what had happened today had nothing to do with adjusting.

Morgan grabbed her keys, got out of the car, stood in the driveway and sized up the backyard. Mother was right. The lawn and flowerbeds needed tending. She strolled down the driveway looking at her house. Its white paint had faded to gray and the green trim had chipped. The flagstone walk needed pointing up. She glanced up and down the block. Compared to her Victorian these houses, with their weary nondescript lines, sagging angles and planes and faded exteriors looked like old school chums, aging badly. She needed repair work done soon.

Morgan went back to the car, got her purse and bags and opened the kitchen door. A wall of heat took her breath away. Sweat beaded at her hairline and above her lips.

Stowing her overnight bag by the door, she took a paper napkin from a holder on the counter, dabbed her face and opened all the first-floor windows. The temperature dropped a tad, giving little relief. Morgan shook her head. No matter how hot it had gotten, Mother always complained about being cold and forbade Daddy and her to buy window units. In retrospect she was amazed at how much they had let Mother dominate their lives.

She spotted her digital camera on the counter, still in its blister packaging exactly where she had left it, both times. She removed the wrap and placed the camera lens down on the counter.

The camera suddenly *whirred* on.

Morgan froze.

A tiny green light flashed. The lens protruded. The liquid crystal display tilted toward her. Sweat rolled down her forehead and face. Stinging eyes riveted to the LCD, she grabbed her pendant and whispered, "This is not happening."

The camera advanced. Its big, square eye blinked, showing shot after shot in a virtual tour of her Lake Placid house in detail-by-chilling-detail.

Images of the dreams and fires connected to her pendant ran through her mind. Was this freaky slide show another way of letting her know that the house or something in it wanted to communicate with her? Voicing that thought would make her sound crazier than her mother.

The next slide, a grainy black and white, clearly unrelated to those before them, winked into view. Dumbfounded, she stared at the camera.

The shot showed the sun either rising or setting on a circle of ragtag wagons and tents near a lake in a scene resembling the barefaced cliff that had appeared in both of her dreams.

Why did this not surprise her?

Men sat in a circle around a campfire. Children and dogs romped near women in peasant blouses, long skirts and kerchiefs tied round their heads. Clothes from another time. Turn of the twentieth century?

She'd read about people who'd pitched tents and traveled in wagons resembling those in the photo. Today they used vans, pick-ups and RVs. They camped on the outskirts of towns, ran bazaars and carnivals, games of chance, sold miracle powders and told fortunes. They were Gypsies. And small-town USA despised them.

Some folks had recalled that when the Gypsies came to town people hid everything that wasn't nailed down, even clothes on the line.

Why would a photo of Gypsies be mixed in with slides of her house?

The camera advanced. Hands shaking, she picked it up, stared at the shot and almost dropped it. In a second black and white, grainier than the first was a small female figure. Morgan frowned. It seemed disturbingly familiar. My God. It appeared to resemble the figure, the hazy apparition she'd seen in the Queen Anne's tower window in May, when Maggie and she had gone back to the house. The day she was so hung over, she thought she'd imagined it all.

A question began forming in her mind that was so wildly off its hinges she shut her eyes against it. Was the haze she had originally mistaken for a misprint in the ad, and the apparition she'd seen in the tower, the person in this photo? She paused and held her breath desperately trying to understand how she could come to that conclusion. But even if it was, what in God's name did it mean, and what did it have to do with her? There was something else. Instinctively, she pressed menu, scrolled down, highlighted the date and gasped. Every color photo was dated 5/22/08. The day she'd called Maggie from home about the ad. Two days before she'd even set foot in Lake Placid! The black and whites were not dated.

The screen faded to dark. The green light went out. The camera whirred off. The lens retracted.

Morgan wiped the sweat from her face. She grabbed a pencil and paper and scribbled a note to Chuck. She turned and looked at the camera. Trembling, she closed all the windows in her house, put the camera in her purse, grabbed her overnight bag and locked the door behind her.

# Bloodfire and the Legend of Paradox Pond

## East Lake Placid October 1924

Under a barren moon and scatter of vacant stars Diamond stood on East Lake Placid shore near the footpath to Pulpit Rock. Clad in a white peasant blouse and a blue and red cotton skirt, she huddled against the wind, waiting for Jared Welcome.

The wind pierced her skin like hundreds of tiny needles. She rubbed the gooseflesh from her arms. Hunkering down, she gathered her skirt and bunched it around her ankles. But for a pair of worn out sandals her feet were bare. Under the full moon her toes looked paler than bloodless slugs.

Her teeth chattered her warmth out in dainty, moist puffs. Shivering with cold she had no one to blame but herself. As soon as Mama and Papa had fallen asleep, she slid out from under her blanket, backed away from the fire and sneaked out of camp so fast she'd forgotten her cloak. She pictured it inside their tent, warming her small trunk.

Diamond pictured her parents and sighed. She hated lying to them each time she'd left to meet Jared, but now that he knew she was pregnant the lying was done. Jared and she would face her parents together. He'd tell them he loved her and wanted to make things right. After Mama and Papa got over the shock, they'd love him as much as she did.

Diamond cupped her hands to her mouth, and her skirt fell away from her ankles. A cold, sharp wind knifed through her flesh and cut to her bones. She blew hard, rubbed her hands together, gathered her skirt tightly around her and smiled at a warming thought.

As Mrs. Jared Welcome, she'd never be cold again. Not with her store full of warm and beautiful clothes. And if she wanted some pretty frock Welcome's Mercantile didn't carry, Jared could order it from one of those fancy New York City catalogues.

Comforted by the thought, Diamond's smile widened. She watched the moonlight melt in the lake like cream in a cup of black coffee. Diamond toyed with her pendant, wondering why on earth Jared had asked her to meet at night when they usually met during the day. Diamond sighed and her smile faded. By his side she felt safe and secure, but pregnant and crouched down alone in the cold she wasn't so sure.

Each time they made love Jared swore if she ever got pregnant he would divorce Elspeth and marry her right away. Hadn't he told her over and over again that compared to their love his marriage to Elspeth was cold and bankrupt? Jared also told her he had a child, a little girl he adored, and for her sake, no one could know that he and Diamond were lovers.

Diamond smiled, knowing all that would change now.

She let her skirt go, stood up and patted her tummy. Soon she'd be mistress of Jared's fancy house, thumbing her nose at all of Lake Placid from high on that snooty hill.

Pincers of cold bit and clawed. She rubbed her arms and blew into her hands harder. Suddenly, she grinned, imagining the shock on Reverend Bradford's beady-eyed, pockmarked face when he found out that Jared Welcome had chosen a Gypsy to be his new wife. Diamond hugged her shivering body and narrowed her eyes. There was no one in Essex County the Gypsies hated more than the evil Ezekiel Bradford.

Every spring when her people returned to town, the good Reverend Bradford would stand in his mucky churchyard glaring, and clutching a bible as flat and as black as his eyes.

As soon as the sun went down, Bradford's mob of good Christian men would storm their camp, wielding torches and threatening to burn it down if they weren't gone by morning.

One year Papa had convinced their people to camp in a place so well hidden the Reverend would never find them. That was the year their camp, which the townsfolk called Gypsy Cove, had turned out to be the best-kept secret in Lake Placid.

Diamond tossed back her mane of saucy black ringlets, exposing large hoop earrings. She might be young, but she already knew why the good Reverend Bradford was worried. The roll of the dice and the sleek, fluid movements of dark gypsy women made Christian men hungry in places their God and their food couldn't touch. The way Jared hungered for her.

Her stomach grumbled and Diamond knew as soon as she married Jared, she would no longer have to fight the dogs for her food, or be forced to travel in hard, wooden wagons. And best of all there would be no more hunkering down near weak fires on stony ground, shivering herself to sleep.

After eating her fancy dinner, Mrs. Jared Welcome would slip out of her fancy dress and into her fancy nightgown. She would slide between fancy sheets on her soft, fancy bed and burrow beneath her billowy, goose down blanket.

Diamond realized she could not feel her toes. They could freeze off and she wouldn't know it. She clasped her hands under her arms and stomped her feet on the ground. To get her blood moving, she walked away from the lake and looked at the stars. The last time Jared and she had met, she refused to make love until he told Elspeth about them.

Diamond's eyes suddenly widened.

Was that it? Was tonight the night Jared told Elspeth about her? Diamond squealed with delight and patted her stomach. The squeal suddenly died in her throat. Was Jared late because Elspeth had refused to let him go?

A mouth of blue-black clouds swallowed the peppermint-disk of a moon. Her dream vanishing with the moonlight, Diamond ran back to the edge of the lake. Standing on toes she could not feel, she craned her neck toward the village and peered down the shore. Any minute Jared would burst through the night, sweep her into his arms and tell her he loved her. Needing to feel secure, Diamond walked to the place on the shore where several short months ago they'd met and fell in love.

Diamond had promised Mama not to go near the village, but daydreaming to the sound of snow crunching under her boots, she wandered further south than she'd meant to. She gazed at the lake, a thawing disk at the base of a bowl of mountains where winter's dying fingers were clinging to jagged peaks.

Warm from the spring sun and her brisk walk, she rounded a bend, stopped to loosen her cloak and saw him, down on one knee, skimming stones over the icy lake. Now and then he would stop, and stare into the distance. Tracking his gaze to a place that only he could see, Diamond moved closer. Ice cracked under her boot. He turned, saw her, lost his footing and slipped. Scrambling, he slipped and fell again and Diamond burst out laughing. He was up on his feet but he kept his eyes down, clearly embarrassed. And Diamond was sorry she'd laughed.

Brushing the frozen dirt from his knees, his muscles strained under his shirt, and Diamond could see that hard work and he were not strangers. He jammed his hands in his pockets and kicked at the ground, dislodging a clump of snow with the tip of his boot. He lifted his chin, looked into her eyes and her heart stopped.

His face flushed under an awkward smile. His black eyes were sad. His dark hair, damp and thick, clung to his forehead and temples. He had a square jaw and strong cheekbones like a Greek statue she'd seen in a magazine once. He gazed down the shore toward the village. He pulled his hands from his pockets as if waiting for her to speak, but all she could do was stare and pray that her heart kept beating.

"I come here to think," he said. "When I see this," he nodded at the lake and the mountains, "it calms me." He shifted and shrugged as if his declaration was of little or no importance. He wiped his palms on his pants and extended his hand.

"I'm Jared Welcome. I own the Welcome Mercantile."

Clearly he thought she ignored his hand, but she just couldn't move. He blushed harder and took his hand back.

"The general store's been in my family for years."

Diamond remembered. On their way through town Papa had stopped at the general store for supplies and he, Jared, had stood behind the counter, reluctantly filling their order.

"I take it you're not from these parts, are you?" he asked, knowing she wasn't, she thought.

She tried to answer but she couldn't move her tongue.

He squeezed his eyes shut as if he were getting a headache. "Well," he blushed harder, "I should head back now." He nodded politely and started down the shore.

"I'm Diamante Rubi O'Day," she blurted.

Jared Welcome stopped walking.

"My mother is Spanish and my father is—"

He turned and looked into her eyes. Her heart had lodged in her throat and dammed up the rest of her words.

"Irish?" he said, smiling.

She laughed and the dam gave way. Words gushed over her tongue and through her lips. "My people camp north of here in Gypsy Cove." Diamond seemed to float toward him. Cradled in her hand was the pendant that hung around her neck. "My mother and I were named for this gypsy necklace. My mother is Ruby. Diamante is Spanish for diamond. That's me."

She looked at her pendant. She wanted to tell him about the pendant and the gypsy legend of star-crossed love, but she thought he would think it was foolish and changed her mind.

They stood very close. She breathed him in and shuddered. He smelled forbidden, like the fruit in that garden in Reverend Bradford's bible.

"It's lovely," he said.

His breath, sweet and warm, brushed her cheek and her skin tingled. He lifted the pendant from her hand. His fingers grazed her palm, and her heart pumped and filled her with urges she never knew existed. "Thank you." Her gazed fixed on his mouth she wondered how it would taste. "I wear it all the time."

The urge to kiss him churned inside. Scared and confused, she mumbled something about needing to go. Mouthing an awkward goodbye, she scampered along the shore and disappeared into the woods, terrified she might never see him again.

It had not been consciously planned, but Diamond met Jared in the same place at the same time often where they walked along the shoreline skimming stones and talking. Whether moving a wisp of hair from her cheek or brushing dirt from her blouse, he always found reasons to *touch* her. He was handsome and rich. And he wanted her. More each time they met. She sensed it. She wanted him too, but—Jared was married.

One May afternoon while walking the footpath to Pulpit Rock, they wandered off the path. She started to speak, when he cupped her face in his hands and brought her lips to his in a kiss that rippled through her in violent, continuous waves. Her head was spinning so fast she almost fainted.

He pulled her to the ground. His hands rubbed. His fingers kneaded. His lips hot and wet found hers. He slipped her blouse off her shoulders to her waist. He pinned her arms to her sides, and devoured her breasts, her nipples, teasing and kissing again and again. Out of her mind with desire, Diamond moaned. Beyond him and the-here-and-now, nothing existed.

He loosened his trousers. Without warning, he lifted her skirt. She wiggled out of her panties. Their breath mingling, he filled her, reaching that place where heat turned to raging fire. His mouth covered hers and sucked in her gasp. Moaning against her cheek, he pushed harder and faster until she—

"Diamond?"

"Jared," she breathed, opening her eyes. Fire still raging inside, she pressed into him. Fighting her hunger, she looked up and said, "Does Elspeth know?"

Clouds held the moon hostage. It was too dark to see his eyes. She held her breath, waiting to hear his answer.

"Yes." He panted, pulling her tight against him.

"Thank God." Relieved, she exhaled and closed her eyes. She slipped her hands inside his jacket and circled his waist with her arms. His heart pounded against her. "When can we tell Mama and Papa?" she whispered.

"Tomorrow."

She sighed into his chest. "What did Elspeth say?" Diamond squeezed her eyes shut, terrified of the answer.

"Your skin's like ice." He took off his jacket and draped it over her shoulders. His hands shook hard and his teeth chattered. She pulled away, squinting, wanting to see his eyes.

"What's wrong?"

He ran his hands through her hair, bent her head back and kissed her. "I'm cold and I missed you." Diamond frowned. His cheeks felt wet as if he'd been crying.

"Jared? What—"

He took her hand and pulled her toward the path to Pulpit Rock. She shook her head and stopped walking. "It's too late now. I've got to get back. If Mama and Papa wake up—"

His lips covered hers in a hard, frantic kiss. Her head was as light as a leaf. He walked his fingers down her cheek and moved them along her neck. "Are you wearing it?" He breathed. His voice was hoarse, raspy. He didn't sound like himself.

"Wearing what?" She squinted, needing to see his eyes.

"Bloodfire." He reached between her breasts.

She shuddered against him. "I need you," she whimpered.

"No!" His voice was harsh. He must've felt her flinch. "Not here," he said softly. He let her pendant go and kissed her saying, "Diamond." She stopped breathing. "Ruby." She stopped thinking. "O'Day."

Consumed with desire, Diamond followed Jared deeper into the woods.

# Chapter 31

## Maggie and Chuck

Maggie sat at Harlan's desk staring at stacks of appointments needing confirmation or cancellation, but all she could see was her birthmark.

*Is Harlan my father?*

July 7, 2008, the day she learned she was Harlan's daughter, would go down as her day of personal infamy. The deception was as old as Adam and Eve and so was the hurt. The betrayal left every piece of her broken heart embedded with anger and bitterness. How could she heal when her heart hemorrhaged every time she extracted a piece of emotional shrapnel? She was mad enough to kill. The question was who should she off first?

After stabilizing Harlan, The Medical Center Emergency Room in Lake Placid sent him to their main branch in Saranac Lake. After further evaluation he had been transferred to the Physicians Hospital Heart Center in Plattsburgh for bypass surgery tomorrow. Mom and she were due to visit Harlan later today after Kevin relieved her. She never thought she'd admit it, but Delaney had been a godsend during this whole nightmare.

Kevin and Natalie. Her blood pressure hit red alert. Maggie had warned Natalie, on the oblique of course, that Kevin cared about one person. Kevin. And that he was using her. She hoped her message had gotten through.

Maggie lost count of the times she'd pictured Harlan on the floor helpless and unconscious. Was this the part where his stunning near-death event made her want to cherish her long lost father instead of strangling him? The event had changed her feelings for him all right, but not for the better. Being her father made what he'd done to Steve and her more reprehensible.

Did Harlan know he was her father? Daughter or not, Maggie would bet her life that Harlan would've acted in the same way.

During the whole debacle, Mom had looked desperate to talk. Maybe it was best they hadn't. She was angry with Mom, Harlan—

everyone but Steve these days. Neck deep in deception, she needed time to sort things out. Maggie checked her watch. It was only 8:30 a.m. and she felt like she'd already put in two days' work.

"Maggie?"

Maggie looked up. Lillian cracked Harlan's office door and stuck her head in. Her face was white and drawn. "Can I come in?"

"Suit yourself," Maggie said, hating the chill in her voice, but hating her mother's deception more.

Clutching her purse under her arm, Lillian opened the door. She looked thin. Fragile. She eased herself into a leather chair and put her purse on her lap. "I never meant," Lillian bit her trembling lip. "Oh God, Maggie." She curled her fingers around the arm of the chair and squeezed till her knuckles were white.

"Can you ever forgive me?"

Maggie glared at her mother.

"I never meant for you to find out like this, but there was never a good time to tell you. If it's any consolation, I never told Harlan either."

"Was Marcy Harlan's daughter too?" Maggie's voice was hostile.

Lillian shook her head. "Can I explain? Please?"

Maggie shrugged and Lillian cleared her throat. "Bob was in Vietnam. I was alone with a house and a mortgage. I needed a second job. Harlan hired me. He was powerful, decisive—"

Maggie rolled her eyes. "I know all this."

Lillian blushed. "It was innocent at first and then—"

"Innocent? You were both married to other people!"

Lillian flinched, and Maggie felt glad and ashamed.

"I know it was wrong. I know we were wrong."

"What about Bob?" Maggie said. "Did he suspect?"

"Bob was so withdrawn and disturbed after Vietnam," Lillian opened the purse on her lap and pulled out a tissue. "I think he was the only one in Lake Placid who didn't know about Harlan and me." She looked into Maggie's eyes. "Even Julia knew—"

"Julia? Bradford? Harlan's late wife?"

Maggie was astounded. Lillian nodded, sobbing openly. She wiped her eyes. "I swear she got drunk, crashed her car and died, because of Harlan and me. Ask Bradford," Lillian paused, waiting, but Maggie did not respond.

"I did everything I could to keep Bob from knowing." Lillian lowered her eyes, "That's how Marcy was born."

Mom's embarrassed, Maggie thought, gratified and nauseous.

"Despite my sins I still loved Harlan, I mean your father, until the Connellys moved into the Welcome house."

Maggie sighed. "If circumstances had been different, maybe Tommy and Marcy would both still be alive."

Lillian raised her eyes. "What do you mean?"

"From the day you introduced us to the Connellys, when Marcy saw those steely-blue eyes, she fell hard for Tommy. She made me take his picture. She mooned over it constantly." Maggie smiled, distractedly. "I'll bet it's still in her wallet."

"Morning, ladies." Kevin walked into Harlan's office.

"Morning, dear." Lillian sniffled, wiping her eyes.

Kevin looked worried. "Is Harlan okay, Mrs. Duran?"

"Yes. Don't mind the waterworks. We're just reminiscing."

"Oh." Kevin smiled weakly.

Now that he'd been a straight shooter for the past few days, Maggie could see why Natalie and half the female population of Lake Placid found him sexy. But she wouldn't dismantle her radar anytime soon.

Lillian looked at her watch. "God. It's ten o'clock I didn't realize I'd been here so long. I'm going to Plattsburgh to see Harlan. Come with me, Maggie?"

"Truthfully, Mom? I think it would put Harlan more at ease if he knew I was here with Kevin taking care of business."

Lillian's fading smile tugged at Maggie Duran's heart, but Maggie *Wainright* was immune.

"Of course." Lillian's eyes glistened. "If that's what you think is best. I understand. Things do have a way of piling up."

Lillian turned to Kevin. "I'll run home first and get Natalie. You've been great looking after her, but I think the worst is over, and I can spell you now."

"I don't mind taking Natalie with me, Mrs. Duran," he said.

I'll bet you don't, Maggie thought, her suspicions showing their ugly heads. Feeling a tad guilty, she smacked them down.

"I know, dear," Lillian said.

Kevin nodded and then headed for the coffee machine.

Lillian turned to Maggie. "Goodbye and, um, thanks for listening," she said. Under normal circumstances they'd hug. These circumstances were anything but.

Maggie managed a weak smile. "Sure," she said.

Gently guiding her mother through Harlan's door, she saw a guy standing in the outer office. He was, tall, good looking, roughly fifteen years her senior, wearing Ralph Lauren jeans, a bonny blue polo and the most radiantly confident smile she'd seen in a long time. His thick blond hair had surrendered to a more distinguished gray, which did nothing to mar his looks. In fact, he was smokin' hot. He held the door for her mother.

"Thank you," Lillian said, sounding slightly less dejected than when she'd arrived.

"No worries, love," said the handsome stranger.

The accent surprised Maggie. She stared at Kevin. From the look on his face the accent had surprised him too.

"G'day. I hear you've been closed due to an illness. Everything's all right, I hope." He looked at her with pale, intelligent blue eyes and black pupils. He seemed cultured, at ease and appeared to come from money. He also seemed concerned.

"I don't have an appointment," he said. "I'm from out of town. I looked in the window and saw you were open."

Maggie and Kevin stared at him. His smile faded. "Sorry. I can see this is a bad time." He headed for the door.

"Don't go," Maggie said. "I'm the one who's sorry. Your timing is perfect actually. Your accent threw me," she laughed.

"Me too." Kevin held out his hand. "Kevin Delaney."

The man shook Kevin's hand. "Name's Chuck—"

"Matthias? Morgan's husband?" Maggie smiled and took his hand. "I'm so happy to finally meet you. I'm Maggie Duran. I sold your wife the house."

Stunned, Chuck took Maggie's hand, thanking God he had chosen this realtor at random and blessing his profession, which prepared him to react with low affect under any circumstance. The young bloke and the rest of the office went blurry. Only the gorgeous, leggy blond with the south-sea blue eyes stayed sharply in focus.

"Morgan said you were in Australia on business, but that you'd be joining her sometime this summer."

*Jesus!* "Right." He smiled, emphatically. A thin sheen of perspiration coated his forehead. He refrained from wiping it. "I'm afraid you have me at a disadvantage, Ms. Duran." His heart pounded. His voice kept steady. "I need directions to the house."

"Easily remedied, Doctor Matthias."

"Thanks. My business kept me on the move, and while mobile phones are a blessing, they do drop calls."

"I hear you." Maggie smiled. "I assume you have a car." Chuck nodded. "Okay. Depending on traffic your house is less than five minutes from here."

Five minutes! He concentrated on Maggie's every direction, trying to ignore his spiking heart rate.

"It's the Stately Queen Anne. You can't miss it."

"Thank you." Trying to keep the ridiculous smile off his face, he held out his hand. "Thank you, Ms. Duran."

"My pleasure." She looked into his eyes. "I'm so glad you're here," she said, squeezing his hand slightly longer than appropriate, but she wasn't flirting. She seemed relieved.

"So am I, Miss Duran."

She let go. "Doctor Matthias. Before you go." She opened her desk drawer and rummaged through a small plastic box. "Morgan left the spare with us." The tag said Welcome.

"Welcome? A key to the city?"

She laughed. "Exactly. Oh, uh Morgan's out of town."

So Parker, the neighbor was right and Lucy had told the truth. The realtor must've mistaken his surprise for disappointment because she quickly added, "I mean Morgan went home to visit her mother. She might be back now, but I'm not sure," she smiled. "I guess there's only one way to find out." She handed him the key.

Chuck squeezed the key. Forcing his lips to smile and his tongue to utter a grateful goodbye, he walked out of the office.

He leaned against a parking sign outside Placid Properties and noticed a neon-green poster taped to it, advertising a Gypsy bazaar on Saturday, July twelfth. He closed his eyes, pressed the key to his lips and replayed Maggie Duran's words over and over again. *Matthias? Morgan's husband?*

He suddenly realized his greatest fear had turned into his greatest relief. Morgan was married. *To him.* And back to his greatest fear again. He pocketed the key and walked back to the hotel deeply immersed in thought.

How do I approach you, Morgan? Do I just knock at the door and say, hi, we lost each other thirty years ago, but according to you, that's not the way it happened. Please, don't misunderstand me. I couldn't be happier knowing you've kept me alive and well in your mind, but *I am a figment of your imagination! And when I finally step into your life, who and what will you really see?*

How in bloody hell could he grapple with what was happening? He must start by isolating and identifying reality piece by piece. Thirty-two years ago he had married another woman. While he had three children and a life with Barbara in Australia, Morgan had been here in America, believing she was married to him. The evil that bloody Lucy had perpetrated on her own flesh and blood astounded and enraged him.

Dear God, hadn't he victimized Morgan too?

Lying on his bed at the White Birch Inn, Chuck stared at the ceiling, paralyzed by the enormity of what was at stake. He must approach this in a way that all his years of expertise fell short of providing. What if he blundered and failed her, again? He shook his head. He was certain of one thing. When they finally met, he would do nothing until he examined every aspect completely and thoroughly. He would ingest and internalize her reality until it became part of him. Like his hand, or his heart. His mission? To know Morgan's delusion better than he knew himself. To understand the intricate way in which she had stitched these pieces of her life together to survive in her own special reality.

He was certain of something else. If Morgan had carried this fantasy to such extremes, she was in deep trouble. She was psychotic and vulnerable. Damn Lucy's bloody soul to hell. Deducing how Morgan had coped with their break-up, he was acutely aware that Lucy had been right. He was as responsible if not more so for Morgan's condition than Lucy was.

But he loved Morgan and now that he knew she still loved him, together they'd make things right—again.

Closing his eyes in painful concentration, he pulled the past into the present, remembering the intensity, urgency, tenderness, and understanding with which they had related to one another in those fledgling months they had been lovers. Because she believed he was real, her trust in him still made Morgan vulnerable despite the ingenious defenses she had erected.

Morgan had built and was living in an elaborate sandcastle to house her version of reality. If she had been his wife and the mother of his children, none of this would've happened.

Speaking of children, he hadn't spoken to his since he left Australia. They must be worried sick about him. He got to his feet, reached into his jeans pulled out his mobile. He'd tried to ring them before, but he had nothing of consequence to say. Chuck frowned. They would have questions. Would he respond with more lies of omission, or the truth? At this juncture, he honestly did not know which would be less harmful—

for all.

He couldn't ring them. Nor could he allow them to ring him. Not until he could offer them a solid outcome and explanation. They lost their mother just a few short months ago. As their father, he owed them that.

Chuck turned off his mobile, turned on his side and planned his re-entry into Morgan Quick's life.

# Chapter 32

**Plattsburgh, N. Y.**
**Maggie and Natalie**

Maggie sat in the PHHC family waiting room, leafing through *Time* magazine, trying to digest a small Caesar salad she'd gobbled for dinner, wondering how she could ever forgive her mother for not telling her that she was Harlan's daughter. She tossed the magazine aside. The clock on the wall read 7:00 p.m. Before Mom went into Harlan's room, the doctors had asked that they visit one at a time to keep his stimulation at a minimum. Kevin and Nat agreed. Maggie stonily abstained.

Needing to switch gears before getting an ulcer, Maggie watched Kevin and Nat, sitting directly across from her. If she could get past their potential treachery and difference in age, they looked great together. She doubted Delaney was sleeping with Nat. He was too smart for that. She wondered how he restrained himself and snickered, enjoying the comic relief.

Nat was a drop-dead beauty who was off the charts in style. Now how did that happen? Maggie smiled, knowingly. Maggie watched Nat read a novel and Kevin scan the *North Country Tribune*, thinking about the night she found out she was Harlan's daughter.

After the Medical Center ER in Lake Placid had stabilized Harlan, Maggie had slipped into the ladies' room, vibrating with shock. She'd called Steve, but refused to disclose details over the phone. Steve named an obscure motel outside Lake Placid and rushed down to meet her there. After tearing each other's clothes off and making fast and furious love, she lay in his arms, sobbing, and told him everything from seeing her birthmark on Harlan's chest to how Morgan Matthias armed with intel from her ally, Jack Bradford, had confronted Harlan and her in front of Kevin. Judging from the confrontation, the Welcome place had already geared up to scare Morgan out of her wits-or worse. She'd been petrified for Morgan, until today. Thank God Chuck Matthias had finally shown up. He could protect his wife while Maggie was otherwise occupied with her *father's* surgery and recovery.

Maggie needed to see Steve tonight, before leaving Plattsburgh.

Everything she'd found out from Morgan today would make Steve's twenty-fifth anniversary article a Pulitzer Prize winner. But, would helping Steve go public again hurt Mom? His ambition and desire for revenge against Harlan terrified her. Would he hurt her again? He shouldn't. They were in it together now. Weren't they?

Time out. That was Maggie Duran talking, not the new and improved Maggie Wainright. She was Harlan's daughter. Not only cold-blooded enough to stomp dear old dad while he's down, but for toe-curling sex, Maggie Wainright would give Steve scoop and cone, because after what her mother did she deserved—

Unshed tears of confusion and shame burned in her eyes. She'd sort things out and make up her mind in Steve's bed. It was 7:10. He should be home by now. If her visit with Harlan ended the same way tonight as it had the past few nights, they'd be heading back to Placid around ten. With Harlan's bypass surgery scheduled for tomorrow, maybe they would leave earlier.

Maggie cleared her throat. "Guys?"

Kevin and Natalie looked up. "Can you keep an eye on Mom and take turns visiting? I've got to hunt for a drugstore. With everything we've got going on I'm low on essentials. Okay?"

"Sure," Kevin said. Natalie nodded and shrugged.

"Thanks." She picked up her purse. "Kevin? If I don't make it back, and Mom and Nat get tired would you take them home?"

"Be glad to."

As soon as Maggie was out of sight, Natalie grabbed her purse, jumped to her feet and held out her hand. "Keys. Now."

"What keys?"

"Yours. Now. Before she gets to the parking lot."

Natalie took the stairs and got to the parking lot just as Maggie was pulling out. She jumped into Kevin's car and eased it from the parking lot into the flow of traffic. Eyes on Maggie's Lexus, she stayed three car lengths behind, noting street signs and landmarks to map her way back. She followed Maggie through Plattsburgh to a complex of condos on Lake Champlain and laughed. "Drugstore my foot."

She parked on the street and watched Maggie lock her car and enter a building. Nat got out of her car and crossed the lot. After a respectable amount of time, she opened the front door. On the right wall were four mailboxes. Each labeled with a unit number and a corresponding name. She ran her finger across the names. Wide-eyed with shock she stopped.

"Steve Rivers," she whispered, remembering his name from the morning she heard Gran and Maggie arguing in Maggie's room. "Why, Aunt Maggie, you slut!" She grinned.

Natalie walked into the PHHC waiting room breathless and grinning like a kid who'd just pulled off the biggest candy-store heist in history.

"I'm glad you got back before your grandmother came out and started asking questions."

Natalie panted, licked those luscious lips and sat. She picked up the magazine and fanned herself. "Where's Gran?"

"Still with Harlan. Why are you out of breath?" He frowned.

"Took the steps. I couldn't wait for the elevator."

"So? Did your little foray into the wilderness pay off?"

"You are *not* going to believe it!"

Kevin listened, mesmerized.

"I've got to hunt for a drugstore ... If ... Mom and Nat get tired would you take them home?" Natalie mimicked. "Really?"

Kevin put his arm around Natalie's shoulder and pressed his lips to her cheek. "That was some piece of detective work, baby," he whispered and smiled to himself.

She looked at him with those *eyes.* "I'll bet you ten bucks Aunt Maggie doesn't get back here in time to take Gran and me home. But who cares? I'd rather go home with you anytime."

Kevin squeezed her, realizing it got harder to let her go. He picked up a magazine and leafed through, thanking God he'd never mentioned the joined-at-the-genitals crack Harlan made about Maggie and Rivers in May. He would never forget how Maggie had stormed out.

So Maggie was back with Steve. Hooo-leee-sheeeeiiiit. He grinned. His mind played chess with the strategy and tactics of Nat's little maneuver. If the old man found out, he'd have another heart attack. *Jesus.* He glanced at Natalie. She was the gift that kept on giving, and she had just given him the keys to the kingdom.

# Chapter 33

## Morgan

Morgan sat at her kitchen table in jeans and a tee shirt, barefooted, sipping coffee and chewing on wheat toast, thanking God she'd slept last night, despite a harrowing drive back with several near misses on the Northway.

The dreams, that camera whirring on, the dated color shots, the grainy black and whites were connecting threads, but in what tapestry? As Harlan's right buyer, was she in the weave too? Why, after all these years, would Mother rip the pendant from her neck, claiming she wanted it back? Mother had always been a control freak. Life at Pine Bush meant surrendering control. Had lashing out been an attempt to take it back? In her hand the pendant doused fires, in her mother's it burned flesh. *Burn* and *fire* were two more common threads connecting her pendant to the house. Were they in that tapestry too?

Morgan grabbed her mug, stood by the picture window and gazed at the backyard. As sunlight dripped through the white birch leaves, she thought about Chuck. Before leaving Port St. John, she'd scribbled a note, begging him to join her in Placid and left it on the counter. If he was there, like Mother had said and their paths hadn't crossed, why hadn't he called?

Morgan suddenly smiled. He must've read her note and was on his way here to surprise her. Now *that* would be very much like him. She checked her watch and glanced at the exterior thermometer. Sixty-five and it was 8:00 a.m. What would it be like at noon? If she were right, Chuck could be here late this morning. She should shower and do some errands.

Last night before going to bed, she'd looked through the window and saw that two streetlights were still out. Maggie and Harlan owed her answers and she wanted them before Chuck got here. She had thought about stopping at PPI and inquiring about the streetlights on her way through yesterday, but the office had been closed. According to Jack, Harlan was a regular shark. Sharks never stopped moving. Something was up.

Morgan grabbed her mug, took the kitchen steps and stopped at the landing where a shinier than usual glint in the hardwood floors caught and held her eye.

As the sound of her lungs drawing in and expelling air resonated in her head, the green area rug seemed richer and lusher. Drawn, she walked down the steps over the cool, naked floor and sank her feet into the rug's deep pile. The long plush fibers between her toes and under her soles were seductively soothing. Her heart thrumming, she slipped into the winged chair, swirled the hot dark liquid around her tongue and sighed. The coffee tasted better than good.

Gazing around the room, she imagined Chuck making love to her on the Prince of Wales sofa. Her eyelids drooping, she gazed at the fireplace and those adorable lamps with their darling ruffle-gowned porcelain ladies and wondered how such dainty little fingers held such tiny fans? Dreamy-eyed, she gazed at the embroidered drapery. Were the vines and flowers moving? She ran her hand over the buds and leaves on the upholstery, breathed in their intoxicating perfume and smiled.

The smell of exotic leather-bound classics from the bookshelves filled her nostrils. The scent of *Canterbury Tales* made her giddy. She imagined Chuck on the sofa, sipping coffee, perusing the paper for local politics or places to explore, when she heard a sigh. A rustle.

Her skin tingled, shattering her elation. Mug in her shaky hand, she carefully raised herself out of the winged chair, made her way up the steps to the landing and turned. Every cell in her body focused and on alert, she scanned nooks and crannies between bookshelves, draperies, tables and chairs.

Rustling. Again. Faint. Elusive.

She looked at the porcelain ladies. When their black, spider eyes met hers, her coffee mug felt heavy as if it were filled with cement.

Their faces frozen in smiles, the tiny ladies bunched their ruffled skirts in dainty porcelain fingers and bowed their hatted, veiled heads. Lifting their ruffled skirts, they exposed their slippered feet. Their petticoats faintly swishing, the tiny ladies bent at their tiny waists and curtsied.

Morgan's fingers went limp. The mug slipped from her hand. Somewhere far away she heard the mug shatter. She looked down. Coffee pooled at her toes. Bits of broken mug like jagged teeth lay on the landing.

Without warning, she watched the stairwell wall whiz by her. It stopped abruptly. Her head spinning, Morgan looked down the steps from the second floor landing. Pieces of broken mug poked through pools of black coffee where she had just stood.

Suddenly, a cold hand cupped the small of her back. The hallway flew by in a whir of pedestal tables and bracketed gas lamps. The rug ran under her feet. Deposited in the bedroom under the tower, Morgan whimpered. The wood in the hearth burst into blood-red flames. She grabbed her pendant and squeezed.

The fire died. Tears welling in her eyes, she was absurdly grateful for the thimble of control her pendant offered. Eyes on the hearth, she held her breath, let go of her pendant and waited for the logs to explode into flame. Nothing.

Morgan stood statue-still. Terrified she'd be dragged off to God knows where, she took in the exquisite fireplace and hearth, the antique mirror and the brass bed. They were the best money could buy, but they masked the truth like fancy French sauces had masked rotten meat set before crowned heads of medieval Europe. Her tears ran, washing away her affection for the house. She sensed the house was vile and for some insane reason her pendant and she by extension were up to the hilt in its evil. No wonder the few buyers Jack mentioned had run from this house, terrified. Of course the house *was* communicating with her. The message? She twirled around—get the hell out or die like the Welcomes and Tommy Connelly. She met her petrified glance in the mirror above the mantle, connecting another dot.

She'd bet her life that Tommy Connelly was the boy in her dream, but she had to be sure. There must be a picture of him somewhere, a newspaper photo—or something. The urge to get the hell out – now, overwhelmed her. She looked at her watch, collected the camera and her purse and ran out of the bedroom, down the stairs and out of the house.

# Chapter 34

## Morgan

Jack Bradford stood in the Bradford House lobby talking to the hostess. Jack turned, spotted Morgan, smiled and held out his hand. She was glad he seemed happy to see her.

"Morgan Matthias."

"I have to talk to you. Now. Please. It's important."

Clearly noticing the urgency in her voice, Jack said to the hostess, "Lea, Ms. Matthias and I will be in the library. Would you have the bar send us two coffees?" He glanced at Morgan.

"Coffee with cream will be fine. Thanks."

Jack guided Morgan into the library room where they sank into a velvet-covered sofa. A waitress brought two coffees, a plate of hot buttered scones and a small cruet of strawberry jam. She set them on a coffee table then slipped away.

Jack lifted his cup. "To your health."

Morgan lifted hers. "And yours." She looked past the plants hanging in the ceiling-to-floor windows and gazed into the manicured, tree-shaded gardens. The coffee felt good going down.

"Now, my dear," Jack put his cup down and picked up a scone. "What's got you so fired up?" He took a bite.

"Do you know why Placid Properties is closed?"

Jack swallowed and dabbed his lip with a napkin. "Harlan had a heart attack." He put his scone down.

"Dear God!" She put her cup down.

"He's in Plattsburgh at PHHC," he said. She frowned and he translated. "Physicians Hospital Heart Center. The best facility in the country. Supposedly, they performed surgery this morning. If something bad had happened, everyone in town would know about it by now. Believe me."

"Do you know if or when Maggie will be back?"

Jack shrugged. "Sorry. Anything else?"

"Something else happened since we last talked." She took a bite of her scone surprised she was hungry. She paused, realizing there was no way to tell Jack her story without him thinking she was crazy. "The house isn't haunting me. I think it's trying to communicate with me."

Jack stopped chewing. The look in his eye pledged his undivided attention.

Morgan explained that before leaving for home, she had confronted Harlan and Maggie with everything, including the two broken streetlights. When she described the apparition she saw in the tower window on Memorial Monday, Maggie had seemed ill at ease, but once confronted, she admitted seeing the same apparition the day before, just as Morgan suspected.

"Apparition." Jack said it as a statement of fact. "That means Lillian had been telling the truth all along."

"What truth?"

"For years, Lillian claimed she saw something in that tower, but no one believed her."

"I told Harlan that thanks to you, I knew about everything, including his obsession with finding the right buyer. I asked if that's why he gave me the house. I ended by saying I had no intention of losing my investment, and when I got back to town I wanted answers."

"Bravo!" Jack popped the last of his scone into his mouth and picked up his cup without blinking. "What did he say?"

"That I got the house because I qualified."

Jack chuckled and took a sip of coffee.

"On my way out of Harlan's office I passed a dark, attractive woman with her Golden Retriever, Jinx, on a leash."

"Lillian," Jack said, putting his coffee down.

"I assumed she overheard my conversation with Harlan because she looked as nervous as Maggie had." Morgan put her scone down, wiped her fingers on a napkin and grasped her pendant. Her eyes met Jack's. "I've got news for them. There is another wrinkle in the old Gothic fabric they do not know about."

Morgan described how the pendant had burned her mother's hand. While explaining how her brand-new-right-from-the-factory camera had pictures in the memory chip that no one had taken, Morgan dug in her purse for the camera. "Check out the dates they were supposedly *taken.*"

"Jesus!" he said, scrolling through the pictures. The sight of the black and whites drained the color from his face. "Gypsies," he said, in a resigned tone of voice.

"You're familiar with them?" She was surprised.

Jack shook his head and waved his hand. "Indirectly. The *Reverend*

Ezekiel Bradford was my great uncle. He loathed the Gypsies for obvious reasons. He led a mob and threatened to burn them out whenever they camped near town. Drove them pretty far north to a place on the lake folks referred to as Gypsy Cove."

"Gypsy Cove. Sounds exotic."

"I haven't been there in decades," he pointed to the lake and mountains in the grainy photo. "This could be it. Talking about Ezekiel after all these years is a bit unnerving." He gave a nervous laugh.

"I'm sorry to drudge up bad memories. I shouldn't have told you," she said, worried that she'd lost her only ally in town.

Jack put his napkin down and signaled a waitress for coffee. "My distress has more to do with my great uncle's rotten history with the Gypsies. I hope this photo isn't another skeleton in the Bradford family closet." Jack frowned and dabbed his lips with a napkin, looking distracted. "Forgive me, Morgan, but I find it hard to believe your mother's pendant is connected, especially if she's never been to Lake Placid. Are you sure about that?"

"Positive."

"You're brave, but you've got to be apoplectic about spending another night in that house."

"After this last scare, I'm pretty sure the house or something is trying to communicate with me, like I said. I'm terrified out of my wits, but to tell you the truth, I've not really been harmed-yet." She shivered, taking a deep breath. "Be that as it may, it's almost as if I have no choice, Jack. I'm compelled to see it through. I just wish I knew what my next step was."

Jack's frown slowly melted into a smile. "For what it's worth, Morgan, I think I can put you in touch with someone who can help. He's a reporter. His name is Steve Rivers. He's a good friend and a staff writer for the North Country Tribune in Plattsburgh.

"Every five years on the anniversary of Tommy Connelly's death Steve does a feature story. This September is the twenty-fifth anniversary, and the buzz is that this year he's going to outdo himself. Truthfully, it's just buzz. There hasn't been a new lead for years," he smiled, "until now."

"Do you think he'd be receptive?"

"Ecstatic is more like it. Steve is obsessed with this story. Finding out how the Welcomes and Tommy Connelly froze to death in that house is his life's mission." Jack took a pen and little note pad from his shirt pocket and handed them to Morgan. "Give me your number. I'll call Steve and set up a meeting."

Morgan finished her coffee. "I believe more than ever that the boy I saw in my house is Tommy Connelly. I wish I knew what he looked like. Have you ever met him?"

Jack shook his head. "I saw Jenna Connelly when she came here for Tom. She had quiet, desperate eyes and seemed as nervous and as timid as a bird. I felt sorry for her. Tom was a hell of a chef, but he was a bully and a loser. He obviously scared her."

"What happened to the Connellys after Tommy died?"

"Tommy died in September of nineteen eighty-three and I believe Jenna and Tom went back to Florida with Tommy's remains. As far as I know, no one has heard from them since. Sorry I can't be of more help."

"Are you kidding? You were fantastic."

Walking Morgan out, Jack frowned and said, "You look like a woman with a mission."

"I need to do a mountain of research. Wish me luck."

"That's a given," Jack said. He took the paper with her cell number. "I'll be in touch."

# Chapter 35

**Morgan**

Morgan stood on the sidewalk in front of the Bradford House. She could go for a coffee and browse the Internet on her phone, but she needed access to a printer. She scanned Main Street and spotted a place that would do her just fine.

The white sign over the front porch said the Lake Placid Library was established in 1884, but the small white building looked like a private home some generous patron had donated. A neon green flyer advertising a Gypsy Bazaar on Saturday, July twelfth was stapled to the porch column. The same flyer in different colors seemed to be plastered all over town.

Morgan entered the library. The reading room, with its fireplace, rocking chairs and panoramic view of Mirror Lake and its mountainous backdrop provided as homey an atmosphere as the building's charming exterior portended. "Do you have Internet service?

The librarian wore short curly gray hair and a pleasant smile.

In a voice as pleasant as her smile the librarian said, "Take the stairs by the exit and follow the corridor."

The room had six computers. Choosing one on the far right, Morgan sat and hit the browser. She typed Google, feeling as if she were sitting at the hub of a wheel whose spokes were leads she felt compelled to follow. Tommy Connelly was uppermost in her mind. Praying for a photo in the breaking story, she accessed the 1983 *North Country Tribune* archives.

**Boy found frozen to death. Bizarre circumstances baffle police**, dated September 30, by staff writer, Mark O'Donnell

Lake Placid—13-year-old Tommy Connelly was found frozen to death in his bedroom at his home on Midlakes Road early this morning. "I'm about to tell you something I don't even believe myself," Lake Placid Chief of Police, Harold Oberdon, said at a press conference this afternoon. "The boy was found frozen solid in his bed, which was also frozen solid. The fact that something like this could happen here, in the month of September is completely baffling.

"Mrs. Jenna Connelly, the boy's mother, said she woke up around 2 a.m. to the sound of terrifying screams coming from Tommy's bedroom. Mrs. Connelly said she jumped out of bed, ran down the hall and found Tommy's room and everything in it covered in ice and Tommy frozen solid in his bed, dead. She ran back to her bedroom and called the police. Mr. Connelly, a chef at the Bradford House on Mirror Lake Drive was at work at the time.

"The only place on the face of this earth with temperatures extreme enough for that boy to have died the way he did is in the dead of winter at the North Pole or on the continent of Antarctica, and I'm not so sure about that either," Oberdon said. "A thorough search of the premises revealed no forced entry, no apparent motive and no form of theft," Oberdon added.

"God knows there's no apparent explanation for what happened here tonight, yet. But we'll keep on it until we come up with one," Oberdon said.

Thomas J. Connelly, the boy's father, relocated his family from Orlando, Florida to Lake Placid in July of 1983 after being hired as chef at the Bradford House, a local historic inn and popular dining spot in downtown Lake Placid. Sources say the family will return to Florida with the boy's remains as soon as possible. The Connellys had no other children.

When asked if the Connelly death was similar in any way to the legendary, mysterious deaths of Jared and Elspeth Welcome, the Victorian's original owners, Chief Oberdon sighed and said, "No comment."

In 1919, Jared Welcome, a Lake Placid merchant, built the house on Midlakes Road as a wedding present for his wife Elspeth. One morning, five years after moving in, the Welcomes were found frozen to death in the same bedroom under the tower where police found Tommy Connelly.

Both cases are pending.

O'Donnell followed up with:

'**Bizarre tragedy continues to stump police,** dated October 12:

Lake Placid—Facts surrounding the death of 13-year-old Tommy Connelly continue to elude police. Connelly was found frozen to death in his bed in his bedroom on Midlakes Road on September 30. Although investigators have placed Connelly's death at around 2 a.m., the rest of the case remains a mystery.

"There are no new leads at this time, but the investigation is ongoing," Lake Placid Police Chief, Harold Oberdon said.

The parents of the deceased boy could not be reached for comment, but acquaintances say that Thomas J. and Jenna Connelly plan to return to their native Florida with the boy's remains as soon as possible. Connelly relocated his family from Orlando, Florida to Lake Placid in July of 1983, after being hired as chef at the Bradford House, a popular dining spot in downtown Lake Placid.

After printing O'Donnell's articles, Morgan found Jack Bradford's reporter-friend's stories. Steve Rivers wrote one each in 1988, 1993, 1998 and 2003, respectively. Morgan read all four. Apparently, what Mark O'Donnell reported in September and October of 1983, and what Jack had said earlier still stood. There were no new leads—until now. Jack was right. Rivers seemed obsessed. Using O'Donnell's copy, Rivers appeared to have searched between every rock and hard place to find and interview Welcome contemporaries and compare stories. The interviewees agreed that in 1924 a fire had burned several buildings to the ground, including Welcome's Mercantile and the old town hall. At the turn of the century, fires were a regular occurrence in wooden buildings with potbelly stoves.

The interviewees had related another strange occurrence. Lake Placid's famous hundred-year flood had hit a few days before the 1924 fire. Rain soaked the buildings clear through, but witnesses said that by the "whump" of the fire, every last person who'd watched it burn swore it had rained gasoline instead of water. Morgan noticed that some claimed the Welcomes had had a child, a little girl who, after they died, had gone to live with relatives far away. Others argued there was no child. In 1924, because fire had destroyed all the records, whether a Welcome child had existed would forever remain a mystery.

A police report, the only remaining legal document, stated the Welcomes had frozen to death in their house, but shed no light on how it had happened or whether there had been a child. The police found no personal records in the house. To Rivers' knowledge neither Elspeth nor Jared had had any surviving relatives.

The old timers concluded that the few people Placid Properties had duped into buying the Welcome house had high-tailed it out within days, claiming that something evil possessed the house, and that they had been lucky to escape with their lives.

Morgan paused and stared at the computer screen. If there had been sixty years between the Welcome and Connelly deaths, why hadn't the house nailed the few buyers in between? Were they really lucky to escape with their lives? Or did the house let them escape because they were the wrong buyers?

If Harlan had thought the Connellys were the right buyers and Tommy died in the tower like Elspeth and Jared had, then the term "right buyers" was not only wrong, it was misleading. Her heart skipped a beat; she grabbed her pendant and squeezed. If she was the right buyer, why had the house chosen to communicate with her rather than kill her?

She scrolled down the page. None of the articles included a picture of Tommy Connelly. Frustrated, Morgan frowned and read aloud.

"Maggie Duran, Lake Placid realtor, said the hype had a ripple effect on sales. No one within miles would come near the place, let alone buy it. Ms. Duran was a childhood acquaintance of Tommy's..."

Stunned, Morgan stopped reading. It appeared as if she'd picked the mother of all days for surprises. She took a deep breath and continued slowly.

"...and the daughter of Lillian Duran, Placid Properties realtor, who sold the house to the Connellys in 1983. Ms. Duran said that on the night Tommy Connelly died, police found her mother wandering Midlakes Road barefoot in her nightgown, claiming she had seen a hazy apparition in the tower window the first day she'd showed the house to the Connellys. Lillian, Ms. Duran's mother, swore the apparition had killed Tommy. When no one believed her, she suffered a deep depression, prompting doctors to send her to High Peaks Sanitarium for rest and recuperation."

Morgan fumed. Not only had Maggie known about the apparition for years, she had also been a personal friend of Tommy Connelly's. Another tidbit she'd forgotten to mention. Swallowing her anger, Morgan clicked, *print.*

While the printer *whirred,* Morgan thought hard. There must be something she'd forgotten. Some stone left unturned. Something relevant. Think! The ad. The apparition. The boy. The fire. The burns on her ankles and wrists.

"The dream," she whispered, staring blankly.

*The lakeshore and cliffs were the same ones she'd seen from her tower ... Maggie had called the bluff Pulpit rock.*

Fingers flying, Morgan searched Pulpit Rock. She found an article and an old regional map in a reference book called the *Geographical History of Lake Placid* and read.

"Centuries of natural erosion had sculpted a cliff towering fifty-feet over East Lake Placid to resemble a preacher's pulpit. "Pulpit Rock" was formed on the exact spot where the water of East Lake Placid runs deepest. Believing this water to be sacred, Indians claimed it as their burial place by *dropping their dead from Pulpit Rock into East Lake Placid?*"

Her dream flashed through her mind. Chilled, she found Pulpit Rock on the map and read.

"The Legend of Paradox Pond: Paradox Bay formerly known as Paradox Pond is located in the southernmost tip of East Lake Placid and is connected to lake Placid by a once famous inlet named after the paradoxical phenomenon for which it was known. Water flowing forward through the inlet would suddenly reverse itself and then flow backward. The phenomenon occurred at brief, intermittent regular intervals. The Indians attributed the "quirk in the current" to restless ancestral spirits that drifted south to Paradox Pond, and then turned abruptly and headed north to Pulpit Rock again. The funeral practice combined with the natural phenomenon to create the "The Legend of Paradox Pond." However, two pieces of information negate the legend: First, there is no evidence, archaeological or otherwise that any Indian tribe(s) had ever lived in that area of Lake Placid. Second, the phenomenon stopped occurring in the early 1900s. (A record of the occurrences in the first written records and travel logs of the area bore testimony that the phenomenon had truly occurred).

In the 1960s a diving club believed that the land bridge separating the southern tip of East Lake Placid and the northern tip of Mirror Lake was honeycombed with underwater caves that connected the two lakes …"

Underwater caves? Finding the land bridge on the map, Morgan put her index finger exactly where her house stood. She remembered the very first time she'd stood in the tower and saw the breathtaking view of both lakes. That must be how Midlakes Road had gotten its name.

Intrigued by the Legend of Paradox Pond and enticed by the possibility that these caves existed, the diving club came to Lake Placid to explore the region, but found neither the caves nor the phenomenon.

Excited by Pulpit Rock, the alleged ancient watery burial grounds reminiscent of her dream, quirky currents and underwater caves, Morgan hit *print*.

Her phone rang. The ID tagged the caller. It was Jack,

"After I read O'Donnell's breaking story and Rivers' anniversary stories, I dug a little deeper. Oh my god, Jack, there's so much I have to tell you!"

"Wonderful! I've got some news for you too. Steve Rivers can see you in Plattsburgh at the North Country Tribune on the twelfth at one p.m."

Morgan gathered and folded the printouts and paid the librarian. She'd grab lunch and then stop by the real estate office. She was angry with Harlan, but hoped he was okay. As a personal friend of Tommy's, Maggie had some explaining to do.

Morgan slipped the folded printouts into her purse, got into her car and headed for Midlakes Road, thinking she would give the world to find Chuck in her driveway.

# Chapter 36

## Morgan

Morgan parked her Buick in front of Placid Properties and walked up to the real estate office. The *closed* sign in the window was gone and the light was on inside. Kevin and Hutch were at their desks on their phones, and Maggie was at her desk with a calculator, crunching numbers and writing, playing catch up for being out the last couple of days, Morgan assumed. It was 2:30. She walked in. They all looked up. Kevin and Hutch smiled.

"Morgan." Maggie got up and held out a hand.

Morgan took it. She sat in the chair beside Maggie's desk, put her purse on her lap and folded her hands.

"How's Harlan doing?" Maggie raised a brow, and Morgan said "I stopped at the Bradford House this morning and saw Jack."

"Thanks for asking. He's doing as well as can be expected. They did open heart surgery first thing this morning. He had four clogged arteries." Morgan whistled. "Exactly," Maggie said. "He's in the ICU. Mom called. She and my niece are on their way home now. Harlan knows we're here taking care of business and it's doing wonders for his recovery. If all goes well his doctors say he'll be home by the seventeenth."

"That's great," Morgan said, meaning it despite everything.

"How's your Mom?" Maggie asked.

"Unfortunately, unlike Harlan, my mother won't get better."

"Sorry. Speaking of family, I met Chuck."

Morgan's eyes widened.

"He stopped by."

My God. Mother had told the truth. Chuck must've seen the note on the counter in Port St. John and he's here!

"You seem surprised." Maggie said, looking surprised.

Morgan's heart pounded. "Surprised at how I've missed him."

"I can see why. He's hot." Maggie's smile was mischievous. "I gave him the other key to the house. Did he get in okay?"

"He sure did," Morgan said, hoping she sounded convincing.

"Good. Now, what can I do for you?"

*Answer this: If Chuck has a key, why haven't I seen him?*

"Morgan?" Maggie touched her arm. "Are you okay?"

Morgan focused in time to see Maggie glance at Kevin and give a slight shrug. She sensed Hutch behind her, listening.

"I'm fine. I've got a lot on my mind, that's all."

"Boy, do I know that feeling." Maggie smiled.

Should she bring them up to speed about the treasure trove of info her research had uncovered? Maggie and Harlan had snookered her. She decided to keep what she knew to herself for now; even the fact that Maggie knew Tommy and had never mentioned it. She had to say something. They knew she didn't come here to get an update on Harlan's health.

"Two of my streetlights are still out."

Maggie hesitated and then looked at her. "Truthfully, Morgan, my mom said as far as she knew those street lights have never worked. But, on the night Tommy died one light came on."

"What?" Another omission. Morgan leaned forward in her seat, thrilled she hadn't told them a thing. She heard Kevin turn around.

"Harlan thought it was just some freaky coincidence. But whatever it was had freaked Mom out so badly, she refused to have anything to do with him until he found out why.

"He put in a call to the Village Clerk and Municipal Electric Department Superintendent. As a favor to him, the superintendent at the time had gone out with his men. After personally pulling lamps and system apart, he gave Harlan his word that there was no earthly reason why those lamps didn't work."

Earthly? The word gave Morgan the creeps.

"Harlan could've pushed for more, but I'll bet bad PR and a prickly hunch made him distance the whole streetlight episode from Tommy's death."

Morgan looked at Hutch who seemed not to have that particular piece of information either. Was Kevin surprised too?

What a fool she was. "Harlan had pretended to be irate about the broken lights for my benefit, didn't he?"

Maggie lowered her eyes and Morgan swore silently.

"I have a question," she said, keeping her voice calm.

Maggie looked directly into Morgan's eyes. "Ask."

"Did you know Tommy Connelly?" Morgan saw Hutch look at Kevin, puzzled and sensed Kevin returning Hutch's stare. Good.

"We went to high school together. Briefly. He was a freshman. I was a sophomore."

"High school?" Excitement cooling her anger, Morgan said, "Would you have a yearbook with his picture in it?"

Maggie's eyes glistened. "He didn't live long enough."

Morgan's pity and disappointment must've shown because Maggie said, "My kid sister had it bad for him. She made me take his picture. Carried it with her everywhere. Mom and I were just talking about it. I bet it's still in Marcy's wallet. Why?"

Morgan was so relieved at the idea of identifying the boy she almost forgave Maggie everything. Should she tell Maggie about her suspicion? Why not? She was meeting that reporter. Her story would come out soon anyway.

"Since I moved into that house, I've seen an apparition of a teenage boy, and I dreamed about him once. I think he is Tommy Connelly."

"Impossible," Maggie bristled. "Why would you say that?"

Touched a nerve, have I? "Oh, maybe because I didn't know he'd died in my house? "Morgan instantly regretted the sarcasm.

"Of course," Maggie sighed, changing her tone. "I'm so sorry. If I find Marcy's wallet, I'll bring you the picture."

"Thanks." Morgan got to her feet.

"How are you doing? In the house I mean? Are you afraid to stay there alone?"

Morgan bristled. "Like the previous buyers were?" she said, to avoid answering.

Maggie's face reddened. "I guess now that your husband's here you're not alone anymore, are you?"

"Right," Morgan said. "Speaking of Chuck, I've gotta run."

Her car was an oven. Morgan cranked up the A/C and moved through traffic as if she were driving underwater, until turning onto Midlakes Road. In sync with her every muscle and nerve, the car climbed the hill fast and joined her heart at the house.

Her driveway was empty. She pulled in, exhaling her disappointment. What if Chuck had had an accident? She was new in town. Few people knew her name. Even if they saw or heard, would they connect Chuck to her and call? Chiding herself for being irrational, she pressed a button and the window slid noiselessly out of sight.

Humidity stuffed its big muggy butt through the window and onto her lap, making it hard for her to breathe. She turned off the motor, pulled the keys from the ignition and set them on her purse. She slumped in her seat, leaned against the headrest and stared at the house. She glanced at the tower and stiffened.

All but two of the house's windows were black.

Every nerve cell and hair follicle electrified, she picked up her purse and keys. Terrified, exhausted and desperate for answers, she opened the car door and hurried across the lawn. She unlocked the door, entered and frowned.

The house seemed a lot cooler, cold in fact.

Praying she was right about the house trying to communicate with her, she singled out the key to the tower...

She unlocked the tower door and entered the stairwell.

The door slammed shut behind her. Morgan yelped and whipped around quickly. She whimpered, jiggled the knob, shouted and rapped until her fists hurt. She lowered her eyes. Her tears blurred the thin line of light that proved the world lay beyond the door.

Cursing herself for being a fool, she leaned her forehead against the door, closed her eyes and squeezed her pendant. The gems bit into her palm like tiny, punishing teeth.

Sensing a strong presence, she remembered the main thing and opened her eyes.

"Who are you?" she asked looking up the dark stairwell. "Show yourself. Why are you doing this to me?" she screamed, peering through the darkness. "What do you want from me? Why did you lock the door?" She turned to try the door again and looked down. The thin line of light framing the door had vanished.

The stairwell was very cold. Winter cold. Cold enough for her to let go of the handrail and rub her arms. Baffled, she turned, looked up the stairs and froze, exhaling frantic breaths.

At the top of the dark, cavernous stairwell a gauzy, elusive *being* extended a slender, florescent arm. Behind the being thousands of stars dotted the black sky. Moonlight filtered through its eyes as if someone had sawed off the back of its skull. The figure stood on a path in the woods where once there had been a house, a stairwell and a gothic tower.

# Bloodfire and the Legend of Paradox Pond

## Lake Placid 1924

Jared had walked this path with Diamond so many times he knew every crooked-toothed stone and twisted arthritic root on the way to their special place. His stomach cramped with self-hatred, bringing up the steak and potatoes he'd choked down for supper. In fifteen minutes he would drag Diamond to the edge of the barefaced cliff and throw her into Lake Placid from a rock shaped like a preacher's pulpit.

Moonlight splashed through the trees and spattered the trail. He walked so fast Diamond fell behind and had to run hard to catch up. He'd tripped twice himself already. Just when he thought about slowing down, Diamond cried out. He stopped and turned. Diamond was holding her ankle. He ran back and caught her before she fell to the ground. Without warning, he pressed her to him. His mouth found hers in a raging kiss that sucked her into his passion and had her arching against him.

Wind swept the clouds from the moon, and Diamond looked into his eyes. He used to thank God she never saw him for what he really was, but now he'd give his life if only she had.

He pressed his cold cheek to hers and closed his eyes. He buried his nose in her hair and breathed in her scent. He loved her more than his life, but Diamond was pregnant and that changed everything.

Her ankle seemed fine. He took her hand, slowed his pace and looked at the sky. Clouds fluffed around the moon like gray cotton batting. Desperate to save Diamond's life, Jared had fine-combed his options again.

Divorcing Elspeth would destroy the Welcome name and subject his family, especially his innocent daughter, to a terrible scandal. Even if he and Diamond married, where would they live? Who would accept them as man and wife? She was a Gypsy. Folks hated and feared them. If only his sister Laura hadn't followed him into the woods that day and overheard Diamond telling him she was pregnant. Fearful his little Gypsy had cast an evil spell, Laura had run to Elspeth instead of talking to him. The ache in his head kicked like a mule. He stopped walking and rubbed his eyes. He watched the moon slip inside a pocket of clouds.

Diamond touched him gently. "Tell me what's wrong. Please."

He took her into his arms and sighed against her cheek.

"I've got a lot on my mind. The store. Elspeth." Your innocent baby. Diamond squirmed but he held her tight, afraid if she saw his eyes, she'd see the terrible truth.

She pulled back. "You weren't fooling me, were you?" Her voice cracked.

"Fooling?" He frowned, confused.

"I mean, you did tell Elspeth, didn't you?"

His eyes welled. Choking up, he cleared his throat. "Elspeth knows." He took Diamond's hand. "Come on," he said, and kissing her fingers, Jared led Diamond to Pulpit Rock.

*"When you get to Pulpit Rock," Elspeth had said, "you'll tie her hands behind her back with a rope you will have hidden in the bushes. Before she goes over the cliff, you'll snatch her Gypsy pendant from her neck. Proof," Elspeth had grinned. "Surely you know why I need it."*

*Her icy calm had unnerved him.*

*"It's the perfect solution." Her eyes, the color of flint and as cold as a reptile's heart, bore through his. "People who really matter don't even know she exists."*

*"You're mad!" His voice had sounded hollow, pathetic.*

*"And you are a stupid fool!" Elspeth clenched her teeth. "While you lay in the woods like a dog with its bitch, did you once think of our daughter, your mother or sister, or me?"*

*His jaws twitching, Jared lowered his eyes.*

*She balled her hands. "You fathered a Gypsy!" She beat his chest with her fists, "humiliated me and dirtied your father's name. When Reverend Bradford finds out, no one will shop at our store. We'll be ruined and die paupers. Did you stop and think about that?" Jared kept his eyes lowered. "I thought not." Elspeth snarled. She grabbed his hair, jerked his head up and stuck her nose in his face. "Your choices are clear."*

*Jared frowned and looked her in the eye.*

*"Kill Diamond and your filthy secret dies with her. Then you can live your respectable life in the house you built with the daughter you cherish," she folded her arms across her chest.*

*"Wander the globe with your Gypsy tramp and her bastard, and you'll never see your legitimate daughter again."*

Jared squeezed Diamond's hand. If her only crime was to love him, how could he kill her? But Elspeth was right about one thing. Without his good name and his daughter, Jared Welcome had nothing. Surely, Diamond would see that.

Jared let her hand go and shoved his hands in his pockets.

Diamond stopped him and took off his jacket. "You're cold."

"No." He smiled and wrapped it around her. "You've got to keep warm." She looked smaller and more fragile in his jacket. He held her close. She smelled like autumn.

"Diamond, you must understand. When I met you my marriage to Elspeth was," his throat closed. He swallowed hard. It opened. He had to get hold of himself. "If things had been different between Elspeth and me, I never would've—"

Moonlight rained through the trees, washing his courage away with the shadows. He took her hand and started to walk.

"I'm not going on until you tell me what's wrong," she said, pulling her hand away.

Her sudden defiance surprised him. Tell her what's wrong? He wanted to scream. My life is falling apart. I could lose everything.

Suddenly, Jared pictured his little girl. With Elspeth's twisted views on their marital bed, it was a miracle she'd ever been born. In all this craziness he realized his little angel was the only one in the world that truly mattered. He couldn't lose her. His mess was all Elspeth's fault. From the day they'd moved into the house on Midlakes Road that he'd built with his bare hands, nothing had turned out the way he believed it would. Elspeth had tricked him. He'd see her in hell where they'd spend eternity. Only a fool fools himself. Deep down inside Jared knew his affair with Diamond would end. But he never believed it would end this badly.

Jared held out his hand, and just like he knew she would, Diamond reluctantly took it and followed him into the woods.

# Chapter 37

## Morgan and Maggie

Morgan came to in a pool of sweat in the tower stairwell. Her heart fluttered like a fish out of water. Her head was spinning, and her mouth was as dry as Antarctica. She made it to the kitchen, stood at the sink and ran the cold water. She opened the freezer, took a glass from the drain board, filled it with ice and stuck the glass under the faucet. She banged back the water. Her mind raced. The last thing she remembered was being locked in the tower stairwell and passing out. She might have dreamt, but she wasn't sure. If Chuck were here, she would not have to run to Jack Bradford.

Someone knocked on the front door. *Chuck?* She opened the front door and sighed.

"You look disappointed," Maggie said, frowning.

"Sorry." Morgan felt drained. "Just deep in thought."

"I found a picture of Tommy."

Morgan perked up. "Come on in. Can I get you a drink?"

"No. Thanks. I'm on my way back to Plattsburgh."

"To see Harlan?"

"Yes," Maggie said, but she kept her eyes averted as if she was lying. Maggie opened her purse and gave the picture to Morgan.

"Dear God." Morgan's hand trembled. "It's him."

Maggie's smile froze. "That's not possible." Her face turned white. "I know you're pissed at Harlan and me, but if this is some kind of a joke, Morgan, I'm not laughing."

"I'd never joke about something like this."

"God, I hate this house." Maggie glanced at the photo. "How could the boy you saw be Tommy? What would that even mean?"

"One more thing, Maggie. Did Tommy ever talk about the house at all?"

Maggie sighed. "He seemed afraid to. My sister and I were his only friends, and he didn't want to lose us. But once," Maggie twisted the straps of her purse with shaking fingers, "he said his mom never had time for anything but the house. If she wasn't scrubbing and polishing floors, she was washing windows and fixtures, and she never wanted to leave, like she was possessed or something."

"Dear God," Morgan said, staring at Tommy's picture.

Standing at the door, Maggie glanced across the living room to the landing, looking worried. "Is your husband here?"

Morgan handed her the photo. "He went to run some errands."

Maggie's eyes flashed. "You're incredibly brave to stay here. She opened her purse, dropped the photo in, took out a business card and jotted another number on the back.

"I'll be at this number in Plattsburgh tonight after I visit Harlan." She pressed it in Morgan's hand. "Promise me if anything happens, you'll get out of here and call me any time day or night at any of these numbers." Maggie squeezed her hand tight. "I don't expect you to believe me, but if anything happened to you, I'd never forgive myself." She stood on the porch. "Do me a favor. Call me when your husband *really* gets here, and I'll sleep much easier tonight."

Maggie had her cell out of her purse before she cleared the porch steps. She hurried across the lawn, dialing, and climbed into the Lexus. When a click replaced the ring, she said, "You're not going to believe what I just found out. I need to see you. I'll be at your place in an hour."

"Whoa, baby. Slow down. Where are you?"

"I'm at the Welcome, I mean Morgan Matthias's house."

"Morgan Matthias's? Really?" She heard the smile in Steve's voice. "Wait until you hear what I've got to tell *you*."

# Chapter 38

**Chuck**

Under the cover of darkness Chuck left his hotel room and drove directly to Midlakes Road. Approaching Morgan's house he noticed only one of the three corner streetlights was lit. He checked his rearview mirror and frowned. The others he'd passed along the way appeared to work fine. He reached Morgan's driveway, turned off his lights, pulled in slowly and turned off the motor. It was late and the house was dark. The porch light was on, but there was no car in the driveway. The thought of seeing her, holding her in his arms. He loved her so much it hurt.

From all indications she loved him as well. But when they actually met, would Morgan love *him* or the man she thought he was? He closed his eyes and gripped the wheel. In the car in the dark his plan to step into Morgan Quick's reality seemed certifiable. The irony brought a mirthless grin to his lips. For a psychiatrist to indulge in a psychotic's fantasy was dangerous. Unethical. Immoral. He could lose his license. But Morgan's and his situation was unlike any he'd encountered. He was still so real to her that she'd taken his name. If not for Lucy, Morgan would be his wife, and they would be living in this house now.

He opened his eyes. Bloody Christ! What if his plan backfired? Chuck ran a nervous hand over trembling lips. What if the shock of seeing him pushed her so far into her psychosis he couldn't reach her? He'd already spent hours agonizing over his options. He even considered contacting a local psychiatrist and then rejected the idea. Why? Because bloody Lucy was wrong. He wasn't partly responsible for Morgan's breakdown.

He was totally responsible.

The thought of the love of his life in a cold, clinical environment with strangers poking and prodding—his eyes stung. No. He broke Morgan and he would fix her. He smiled, mirthlessly. How could he fail? Against all odds it appeared that·their bond had never been broken, and their love had not been destroyed.

According to Maggie Duran, Morgan was expecting him, any time now. Wasn't that endorsement enough? His plan was simple. He'd let himself into her house and into her life. She'd wake up and see him in the morning like she had so many times before. But, what if—

Chuck faced himself in the rearview mirror. No buts. His mind made up, he felt his shirt pocket for the key, slammed the car door behind him and took the porch steps.

There was a mailbox to his right. He wiped his feet on the welcome mat. On a whim he reached inside. His eyes widened. There were supermarket flyers and a few coupons from outlet stores addressed to Morgan Matthias, confirming what? Her reality?

Shaken but gratified, he let himself in.

The house was still. By the scant light of the one working streetlight, he made his way past a fireplace, sofa and chairs to a set of steps on the far side of the living room.

From what he could see, the house had been furnished with valuable antiques. Amazed she could afford them he climbed to the landing and peeked into an empty kitchen.

He took the steps slowly, wincing at every creaky floorboard and peeked into two bedrooms. Both were empty. One remained at the end of the hall.

Chuck entered the third bedroom which appeared to be as lavishly decorated as the rest of the house. Bookcase, night table and Victorian lamp, chest of drawers, queen-sized bed. There were two doors opposite the front window. One was a closet. He opened the other and saw steps leading to the tower.

The stairwell was dark. He felt for a light switch. Finding none, he climbed the stairs to the tower, ran his hands over the walls, located a switch and threw it. The tower was empty.

Chilled, he shivered. His teeth began chattering. He saw his breath. Frowning, he backed away, rubbed his arms and shivered harder. He breathed in and the hair in his nostrils began freezing. He turned and bumped into Morgan.

She threw her arms around his neck. "Thank God you're finally here." Tears spilling, she pressed her cheek to his. "I missed you so much, and I was so scared and lonely I thought I'd go crazy."

Stunned, Chuck frowned deeply. His eyes welled with tears. He wrapped his arms around her and held her tight. "I'm here now, darling. And as Christ is my judge. I'll never leave you again."

Chuck and Morgan sat across at the kitchen table over two cups of steaming tea. She lifted his hand to her lips.

"So, how was Australia, and how was the mental health symposium?"

Chuck smiled. "Plenty of time for that later, love. So, tell me what you've been up to since I've been, uh, gone."

Morgan yawned. "I don't know where to begin."

Morgan slipped into bed and reached for Chuck. Her touch sent a bolt of lightning through him. The doctor in him waged war, but years of yearning for this moment, the man surrendered. Morgan straddled him. He buried himself inside her. She tossed her head back and moaned. Unable to restrain himself, Chuck plunged deeper with each thrust. Stiffening, she cried out. He groaned, shuddered hard and emptied himself inside her. After making less urgent love, Chuck and Morgan fell asleep in each other's arms.

Resting on Morgan's chest in a pool of moonlight, the pendant suddenly rose, unclasped and floated above her.

Startled awake, Morgan sat up and gasped. An amorphous haze hovered at the foot of her bed, the same haze that had appeared in the tower window? Her blood running cold, Morgan shivered. She reached for Chuck. Hearing his rhythmic breathing, she changed her mind. As the haze shed its ghostly scraps, a petite girl stared at Morgan. Crystal-clear in every grotesque detail, the girl, most definitely dead, was wearing Morgan's pendant. Morgan shivered harder. Her teeth chattered her breath out in lacy puffs. A thin film of ice sheathed her heart.

The girl's eyes, bottomless and cold, peered out from a chalky white face. Her lips, the color of cinnamon candy curved up in a chilling smile. Deep dimples, most likely beguiling in life, made her face gaunt and hollow in death.

Her sopping wet hair, tucked behind two perfect ears, fell to her marble-white shoulders in springy black ringlets. She wore gold hoop earrings. Her white peasant blouse, caked with muck, hung off her shoulders and clung to the swell of her breasts, tapering to a V at her tiny waist. Her skirt, a rowdy red and blue print, stayed molded to her hips and thighs as if she had dragged herself from a lake after-oh my God-*drowning!*

Morgan had seen girls dressed like her at bazaars, parties and in movies. She was a Gypsy, and Morgan would bet her life this was the girl in the grainy black and white photo.

Suddenly, Morgan realized she'd been wrong. Her dream did not foretell her own death. It showed how this girl had died or was murdered!

But why and who was she?

The Gypsy girl turned and glided out of the bedroom.

Shivering violently, Morgan followed her through the hall and down the stairs. Morgan stood in the living room and watched the girl *pass through the front door.*

She grabbed the frozen knob, yelped and pulled away. She gingerly reached for the knob again and opened the door.

The girl was gone. Morgan looked down and saw her pendant pooled on the welcome mat. She picked it up, gasped at her wrists and stared at her ankles.

The burns looked black in the silvery moonlight.

# Chapter 39

**Chuck and CJ**
**July 12**

Chuck sat at the kitchen table awake in a dream, veering from total bliss to feeling like hell for making love to Morgan, when he bloody well knew she was vulnerable. He had no defense except that right now he couldn't love her more. He swore it wouldn't happen again, until her personality had been fully integrated.

Watching her fry bacon and eggs and butter toast, he wondered how he'd survived all these years without her. She put the billy on for tea, and Chuck was amazed and gratified to find that from her point of view theirs was a very happy marriage. Except for a dusting of gray in her hair and faint lines about her eyes and mouth, time appeared not to have touched her. She was as fit, trim and as beautiful now as she had been then, despite the pain he must have caused her. That worried him, because he saw none of it in her eyes.

"You're staring at me," she said.

"I can't even begin to explain how I've missed you."

Morgan smiled, clearly pleased. She sat across the table eating her eggs and telling her hair-raising story so matter-of-factly, his heart raced. Her delusion was deep and complicated. Her trust in him made her even more vulnerable. She squeezed her pendant now and then when she talked. That hadn't changed.

"Something weird happened last night," she said.

"Usual weird or weirder than usual?" he laughed.

"I'm serious."

"And I'm not?"

"I need you to believe me."

He kissed her lips softly. "That is a given, love."

A few minutes later, Morgan said, "That Gypsy girl wanted me to know that my pendant had belonged to her."

"Darling, please—"

Morgan jumped up and pulled some papers from her purse.

"I did some research. I don't quite have a connection between these and what's going on and what happened last night." She handed him the papers. "Jack Bradford verified that the Gypsies have been coming to Lake Placid for over a century. In fact, he said his great uncle, the Reverend Ezekiel Bradford, had made it his mission to drive the Gypsies away.

"Our house is built on a land bridge between the two lakes. There were rumors about underwater caves. I searched the newspaper archives and found the breaking story and subsequent articles on the Welcome-Connelly deaths," she paused. "I have an appointment today with Steve Rivers, the reporter who wrote these follow-up stories. I know there's more," she said, excited.

The articles were intriguing. He knew why she was so excited. His civilian side was tempted to explore the titillating, intricate mesh she'd created, but as a doctor he was deeply disturbed at how Morgan Quick, excuse me, Matthias, had made love and conversation with him as if she'd been doing it for three decades!

"Believe it or not," she gathered the dishes, "the events I mentioned are the tip of the iceberg. I haven't told you the rest for fear of overwhelm—"

He watched her watch his eyes darken. She stopped moving. "You don't believe me." She stopped him before he could speak. "It's okay." She grabbed her purse and handed him the camera. "Jack Bradford had a hard time believing until I showed him this. Go on and check out the dates. The color photos are dated May twenty-second. Two days before I set foot in Lake Placid."

Chuck's eyes widened at scores of digital slides of the house on the display and their dates. The last two slides, grainy black and whites, were clearly out of place.

Morgan suddenly frowned, took the camera, advanced to the last photo and zoomed in.

The Gypsy girl was clearly wearing her pendant. "Oh my God, how did my mother end up with this pendant?"

Chuck got to his feet. "I don't know what to say."

Morgan's kiss stopped him. "You don't have to say a word."

Morgan started the Regal and turned on the A/C. She lowered the window and smiled at Chuck, who said, "Good luck with Steve Rivers this afternoon."

"Thanks. I'm going to need all the luck I can get. There's tons more I haven't told you."

"Take your time." He leaned in the window and kissed her.

"I'm dying to tell Steve Rivers what I know. Jack was hot for putting us in touch. Maybe Steve can shed some light too."

"Have I told you how much I love you and how much I've missed you?" Chuck grazed her cheek softly with his fingertips.

"Back at you." She smiled, put the car in reverse and hit the break. "God. I almost forgot." She grabbed her cell, Maggie's card and dialed the number in pen on the back.

"Maggie was worried about me being here alone." She paused, listening to the ring. "Hi, is Maggie Duran there?" Morgan pulled the phone away and whispered, "A guy answered. Must be her lover." She winked. Chuck smiled and kissed her cheek.

"Maggie? It's Morgan. Just wanted to let you know that Chuck got here last night." She blushed. "You're welcome." She pressed *end,* kissed Chuck and pulled out of the driveway.

Alone in the kitchen Chuck poured himself another mug of black coffee and set it on the marble top table in the living room. Morgan's appointment in Plattsburgh gave him time to think. From what he observed, the psychological blow he'd caused her must've been devastating for her to reinvent this incredible reality in order to cope and function, but it appeared she'd succeeded. As far as the camera and sundry, there had to be a rational explanation. In his opinion she suffered from an extremely rare form of schizophrenic reaction, one he'd read about in textbooks, categorized as a delusional disorder. Recorded cases showed patients exhibited unshakeable beliefs in something untrue. Symptoms lasted for a month. As far as he knew not one had lasted longer. Certainly not thirty years!

She seemed to be functioning exceptionally well in all other areas. He marveled at the human mind's ability to adapt to life and circumstances when necessary. That said, Morgan was in deep trouble and he was to blame. Overwhelmed with guilt, Chuck sat on the sofa and sipped his coffee. He had to craft a strategy to take her back through the experiences that had destroyed her real life and forced her into this fantasy.

It might take a protocol of neuroleptic, anti-psychotic drugs, and months, maybe years of in-depth therapy. There was also a question of ethics. His colleagues would say he was too closely involved with the patient. He'd face his professional community later. Now he vowed to stand by her side and help her confront her past, and together they'd make her whole again.

He kicked off his loafers and ran his toes through the deep moss green area rug, admiring the fireplace. He leaned over the marble topped coffee table, pushed his car keys aside and scanned an array of brochures he'd scooped up in town, looking for a good restaurant, when he heard a car crunch to a halt on loose stones in the driveway. He looked at his watch. Morgan had left fifteen minutes ago. Had she forgotten something? He hurried out the door, down the porch steps and froze.

CJ stepped out of an emerald green Camry, looking uncharacteristically rumpled. Their eyes met and Chuck's blood ran cold. His son never would've come halfway around the world to find him unless something was terribly wrong. Why hadn't CJ rung him first? Suddenly, Chuck realized he'd turned his mobile off. He broke into a sweat. His heart plunged. Was it Elizabeth? Phillip? What a fool he'd been for not ringing Australia.

"Dad!" CJ looked pale as a ghost and exhausted.

Suddenly, Chuck realized if Morgan had forgotten something and pulled into the driveway now, what would she do? In her state of mind anything could happen. How could he think of Morgan with CJ's eyes so full of pain? He forced his legs forward one leaden step at a time.

CJ stumbled across the lawn and met him halfway. Chuck opened his arms, and CJ collapsed against him. He felt CJ's heart fluttering like a frightened child's. Chuck closed his eyes and rocked his son in his arms. "What," Chuck's voice caught. He cleared his throat, let CJ go and looked into his eyes. "What happened? How did you find—"

"I took a key to your house," CJ panted, lowering his eyes, "and searched the desk in your study," He looked up. "I'm sorry, Dad. I broke into a black box and found some letters–"

"No worries, son." Chuck squeezed CJ's shoulders and took a deep breath. If CJ had found his letters, his children knew about Morgan. Dear God, what must they think?

"I went to Port St. John to the return address on her letters. Talked to a neighbor, Art Parker. He mentioned something about her buying a house here. That big red and white realtor's sign in the middle of town caught my eye so I stopped in. Look, Dad, I think I know why you're here." His eyes glistened. "You can explain everything on the plane ride home."

"Home?" Chuck shook his head. "I can't leave now, CJ. There are things you don't--."

CJ grabbed his father. His eyes shimmered, alarming Chuck. CJ's tears spilled.

"Tell me what's wrong. Now!"

CJ's chin trembled. "It's Liz's Jimmy, he—he's dying".

Speechless, Chuck stared at CJ.

"Phillip's with Liz, Dad. She needs us. She needs you."

Chuck pictured Morgan. How could he leave? He pictured Liz. How could he not? Chuck put his arm around CJ's shoulder.

"You look like you haven't slept since you left Australia. Come with me." Thanking God he hadn't checked out of the White Birch Inn, Chuck led CJ inside and grabbed his wallet. He lifted his key card from his wallet, pressed it into CJ's hand and took his car keys from the coffee table. "Follow me into town to the hotel. We'll get you a bit to eat. I'll take you to my room. Important decisions will take time and clear thinking to arrange. After you've had a long hot shower, a bit of a sleep and I've had a chance to prepare Morgan," Chuck turned on his mobile, "I'll come and get you."

# Chapter 40

## Maggie and Kevin

Naked under Steve's robe, Maggie held his phone in her hand and looked at Lake Champlain through the sliding glass doors in his family room. "Thanks for letting me know, Morgan," she said, hung up and put the phone down.

Steve closed his robe tight around her and took her in his arms. "Feel better now?"

"In more ways than you know." Maggie slipped her arms around Steve's neck and kissed him. Steve moaned. Maggie smiled, pulled away and pointed to his coffee mug. "Can I top you off?"

He checked his watch. "Coffee is all I have time for. Evan will can me if I'm late for my meeting with Morgan."

"With the readership your anniversary stories bring, I doubt it." She reached for the carafe and filled his mug.

"So, tell me all the ways you feel better," Steve said.

"Considering Mom's history with Julia Bradford Wainright, Jack would bust a gut if he knew the huge favor he did me by putting Morgan in touch with you. Now Morgan can tell you everything and I won't have to—" Her voice trailed off and she blinked back tears.

"Betray your father?"

"Why should I care about betraying Harlan after everything he's done to us?"

Steve lifted her chin and kissed her. "Truth will set everyone free. I love you. I've got to go."

Maggie smiled. Her purse was on the counter next to the phone. She reached in for a tissue and saw Tommy's photo.

Steve checked his watch. "Gotta split. I'm really late."

"Not until you hear this." She handed him the photo. "I can't believe I forgot why I rushed down here in the first place." Steve looked at the photo. Maggie said, "This is Tommy Connelly. Morgan identified him as the boy haunting her house."

He picked her up in his arms, swung her around and then set her down. The smile dropped from his face. "Sharing this with me, does it mean that you trust me?" Maggie kissed him hard.

Kevin pulled into Steve Rivers' condo complex and spotted Maggie's Lexus. She had the hots for the lucky guy all right. Damn! Nat was right again. She'd called him as soon as she found out Maggie had lit out for Plattsburgh last night. He decided to pass by on his way to the hospital.

The condo door opened. Kevin recognized Rivers from his photo in his column. He watched Rivers hurry across the parking lot to a 2008 dark blue Chevy Blazer.

"What's got you running from Maggie in such an all-fired hurry?"

Kevin followed. He watched Rivers ease his Blazer into a parking space across the street from the *North Country Tribune* building, jump out of the car and cross the street.

"You left a babe like Maggie Duran alone in your bed to go to work?"

Suddenly, Kevin spotted Morgan Matthias standing in front of the *North Country Tribune* building next to a tan Buick Regal. As Kevin drove by, Rivers was shaking her hand and appearing to introduce himself. He took her by the arm and led her into the building.

Holy double-chocolate-dipped shit! Not only does Maggie get back with Rivers, she puts him in touch with Morgan Matthias!

Suddenly, Kevin felt nuclear-bomb proof about his future with Placid Properties. His arsenal bulging with weapons to neutralize Maggie Duran and his spirits in high gear, Kevin drove to the hospital.

# Chapter 41

## Morgan

Morgan stood in front of a brown brick building with glass doors, watching a new midnight blue Chevy Blazer ease into an empty space across the street from the *North Country Tribune.* The driver, a guy in his late thirties, saw her and waved. He had to be Rivers. He darted across the street through traffic.

"Morgan Matthias?"

"Mr. Rivers."

Steve Rivers was ruggedly handsome with dark, intense eyes and a firm handshake.

"Have you had lunch, Ms. Matthias?" His smile was disarming. "I had a big breakfast, thanks. Call me Morgan." She warmed to him instantly.

"I'm Steve."

He led her through the *North Country Tribune's* main entrance. There were small cubicles and several manned desks behind the reception area. The editor's office was in the back.

A petite blond with big brown eyes and a winsome smile said, "Glad you found time to fit us in today, Stevie."

Steve blushed and Morgan smiled, wondering what he had going on. He guided Morgan around the newsroom through a jovial chorus of "oooh, Stevie" from his smiling coworkers. He grinned, blushing harder, motioning good-naturedly for them to stop.

He came to a metal desk, his, she presumed, and grabbed a bulging manila file folder labeled "Welcome-Connelly". He scooped up a note pad and pencil and led her to a table in a conference room. He placed the file folder, notepad and pencil in front of him on the table.

"Can I get you a cup of coffee?"

"I'm fine. Thanks," she said, easing into a chair.

"Steve noticed her pendant and eyed it oddly.

"That really is a beautiful necklace."

"Thanks. It was my mother's. Jack tells me you're getting ready to run a twenty-fifth anniversary story on my house and the Welcome-

Connelly murders."

"Murders?" He smiled politely, but his expression seemed skeptical. "Last time I looked, the record showed that the Welcomes and Tommy Connelly had frozen to death," he said.

"Buckle up, Steve. You're in for one helluva ride."

Morgan talked. Steve clicked his pen and scribbled furiously, interrupting now and then with clarifying questions. Omitting one event, Morgan finished and frowned asking, "Can I ask why you didn't record me?"

Steve dropped his pen. "Got burned one too many times with recordings getting deleted by mistake." He slouched, laced his fingers behind his head and stared at her.

"You're preaching to the choir, Morgan. Wondering how these people froze to death in that house has driven me nuts for over a decade." His eyes lost their glitter. "Almost cost me the woman I love." Eyes glistening, Steve cleared his throat. "That said, your story, replete with a Gypsy, is so fantastic even I find it hard to believe. And that's saying something." He paused and smiled good-naturedly. "Of course, you can back this all up."

"Absolutely."

Steve's eyes glittered again. He seemed excited but guarded. Morgan shoveled through her purse, dug out the camera and pressed *power*. Steve unlaced his fingers and scrolled through the pictures, smiling.

"Observe the dates. The twenty-second is the day I called Maggie about the house. I took the camera out of its packing well after July fourth."

His smile faded. He sat steel-rod straight. Their eyes met.

Morgan took the camera. "There is one thing I omitted, but first I have to tell you what happened last night." A few minutes later, Morgan advanced the camera to the last black and white and zoomed in on the figure.

"My God." Steve gasped. "The girl is wearing the pendant."

"I'll ask you the same question I asked my husband. How did my mother end up with this Gypsy's pendant?"

"Are you sure your mother has never been to Lake Placid?"

"Positive. You know, Steve, Jack Bradford referred to the location in the photo as Gypsy Cove. Ever hear of it?"

"Back in the day there was a trail that ran north along East Lake Placid to a hidden place where the Gypsies set up."

"Back in the day? Like the early 1900s?"

Steve nodded. "From what I know most folks wanted nothing to do with Gypsies, but apparently they drew enough of a crowd to make it worth their while to return every few years.

"Hold on!" Steve opened the Welcome-Connelly file and leafed through a stack of papers. "This is an excerpt from a book called *American Gypsy Legends,* by Penny Halliwell. Read."

"Five generations ago King Phillip V of Spain fell in love with Magdalena, a Gypsy woman. He gave her a ruby in a heart-shaped setting of diamonds. The king called the amulet "Bloodfire" and said it came from origins unknown. Angry and fearful the gypsy had put the king under a spell, the queen ordered the Gypsy found, dead or alive. After Magdalena told the king she was pregnant, Phillip made arrangements for her to flee to the New World. Magdalena never saw Phillip again."

Pale, Morgan looked at Steve and touched her pendant. "I've worn this all my life, thinking it was paste and glass. But it's real? And it belonged to the king of Spain who gave it to his Gypsy mistress?" Her heart thrumming, Morgan kept reading.

"After giving birth to a girl, Magdalena had languished for years. Before she died she gave her daughter the amulet and related the story of her never to-be-claimed royal birth. Because their love had been doomed from the start, Magdalena feared the amulet was cursed and begged her daughter not to wear it.

"In 1924 a Gypsy couple camping on Lake Placid north of Mirror Lake reported their daughter, Diamond, had been missing for several days. They claimed that when last seen, the girl had been wearing the amulet. The girl's parents claimed the necklace existed, but the story was legend and the necklace was worthless. Without proof, the police reported the girl as missing and the necklace as stolen. Neither was ever found.

"Not only was Bloodfire real, it was a dead Gypsy girl's ruby and diamond namesake, complete with a star-crossed-lovers' curse, just like *Romeo and Juliet.* And everyone knows what happened to them. Don't you see, Steve? Events are shaping up to look like Diamond, this Gypsy girl, was murdered."

"I think you might be onto something."

Morgan's head swam. Her skin felt clammy. A wave of dizziness was sucking her under.

"Are you okay? Can I get you some water?"

"I'm fine," she said. "I just need a tissue."

"Your pendant is so distinctive I knew I'd heard about it before. With your pendant, those pictures and Halliwell's report, my twenty-fifth anniversary story will go radio-active!"

Along with the tissue Morgan pulled out the neon-yellow flyer from her purse, announcing a Gypsy Bazaar on July twelfth. "Do you suppose the Gypsies know about the Welcomes or Connellys?"

Steve jumped up. "Do you know what today's date is?"

# Chapter 42

**Morgan and Steve**

Morgan saw Steve toss the Welcome-Connelly file onto the Blazer's passenger seat. He followed her south on the Northway. At exit 30 they took 9N to 86 through Lake Placid past the real estate office. Someone waved, but deep in thought, Morgan had already passed before she realized the person waving was Maggie's niece, Natalie. She put her right directional on and pulled her car into an empty space in front of Band Shell Park in the middle of town. Steve pulled in behind her. She got out of her car and locked the doors. She grabbed Steve's file from the passenger seat, slid in and closed the door.

Steve shifted into park. "What's up?"

"My husband's at the house." She put Steve's file on her lap, "and I'm feeling guilty. Can we swing by and pick him up?"

Steve looked at his watch. "Sure thing." He checked his rearview mirror and pulled out. "We might be short on time. Ride with me. We'll get your car later."

He took Main to Midlakes. There was no car in Morgan's driveway.

"That's odd. Be right back," she said. Steve looked at his watch and Morgan said, "I promise."

She unlocked the front door, stuck her head in and called out. No answer. She stood on the landing calling out. Nothing. She returned to Steve's car, perplexed.

"Where could he be? He doesn't know anyone here."

"Maybe he needed something at the store."

"Maybe."

Checking her watch, she frowned, and Steve said, "Hey, when we're done with the Gypsies, I'll bring you to your car, follow you home and we'll fill your husband in on everything together."

Morgan smiled. "Fair enough."

Steve shifted into reverse and pulled out.

"We need a location. I'll check the flyer," Morgan said.

"I remember an article the paper ran the last time the Gypsies were in Lake Placid. A colleague of mine listed some of their favorite haunts," Steve said.

"Don't people need permits to run carnivals or bazaars? Why not start with the police or town hall?"

Steve smiled. "I'd rather not alert the authorities."

"Good thinking," she said, frowning. "I don't see a location on this flyer."

"Truthfully, there usually isn't. Gypsies let their location be known by word of mouth."

"Really?" she said. "Can I ask you something? How can a band of Gypsies come through town and put flyers up without being noticed?"

"This isn't the early 1900s with Gypsies in scarves and tambourines. Thousands of tourists come through town every season. Today's Gypsies look like anybody else and can disappear in a crowd easily. To make a killing, the Gypsies only need a couple of days and a little cooperation from some disgruntled landowner with a hard-on for the establishment. They'll make him an offer he can't refuse and move on when they're done."

"I suppose," she said, playing with the folder on her lap.

Steve glanced sideways. "Have a look at that file."

Morgan opened it and recognized the newspaper articles. "These are some of the articles I copied from the library." She read out loud, "Some claimed the Welcomes had had a child, a little girl who, after they died, had gone to live with relatives far away. Others argued there was no child. In 1924, because all records were destroyed in a fire, whether a Welcome child existed would forever remain a mystery." Morgan sighed. "If the Welcomes did have a little girl, what could have happened to her?"

"My instincts tell me if we keep going," he smiled confidently, "we'll find out everything. Speaking of which, I've got some info on the Connellys as well."

"I've got it." Morgan read aloud. "Jenna Connelly, born in Orlando, Florida in nineteen forty-nine, attended the University of Central Florida, where she met Tom, her husband. They had one child, Tommy. He died on September thirtieth, nineteen eighty-three in Lake Placid, New York. Cause of death unknown. Tommy was thirteen.

"Pity he died so young." Morgan shook her head then continued. "Thomas J. Connelly was born in nineteen forty-seven and raised in Florida by adoptive parents. He graduated from college then attended The Culinary Institute in Austin, Texas. An opportunity to serve as head chef at the Bradford House brought the Connellys to Lake Placid in nineteen eighty-three.

"The Connellys left the house immediately following the death of their son, but remained in Lake Placid pending the outcome of the investigation. Findings were inconclusive. The Connellys returned to Florida shortly thereafter. The investigation is still pending."

"Oh – oh," Steve said, and Morgan looked up.

Two unshaven men in a rusted out red and gray Chevy Silverado passed Morgan and Steve and turned right off Route 86 five miles west of Lake Placid. Steve followed them. Morgan frowned and Steve said, "With a little luck that Silverado is headed for the same place we are."

The narrow dirt road was veined with roots and pitted with rocks and ruts that made the Blazer kick under Morgan and Steve like a bucking bronco. Morgan caught the afternoon sun peeking through the trees like a bloodshot eye near the end of a long, hard day. Steve pointed to light at the end of the wooded road.

"I think we found our Gypsy camp."

Her heart spiking, Morgan grabbed her pendant and squeezed.

Steve pulled into an open field where about thirty cars worse off than the Silverado were scattered as if some kid got bored playing decades ago and left them to rust in the grass.

An old, beat up green Ford Taurus pulled in and parked next to Steve's new Blazer. Two teens, a boy in jeans and a girl in shorts and a tank top jumped out and headed for the crowd.

"It's now or never," Steve said, opening his door.

Morgan shut the door behind her, feeling uneasy. Steve's Blazer stood out like the proverbial sore thumb. She followed Steve, absorbing the people and the lay of the land.

Beyond the parking area was a caravan of pickup trucks, microbuses and minivans parked in a horseshoe, looking like they'd barely passed inspection. Clusters of women in tee shirts and jeans chatted with tourists near tables piled high with silvery arm bracelets and earrings.

In a large canvas tent to their right several men ran shell and card games. Women in hoop earrings and brightly colored dresses sat under canopies telling fortunes with tealeaves and tarot cards. Exotic girls with dark mysterious eyes seduced the crowd with jangling bracelets and sleek movements to canned music. Boys in worn out sneakers and faded jeans juggled hula hoops and tennis balls.

Morgan noticed a tall man of undetermined age in overalls and a red bandana. He folded two beefy arms across his chest and watched Steve and her with narrowed eyes. A cigarette dangling from his lips, he leaned on the hood of a car full of young kids with smudged faces. They stared at Morgan and Steve with runny noses and flat, uncurious eyes through dirty windows, giving her goose bumps. In the woods off the clearing several dogs snarled and growled. One yelped and the growling stopped. Without averting his eyes, the big, beefy man walked toward Morgan and Steve in slow, confident strides. Fearing he'd recognize and claim her pendant, Morgan hid it under her blouse.

His hair was fastened in a ponytail at the back of his neck. He took a drag on his cigarette. "We pay money for field." His heavily accented words were shrouded in smoke. He flicked the butt to the ground and pulled a pink paper from his hip pocket. "We got permit to camp here and make fire." He pointed and Morgan noticed strategically hollowed out grounds filled with kindling.

Steve shook his head. "We're not the police." He held out his hand. "I'm Steve Rivers, a reporter for the North Country Tribune and this is Morgan Matthias."

His eyes in a nest of hard lines, the man looked down his hooked nose at Steve's hand with disdain. Appearing unruffled, Steve gave a good-natured shrug and withdrew it.

"Baro!"

Morgan and Steve turned in sync toward the gravelly female voice coming from behind them.

"Who are these?" Baro's age mate, a pleasingly plump woman with long gray hair, dark suspicious eyes and tattoos on her neck and hands glared at Morgan and Steve. Resisting the urge to clutch her pendant, Morgan cleared her throat instead.

"We don't mean to intrude. We're looking for information."

Before the woman responded, Morgan launched into her story. She described events pertaining only to the Gypsies, including the pendant. She combed through her purse for the camera, advanced to the black and whites and handed the camera over.

Her eyes glistening, the woman let out a wounded cry. Trembling, she handed Baro the camera. He gazed at the photos. The lines around his mouth and eyes softened before getting harder. His icy gaze impaled Morgan.

"Where you get these?"

Shaken, Morgan gambled with a long shot. Gypsy culture with crystal balls and tarot readings was steeped in the occult. Sensing the

Gypsies would be receptive, she told the truth.

"The camera's brand new. I unpacked it and put it on the table. It clicked on and lit up and these pictures were just there."

The white-lipped woman grabbed Baro's arm and mumbled something in a foreign language. He answered in the same language. Without knowing the tongue, Morgan knew Baro was dead set against whatever his woman wanted him to do. Steve must've noticed it too. He opened his wallet, took out a roll of bills and peeled off two twenties. Looking at Steve through narrowed eyes, Baro snatched the bills and nodded to his woman.

"Almost hundred years ago young girl, Diamond, disappear from Gypsy Cove, old Gypsy camp on Lake Placid. These," she pointed to the Gypsies in the photo, "Diamond family. They beg sheriff help find her. Sheriff search day, maybe two, then stop. Gypsies search until too cold to stay in mountains. Gypsies leave. Never hear nothing about girl again."

Steve started the car. "Good work, Morgan. Now we have two names to go on. Diamond and Bloodfire. Ever think of doing investigative reporting?"

Morgan laughed. "Thanks for the vote of confidence, but I'll keep my day job." The smile slipped from her face. "The problem is if the Gypsies didn't kill the Welcomes or Tommy, who did, and where do we go from here?"

Steve headed east. "For starters, we head back to Lake Placid."

# Bloodfire and the Legend of Paradox Pond

## Lake Placid 1924

Fighting the wind, Jared hurried along the footpath to Pulpit Rock, crushing twigs and leaves under his boots as broken and dead as his heart. From time to time he glanced over his shoulder at Diamond lagging behind him. She was the lucky one. Pregnant or not, Diamond was free to escape, but he and his daughter were prisoners in Lake Placid.

Elspeth was right about something else. Having a Gypsy child would put his family in the biggest Lake Placid scandal of their lives. But ruin business and make them paupers? Jared stopped walking. That didn't make sense. Theirs was the only store in town. As tasty as gossip is, it wouldn't fill grumbling bellies with food or fit cold, growing backs with warm clothing.

Jared grinned, pleased. For the first time since Diamond had said she was pregnant, he began thinking clearly. Maybe there was a way out of this after all. Diamond caught up, hooked her arm in his, and they started walking.

His mother and sister might be the butt of cruel jokes and harsh judgment. Embarrassed, they'd shut themselves in—for a while. But that was no reason for him to kill Diamond—on Pulpit Rock. A harsh laugh escaped his lips and died in the wind. How like Elspeth to turn Pulpit Rock, his shrine of beauty and love, into a hell of guilt and torment.

Jared pictured his daughter drowning in his shame, and his eyes shimmered with tears. She was innocent. She had nothing to do with his sins, and he'd be damned if he'd let her pay for them. Elspeth was right in the first place. He was a fool who'd destroyed his family. Damn Elspeth, her logic was flawless—tears stung his eyes—but it was not convincing enough for him to kill Diamond. Jared swallowed and licked his lips. His mouth tasted bitter. His eyes blurred. Tears spilled down his cheeks. He sniffled, wiped his face, lifted his head and stopped walking. Diamond bumped into him, panting. He heard her teeth chatter. Her body, pressed against him, shook like an autumn leaf. Her breath, hot and moist, warmed the back of his neck. He glanced to his right at a clump of wild rhododendron. Elspeth's words echoed.

*When you get to Pulpit Rock, you'll tie her hands behind her with a rope you will have hidden in the bushes. Before you throw her over the cliff you'll snatch her Gypsy pendant. Proof, ... Surely you know why I need it.*

Jared bowed his head, loathing himself, wondering how Elspeth had known about Diamond's pendant. A coward, he'd never asked. And what did it matter?

"Jared?" Diamond pulled at his shirt and rubbed his back gently, sounding frightened.

He lifted his head, wiped his nose and narrowed his eyes. To hell with Elspeth! He loved Diamond, and he refused to kill her.

Not now. Not here. Not ever.

He ignored her plea and kept walking. He pictured his mother. Widowed young, she'd raised Laura and him alone and made the store turn a profit. Laura was engaged. Her husband would take care of her. When the scandal broke, all three would find a way to cope. That left his daughter. He pictured his little darling, sitting in his lap, winding her slender arms around his neck, kissing his cheek, begging him to read her a story, and he groaned like a wounded buck. He had to save her and Diamond.

"Jared." Diamond stepped in front of him. She looked up into his eyes. "I know something is wrong. Please tell me what it is."

Suddenly, Jared looked at Diamond and realized the solution to his problem had been staring him in the face all along. Wasn't honesty the best policy? He would tell Diamond the truth: That Elspeth wanted her dead, so she must leave with her people.

Relieved, he kissed the top of her head and shrugged out of her arms. He took her hands. Her fingers were cold. He squeezed and kissed them, then walked off the trail to the clump of wild rhododendron. Diamond followed behind him. The rope was where he'd left it, coiled behind the bush like a deadly snake. Diamond stood alongside him. The cold clearly sapping more of her warmth, she rubbed her arms and stared at the ground.

"Rope?" she said. He pictured her frowning. "What's it for?" Her breathless curiosity, so much like his daughter's, was one of the things he loved most about her. He wouldn't let her die. He'd miss her, but when she left, his life would go back the way it was before. Loveless but less complicated. Down on one knee he looped the rope on his arm.

"What are you doing?"

He stood up and faced her. "I can't marry you, Diamond." His words were soft, more of a plea than a statement.

"What?" Her whole body shook. "I don't understand." She hugged his jacket around her. "You said Elspeth knew."

His face burned. He lowered his eyes. "She does."

"But you said if I got pregnant—"

Jared looked into her eyes. "I know what I said." He unwound the rope. "But things," his voice cracked, "have changed. When your people break camp, you've got to go with them. It's the only way out of this mess for both of us."

"Mess?" She stroked her belly. Her chin trembled.

He held the rope up. "Elspeth wants me to kill you."

Her mouth an astonished O, Diamond stopped trembling and shook her head. Her knees gave way. She sank to the ground, stared at the rope in his hand and shivered.

"But it won't end that way. I promise," Jared said.

"End?" she whispered, looking up at him. "What are you talking about? Nothing's going to end. It's just beginning."

"Diamond, you don't understand—"

"But you love me," Diamond shouted, shaking her fist. "You promised if I got pregnant, you'd divorce Elspeth and marry me!"

Once Diamond realized he'd worked things out despite Elspeth's threats she would be calm. Jared stepped closer and Diamond's eyes bulged at the rope. She shrank back. Jared looped the rope back on his arm and pulled her to her feet. Diamond backed away, looking as if she'd turn and run. He couldn't let her. She had to hear him out and do what he said. He wasn't going to kill her. He grabbed her wrist. "Please, Diamond. Let me explain."

Diamond jerked her arm and loosened his grip. He tightened it. She lowered her face to his hand and bit down hard on his fingers. Her bite stung. His eyes watered. He let her wrist go, dropped the rope and waved his hand hard, shaking the pain from his fingers. She turned and ran a few feet, but Jared ran faster and grabbed her. He locked his arms around her waist and pegged her back to his chest. Her curls were cold against his lips.

"I won't do what Elspeth wants. I'm not gonna kill you."

Diamond bent forward and twisted and turned in his arms.

He spread his legs, planting his feet firmly on the ground and held her tight. "You've got to believe me."

She screamed and stomped his foot with her heel. He gripped her tighter. He leaned his face over her shoulder and pressed his cheek to hers. "There's a way out."

Diamond panted hard.

"I have a plan. I love you."

Slowly, her chest stopped heaving. Jared felt her go limp in his arms. He exhaled a sigh of relief and closed his eyes.

"Let me go." She exhaled, sounding exhausted.

"Promise me you won't run."

She hesitated then nodded. He let her go. She turned slowly and faced him. He took her shoulders. Moonlight spilled through the trees and spattered her face. Panting, she waited. He swallowed hard and looked into her eyes. He squeezed her shoulders gently. Without the ugly details he summed up Elspeth's threats.

"If I don't kill you," he felt Diamond stiffen, "I'll lose my child."

Diamond's eyes flashed. "What about my child?" she said, touching her stomach. "Doesn't he count?"

Didn't she hear what he said? Jared looked at her stomach. The thought of *her child* suddenly repulsed him. "Of course he counts." He forced the words off his tongue.

"You said you hated Elspeth." She shrugged his hands off her shoulders, put her hands on her hips and jutted her jaw out. "You said you loved me!"

"I do," he said, stunned. She sounded just like Elspeth!

"You said we'd get married and live in your house!"

"It's not that simple. If people find out you're pregnant, I'll lose my child—my good name. You've got to leave town with your family until we can figure things out."

"That's your plan? I leave pregnant so you can keep your child and your good name. What about my child and my good name?"

Her good name? He was astounded. If this weren't so serious, he'd laugh in her face. "You don't understand," he said, trying to hide his annoyance. "The scandal—my family—"

"Your family?" She moved closer. "I hate your family!" She raised her arm and swiped his cheek with her nails.

Jared's eyes watered. His face stung. He ran the back of his hand across his cheek and frowned. His hand was smeared with blood. She pummeled his chest with her fists. He grabbed her wrists. She wormed free.

"I hate you!" She slapped his face.

He grabbed her arm. "Do as I say. It's the only way."

She raised her hand, curling her fingers, ready to claw him again, "You promised—"

He grabbed her wrists. "I can't marry you."

"I'm pregnant! You have to marry me. When my father finds out it was you," she screamed, wriggling free, "he'll kill you, your wife and your precious daughter!"

*Jared snapped. The full autumn moon, naked and shameless, focused his mind, honing his primal senses.*

Her taste filled his mouth. Her scent filled his nose. Never averting his eyes, he stooped down and slowly picked up the rope.

Her eyes as wide as saucers, Diamond backed up. Like a doe in a starving wolf's sight, she turned on her heels and ran down the path, vanishing into the darkness.

Jared dropped the rope. He got to his feet and smelled her fear. It was fetid and fading fast. He ran down the path, his legs and heart pumped hard, closing the gap between them. He rounded the bend. She saw him and ran harder. Her fear, hot and fresh, filled his nostrils. Gaining quickly, he hooked her waist with his arm and dragged her back up the trail. She fought all the way, kicking his shins and punching and scratching his arms. He spotted the rope and dropped her face down. Her face to the ground, she coughed and choked. He'd clearly knocked the wind from her lungs and she breathed in dirt. He put his knee in her back and forced her arms behind her. She squirmed under him, kicking her legs. Her feet were bare. Her heels were bleeding. She must've lost her sandals on the trail. He held her wrists with one hand and grabbed the rope with the other.

She turned her head sideways and screamed. "You're hurting me!" He wound the rope around her wrists and ankles tightly. "No. Please let me go." She coughed again, deep and hard.

He turned her on her back. Her tears mixed with her dirt streaked her face.

"I'll do what you say. I'll go with my family and never come back," she begged, coughing and panting. "I swear! Please."

His eyes were blank. His face was as rigid as stone. Did he even hear her? She felt him grab her ankles and drag her across the ground like a sack of his store flour. Her skirt rode up. Her blouse slipped out of her waistband. Rocks and stones bit and tore at her bare back. Twigs scraped her buttocks and thighs, stinging her flesh. Suddenly, he stopped moving. Diamond watched him. Her heart leapt to her throat. He walked to the edge of the cliff and stared into Lake Placid.

She was a fool. He lied. He never loved her. He used her and now he'd throw her and his baby away. She must be dreaming. This wasn't happening. Panting, she twisted her arms, kicked, and rubbed her wrists and ankles raw. The rope was so tight.

Suddenly, he knelt by her side. He shoved his hands down her blouse and groped her breasts. Too stunned to scream she squeezed her eyes shut and shrank from his touch. He grabbed her chain and yanked Bloodfire from her neck. She opened her eyes realizing she would never know why he took Bloodfire because—

*Jared was going to kill her.*

Her chest heaving, she breathed deep and screamed out.

"NOOOO! Please, Jared," she shrieked and panted. "Please don't. Please. Please. Please. Don't. Please don't kill ... us."

He jammed her pendant into his pocket.

"Please, Jared. Please don't kill my baby. Please."

*Jared was going to kill her.*

Diamond sobbed, picturing Mama and Papa. When they realized she was missing, they'd go to town and report it, but no one would help. *Decent* folks wanted them gone. Her people would search. But sooner or later they'd give up and leave town.

He swept her up in his arms. Under the barren moon and scatter of vacant stars Jared held Diamond over the cliff. With eyes flatter and deader than Ezekiel Bradford's, he let her go.

The rope biting into her wrists and ankles, Diamond falls into water so dark and cold the impact slams the air from her lungs and wracks her body with spasms. Sinking fast, she struggles to hold her breath. Blood surging in her temples, she exhales, forcing her body to spin head over heels. Her lungs are on fire. Her calves and thighs twitch. Seconds before blacking out, she kicks hard and makes her way up. Her pulse throbs in her throat. Fireworks burst behind her eyes. Breaking the surface she chokes, coughing up water. She tips her face to the sky, gulps in mouthfuls of frosty night. Her life shivers out in small, wispy puffs. Her body shakes. She can't stop her teeth from chattering. She kicks her bound legs, squints at the shore and sees the barefaced cliff. Its proud granite jaw juts over the water while moonlit waves lap at its craggy chin.

Diamond is so cold she can't move, but she needs to move now or she's not gonna make it. She kicks hard to stay afloat. The rope bites into her ankles. She bows her wrists and tugs at the knot, but her fingers are stiff and numb and the wet rope feels tighter.

She stops shivering. Her confused mind wanders. Her head slumps forward. Her nose and mouth fill with water. Startled, she wakes up coughing.

Diamond can't feel her legs. Is she still kicking? She tips her chin up. Water rises around the island of her face and above her chin, circling her nose and mouth. Is she sinking? Water covers her lips and laps at her nostrils.

She pulls air through her nose, fills her lungs, holds her breath and sinks. Her frantic heart pummels her breastbone. Her stingy lungs exhale miserly bubbles. Jerking herself hard, she ripples water she can't feel and no one will see. Her lungs burn and twitch. Her eyes bulge.

Against her will, Diamond breathes. A thousand suns burst in her brain. Her bladder empties itself, warming the water around her, briefly.

# Chapter 43

## Kevin and Maggie

Kevin walked into the PHHC family-waiting room and groaned. Natalie was dressed in white, pouting and leafing through a magazine with her legs crossed in a way that ought to be illegal. He moved his gaze up her calves past her knees and thighs to the curve of a luscious butt cheek.

Damn. He was getting hard. He had to ditch Nat and soon. He had everything he needed to banish Princess Maggie from the royal business forever, but if he broke off with Nat before filling the old man in on his golden girl's extra curricula activities, Nat could tell Maggie and nuke him. He saw Maggie's Lexus in the parking lot; ergo she had to be in with Harlan. Lillian sat on Natalie's right. She looked up.

"Hello, dear," she said and smiled.

"Ladies." Kevin sat on Nat's left.

Smiling, Natalie put the magazine on the coffee table and looked into his eyes. "Kevin."

She sighed his name in a way that went straight to his groin. Kevin coughed and leaned forward. He rested his arms on his knees, clasped his hands and looked past Natalie.

"How's he doing, Lillian?"

"Good. Doctor says he might be out by the seventeenth."

"Great." The seventeenth. At least that was something. He'd tell the old man everything as soon as the doctor said he could work. He should be well enough to handle it by then.

Lillian stood. "I'll tell Harlan you're here, Kevin."

She left and Nat grinned and uncrossed her legs. "Kevin. Guess what?" Excited, she didn't wait for him to answer. "A super hottie named CJ Matthias came into the office looking for Morgan and his *father*!"

"I didn't think Morgan had kids."

"She doesn't. Apparently Morgan's the second wife, and the Australian hottie is her stepson."

"Interesting."

She slid to the edge of her seat, "What did you find out?"

His gaze drifted to the shadow between her thighs. "Maggie stayed with Steve last night, just like we suspected."

"I knew it!" She gave a victory fist-clench.

"I was leaving when Steve came out, jumped in his car and took off. I got curious and followed. Guess who he met in broad daylight right in front of the North Country Tribune building."

"Who?"

"Morgan Matthias."

"No!" Natalie giggled and clapped her hands. Kevin shook his head and laughed softly. "Boy, Maggie must hate Uncle Harlan big time to set Morgan up with Steve Rivers."

"That's what I thought." Kevin said, looking at Natalie. She laid those luscious brown eyes on him. "What do we do?"

"Nothing until Harlan gets back to work." Damn, he hated having to cut her loose already. Why was she born too late?

Maggie stood in Harlan's room at the foot of his bed watching him sleep. The change in him since the operation was dramatic. The shadows under his eyes and tightness around his nose and mouth were gone. He breathed easily. His cheeks had color. As soon as he realized he wasn't in a private room he'd have a hissy fit, proving he was on the mend more accurately than any state of the art test.

Maggie put her white leather purse on his nightstand and glanced around. The room was equipped with the usual hospital fare. Nightstand, phone and bedside lamp, intravenous stand, over-bed table, privacy curtain and patient chairs. She watched Harlan with mixed emotions. Where to from here, Dad? Would she say she's his daughter? Or would Mom do the honor?

As much as Maggie would love to take him down, if Steve got his intel elsewhere, she'd be on high moral ground, a place, she'd bet, Harlan Wainright never even knew existed.

Maggie looked at her watch. It was 4:30 and she was getting hungry. Steve had promised he'd be home by five. Maybe they'd eat out tonight. Italian sounded good. She gazed out the window at the mountains, imagined dessert and grinned.

"If you're here," Harlan said, "who's minding the store?"

Maggie faced him. "Hutch. How are you feeling?"

"Anxious to get the hell out of here and back to work." He felt the mattress for the bed's control button, found it and pressed. The bed rose.

"Is Morgan Matthias still in the house?"

"She is." He clearly blew out a breath of relief. "You look good," she said, meaning it.

"Thank you." The bed raised him to a sitting position. "You do too." He regarded her with clear, keen eyes and a solemn expression. "Better than you have in a long time, and frankly, Maggie, I've spent the last few weeks wondering why."

Damn him. She picked up her purse and scratched at a speck on the strap. "I don't know what you're talking about." But she did. He knew her as well as her own mother. Did he sense she was back with Steve? Her mouth felt dry. "I should look good." There were two beige plastic cups and a pitcher of ice water on his over-bed table. She put her purse down and picked up a cup. "I sold the Welcome place for you, didn't I?" She filled it.

"You did and I'm delighted. But that's not what I'm talking about, and you know it."

"Jesus, Harlan." Her gaze never wavered, but her heart fluttered behind her ribs. "You just had a heart attack. Scared us all to death. You're in a hospital bed recuperating from major surgery. Stop playing games. If you have something to say just say it." She drank.

"Fair enough," he said.

She put the cup down and braced herself.

"I'm talking about our post-Memorial-Weekend meeting."

She tilted her head forward and rubbed the back of her neck.

"You stormed out in a rage, disappeared for days then came back to work as if nothing had happened."

She lifted her head and stared at him.

"I want to know why."

Maggie felt a familiar arm encircle her waist and turned. "Mom," she said, angry with herself for feeling relieved.

Lillian squeezed her. Maggie stiffened. A pained look in her eye, Lillian let Maggie go and smiled at Harlan. She looked genuinely happy to see him awake. Maggie was amazed and pissed that her mother still loved the bastard.

Lillian fluffed Harlan's pillow. She combed his hair with her fingers and kissed his forehead. "How do you feel?"

Harlan slipped his arms around Lillian and hugged her to him. "Now that you're here," he said, stroking her cheek and looking over her shoulder at Maggie, "I couldn't be better."

Maggie cleared her throat. "Listen guys, I gotta bounce."

On her way out of Harlan's arms, Lillian kissed his cheek and then looked at Maggie. "Where are you going?"

"Placid." Maggie felt Harlan's eyes bore into hers. She kept her eyes on Lillian. "It's not fair to leave Hutch alone."

"Nonsense. You know as well as I do that Hutch would do anything for Harlan." Lillian looked at Harlan and smiled. "I think she's been secretly in love with you for years."

Harlan laughed and Maggie, who'd suspected the same, smiled.

"Let her go." Harlan's smile vanished. The coldness in his eyes left no doubt in Maggie's mind. The topic they'd discussed was not closed. "She's right. We mustn't take advantage of Hutch's loyalty." The clock on his nightstand read five-thirty. "My goodness. You look tired, Lilly. Did you drive here alone?"

"Natalie and I rode up together."

"Why not follow Maggie's lead?" His eye on Maggie, he took Lillian's hand. "Take Natalie back to Placid and have a nice dinner. On me." He pressed Lillian's hand to his lips.

Was it Maggie's imagination or did Harlan know she had no intention of going home?

"But—"

He patted Lillian's hand, cutting her off. "You've been with me every day since my heart attack. There's no need to stay late again tonight." She hesitated but he said, "Go. I mean it."

"If you insist." Lillian kissed his cheek and smiled. "Sleep well. I'll be back tomorrow."

"Goodbye, Harlan," Maggie said. She kissed his cheek. He looked surprised. He'd freak if he knew that she and Steve were joined at the genitals for good. She almost laughed out loud.

As Maggie and Lillian were leaving he said, "Maggie," stopping them. His eyes narrowed to slits. "Where's Kevin?"

A knot formed in Maggie's stomach. "In the waiting room."

"Send him in before you leave, will you?"

Maggie nodded, wondering what Harlan was up to now.


Kevin walked in slowly and on guard, trying to size the old man up. Failing miserably, he plastered a smile on his face.

"Hey, Harlan. I'm glad—"

"Save it." Harlan pointed to a chair near the foot of his bed. "Tell me what the hell's going on with Maggie."

"I don't—"

"Cut the crap. I know you suspect something."

Well, what do you know, Kevin thought, delighted he didn't have to wait till the seventeenth to clue Harlan in after all. The old man was a pro at hardball. Kevin shifted gears.

"Give me specifics," Kevin said, stalling. He needed to know what this was all about before he admitted anything.

"Fine," Harlan growled. "You were at the staff meeting after Memorial Day Weekend. You saw how Maggie stormed out. Tell me what happened during the time she went missing to make her return to business as usual instead of going for my jugular."

Goddamn! There *was* a pot of gold at the end of the rainbow. And this one had Kevin Delaney written all over it. He took a breath. "You don't miss a trick, do you, Harlan?"

Harlan gave a frosty smile. Kevin clasped his hands tight. Cool, man. Be cool. He remembered the day at the White Birch Inn when Harlan had seen Natalie's phone number on his receipt. His instincts screamed to omit Natalie. He looked at Harlan.

"You're right, dude. I noticed it, and I think I know why."

Kevin told Harlan everything including Steve's interviewing Morgan Matthias. Harlan looked at Kevin with stone-cold eyes.

"And just when the hell were you planning telling me?"

Kevin resisted the urge to wipe the sweat from his brow. The old man hated wimps. If he didn't play this right he'd be out on his ass— fast. "Jesus, Harlan. They just plowed your arteries. Did you want me to rush right into ICU and blow your aortal wall?"

"Save the histrionics for Natalie. Tell me."

"I was gonna sit tight till the seventeenth. If I told you before that and something happened," Kevin shrugged.

Harlan shook his head. His expression softened to a smile.

"You did good. Now, get the hell out. I need to think."

# Chapter 44

**Morgan and Steve**

Morgan pulled the Buick Regal into her driveway. She shifted into park and stared at her house. The upstairs was dark, but the living room was lit. Chuck might be waiting up. She killed the ignition and lights. Steve pulled in behind her and did the same. By the time they got out of their cars, Chuck had opened the front door and was out on the porch. Morgan climbed the steps and slipped into his arms. She pressed her face against his cheek and closed her eyes.

"Missed you, sweetheart." he said, hugging her to him.

"Me too." She pulled away gently, looked into his eyes and smiled. "Chuck, this is Steve Rivers, the reporter for the North Country Tribune. Steve, my husband, Chuck."

Steve extended his hand. "It's a pleasure, sir."

Chuck smiled and shook hands. "Pleasure's mine, mate."

"You've got one heck of a wife," Steve said, smiling at Morgan. "I'm trying to convince her to team up with me."

Chuck laughed. "Come on in," he said, gesturing toward the front door. "You both look like you can use a bit of a drink."

"If a Manhattan on the rocks is what the doctor orders," she said, walking through the front door, "count me in."

"Done. Steve?" Chuck closed the front door.

"I'll take a beer. Any kind. As long as it's not light." Steve followed Morgan into the living room.

"Have a seat," Chuck said on his way to the kitchen.

Morgan sat next to Steve on the Prince of Wales sofa, listening to Chuck clink ice cubes into a glass. She watched Steve take in her well-appointed living room.

"Looks like Harlan spared no expense." He looked at Morgan, and quickly added, "I mean, I assumed this stuff came—"

"You assume correctly. The stuff came with the house." Suddenly, Morgan frowned. "I'm sorry. I thought that since you wrote about this house you'd be familiar with the inside."

Steve shook his head. "Not for quite a while. It's a long story," he said, sighing. He pointed toward the hearth filled with logs and the mirror above the mantle. "Is that where the fire roared out of control?"

"The second fire. The first was in my bedroom."

He turned away from the mirror and faced her.

"About your long story. I'm all ears."

"That makes two of us, mate," Chuck said. "But, first things first." He set a tray with a Manhattan, two clear, frosty mugs of beer and three clear, acrylic coasters on the coffee table. He sat opposite Morgan and Steve and raised a frosty mug.

"Cheers," he said.

"Cheers," they replied, doing the same.

The Manhattan was cold and burned Morgan's throat going down. She swirled the amber liquid. Ice cubes clinked against glass. She took another sip, grabbed a coaster, set the coaster and glass on the table and looked at Steve. He took a long swallow, closed his eyes, sighed and put the mug on the coaster.

"Maggie Duran and I are lovers."

Morgan raised her eyebrows at Chuck, and then looked at Steve. "Did you answer the phone when I called Maggie to let her know Chuck was here at the house with me?"

"Yes." Steve grabbed the mug and took another swallow. "Maggie and I go back a long way. As a matter of fact" he said, looking around, "this house brought us together in the first place. Then with a little help from Harlan it tore us apart."

After Steve finished explaining, Morgan was appalled.

"Funny thing. When the Welcome-Connelly stories settled into a rehash of the past despite my spin, I found myself wondering if losing Maggie over them years ago had been worth it." Steve drained the mug and put it on the table. Chuck followed suit. Foam ringed the insides of their glasses.

"When Jack called and told me about you, Morgan, I almost blew him off." Leaning forward, he placed his forearms on his thighs and clasped his hands. "Maggie and I are together and better than ever. I swear I'll never risk losing her again."

"I hear you," she said. "By the way, how's Harlan doing?"

"From what I hear, he'll be wreaking havoc in no time."

Chuck stood. "Okay, Rivers," he said, scooping up the empty mugs, "I'll replenish your brew under one condition. When I get back I want to hear everything that happened today."

"Deal," Steve said.

Chuck pointed at Morgan's glass. "Love?"

"I'm fine," Morgan said, sipping. Chuck headed toward the kitchen. "Honey?" she said. Chuck stopped and faced her. "Steve and I stopped by earlier to pick you up. Where were you?"

Staring oddly, she thought, Chuck frowned.

Morgan frowned in kind. "Is something wrong?"

"Oh. Sorry, love. No, of course not. I forgot to tell you. I had to run into town and check out of the White Birch Inn."

"Oh." Morgan smiled. She watched him disappear over the landing into the kitchen. She heard Chuck open the door to the back yard off the kitchen and looked at Steve.

"Well," she heard Chuck say with a smile in his voice. "What's a good little dish licker like you doing here?"

"Dish licker?" Steve said.

Morgan laughed. "That's Australian for dog,"

As if on cue, a dog bounded over the landing, down the steps through the living room to Morgan and licked her hand.

"Jinx? There's a good baby. What are you doing here?" Morgan said, laughing and scratching Jinx behind the ears.

Chuck appeared with a frosty mug of beer in each hand and placed Steve's on the table in front of him.

"Thanks, man." Steve lifted the mug and took a swig.

"My pleasure, mate," Chuck said, doing the same. He licked the foam from his lips, put the mug down and watched Morgan pet Jinx. "I think you've charmed the coat off that dog, love."

Morgan cupped Jinx's chin in her hand. "I know," she said, looking into the dog's big sad eyes, "and I'm so glad, but I haven't got the faintest idea why I deserve such adoration."

Morgan lifted her glass and sipped. "Mmmm. I think our barkeep has earned his story fee."

"I agree," Steve said. "Why don't you do the honors?"

"Okay. Sit back and relax, sweetheart," Morgan said. "The account of our adventure may take a little while."

Morgan finished. Chuck said, "That is one helluva tale."

"It sure is." Morgan scratched Jinx under the chin and frowned distractedly. "We know Diamond was murdered, pushed off the cliff, but why is she haunting this house? And how did her ghost get in? Swim?" Suddenly, Morgan's eyes widened as two gigantic pieces of the puzzle locked into place. She stopped petting Jinx.

"What is it, love?" Chuck said.

"Maggie said one of this house's biggest selling points is that it stood on a hill high enough to escape some proverbial hundred-year flood." Her body rigid with excitement, she looked directly at Chuck. "At the library I found an article about some diving club in the sixties that had explored the land bridge our house sits on for underwater caves, connecting the two lakes."

"But the diving club came up empty," Steve said.

Morgan stood and looked from Chuck to Steve. "That doesn't mean the caves don't exist."

His eyes shining, Steve said, "If the last flood happened a hundred years ago, give or take, the timing might be right." He sat up straight. "The current could've carried Diamond's body from the lake to a cave right under this house!"

"One flood that happened a hundred years ago? I wouldn't be too sure about that," Morgan said, frowning. "Unless—"

"Unless what?" Chuck said.

"Unless the flood had help."

Steve snapped his fingers. "The Legend of Paradox Pond."

"You lost me," Chuck said.

Morgan rummaged through her purse and handed him the article and an old regional map she had copied from the *Geographical History of Lake Placid*.

Chuck mumbled through. The more relevant the information became, the harder he frowned. He finished and looked up. "The last few sentences negates everything about the Indians and—"

"I know," Morgan said, "but—"

Suddenly, Jinx took off. Clearly surprised, they followed her to the hallway off the kitchen. Jinx raised a paw, growled and scratched at the cellar door. Morgan remembered seeing those scratches on Memorial Day Weekend. Jinx barked frantically, jumped up, chewed on the knob. She let go, barked and looked up at Morgan. Morgan patted Jinx's head.

"You know something, girl, don't you? In fact," she looked at the scratches, "you've known something all along."

She patted the dog's thick, golden coat and Jinx's cry turned into a bark. Morgan opened the cellar door and hit the switch. Light flooded the stony stairwell. "Go on, girl, show us."

Jinx bounded down the steps and they followed.

At the bottom, Morgan found another switch. It lit up space the size of her kitchen. Threadbare light wrapped Jinx in sinister shadows that disappeared in the crawl space.

Jinx paced, stopped and sniffed the hard-packed dirt floor.

"I don't know love, can dish lickers really sniff out dead bodies under solid ground?"

"Maybe with a little help from a Gypsy friend," she said.

Jinx stopped, sniffed and moved on, then stopped and sniffed again. Settling on a spot near the far right stone foundation, she yelped, frantically clawed the dirt floor, stopped, barked at Morgan, and then frantically clawed again.

Not having gone into the cellar since May, Morgan darted her eyes through the tattered light and scanned the uncluttered room. Along the stone foundation were several wooden bins with iron hinges and handles, stacks of empty wooden crates, an old-fashioned apple cart with big, rusted wheels and two wooden barrels. To her left in the corner were the tools they needed.

"Guys. Look." she said, pointing.

Chuck smiled. Clattering several tools aside, he went for a shovel. Steve grabbed another and Morgan, a pickaxe.

"Good girl." As Chuck scratched Jinx's ears, she lowered her head and wagged her tail. "You can step aside now."

Chuck pierced the dirt floor with the tip of the shovel. His foot to the metal, he pushed down hard, trying to break ground. Exchanging his shovel for Morgan's pickaxe, he raised it high above his head and swung and stabbed, loosening the hard-packed dirt floor. After several swings, he blew out a breath, handed the pickaxe to Steve, scooped up and tossed a shovel of dirt aside. A few feet from Chuck, Steve swung the pickaxe and loosened more earth. Every few shovels and swings, the men stopped to wipe their brows, Morgan picked up a shovel and dug.

The six-foot hole was as dark as the rectangles of night framed in the cellar windows. Seeing Chuck and Steve stripped to their bare, sweaty chests, Morgan ran upstairs to the kitchen. She pulled a metal pitcher and three large glasses from a cabinet above the sink, filled one glass, drank, and then filled the pitcher. She turned off the tap, scooped up the pitcher and two empty glasses and headed back. She filled the glasses. Chuck climbed out of the hole. She gave each a glass then put the pitcher on a crawl space ledge. Chuck banged the water back.

"Thanks, love." He poured another. "Not to whine, mates, but I'm about worn out."

Steve stood in the hole and drank. He ran a sweaty arm over his lips and handed Morgan the glass. "Thanks," Steve panted. His face pinched with pain, he winced at his blistered palms.

"You know," he rubbed his hands together and raised the pickaxe above his head. "I'm thinking old Jinxy buried a bone here so long ago," he lowered the pickaxe. "It's an artifact."

He struck something hard, let the pickaxe go, looked up at Morgan and Chuck and dropped to his knees. Chuck jumped into the hole. Both men clawed at the dirt with their bare hands and unearthed a surface of rock almost the width and length of the hole. Chuck raised the pickaxe above his head, swung and broke through a patch of ground at the edge of the rock to a hollow space beneath. He gawked at Steve.

"What is it?" Morgan said.

His face streaked with dirt and sweat, Chuck said, "I saw a flashlight on a shelf near the back door, love."

Gone and back, Morgan snapped on the flashlight, dropped down into the hole and lit up the hollow. Chuck grabbed the pickaxe and swung. Mining an opening large enough for two men to fit through, Chuck put the pickaxe down and stepped back and nodded to Morgan.

Morgan dropped to her knees and shined light into the hollow. They looked over her shoulders and peered into a cave.

"Jesus bloody Christ!" Chuck said.

In a cone of light a human skull stared at them with empty eyes and a vacant grin.

Remnants of rope braceleted its slender wrists and ankles.

White-lipped and teary-eyed, Morgan said, "Call the police."

# Chapter 45

## Maggie and Steve

Meeting Steve thrust for thrust, Maggie arched and cried out. Steve shuddered and collapsed against her. Her heart drumming, she buried her fingers in his hair and pulled his head back. She tightened her legs and locked him inside her. Her hungry mouth found his.

"You're like the seven deadly sins in one tasty package," he said.

Maggie laughed. "I'm still trying to process everything you told me," she kissed him in between words.

"I listened to us give our statements to the police with my own ears," Steve kissed her, "and I still don't believe it."

He slipped out of Maggie's arms and out of bed.

"Are you taking Morgan's word and running her *whole* story?"

He slipped into a T shirt and pajama bottoms, nodding. "Morgan appears to be a stable person with a firm grip on reality. She's been an English teacher in the same district and married to a bona-fide psychiatrist for over thirty years. She had no prior knowledge of the Welcomes. She knew nothing about the house before moving in. Morgan and Chuck are the real heroes. They provided a solid lead toward solving a very old, very cold case."

Steve turned his computer on.

"That's for sure," Maggie said, distractedly.

Steve took her chin in his hand. "What is it, Maggie?"

She looked into his eyes. "Can I change the subject?"

"You can do anything you want." He kissed her nose.

"Harlan suspects us. I saw it in his eyes earlier. If he finds out we're together, he'll make the rape charges he's been blackmailing you with go public. You'll lose your job."

"I'm not a kid he can scare anymore. I've been around awhile. I have a good reputation." He pulled her against him. "I don't care what he does. I love you. I won't lose you again."

"I love you too." The covers slipped from her body. Maggie shivered and slipped out of bed. She looked at his computer.

"You've got a story to write, and I've got to go. I feigned an appointment to get out of driving back with Mom and Natalie. Mom knows I'm still angry, but she'll wait up for me."

Maggie showered and toweled off. Steve stopped typing and watched her finish dressing. "Before I left the hospital tonight, Harlan asked me to send Kevin in to see him."

"Why would that upset you?"

"You had to be there." She stuffed the brush into her purse and took out her car keys. "I don't like it, Steve. I'm going to be in the office first thing tomorrow morning and find out what Harlan said to him."

# Chapter 46

**Natalie and Kevin**

Natalie pulled Lillian's white Subaru Outback in the driveway and shifted into park. Lillian opened the door and swung her legs out. She paused and looked over her shoulder at Natalie who sat behind the wheel, scowling.

"Coming in, sweetheart?"

"I don't think so, Gran. I'm going out for a little while."

"Where?" Lillian looked at the dash clock and frowned. "It's almost ten o'clock."

"I know, Gran." Annoyed, Natalie closed her eyes and sighed. She didn't give a damn how desperate she was to see Kevin alone. She wasn't in high school anymore. She refused to beg for a night out. God. She couldn't wait to go to college and be her own boss.

"Is something wrong?"

Natalie made a frustrated fist and hit the steering wheel lightly. She heard Lillian pull her legs back into the car and close the door. "I'm either visiting Uncle Harlan or helping Hutch man the office." She faced her grandmother. "I haven't seen my friends since I graduated."

"I understand, but if Maggie comes home and you're not here," Lillian's unspoken words hung between them.

Natalie felt like exploding. If Maggie hadn't skipped out to screw Steve, and if Harlan hadn't called Kevin in at the last minute, she wouldn't be lying to Gran through her teeth.

"What time will you be home?"

"I don't know," Natalie said, locking her temper down. She was sick of that stupid question. She took a deep breath and sweetened her voice. "Not late. I'm going to the park to see if my friends are hanging out. If not, I'll come home."

"Well," Lillian sighed, I suppose it's all right, dear, if you don't come home too late. You have to cover the office tomorrow."

"What?" *Damn!*

"I forgot to tell you. Hutch has a vacation day tomorrow."

Natalie gritted her teeth and glared out the windshield.

"Drive carefully," Lillian said. She opened the door and stepped onto the driveway. "I hope you find your friends."

"Me too. Thanks, Gran. Bye."

Natalie drove down North Woods Road, left onto 86 then right onto Essex. Kevin had an apartment on the top floor of a white, two-story house in the middle of the block. She'd driven by hundreds of times but never stopped. He was paranoid about them being seen together. He'd be mad, but it was dark. Besides, with all their snooping on Maggie they were closer than ever.

She pulled Lillian's car behind Kevin's red Acura, opened the door and the courtesy lights blinked on. Checking her face in the rearview mirror, she pulled her lipstick from her purse. She could've changed when she dropped Gran off, but by the look on Kevin's face she knew her white dress had definitely turned him on. Natalie smiled. Best buy she'd ever pulled off.

She crossed the sidewalk, took the steps to the outside door and tried the knob. It was unlocked. She ran up the steps quickly and quietly and paused outside his apartment door to catch her breath. If they'd met privately instead of publicly they would've made love by now. She wanted to feel him inside her more than she wanted to live. Natalie swallowed, held her breath and knocked.

No answer. He had to be there. His car was outside. She knocked again and put her ear to the door. She heard footsteps.

"Who is it?" he whispered harshly through the door.

"Me."

"Natalie?"

She frowned. Why was he whispering? She heard him fumble with the lock and unhook the chain. He opened the door and she sighed. He looked lean and sexy in the hall light. He had to be naked under his blue pajama bottoms. His shaggy hair covered one eye. He ran his fingers through it and stepped into the hallway.

"What are you doing here?" He seemed on edge.

How could she be so stupid? Except for wanting to jump in his bed, she had no reason to be here on a weeknight at 10 o'clock. She felt the heat. She wanted him so bad she ached.

"Well?" he pressed.

"You're mad." She crumbled inside.

"Damn right I am."

Her eyes stung. "I know how you feel about us being seen—"

"Kevin?" Wearing only his blue pajama top, Kellie slipped into the doorway behind him. Draping herself on him like a cheap boa, she twirled a glass of vodka. Ice cubes clinked against the side. "I freshened this up for you, sweetie."

He took the glass. She brushed her lips lightly against his.

"You said—" Natalie's voice caught. Her eyes welled. She wanted to rip them out to stop the tears. "You were done with—"

"Well," Kellie said, running her tongue along Kevin's earlobe, "I guess he lied."

Nat's eyes flashed. Had he pulled her heart out with his bare hands, the pain could not have been more intense.

"Maggie was right about you." Her lip quivering, she shivered with shame. "You used me!" If she didn't leave she'd vomit on their feet, adding disgust to her embarrassment. Tears streaking her cheeks, Nat ran down the stairs into the street.

Kevin stood in the doorframe, watching Natalie disappear. He lowered his head. A lock of hair covered in his eye.

"Come on, baby, let's finish what we started," Kellie whispered, nibbling on his ear.

Dumbstruck, he stood there, thinking, he was a first class jerk. He shut his eyes tight, hating himself for hurting Nat. He felt like crying. He'd never forget the look in her eyes when she saw Kellie in his pajama top.

"Kevin?" Kellie said, sounding puzzled. She pulled away.

Seeing Nat in her white dress earlier at the hospital had made him so goddamned horny, that after leaving Harlan he'd raced to the White Birch Inn service entrance. He got Kellie out of the kitchen, shoved her into the shadows against a brick wall in the alley, apologizing out the yin yang for being a jerk. She got so juiced she believed it was her idea to drop by his place as soon as her shift was over.

Kellie grabbed his chin, turned his face toward her and looked into his eyes. "You bastard!" She pushed him away and ran through his kitchen into his bedroom. He followed, spilling vodka on the kitchen floor. He set the glass down on the counter and walked into his bedroom. She was stepping into her panties.

"Seems that little bitch wasn't the only one you lied to."

"What are you doing?" It was a pretty lame line, but it was the best he could do.

She glared and ripped his pajama top off. Her breasts bounced. He gaped. "Forget it!" she snapped.

He took her arm. "Don't go, Kel, please." His heart wasn't in it, but for her sake he had to make an effort. What the hell was wrong with him? Why was he suddenly so considerate?

"Why? So you can screw me and pretend I'm her?"

"I wouldn't do that," he lied. "Besides, she's a kid."

"From where I stand it looks like she's woman enough."

Kellie slipped into her black WBI uniform. "Take a good look in the mirror and tell yourself you don't love her, because I don't buy it anymore." She picked up her purse and car keys from his dresser and stormed through his apartment.

"Come on, Kel," he said, following her. "Gimme a break."

"We're so over, Delaney, that if I see you crossing the street, I'll hit you with my car." She opened the door, stepped into the hallway, paused and turned. "Oh, and by the way, Kevin, *you* have a nice life."

He stood on the landing and watched her disappear down the stairs. She slammed the door on her way out, and he flinched. If his neighbors were home, they'd be all over him.

He was alone. The girl he most cared for hated him.

He closed his door, shuffled inside and slumped on his couch. Natalie's eyes, large and hurt, filled his mind. He closed his eyes tight to block them out. It didn't help.

*Kevin, why don't you take a good look in the mirror and tell yourself you don't love her.*

Kellie was nuts. His heart hurt like hell. Let it. He did what had to be done even though he hadn't consciously planned it that way. He just went with the flow. Or did he?

After Harlan had forced him to rat Maggie out, his mission was accomplished. There was no need to keep leading Nat on, unless he wanted to get himself into a whole mess of serious trouble. A clean break was the only way. Isn't that what everybody said?

Kevin opened his eyes, dragged himself off the couch and walked into the kitchen. Let Natalie think what she wanted as long as she knew they were over. He did it for her, really.

She was so in love with him she couldn't see straight. He opened his freezer, grabbed some ice cubes and clunked them into his glass. He took a bottle of Grey Goose from the freezer and filled the glass. He slammed the freezer door and walked into his bedroom. He drained the glass, put it on his nightstand and lay on his bed. He closed his eyes and gazed into hers until he fell asleep.

# Chapter 47

**Natalie and Maggie**

After talking Gran into hitching a ride into town later with Maggie, Nat pulled Gran's car into Maggie's spot in front of the office and breathed a sigh of relief. Kevin's Acura wasn't there which meant he wasn't in yet. Every time she pictured Kellie in his blue pajama top she wanted to die. Natalie's eyes welled. Would her tears ever stop?

She'd nodded off about six. Exhausted, she looked in the rearview mirror. Her eyes were red and puffy despite her expensive make up. When she'd gotten home last night, Gran was in the living room watching TV. She rushed past saying no one was at the park, and if she had to work in the morning she needed to get to bed. Thank God Maggie hadn't been home.

Natalie got out of Gran's car as Kevin pulled up in his Acura. She ran toward the office. How in God's name would she get through the day? She stood at the locked door, terrified. Her trembling legs buckling, she rummaged through her purse for the office key. Her hands were shaking so badly she barely fit it into the lock. She heard his car door shut just as she rushed inside. She wanted to slam the office door in his face.

He ran in behind her, locked the door and left the *closed* sign in place. His eyes met hers. Trembling, she backed away. He took her into his arms. She slapped his face. He picked her up and carried her into Harlan's office. Using his foot, he nudged the door closed and put her down. She got past him and opened the door. He kicked it shut.

"Leave me alone," she sobbed.

He leaned her against the door and devoured her mouth. She felt him getting hard. He ran his hands down her breasts, past her belly. His fingers explored between her thighs, making her vibrate. Suddenly, last night no longer mattered. Her clothes and his were the only things between them. She lifted her skirt, wiggled and tugged. Her panties slid down her to her ankles.

"No." His voice was weak and hoarse.

She stared at him, crushed. The blood drained from her heart. He closed his eyes, leaned against her and tapped his forehead against the door. He was still hard.

Panting, she pressed into him. "Please, Kevin."

"No." His voice was stronger.

He slid down her breasts and belly to his knees and kissed her *there*, making her sizzle.

Fire raging between her legs, Natalie trembled and closed her eyes. His forehead pressed to her stomach, he kissed her navel and pulled her panties up over her legs and hips. He got to his feet and pulled her skirt down. He ran his hands up her sides and stopped without touching her breasts. She felt his arms drop. Burning with love, she opened her brimming eyes.

"What are you *doing?*" Dripping with desire, she wrapped her arms around his neck and drew his mouth to hers. "Please," she exhaled and felt him inhale the word.

He tensed and pulled back. He ran his hands through her hair, bunched it in his fist and bent her head back. He looked into her eyes. "You're driving me crazy." His eyes glistened.

"With Kellie warming your bed last night?" she breathed, aching to feel him inside her. She tried to move her head, but he pulled her hair tighter, exciting her even more.

"Believe it." He kissed her eyes.

"Then why don't you want me?"

"How's your math?" His voice was husky. He let go of her hair. It fell to her shoulders. He rubbed a few strands between his fingers and looked into her eyes.

"What are you *talking* about?"

"Math, you know. Subtraction. Seventeen take away sixteen."

"One?" she said, frowning.

He laughed, backed away and sank into a chair in front of Harlan's desk. He sighed and rubbed his eyes. "I can see math's not your thing. But I bet Maggie got straight A's."

"Kevin—"

"The difference between seventeen and sixteen is twenty— as in years." He laughed, bitterly, she thought.

"But with my consent—"

"There are no buts and no consents. I have sex with you and I'm breaking the law. Period. That's just the way it is, squirt. It's called rape, whether I love you or not." He rubbed his eyes. "Maggie catches me," he looked at her, "and I'm history."

"Sex? Is that why you and Kellie—" she stopped. Suddenly, her eyes got wide. Did he just say he loved her? She sat in the chair next to him and said, "You love me?"

"I never said I loved you. I said, 'whether I love you or not.' Right now I don't know what I feel."

Suddenly, someone yelled from the outer office. "Hello."

"Maggie!" Natalie rushed into Harlan's washroom and finger-combed her hair. She ran her hands over her breasts and hips, smoothing the wrinkles from her tank top and skirt.

"They must be here. Their cars are outside." Lillian said.

Kevin got behind her. "See what I mean?" He kissed the back of her head. "If we did what we wanted—" he shrugged. She nodded and Kevin said, "Get yourself together. I'll cover for you."

Kevin stepped out of Harlan's office and smiled at Lillian and Maggie. "Morning, ladies."

"Morning, Kevin," Lillian smiled, sniffed and said, "Forget to put the coffee up this morning?"

"What are you doing here so early?" Maggie said, frowning. She watched her mother head for the counter, pull two carafes from a cabinet above the sink and turn on the faucet.

Lillian took two packets of coffee from the drawers and brewed one regular and one decaf. "Where's Natalie?" Maggie turned and looked over Kevin's shoulder at Harlan's office door.

"One question at a time, sunshine."

Kevin smiled and walked toward her, stalling for time, Maggie thought.

"When I got here Nat was already in Harlan's office. His desk was piled with a flock of "while you were outs." He'll be back on the seventeenth, so we thought we'd thin the herd."

"Really." Maggie leafed through her messages and mail.

"What's that supposed to mean, princess?" Kevin smiled.

Maggie heard Lillian grab two Placid Properties mugs from the cabinet. "Hmmm." She swept her mail aside and looked at her calendar while he watched. She imagined his pea brain doing cartwheels, second-guessing what she was up to. "The seventeenth is in three days."

"I see math's your forte," Kevin said, smiling.

"It's odd. You're usually so constipated about your morning coffee, so why did Harlan's mail take precedence today?"

"Speaking of coffee." Lillian walked to Maggie's desk with two steaming mugs.

Maggie heard the front door open, saw a man enter, looked at him and frowned.

"Oh my God!" Lillian said, sounding shocked.

Maggie faced her mother and watched both mugs slip from Lillian's hands and hit the floor with a muffled thud.

Coffee beaded on the Berber weave rug. She followed Lillian's gaze to the man and gasped. He obviously didn't remember her, but she'd never forget Tom Connelly's face.

There was something dark about Tom Connelly. Maggie remembered that even back in the day, for a guy in his mid-thirties, Tom had racked up more miles than his rusted out Barracuda.

Wearing snug jeans, scuffed boots and a faded Miami Dolphins T shirt, he had hooked his thumbs on his frayed waistband and had listened to Mom pitch the Welcome house with a bored, make-my-day smirk on his face.

Maggie remembered Jenna, Tom's wife and polar opposite, as being thin and blond with a meek smile and features so pale, Maggie had needed to squint hard to see them. The moment Jenna had looked at the house her lifeless eyes seemed to sparkle. Her reed-like arms had loosened and slipped from her waist. Her stooped shoulders had straightened as if they'd shirked a heavy, invisible burden.

Then there was Tommy, their son. He was tall and dark with Jenna's fine nose and mouth and the most astonishing blue eyes Maggie had ever seen. She remembered thinking those eyes had not come from either of his parents. Tommy clutched his basketball, looking like he'd rather be in a cage full of man-eating tigers than there with them.

"Hello, Lillian," Tom said. "You look as lovely as ever."

Maggie noticed that Tom looked thicker in the jowls and crueler around the eyes and mouth. His hair was graying, but with dimples that rivaled Delaney's, he still could turn some vintage heads. He wore a white T and faded jeans. His black, off-the-rack-shabby sport coat barely hid his paunch. Booze and his age didn't mix well. Why the hell was Tom Connelly here after all these years?

Lillian's face went from healthy pink to apocalyptic white. "Tom Connelly."

She knelt and grabbed the mugs. Her hands shook the way Maggie had never wanted to see them shake again. Watching Tom size her mother up, Maggie felt the impenetrable iceberg she harbored against her mother thaw.

Lillian forced a pale smile. "I'm surprised to see you."

"Well then," he said, "to quote the best president these United States ever had, 'Mission accomplished'."

Natalie walked out of Harlan's office. "Hey, Gran," she said, clearly startling Lillian.

"Damn it, Natalie, don't sneak up on me like that!" Lillian said.

*Sneak up?* Maggie thought, surprised. Mom never yelled at Natalie—a major bone of ongoing-contention between Maggie and her mom. Normally Maggie wouldn't get a ticket for speeding, coming to Nat's defense, but Nat looked devastated and confused. Mom saw it too.

"I'm sorry, Nat." Lillian's lip trembled, breaking Maggie's heart. She looked like a fawn caught in a Mack Truck's headlights with Tom Connelly behind the wheel. "I didn't sleep well last night. I shouldn't take it out on you."

"It's okay, Gran," Natalie's voice cracked.

Maggie cleared her throat. "Tom." He frowned. She held out her hand. "I don't know if you remember me. I'm Maggie Duran."

"Of course." His frown turned into a cold smile. He took her hand. "Lillian's beautiful daughter and Tommy's friend."

She withdrew her hand. "Let me introduce you. The beautiful young lady you see is Natalie, my niece." Tom nodded. Natalie smiled, hesitantly. Maggie pointed at Kevin. "And this young man is Kevin Delaney, another realtor. Kevin, Tom Connelly."

Kevin and Tom nodded. Kevin looked as astonished as Natalie. The Connelly name still held dubious distinction.

"Can I ask what you're doing here?" Might as well get to the point. She could feel the suspense and tension running through all of them.

"I'm here to see Harlan."

"I'm afraid that's not possible." If Harlan knew Tom was in town, he would swear Tom was here to scare Morgan out of the house. Knowing Morgan, however, she doubted he'd be able to do it. "Harlan's out of town. Perhaps I can help you."

"I'm here about the house," he said.

Maggie glanced at her mother, who looked like she was wound tighter than a weed whacker and said, "It's been sold."

"Well, in that case," he frowned, "you've got a problem."

We'll see about that, she thought, but said, "You lost me."

"Legally that house is mine, and I can prove it."

"Oh?" He really was crazier than she remembered. "How?"

Kevin and Nat traded looks. Lillian stared, tight-lipped.

"Don't worry about that. Who bought it?"

"A woman from downstate. Morgan Matthias." Maggie could've kicked herself for slipping. The sale was public knowledge. Tom would find out sooner or later—unless he already knew and was lying.

"Matthias?" he said, frowning as if something didn't fit, she thought. "I just came from the house. No one's home."

"I saw her yesterday," Nat said. "She drove past, looked like she was heading out of town." Tom stared at Natalie. Maggie glared, Natalie flinched. "I waved," Natalie hesitated, but—"

"Was her husband with her?" Maggie asked.

"No. Maybe he went back to Australia."

"I don't think so," Maggie said. She shot Nat a guarded look, praying Chuck's potential whereabouts got by Tom. Natalie looked scared. Maggie looked Tom in the eye.

"Morgan called me last night and told me Chuck was at the house with her," Maggie said. "Natalie might be right. Morgan could be out of town. Her mother's downstate in a nursing home."

"In that case, I'll try her later on," Tom said.

"How could you want that house?" Maggie said. "Your son died there."

"I'd already have it, if it wasn't for a certain thieving realtor." He looked at Harlan's office. "When will he be back?"

"A week. We're not sure exactly," Maggie lied. "Tom?"

"Yeah?"

"I'm curious," Maggie said. "Where's Jenna?"

"Fuck knows. Probably shacking up with the prick she left me for." He grabbed the doorknob. "I'll be back."

Lillian sank into Hutch's chair.

Natalie looked worried. "I said something wrong, didn't I?"

"Actually, you may have helped buy some time," Maggie said.

Kevin looked at Maggie and said, "He has no claim. Harlan owned that house legally. Didn't he?"

"Yes. And now Morgan does," Maggie said. Kevin followed Maggie to Hutch's desk.

Nat hugged Lillian. "Are you okay, Gran?"

Nat sounded scared. She wasn't the only one, Maggie thought.

Lillian patted Nat's hand. "I'll be fine, sweetheart." She looked at Maggie. "Harlan almost died. I feel that we've been given another chance. I don't want to lose—" Her eyes welled.

Maggie hugged Lillian, let her go and then smiled at the pleased look on her face. "You're not going to lose anything," she said, knowing more about second chances than Mom realized. She would tell Mom about Steve. Soon. "Harlan's tougher than ten Tom Connellys."

"That Connelly guy is big trouble." Kevin frowned. "What if we use the time Nat bought us and leave town for the day?"

"What?" Maggie shook her head. "What is this? *High Noon*?"

"Hutch won't be back until tomorrow. If you're right and Morgan *is* visiting her mother, then she's safe from that wacko."

"Safe?" Lillian shivered. "I don't like the sound of that."

"If we close up and head for Plattsburgh, we can plan our next move without worrying about Tom showing up again," he said.

"What if Morgan gets back while we're gone?" Lillian said.

"Her husband's with her, I hope," Maggie said. She stared at Kevin. Was she dreaming or was he becoming more of a team player than her arch-competitor? She must be getting old, but it felt good to have him on her side.

"Kevin?" Maggie smiled. "Thanks." He winked and smiled half-heartedly. He seemed distracted. Maggie wondered why.

"Okay. One more thing," Kevin said. "Nat, you ride with your grandmother."

"What? Why?"

Maggie smiled. Nat almost stamped her foot like she was two.

"Please, baby," he said.

*Baby?* Maggie raised her eyebrows.

"Do what I say, Nat," he kissed her on the forehead.

"Maggie, you ride with me. I've got something important I need to tell you."

# Chapter 48

**Maggie**

Kevin pulled his red Acura into the Physicians Hospital Heart Center parking lot. Lillian pulled her white Outback into the neighboring space. Natalie sat in Lillian's passenger seat.

Maggie jumped out of Kevin's car and slammed the door. She crossed the parking lot in long diagonal strides, swinging her hips harder than she swung her purse. Oblivious of cars pulling in, she moved between them carelessly. Drivers shook their fists, swore and blew their horns. Kevin jumped out and ran after her. He caught her by the arm and turned her around.

"I said I was sorry."

"Yeah? Well sorry doesn't cut it." She jerked her arm free and started to walk away, changed her mind and faced him. "You son of a bitch!" she screamed, startling two young women in shorts and tank tops.

The women's faces registering shock, they veered wide, giving Maggie and Kevin lots of room. Looking over Kevin's shoulder Maggie saw Lillian running after Natalie, who was heading toward them.

"How dare you tell Harlan about Steve and me!"

Kevin tensed his jaw. Lillian got to his side on Natalie's heels. Their faces frozen in disbelief, Natalie and Lillian stared at Maggie. She glanced at them, and then glared at Kevin.

"Forget it, Delaney. How could I be dumb enough to think you'd really changed? For a buck I'd choke the shit out of you."

A pudgy, elderly couple in Bermuda shorts and white Martha's Vineyard T shirts walked by. The woman stopped. The man, oblivious, kept walking. Realizing he was alone, he scowled, doubled back, tugged on the woman's arm and nudged her along.

"I *have* changed. I didn't have to tell you anything. Harlan never would've ratted me out, and you would never have known."

The thought gave her pause, but she shook it off and walked. Before she was out of reach, Kevin grabbed her arm.

"I told you the truth because I wanted to," he said.

Her eyes, two green flames, bore into his. "You don't do anything unless something's in it for you. You've had your eye on the king's throne since you came on board."

"That may have been true in the beginning, Maggie," Natalie said, staring at Maggie accusingly. "But Kevin *has* changed."

Maggie flexed her fingers. She felt like twisting Nat's hair around her fists and wiping up the parking lot with her.

"*He told me everything,* you little Benedict Arnold."

Natalie frowned, clearly confused and Maggie laughed.

"Do you even know who Benedict Arnold was?" Natalie stared blankly. "Figures." She looked at Kevin. "How can a stud-muffin like you want a girl who's too dumb to be insulted?"

Natalie's face flushed and she burst into tears.

"Stop it right now!" Lillian hugged Natalie to her. "I won't let you speak to this child that way."

"Child? You have no idea what he and this little—"

"Don't act like your father, Maggie. It doesn't become you. Harlan has strong traits. Some of which aren't very nice. When I see them in you it frightens me."

Shock hermetically sealing her feet to her Prada sandals and her sandals to the blacktop, Maggie glared at her mother.

Natalie sniffled and wiped her tears. "Maggie's father?"

"Go on, Mom. Tell her," Maggie jutted her chin defiantly.

Lillian took a deep breath. "Harlan is Maggie's father."

Natalie stared at Maggie. "Why didn't anyone tell me?"

"Because no one knew. Not Maggie. Not Harlan." Lillian said. "The night Harlan had his heart attack Maggie saw the birthmark on his chest. She has the same birthmark in the same place." Tears pooled in her eyes. "Harlan doesn't know, yet."

Natalie looked at Kevin. "Did you know about this?" Kevin nodded and she said, "Why didn't you tell me?"

"Why? Hmm. Let's see." Maggie folded her arms across her chest. "Could it be because he's using you to get intel on me?"

"I thought it would be better if you heard it from Maggie or Lillian," Kevin said calmly.

Maggie smirked and shook her head. "Besides, I knew Maggie would go radioactive if I did."

"Now we're knee deep in the nitty-gritty."

"Look, I don't know what I can say to—" Kevin's voice trailed off.

His face looked pinched with worry.

*I didn't have to tell you anything. Harlan never would've ratted me out and you'd be none the wiser.*

Kevin's words echoing through her mind, Maggie frowned. Her arms fell to her sides.

"Actually, something you said before makes a teeny bit of sense, Delaney." She watched the tension around Kevin's mouth ease. "You're right." She put her hands on her hips, blew out a relenting breath. "Harlan would've kept the truth secret until he could use it against me, but you told me anyway. If, as they say, forewarned is forearmed, then I owe you."

Coming clean like he had just now must mean that his feelings for Natalie ran deeper than she'd realized. "And as much as I hate to admit it your instincts are good. You were right about us getting out of Placid today."

"Thanks." Kevin smiled.

"All right, listen up, the two of you," Maggie said, "I'm still mad as hell at both of you, but we'll work that out later. Right now we've got to decide on a few things before we face Harlan." She had their attention.

"Yeah," Kevin said, "like whether to tell him about Tom Connelly and a lawsuit Connelly may think he has."

"Right. Being powerless in that situation may be more stressful to Harlan than waging all-out war," Maggie said. She looked at Kevin. "What does Connelly have that makes him think he can boogie on in and snatch that house?"

"Whatever it is," Lillian answered, "please keep it from Harlan. At least until he's out of the hospital."

"Fine by me," Kevin said and Natalie nodded.

"Listen, you guys go see Harlan. I need to talk to Mom."

Kevin took Nat's hand and walked her toward the building.

"Mom," Maggie's eyes glistened, "that business about not telling me about my father—"

Lillian's eyes shimmered with tears. Maggie put her arm around Lillian's shoulders.

"When Tom Connelly walked through the office door and I saw the terror in your eyes—the thought of him harming you," Maggie's tears rolled down her cheeks. "God, Mom. I'm so sorry for not even trying to understand how horrific this Harlan-Welcome-Connelly stuff must've been on you all these years."

"The important thing is," Lillian wiped her cheeks with the back of her hand, "it's out in the open. I don't have to fear you'll find out and hate me. Maybe now we can move forward."

"I could never hate you, Mom. But, speaking of moving forward, there's something I need to tell you."

Maggie revealed everything but the alleged rape charges against Steve, or that Harlan had threatened to expose Steve if he didn't break up with her.

"That behavior is exactly why I can't marry him. I couldn't live with it then, and I can't live with it now."

Maggie sniffled. "If it hadn't been for Steve—" Lillian put her arm around Maggie and squeezed. They started across the parking lot toward the hospital. "I might get past it, Mom, but I don't know if I can ever forgive Harlan or forget it."

# Chapter 49

## Maggie

Kevin and Natalie stepped out of Harlan's hospital room and stood in the hall. "He wants to see you, Maggie," Natalie said.

"Did he say why?" Maggie's heart skipped a beat.

"No," Kevin said, "but my guess is it's my fault."

"Quit beating yourself up, Delaney. He had to find out about Steve and me sooner or later," she said.

"Wait, Maggie, I'm coming with you," Lillian said.

The *North Country Tribune* draped on his lap and the pillows puffed up behind his back, Harlan heard them enter and looked up.

"Lillian," Harlan smiled and held out his arms. Lillian complied hesitantly. His smile fading, he kissed her cheek.

"You're looking well," she said, coolly.

He frowned. Maggie knew the look. He was like a secret weapon, sensing trouble by the slightest change in room temperature.

"I'm sure I'll feel that way as soon as I can get the hell out of this place and get back to work." He patted her arm, appearing to dismiss his suspicion, but Maggie knew better.

"Maggie." He nodded, acknowledging her. His eyes twinkled.

"Harlan." Keeping her face neutral, she sat in a chair at the foot of his bed, waiting for him to drop the Steve bomb.

"Lillian, my dear," he pushed the control button and lifted his bed to a higher sitting position. "Could you give me a few moments alone with Maggie? It's business, very boring."

"What you say to my daughter you can say in front of me."

Harlan narrowed his eyes. He relaxed his expression and smiled. "Well, I suppose it can wait until we get home."

"The hell it can!" Steve said, walking through the door. He looked exhausted. His eyes burned with anger. Kevin and Natalie were right behind him.

Maggie jumped up. "What are you doing here?" She looked at Harlan.

Steve glared at Harlan. "Tell them what you did."

"What the hell *are* you doing here, Rivers?" Harlan said.

"You know goddamn well." Steve clenched his fists.

"I think you've been sniffing printer's ink again." Harlan smoothed out his sheet and blanket. "*I'm* not the one who *did* anything," he said, smiling at Steve.

"What's going on, Steve?" Maggie said.

Steve's face was ghost-white. "Your little plot to destroy me backfired. After you called Evan and told him about the charges and transcript he called me." Steve's eyes bore into Harlan's." I told him the *whole* story, and I'm still standing."

"What charges? What transcript?" Lillian stared at him.

Anger simmered in Maggie's eyes. "How could you?"

"How could I? You traitorous slut!" Harlan glared at Maggie.

Lillian gasped and flinched as if Harlan had smacked *her*. Stone-faced, Steve clenched his jaws until his facial muscles twitched. Eyes wide, Kevin put his arm around Natalie.

Harlan pressed his palms down hard on either side, practically lifting himself off the mattress.

"Every five years his anniversary stories buried us in rumors and speculation that were inadmissible everywhere except the goddamned North Country Tribune." The vein in Harlan's temple swelled. He looked at Maggie and spat words out like semi-automatic rounds. "Your reprobate lover gleefully exploited you for information and then profited at your mother's and my expense!" Harlan eyes narrowed. "After all I've done for you—"

"What have you done for me besides use me to make yourself rich?" Maggie said. "I loved Steve and he loved me. I was in agony for years because of your lies and omissions. You had the power to help but you used it to hurt me instead."

"What charges, Harlan?" Lillian said. "What's this about?"

"Go on, Harlan. Tell her." Maggie clenched her fist. "Tell her, damn you!" She pounded his bed. Harlan locked her in his frozen gaze. "That's right. That's your style. Don't say a word. You'd better change. After you stonewalled Morgan Matthias you had a heart attack."

"Harlan, you tell me what she's talking about right now."

Harlan never averted his eyes, but the force of his anger slammed into Maggie. Steeling herself, Maggie looked at her mother and made Harlan's confession for him. "Years ago in college a girl accused Steve and some of his fraternity brothers of rape. They went to trial. Thank

God the courts had recognized DNA testing, and they were acquitted. They were young and their records were sealed."

A tear rolled down her cheek.

"Harlan got hold of the records and threatened to expose Steve." She bit her lip, sniffled and wiped the tear away. "He swore Steve would never work anywhere in the northeast again if he didn't break up with me."

Lillian trembled. Her eyes sizzled. Harlan's eyes softened. He looked at Lillian, nervously.

"I watched you disintegrate after the Connelly kid died." His eyes watered. "You were a fragile, broken doll when I drove you to High Peaks." He grabbed and squeezed her hand. "I watched you inch your way back to mental health," he glared at Steve, "until he dredged up the filth and knocked you back down."

Lillian pulled her hand away. "Bullshit!" Harlan flinched. "You never did it for me. You did it for yourself!"

"I did it for all of us, Lilly. Maggie was Rivers' direct pipeline to new information about the house. Their affair posed a clear and present danger to—"

"To your little empire," Lillian said.

"To the main means of all our support." Harlan countered.

"You knew my reasons for informing Steve," Maggie said.

Harlan laughed derisively. "I remember them well. Anything to generate activity. Bad PR is better than no PR. You were so young and naïve, you actually believed his bullshit about prospective buyers flocking to the scene because of his stories. The people who lived in that Long Island house after the owners sold it claimed it wasn't haunted at all," Harlan said. "Was that his bullshit, or yours?"

"It was in their book."

"Look at him." Harlan turned his mouth down in disgust. "You can't tell me you weren't afraid of what his stories might do to your mother, because after a while you came to your senses and begged him to stop. Don't you remember?"

"Yes." Maggie whispered, remembering the gamble she took. As always Harlan had hit a nerve and her doubts about Steve bubbled up. She fired back. "In retrospect, Steve's stories never hurt Mom like you said they would, did they?"

"I know all about your filthy trysts." Harlan glared, dragging her in another direction. "Is sex what you want, Maggie? You can have sex without betraying me. What about young Delaney here? I've seen the way he looks at you."

"That's enough!" Lillian's mouth turned down in disgust.

Natalie burst into tears and started out of the room. Kevin grabbed her. "Not true," he whispered, "not anymore."

Rage contorted her face. Burning with humiliation, Maggie said, "Do you know who you're talking to?"

"No, please, Maggie," Lillian begged. "Not like this."

Harlan shot Lillian a quizzical look.

"I'm talking to the girl I took under my wing years ago and made her the businesswoman she is today. And what do I get for it?" His face twisted with anger. "Betrayed. Again."

"What are you talking about now?" Maggie said.

"The meeting you arranged between him," he glared at Steve, "and Morgan Matthias."

"Maggie didn't arrange any meeting, Harlan," Steve said. "Jack Bradford did."

Glaring at Kevin, Harlan said, "You're lying, Rivers."

Maggie shook her head. "I rode with Kevin on the way here. He told me everything, Harlan. He saw my car in Steve's parking lot. He followed Steve to work, saw Morgan and drew the wrong conclusion." Harlan's eyes searched hers, his anger held solid.

"Don't be a fool. Can't you see he's still using you?"

Maggie sat on his bed. "Right again, Harlan. I am a fool. I was so happy when Steve told me that Jack had arranged that meeting with Morgan." Her stone-cold eyes bore into his. "I didn't want to be the one to tell Steve what I knew. She unbuttoned her blouse. "Why?" She hooked her finger in the center of her bra, pulled it down and exposed her birthmark.

"Because I didn't want to betray my own father."

*His senses in lockdown, Harlan moves his gaze down the long, bronze column of Maggie's neck. Strawberry red, the size of a dime and shaped like a crescent moon, her birthmark is identical to his grandfather's, his father's, and his! Blood roars in his ears like the falls over Niagara, drowning out sound. The need to process the truth turns his mind into a lockbox where the trapped unspoken question ricochets aimlessly until it turns into a statement.*

*Maggie Duran is his daughter.*

*His elated heart pushes blood through his veins like a brand new, straight-from-the-factory pump. Of course she's his. Isn't her know-how always in sync with his? How many times had she verbalized his thoughts or completed his sentences? Her uncanny knack for real estate isn't uncanny at all. She excels, because like her father, Maggie was born to.*

*He sees her as a child, wrapping her arms around Bob Duran's neck, laughing and kissing his cheek, calling him daddy, telling Duran she loves him.*

*Suddenly, like a pin to a balloon, reality punctures his elation. Now, instead of thousands of memories to warm him in old age, like Dickens' Marley, Harlan Wainright would spend eternity regretting the ruthless manipulations he'd perpetrated on his own flesh and blood.*

He watched her next to Rivers, the other man in her life, so much in love she glowed. He realized he'd been so hell-bent on using her to line his pockets, he'd plundered the only real treasure he'd ever had. A tsunami of anguish for time wasted and opportunity lost ravaged the shores of his heart, drowning him in grief. If only he'd known, he *never* would've—

Harlan leveled a cold, hard glare at Lilly that clearly hit her heart like a bullet. Her face turned chalky white. Watching her slump into a chair at the edge of his bed, he cursed the pain in her eyes for turning his resolute anger to JELL-O.

"I understand that telling the truth while she was a child and Duran was still alive would've confused her," Harlan choked out the words, "but I need to know, Lilly, if it wasn't for my heart attack would you ever have told me the truth?"

Lillian buried her face in her hands and sobbed. After everything she'd done, why did he still hate to see her cry? Natalie moved away from Kevin, bypassed Maggie and wrapped her arm around Lillian's shoulder and murmured consoling sounds. Crushed, Harlan laid his head on the pillow and closed his eyes.

"Oh no you don't, Daddy dearest." Startled, he opened his eyes. "You're not getting away with it that easy." Maggie said, narrowing her eyes. "You owe me some answers."

Christ, Harlan thought, he was tired.

"I'm curious," Steve said, "why use the alleged rape to blackmail me when you could've run me out for good?"

Harlan grinned mirthlessly. "Come on, Rivers. What the hell kind of an investigative reporter are you anyway?"

"I have my theories," Steve smiled coldly, "but I'd rather hear it from you."

"That makes two of us," Maggie said.

"I could've kicked myself for not investigating you sooner. Then I realized the delay had worked to my advantage for two reasons. One, if I got you fired prematurely, Burke would've replaced you with another ambitious little bastard, because like it or not, those anniversary stories of yours were a goldmine."

"And," Steve smiled, tightening his arm around Maggie, "Maggie would've sided with me," he said, looking gratified.

"Something like that." *You insolent little prick!*

"And the second reason?" Maggie said.

"Listen here, young lady." Harlan straightened up. "If you weren't Lilly's daughter, I'd have canned you the minute you took up with that arrogant son of a bitch."

"Nice try, Harlan, but I can see right through your transparent red herring. You didn't fire me because I'm the best realtor you'll ever have. Now, give me the second reason."

Touche, Harlan thought, proud of his daughter. A faint smile played at his lips. "I knew I couldn't stop the press even before I talked to Burke, but I could do the next best thing."

"Which was?" Her eyes sparked.

"Get Rivers out of your life for good."

"So that's why you chipped away, creating doubt in my mind about Steve, then dared me to ask him to stop the stories."

"I knew Rivers would choose his career over you. He'd be a fool not to, but just in case, I had an insurance policy."

The rage in her eyes ignited. "The rape charges."

Harlan hadn't seen her so angry since the day he'd humiliated her in front of Hutch and Delaney. Desperate to avoid pushing her further away, he looked into her eyes and let her do the talking.

"Those charges were the gift that kept on giving, weren't they, Harlan?" Her eyes were on fire. "You knew if Steve bailed, Whiteface would grow palm trees before I'd give him one shred of new information." Tears rolled down her cheeks. "And you made it your mission to keep it that way," she said, shaking.

A lump of despair in his throat, Harlan said, "You wanted answers, Maggie. You got them."

"Not quite," she said. "There was one loose end."

"The anniversary stories and bad PR," Steve said.

"But you probably figured five years between anniversary stories is a long time and a lot could change," Maggie said.

Harlan nodded. "I did and they have. But now that I've found the right buyer," Harlan smirked at Steve, "nothing you write or your rag prints will ever scare Morgan Matthias away."

Lillian raised her eyes. "I wouldn't be too sure about Morgan not going away, Harlan," she said, sniffling.

"What do you mean?" he said, wondering how in God's name he could still love her.

"Tom Connelly paid us a visit at the office this morning," Lillian said, alarming him.

Back on familiar turf Harlan was all business and clearly in charge. "After all these years? What the hell did he want?"

"He said you sold the house illegally," Maggie said.

"That's absurd," Harlan said. "Looks like the booze has pickled what's left of that bastard's brain."

"It was Kevin's idea to close up shop and get out of Dodge, Uncle Harlan," Natalie said, smiling.

"Delaney." Harlan lifted his blanket and sheet and swung his legs over the side of the bed. He pressed the call button. "Get me my shoes, trousers and shirt. They're in the closet."

"What are you doing?" Lillian asked, wringing her hands. "You had open heart surgery. You can't just leave the hospital."

"The hell I can't, Lilly. Damn it, Delaney," he shouted. "Did you hear what I said?"

Harlan stood up. The room started spinning. His legs buckled. Steve and Maggie caught him before he sank to the floor and helped him into bed.

"Harlan, please don't do this. If anything happened to you," Lillian looked at Maggie, "before I had a chance to explain—"

"Mom's right, Harlan," Maggie said, tucking him in like a helpless kindergartner.

He curled his fingers around her wrist. "I may be ruthless, but Connelly's a ruthless sociopath. I know how he thinks. Without me there to—" He started to lift the covers again.

"No!" Maggie said, forcefully. "What good will you do PPI or us if you leave the hospital prematurely and suffer a setback," she paused, "or worse?"

Harlan fell back against the pillow and looked into her eyes. "Connelly's always been a crazy, ginned-up fuck," he said, panting. "But now that he smells money, he'll stop at nothing to get it. What if he hurts you, your mother, or Morgan Matthias?"

Suddenly, Lillian was at his side, smiling.

Surprised, Harlan frowned. "Did I say something funny?"

"On the contrary. This is the first time I've ever seen you put us before the business and mean it," she said, smoothing his covers around him. "I never thought being a father would agree with you, but I'm beginning to think I was wrong, Harlan."

Harlan saw Maggie nodding. His eyes shimmering, he patted Lillian's hand then cleared his throat. "All right, children," he said, with authority, "we've got a problem."

"Tom Connelly," Lillian said.

Maybe not," Maggie said and Harlan's eyes widened. "Well, what I mean is maybe not right away. Morgan's husband's in town and he looks like he could give Connelly something to worry about.

"In the meantime, *Dad*," Maggie fluffed Harlan's pillow up, "there've been a few extraordinary developments in the Welcome story that ought to make this anniversary installment light up like the fourth of July. And because they came from Steve's meeting with Morgan, Steve should be the one to tell you."

# Chapter 50

**Tom Connelly**

Tom had driven his black Dodge Caravan to Midlakes Road twice getting more agitated each time he passed the Bradford House. Bradford had been the mother of all assholes for shit-canning him years ago. Drunk or sober Tom was the best, goddamned chef Bradford ever had. That Morgan woman still wasn't home and that pissed him off too. If that sexy little witch Natalie was right and Morgan's husband was in Australia, that'd work for him, big time. Convincing Morgan to see things his way would be easier without her pain-in-the-ass husband screwing things over.

Tom stopped at Placid Properties. The office was dark. He banged on the door and tried the knob. Shit! Were those bastards realtors or bankers? He turned and spotted the Lake Placid Liquor Store across the street, thinking what the hell. He went in and grabbed a fifth of Jack Daniels off the shelf. His plastic maxed, he peeled a fifty from his dwindling roll, scooped up the change and then drove to The Budapest Inn a few miles south of town, imagining how sweet the cash from selling *his* house would smell in the palm of his hand.

His was a run-of-the-mill-off-white room with the usual motel junk. He looked at the TV *bolted* to the dresser, a winter scene *bolted* to the wall, a refrigerator *bolted* to the floor and set his bottle of Jack on the bathroom counter, shaking his head and wondering what the world was coming to. After filling a white plastic bucket at the ice machine, he plunked the bucket down on the bathroom counter, grabbed a glass and scooped up ice. He ran the back of his hand across his mouth, opened the bottle and licked his lips. He drowned the ice in bourbon and held up his glass.

"Well, Jack, here we are in Lake Placid again." He drained the glass. It burned going down. He grabbed the bottle and glass, walked out of the bathroom and cranked the A/C.

"What's that, Jack?" Tom cocked his ear. "Don't mind if I do." He poured the fragrant sour mash over ice, stuck the bottle on his nightstand, kicked off his shoes and sat on the bed.

"Lots of water under the bridge since you and I were here last, Jack. To old times, buddy." He raised his glass and toasted the bottle. "Bottom's up." He drained the glass, poured himself another and drank half. It no longer burned. He was on his way.

Tom pictured the Victorian on Midlakes Road and remembered the last time he'd thought he was on his way. Things had been going great. Then suddenly, he lost his job, his kid, and his wife. It wasn't his fault— completely. If Jack, the-arch-prick Bradford, had given him one more chance things would be different today.

Tom drained his glass and then lay on the bed and folded his arms behind his head. Standing on the back patio, looking into the kitchen on Midlakes Road earlier today reminded him of the last time he'd peeked in that kitchen window twenty-five years ago on the night his son Tommy died. Tom grabbed the bottle of Jack off the nightstand next to his bed and put it to his lips. That house owed him. It was his no matter who the fuck owned it. The bottle slipped from his hand. While his bottle of sour mash hemorrhaged on the hotel rug, Tom fell asleep.

# Chapter 51

## Morgan

With Steve's blessing, Morgan had called the others and asked if they could meet for brunch at the Bradford House. She was anxious to share their discovery.

She watched the first real friends besides Chuck she'd ever had heap their plates from a buffet laden with eggs and bacon, sausage, crepes, waffles and pancakes, yogurts and fruit and pastries. Morgan smiled. Jack had gone all out.

At their table were advance mock-ups of the Welcome-Connelly anniversary edition, complements of Steve Rivers, chronicling events including finding Diamond's remains.

Chuck poured a mimosa for Morgan and one for himself from a crystal pitcher on the table. Morgan raised the delicate crystal glass to her lips. Watching her friends read she was amazed at how her world had been rocked since the first time she'd eaten here.

She glanced at Maggie and Steve, sharing a paper, looking very much in love. But they weren't the only ones. She smiled at Kevin and Natalie and squeezed Chuck's hand grateful that her wishing-he-were-here days were gone for good.

Jack, who'd graciously closed The Bradford House to the public for this special occasion, picked up his fork and pierced a wedge of egg and broke the hushed silence.

"For the first time in decades I'm speechless." He looked at Maggie and shook his head. "I can't believe Harlan's your father." He popped the egg into his mouth. Everyone laughed.

"If you're speechless," Maggie said, "imagine how I feel."

Everyone laughed harder. Morgan was pleased that Jack spoke without rancor. Perhaps he was letting his bitterness go.

Natalie blotted her lips with a pink linen napkin. "I don't know about you guys," she said, placing the napkin next to her plate, "but I get a feeling this still isn't over."

"Nat's right," Maggie said, sipping her coffee.

Morgan shivered and Chuck said, "Are you all right, love?"

Morgan nodded. "What makes you guys say that?"

Maggie put her cup down. "Tom Connelly showed up yesterday asking about your house."

Jack paled. "He probably wants to stake some bogus claim. And it's my fault."

"No, it's my fault," Maggie said. Jack looked surprised. "If I hadn't given him Morgan's name at the office that day—"

"No, my dear." Jack interrupted gently. "If I hadn't let Harlan blackmail me into paying that bastard enough to afford that house all those years ago—"

"Harlan blackmailed you, too?" Lillian stiffened.

"You didn't know?" Lillian shook her head. Jack put his fork down and shrugged, looking embarrassed. "Sorry."

"Something told me Harlan was behind that," Lillian said. "I'm the one who's sorry for not checking into it."

Jack turned to Chuck and Morgan. "Be warned. Tom Connelly's a very bad man, a wild card. He's an abrasive, abusive, animal. And those are just the A's. If he shows up and you need help—"

"Count me in," Kevin said.

"Thanks. I'll keep that in mind, mates." Chuck leaned back and draped his arm on the back of Morgan's chair.

"Morgan," Lillian said, "the way you courageously dove into that mystery speaks volumes. Poor Diamond, so brutally murdered. But who killed her and what did it have to do with the house?"

"Million dollar questions," Morgan said, staring blankly. "I don't know how we would ever find out."

"And, Steve, the way you wove geography, legends and Jinxy," everyone chuckled, "into the story was absolute magic."

Steve took Lillian's hand gently in his. "You have no idea how much that means coming from you, Lillian. Thank you."

"Good job, mate!" Chuck raised his coffee cup and the others raised their cups saying, "Job well done."

"Thanks, everyone," Steve said.

Looking wistful, Lillian smiled and patted Maggie's hand, prompting her to ask, "Is something wrong, Mom?"

"I'm mad as the dickens at Harlan all over again for this blackmailing business, but I still wish he was here."

"He'll be out of the hospital in a few days," Maggie said. "If you like we can stop by the office, grab Hutch and run up to Plattsburgh." She smiled at Natalie and Kevin. "All of us."

"The truth is out, and Morgan's here to stay. That should wipe away any bad blood between Steve and Harlan," Kevin said.

"One would think, dear." Lillian said.

Jack signaled the waitress for more coffee.

"None for me, mate," Chuck said. "I'm ready to explode."

"The Bradford House has outdone itself," Morgan smiled at Jack.

Chuck and Morgan walked out the front door into the fresh air and sunshine. The crowd thinned, promising to keep in touch. Morgan and Chuck headed for Midlakes Road.

"I'd say that went smashingly well."

"I guess." Morgan smiled listlessly and continued walking.

"Ah," Chuck said, "the letdown."

She stopped walking and frowned. Chuck took her hand in his, squeezed it gently and coaxed her up the hill.

"Your extraordinary adventure is over. After living on adrenaline for weeks, feeling let down is natural."

"That's not it," she sighed, walking down the driveway.

"What then?" Chuck said, following her up the porch steps.

She opened her purse and grabbed her key. "Besides not knowing who killed Diamond and why" she said, "how do my mother, the pendant and I fit into this? And, why did Tommy Connelly freeze to death like the Welcomes? That makes no sense at all."

Suddenly, a car squealed into the driveway. Popping gravel under its tires, it skidded to a stop behind Chuck's Impala.

He looked at the driveway. "Bloody Christ!" His face ghost-white, Chuck turned to Morgan. "Go inside, love." She started to protest. Perspiration beaded above his lip. "Please. I'll explain later." He left the porch and hurried across the lawn.

Morgan watched the car door open. A guy, a little younger than Kevin Delaney, stepped out of the brand new emerald green Camry. He looked familiar, but before Morgan could place him, Chuck had reached the car and blocked her view.

Morgan descended the porch steps and walked toward the driveway. Chuck's legs buckled. The young man must've brought bad news. Holding Chuck steady, the young man looked up.

*And Morgan saw Chuck ... the way he'd looked thirty years ago!* If she didn't know better she'd swear—

*The young man was Chuck's son.*

Her legs turned to rubber. Her hands got cold and clammy. She rubbed her palms across the front of her slacks. Something shattered behind her eyes, and Chuck and his son shimmered like a mirage on some parallel horizon in some other time that was meant to happen but never did. Without warning, the world spun. Round and round the vortex went, taking Chuck and his son with it.

"Not again. Oh God. I can't do this again," she screamed.

Startled, Chuck and his son rushed toward her and caught her before she sank to the ground. "My darling, I'm so sorry."

"Dad," CJ said, "we have to talk."

*Dad?* Morgan struggled to get free. Chuck touched her face. She recoiled.

"Please. I need to explain," he said.

Lucy's voice filled her head, drowning him out.

*God damn you! Stop with this pretend marriage to Chuck! I've listened to your insane fantasy for years and I'm sick of it.*

Morgan clamped her hands over her ears. She shut her eyes tight and sobbed hysterically. But the truth was inside her. Devastated, she screamed, "Pretend? Is that what I've done all these years?"

Chuck looked frantic. "It's not that simple."

Morgan suddenly lowered her hands and stared blankly. "Oh my God," she flinched as if slapped. "I remember now." Her face was stone, her voice eerily monotone. "You went back to Australia and got Barbara pregnant."

Chuck darted a nervous glance at his son whose eyes were swimming in tears.

"You said you'd straighten things out," her voice robotic, her eyes blank, she continued. "You said you loved me and that when you came back we'd get married. You bought me another semester and begged me to stay at the university. You begged me not to go home to Mother. I stayed in the dorm and waited. I wrote and waited. Your letters never came. I disintegrated until I couldn't function. They found me and sent me home to Mother."

Chuck's chin quivered. "Morgan, please." He took her hand.

"No! Let me finish." She pulled away. "You owe me that much."

Clearly grief-stricken, Chuck nodded.

"Awake I was fragile and broken. Asleep I was whole and strong. I dreamed about us. I wished my dream was my life and my life was the dream. You lived in my heart. I needed you in my life. One day I woke up and you were lying beside me."

"I'll make it right. I can get you the help you need."

"I should be grateful," she said, devoid of emotion. "Reality ties up the loose ends I couldn't. Like why we never had children. Why Mother insisted I was crazy, and why she became apoplectic whenever I said your name. My God," she whispered, "and why you were *never around whenever I desperately needed you.*"

"Morgan, it's so much more complex than that."

"That's where you're wrong, Chuck. It's simple, really. As a psychiatrist you of all people should know that weak, pathetic, Morgan Quick could never have survived her abusive mother after losing you. But Morgan Matthias could."

"Please, Dad, we need to talk," CJ said.

"You begged me to stay at the University because you knew Mother would intercept your letters," Morgan said, ignoring CJ.

"Lucy admitted pinching them," Chuck said.

"What? When?" Stunned, Morgan looked at Chuck.

"I tracked her down in Port St. John. That's how I knew you'd bought a house in Lake Placid."

"You bastard!" she screamed and Chuck flinched. "Now you tracked her and me down?" Her eyes flamed with rage. "You should have done it thirty years ago!"

"I tried. I swear," Chuck sobbed openly. "I called and called. Lucy hung up."

"She hung up and you gave up? Without a fight? You could've flown back, sailed back, swum back." Morgan closed her eyes.

"Bloody Christ. I shouted down family, friends, the whole world until my throat was bloody raw. I have no excuse except that I was CJ's age, half a world away and outnumbered. The pressure crushed me." He ran his hand across a drenched cheek. "I would do everything and anything I could to take it all back."

For the first time in decades Morgan saw the whole truth.

*Chuck knew Mother would intercept his letters.*

She narrowed her eyes. *Mother did this.* Morgan's head pounded. Her legs gave way and she sank to the ground.

Fingers encircled her arms, standing her up. Hands brushed dirt and grass from her pants and calves. Strong, muscled arms slipped under hers, braced her and lifted her up.

She felt grassy ground skim under her shoes. She watched the porch slide under her feet. The living room glided past her. Chuck and CJ buoyed her up the steps and down the hall to her bedroom as if she weighed nothing, while the truth raced through her, picking up steam, picking up speed faster and louder.

*Mother did this, motherdidthismotherdidthis.*

Until it exploded.

Morgan lay in her bed as still as death with her eyes closed, petrified her egg-shell-thin world would crack if she moved. Chuck and CJ stood in the hall outside her door. Their words buzzed into her room like a swarm of agitated bees.

She heard Chuck say, "I can't abandon Morgan. It's my fault the last thirty years of her life were a lie!" She listened to CJ plead his case. He seemed kind and understanding, which puzzled and surprised her.

"My God. My poor Liz." Chuck's voice cracked. "My poor little girl! And what about Phillip?"

*Liz and Phillip?*

Morgan opened her eyes to accommodate her tears. The lump in her throat wouldn't let her swallow. No wonder CJ measured his words. Whatever he thought of her, for his sister's and brother's sakes, he could not afford to alienate his father. Morgan heard Chuck sniffle and clear his throat. He stood outside her door.

"She must be hospitalized." Chuck sounded desperate. "She needs a protocol of anti-psychotic drugs to absorb the shock. She needs deep therapy to unravel the psychological hell her mother and I put her in."

Eerily calm, Morgan knew Chuck was right, because if Mother had left them alone thirty years ago, Chuck and she would've figured out what to do about Barbara, together.

Mother had made a decision that was Chuck's and hers to make. Mother had stolen decades of their lives, her lip quivered. She stole the children and grandchildren they should've had! She robbed them of thirty Christmases, Easters and birthdays. Morgan glanced at the doorway through a web of wet lashes. Chuck walked into the room. CJ was behind him. His likeness to Chuck still took her breath away.

"Dad."

The word broke something inside her. Suddenly decades of grief wrung her heart and squeezed tears from her eyes.

"You've got to come with me. Liz needs you. We all do. We can get someone to look after her, until—" His voice cracked.

Chuck's eyes were closed. He held CJ in his arms. CJ's shoulders shook. Morgan saw Chuck nod against his son's head and realized Chuck had made up his mind. Missing her own father for years after he'd died, Morgan understood more than anyone in all this craziness, how desperately Chuck's daughter needed him.

Chuck sat on her bed. His thigh pressed against her, warm, strong and familiar. He cupped her face in both hands and looked into her eyes.

"I never wanted you or my kids to learn the truth like this. I swear before God and my son, I've never stopped loving you. You've got to believe me." He kissed her face. His tears fell like hot rain against her cheeks. "My grandson, Liz's baby, died." Morgan drew in a sharp breath and Chuck said, "Liz needs me." Chuck sighed and took her hands. "Liz, Phillip and CJ lost their mother the end of May."

Their tears mingled. How had her life gone from *terra firma* to a Calcutta mudslide in fifteen minutes? Or had she been unwittingly living on a mudslide for thirty years? Pain ripped through her heart. Her flesh turning cold and clammy, Morgan took rapid, shallow breaths. Suddenly, she felt Mother's venomous tentacles sinking into her heart.

"Morgan?" Chuck sounded alarmed. "Oh my poor darling."

He pulled her shivering body against him, and one-by-one Mother's tentacles loosened. Pain subsided. Her heart slowed. Morgan closed her eyes, breathed him in and knew that despite his betrayal, her mother's lies and against all odds, they'd found each other again. Morgan also knew above all, she must put aside her anger and confusion immediately in order to survive. Right now she had to go home. Alone. She had a score to settle, and she needed answers. Morgan opened her eyes.

"CJ's right, Chuck. You've got to go with him and help your daughter." She squeezed his hand. "It's the right thing to do." She kept her eyes clear and her voice calm and steady.

"But I can't leave you like this."

"A girl needs her father. No one understands that better than I. We have the rest of our lives to sort things out."

"You see, Dad?" CJ was all over it. Morgan almost smiled. Looking relieved, he reached out then changed his mind. "Thanks."

Morgan thought he'd say her name, but he didn't. Why should he? She was the other woman. He put his hand on Chuck's shoulder.

"I don't know." Chuck looked skeptical. His gaze never wavered. "I love you, Morgan, and I want to believe you, but I'm a doctor. Miraculous recoveries just don't *happen*. This all feels off."

"Please, Dad. We've got a long way to go."

Chuck closed his eyes and rubbed his temples. "All right," he said, opening his eyes. "I need to go back to Australia to help Liz with—" His words trailed off. His eyes brimmed. He cleared his throat. "And God help me, I owe Liz and Phillip an explanation in person." He took a deep breath. "I'll leave, if and only if you vow to do exactly as I say."

# Chapter 52

**Morgan**
**High Peaks Sanitarium**

Morgan had kept her promise to Chuck. Two agonizing weeks ago she checked into High Peaks Sanitarium for observation. In their first session Dr. Martin Spinelli said that getting well-meant facing the truth and accepting reality. Even though doing just that had landed her here in the first place? Well, Spinelli was right in one way. Facing the truth had set her free.

There was something else Morgan had faced. For as long as she could remember the monster she called mother had never tossed her a crumb of affection. Never smiled or kissed or hugged her. That monster had made it her life's mission to destroy Chuck and Morgan's love. Needing to find out why before Mother turned completely senile, Morgan realized that instead of telling Spinelli the truth *again,* she must tell him what she prayed he wanted to hear.

Today her case was up for review, and she was terrified. What if she screwed up, and Spinelli refused to release her? Morgan knocked and opened the door.

"Good afternoon, Morgan."

Spinelli motioned her through his office door to a brown leather chair in front of his desk, folded his hands on a file marked "Morgan Quick" and smiled.

"Dr. Spinelli." Morgan smiled. She slid into the chair, gazed at his medical books and his degree and license in gilded frames, thinking if she didn't get out of here soon she really would go crazy. To stay calm, she folded her hands in her lap and focused on the good doctor. Again.

He was tall, fit, graying at the temples and evenly tanned. Today his shirt was Dolce and Gabbana. His dark blue slacks, Armani—very high end. Morgan concluded that his patients' mental misery had earned him enough to live in a Mirror Lake mansion, golf at the country club and drive a Cadillac hybrid. Spinelli folded his hands on top of her file and his cuff rose above his wrist, exposing a Rolex. Smirking inwardly, Morgan rested her case.

Unfortunately, her smirk was short-lived. On Spinelli's desk next to her file was a newspaper. It was her advance copy of the Welcome-Connelly anniversary mock-up Steve Rivers had given her at the restaurant. Spinelli picked up the paper.

"Although this makes sensational copy," he said, frowning, "these anniversary stories deviate from Rivers' normally sober, factual style." Spinelli put the mock-up aside, peered down his nose, opened her file and consulted some notes.

"Steve Rivers and several other prominent Lake Placid citizens petitioned on your behalf." He looked up from his notes. "I must say I'm duly impressed, Morgan," he blinked, "but frankly, I'm still uncomfortable with how your original story and Steve Rivers' fantastic account are so closely aligned."

Her thrumming heart sank. Apparently her painstaking efforts to revise her original story had failed. She kept her face blank and listened in silence. For all she knew about loony bins, one wrong word might make her a permanent resident.

"Having said that, I've maintained contact with Dr. Matthias, eminently respected in the field, who conferred with me constantly after leaving for Australia.

"I understand from you and Dr. Matthias that the first devastating blow you suffered created your delusional disorder and the second shattered it."

Despite her anxiety, Morgan kept her cool and nodded, conveying she understood.

"I concur with Dr. Matthias. Despite overwhelming trauma, you've managed to function highly in most areas. While at High Peaks, you've been cooperative and have had a positive attitude, two crucial steps that demonstrate your desire to get well." Spinelli cleared his throat. "You signed in voluntarily and unless I have good cause, I can't keep you here."

Weak with relief, Morgan exhaled a sigh.

"Based on my observations and Dr. Matthias's input, despite his emotional involvement with you, I don't believe you're a danger to yourself or to others."

Eyes glistening, Morgan leaned forward and whispered, "Does that mean I'm free to go?"

"On two conditions," Spinelli said. Morgan held her breath. "Continue your medication. I need to see you in two weeks and monthly thereafter until I see fit to stop the sessions."

"Yes, doctor." Morgan stood, extending her hand. "Thank you, thank you so much, Dr. Spinelli." She smiled brightly.

"Good luck, Morgan," he said, taking her hand. "A nurse will come to your room with a prescription and your paperwork."

Her back to Spinelli, Morgan's smile vanished. She opened the office door. Her eyes cold and flat, she walked down the hall to her room and waited to sign her release form.

Morgan sank into the Prince of Wales sofa and gazed around her living room. She opened her purse, pulled out Spinelli's prescription and tore it to shreds. They landed on an array of pamphlets promoting restaurants in town. Apparently, before her world blew up, Chuck had been planning to take her to dinner. Physically drained and emotionally bankrupt, she closed her eyes and leaned her head back. How in God's name had she believed that Chuck and she had been married for over thirty years?

Suddenly, the full force of the truth slammed through her, drowning her heart in pain and rage. An urge to claw and hit and kill smothered her like a huge wet blanket of sadness and grief. Would she ever be able to crawl out from under? She honestly did not know.

She pictured Mother at Pine Bush Acres, carping about being left in the care of strangers. She pictured Chuck in Australia with sons and a daughter that should've been hers. Anger boiled in her heart like acid in a vat. But, giving Satan *her* due, Morgan agreed with one teeny part of Mother's point of view.

*A mother should be with her daughter.*

Morgan got to her feet and took the stairs down a hall that seemed longer than she remembered. For reasons beyond her grasp, her mother belonged in this house. For reasons she grasped too well, she had a score to settle. She'd head home tomorrow, pack Mother up and bring her back.

She stood in the bathroom and looked in the mirror. Her cheeks were gaunt, her color sallow, her eyes dark with rage. She should be grateful. What if her world had cracked while Chuck had been in Australia still married to Barbara?

Morgan ran the tap, doused her cheeks and reached for a towel. Her head throbbed. She needed sleep. She spread the towel on the rack, hit the light switch and headed across the hall.

# Chapter 53

## Morgan

Morgan pulled into Pine Bush Acres, shaking violently at the realization of what her mother had done to her. She parked the Buick in an empty slot near the main entrance, turned off the motor and looked in her rearview mirror. Her eyes were red-rimmed and bloodshot. Her stomach churned with nausea. Her chin pressed to the steering wheel, she closed her eyes.

Sunlight blared through the windshield against her face. The cabin temperature approached hellfire. She sat up, opened her eyes and ran a hand through her damp hair. She remembered Diamond's remains in her cold, dank grave under her house. Sweat rolled down her forehead. She grabbed her purse from the passenger's seat and rifled through for a tissue. She got that Diamond haunted her house, but what did Diamond have to do with Tommy, her mother or her? And how had Mother gotten Diamond's pendant?

She dropped the key in her purse, got out of the car, stood on the pavement and stared at Pine Bush Acres. She pictured Mother safe in her bed and slammed the car door. She followed the walkway and entered the building.

Ms. Alvarez, Pine Bush Acres' director, a tall, full-figured woman with large brown eyes, sat at a reception desk, staring at a computer screen. She looked up and smiled.

"Morgan, it's good to see you."

"Likewise," Morgan returned a mechanical smile. "I'd like to sign my mother out."

Alvarez looked at the screen and typed. "Quick, Lucy." She moved her fingers across the keyboard. "Taking Mom on vacation?"

"It's cooler in Lake Placid. She'll be more comfortable there," Morgan said, tonelessly.

"I see. How long will you keep her?"

*As long as it takes.* "I'm not really sure."

Alvarez entered the information, Morgan supposed.

"If she's gone over thirty days she'll lose her place."

"Yes, I know."

Alvarez printed a release form and gave Morgan a pen. Morgan returned the signed form. "Your mother's a lucky woman. Pity more of our residents don't have daughters like you."

"Thank you," Morgan said, the smile still frozen on her face.

Her smile thawing, Morgan passed the bulletin board, noting the menu, then walked down a beige and mauve hall, past three old folks' rooms. Two were empty. In the third, a frail woman dressed in a print cotton bathrobe sat in a rocker, watching a game show.

Morgan stood in the doorway, surprised to see her mother sitting in a chair and looking out the window. Apparently, Dr. Mendoza's controlled diet had finally kicked in. Once upon a time, Morgan would have been thrilled. But after two solid weeks in a mental ward, wondering how a mother could destroy her daughter's life, Morgan had nothing left to feel. Hands in her lap, Lucy twiddled her thumbs. Not exactly her mother's style.

"Hello, Mother." Morgan walked into the room.

Lucy jumped and raised a palm to her chest. "Jesus! You gotta stop scaring me half to death."

"Aren't you glad to see me?" She headed for Lucy's closet.

"Nice of you to spare me a few moments of your precious time. I suppose after lunch you'll be off to—"

Morgan looked into her eyes. "Right, with one exception."

Morgan opened the closet door. Rifling through Lucy's closet, she pulled out a gray, hard-shell Samsonite suitcase and put it on Lucy's bed. She grabbed several light cotton, floral print dresses, several pairs of light cotton slacks and summer tops. They looked a bit large now, she thought, folding them into her mother's suitcase, but they would have to do.

Lucy's eyes widened. "You put those clothes back."

"No." Her brow furrowed, Lucy gaped at Morgan.

"Don't look surprised," Morgan's lips formed a frosty smile, "I've decided you're absolutely right." She opened Lucy's dresser and pulled out a sweater, nightgowns, socks and undergarments.

"Right about what?" Lucy grasped the arms of her chair, grunted and lifted herself up, surprising Morgan again.

"You need a vacation, so this time you're coming with me."

"Vacation?" Lucy plopped back down and stared blankly at Morgan. "You mean you're getting me the hell out of this place?" she said sarcastically, "Where are we going?"

"Lake Placid."

Lucy regarded Morgan with narrowed eyes. "*You* want *me* in Lake Placid?" Lucy rubbed her bare arms and looked around the room. "*Damn* them. How many times do I have to tell them to raise the temperature in this room? Aren't you cold?"

"Mother, it's hotter than hell in here and worse outside."

"Put my clothes back. I'm not going." She folded her arms over her still ample belly, defiantly. Her flesh hung on her arms like beef on a butcher's hook.

"I'll be right back with a wheelchair."

Lucy was snoring before Morgan had reached Saratoga Springs. Taking the Northway through the mountains to Lake Placid was like driving in a post card, normally, but today Morgan saw only the landscape of her life as it should have been, if not for Mother.

Grateful for some think time, she mustered the loose ends. According to Jack, Tom Connelly, a bad man, a wild card, was out there. Not knowing what he looked like worried her. She got that he wanted, the house, but what did he or his son have to do with Diamond and the Welcomes?

After several pit stops, Morgan turned off the Northway at Exit 31 and took 73 to Lake Placid. She drove past the real estate office. Maggie and Kevin's cars were nowhere in sight. Harlan must be out of the hospital. Maybe they were with him.

A guy in faded black jeans and a white T shirt was out front, near a black Dodge van, frantically looking up and down the street. She caught a glimpse of him and frowned. He seemed familiar. That was odd. But wasn't everything these days?

She left Main St. and took Mirror Lake Drive to Midlakes Road. She turned and drove up the block slowly. Lucy opened her eyes. She yawned and looked out the window. Judging by her calm, almost blank expression, Mother didn't recognize the street or the houses. Then again, how could she if she'd never been here?

Morgan pulled into the driveway and turned off the motor.

"Well, Mother, here we are," she said, opening her door.

"Where?" Lucy squinted at the house and yard.

"Lake Placid. This is the house in the ad. The one I bought." Morgan dropped the keys into her purse. She was out her door, around the car and opening Lucy's door, before Lucy could reply.

"I don't remember any ad." Lucy stared at the house.

"Come on, Mother. Slide your legs around and I'll take you inside." Lucy was still huge despite her weight loss.

"Where are we?"

"Midlakes Road in Lake Placid."

"Midlakes—" Her jaws dropped. She looked into Morgan's eyes and shook her head. "I'm not going in there."

Stunned at her reaction, Morgan frowned. "Why not?"

"I don't have to explain anything to you. You take me back to—" She searched the sky for the answer, "to my place."

"It's a three-hour trip. We just got here, and I'm tired."

Morgan reached in and started to pull Lucy's legs to the side of the seat, one at a time. Lucy made a fist and punched Morgan's hand. Blindsided, Morgan gasped.

"I don't care if you're unconscious. I don't want to be here. I'm cold. I want to go home."

"Cold?" Morgan stood up. "It's eighty-five degrees."

"I'm not getting out of this car." She clenched her jaw, folded her arms and stared straight ahead.

"You haven't had anything to eat since breakfast," Morgan said, trying to stay calm. "It's six now. If I don't get started with dinner, we won't eat until eight."

Lucy unfolded her arms and relaxed her jaw. Morgan seized the new opportunity to ease her mother's legs out of the car.

"There we go," she said, pulling her mother to her feet.

"I'll get your cane." She opened the rear door and reached into the seat. With Lucy's weight still bowing her legs, they made their way over the lumpy lawn at a turtle's pace.

"Stand right here." Morgan walked to the car, hefted the gray Samsonite suitcase from the trunk and rolled it over the lawn. "Take my arm. Up we go." Morgan held her arm out. Lucy curled her fingers around Morgan's wrist and took the porch steps one at a time.

Morgan unlocked the door and led her mother into the house.

# Chapter 54

## Lucy and Morgan

Lucy sat in Morgan's kitchen wondering why some things seemed so familiar. The picture window overlooking the back yard and the porcelain sink fit, but the cherry wood cabinets, brass faucets, and Tiffany lamp didn't. Gazing at tile rosettes on the tin ceiling, she tightened her fingers around her cane and waded through the fog shrouding her memory.

*Suddenly, a tiny rat opened his eyes and yawned. Asleep for a long time, he sniffed and skittered through the fog in her mind.*

Lucy was getting a migraine. She rubbed her temples and watched Morgan fill a large pot with salted water, put it on the burner and turn up the gas. Morgan pulled a frying pan from a cabinet next to the stove. From the fridge she grabbed grated cheese, a jar of capers and chopped garlic. She took a bottle of olive oil, a can of plum tomatoes, sliced black olives, and several spices from the cupboard.

Even the hallway off the kitchen seemed familiar, Lucy thought.

Morgan went to the fridge and pulled out a head of lettuce, two tomatoes, a cucumber and a bottle of blue cheese dressing.

"I'm making *Marinara* over *farfalle*," she said, nudging the fridge door closed with her hip. "We'll eat in half an hour." The sauce smelled good, but oddly enough, despite her creeping migraine, Lucy was not hungry. The phone rang.

"Hi, Chuck."

*Chuck?* Jesus. Was she crazy or was Morgan still talking to a figment of her imagination?

*The little rat in Lucy's head stopped, stood on his hind legs, peeked above the fog and listened.*

Morgan talked as if the goddamn phone call were real.

"No worries," Morgan laughed, "I got out yesterday."

Morgan sounded as if Chuck really was on the line. Her heart pounding, Lucy closed her eyes. The call had to be real. She heard the phone ring herself, didn't she? Lucy opened her eyes and stared at Morgan in confusion.

"Mother's here with me." Morgan looked at Lucy. "I went to the home and picked her up." Morgan frowned. "Actually, love, I'm better than I've been in years."

Her cool smile made Lucy ill at ease. Morgan pivoted and pulled a box of *farfalle* from a cupboard above the range, ripped it open and dropped half the pasta into the boiling water.

"Are you in Melbourne?"

Melbourne?

*The little rat burrowed under the fog and clawed.*

Christ, her head hurt.

"I'm so glad you made the service." Morgan sounded so convincing. "Love you too. I'll be waiting." She hung up.

*Its stomach rumbling, the rat stuffed its mouth and chewed.*

Her head pulsating, Lucy remembered. Chuck *was* back. He had come to see her at her new place.

Morgan opened the cupboard and grabbed a large pasta bowl and two dishes. "We'll be eating in five minutes, Mother."

Lucy narrowed her eyes. Morgan hated her enough to dump her in that place. So why the sudden urge to bring her here on vacation—Lucy sniffed at the frying pan—to poison her?

"It's cold in here," Lucy said, seeking familiar ground.

"Please, Mother." Morgan said impatiently. "Don't start."

She pulled a salad bowl from the cupboard and banged it on the counter. Lucy stole a smile. She felt better, despite the drummer jamming in her head. Morgan opened a drawer under the counter and pulled out knives and forks. She rinsed the lettuce, broke the leaves and plopped them into the bowl.

"I don't want dinner," Lucy squinted. Her headache was in rip-roaring form, but she was back in control. She *knew* if she left that Pine Bush place she'd be her old self again, and she was right. "I want to sleep."

Morgan diced tomatoes and cucumbers and tossed the salad. "It's not good to go to sleep on an empty stomach."

After she put the salad in front of her mother and set their places, she drained the pasta into the bowl, poured the sauce and set both on the table next to a bowl of grated cheese.

"I said I don't want to eat."

The migraine cracked her skull like a machete through a melon. She hadn't eaten since lunch, so why wasn't she hungry?

"You? Not eat? That's hard to believe."

"Is it? Then believe this."

She swept the bowl off the table. It fell to the floor and shattered.

Morgan pounded the table with her fist and their place settings jumped. "Damn!" She closed her eyes and Lucy stole another smile. Morgan opened her eyes. Lucy stared at her blankly. Morgan got to her feet, grabbed a broom from the hall closet next to the bathroom and swept pasta, sauce, and porcelain chunks and slivers into a dustpan.

"Turn up the heat." Lucy said. Her head felt a bit better now. Not much, but at least it was something.

Morgan dumped the pan into the trash. "It's eighty-five degrees in here. Honestly, Mother, don't you know it's summer?"

*Honestly, Morgan, don't you know I'm not, your, mother?*

Morgan leaned the broom against the counter. She left the pan on the floor and checked her watch. "We've had a long day and we're both tired. At least have some salad."

"I want to go upstairs, now." Suddenly, Lucy felt exhausted.

Morgan ran her fingers through her hair and blew out a breath, looking disgusted. "Suit yourself."

Lucy pressed her palms on the table, grunted and got to her feet. Cane in one hand, she grabbed Morgan's arm with the other. Making her way to the landing, she glanced into the living room. The bookcase against the wall. The fireplace and mirror above it. The ceiling-to-floor windows. They all looked so familiar.

*Famished, the little rat gnawed, burrowing deeper.*

"We'll get there, Mother, come on." Morgan took the cane.

With one hand on the wall and the other on Morgan's arm, Lucy took the steps one at a time at a glacial pace.

"That's the girl." Morgan said, moving beside her mother.

They reached the top. "Stop treating me," Lucy panted, "like a child." She jerked her cane out of Morgan's hand, surprising her, and looked up and down the hallway.

"Your room is under the tower. The one with the view."

Groaning, Lucy leaned on her cane and followed Morgan down the hall. They stood at the bedroom door.

*Frenzied, the little rat gorged.*

"Why do I know this house?" Her brain seared with roast-on-a spit pain. "Have I been here before?"

"I don't know, Mother, have you?"

Morgan opened the door and walked Lucy to the bed. "There's really not much I do know about you. Is there, Mother?"

"Stop calling me that." Her empty stomach growled.

"Stop calling you what?"

"Mother. I'm not your mother." Christ that felt good.

*"What?"* Morgan gaped at her mother, sitting on the bed.

"I said—" her head feeling like it was caught in a vise she glared at Morgan, *"I am not your mother!"*

*Its stomach stretched to bursting, the little rat lay on his back. He huffed and he puffed and he blew the fog out.*

The migraine cut through her skull like a chainsaw, but Lucy felt better and more aware than she'd felt in years. Her nerve endings sizzled. Her flint-blue eyes sparked.

"Look at your face! You are such a fool," she giggled. "Do you honestly think if I had a daughter, she'd be anything like you, weak and scared of her pathetic, insipid shadow?"

Morgan looked stupefied. Lucy giggled harder. "My God, you really don't remember. Well," she reached out and patted Morgan's hand, "allow me to catch you up on old times.

"I'll bet you didn't know that your real mother was an English teacher too. Isn't that sweet? Must run in the family."

Morgan's mouth dropped. She blinked back tears.

"Lucky for you those old memories of mine are the last to go. Your mother's name was Martha. Your father called her," Lucy tilted her head and winked one eye closed, pretending to concentrate. "Um, Marty. Your mother, Marty, named you after Morgan le Fay, King Arthur's half-sister. Can you believe people like this really exist, *Morgan?"*

Morgan moved her lips, but no sound emerged. Lucy burst into peals of laughter, shaking the mattress. The migraine chewed her skull like a nest of termites, but this was so much fun, she ignored the horrific pain.

"No? Well, for once we agree, because I couldn't believe it either. From the way your father talked about your mother, she must've been more boring and tedious than he was, if that were even possible. No wonder you turned out like you did." She looked Morgan over slowly and with disgust. "With an accountant and an English teacher for parents, you didn't stand a chance!"

Dazed, Morgan whispered, "Why didn't you tell me?"

"Found our voice, have we? Pity. I did so enjoy our one-way conversation."

"Tell me!" Morgan clenched and unclenched her hands.

"Fine." Lucy snarled. "After your father forced me to move upstate to that piss ant town, he spent *my* money on your education. You owed me! And I aimed to collect."

"What about Chuck?" Morgan's voice was husky with shock.

"You mean the nervy, know-it-all, bastard who walked into my house, thinking he'd whisk you to Australia and leave me to rot, penniless and alone?"

"You doctored Chuck's letter."

"You're goddamned right. You were my retirement fund. My own personal little nest egg. When your precious Chuck ended up doing what men usually do, I made a few corrections and additions and collected for thirty years. No!" she gasped, mockingly, "does that mean I owe him? With interest?" She looked at Morgan and laughed. "Poor, pathetic Morgan. You're not my daughter," she said, sniffling with contempt. "A daughter of mine would've been strong enough and smart enough to figure all this out decades ago. You were *his* daughter. I had a son I gave up for adoption, who had nothing to do with your father," she spat.

*Lucy wasn't her mother. Chuck wasn't her husband.*

Lucy's words cut Morgan's heart like a straight-edged razor. Dazed, she sank to the floor and grabbed and squeezed Bloodfire hard. The ruby and diamonds bit into her palm but tears wouldn't come. She closed her eyes and searched for the part of her life that had not been a lie. Her father loved her. Despite Lucy's treachery, Chuck and she had survived. She vowed to find her way back to him. Morgan opened her eyes and stared up at Lucy.

"You had a son? You're not my mother. You knew Chuck wasn't my husband. How could you let me live a lie?"

"I tried to tell you about him over and over, but you wouldn't listen. Goddamn you, it's cold. Turn up the heat.

Suddenly, Morgan shivered and frowned, realizing this time Lucy was right. It felt as though the temperature had dropped drastically. She rubbed her arms, saw her breath. Eyes bulging, she jumped to her feet.

Shivering harder, Morgan watched a white haze seep into the bedroom from under the door to the tower. She heard *crack and* looked up. Ice began growing on the ceiling, creeping down the walls and inching across the floor.

The haze swirled, fusing into a petite girl with bottomless black eyes and a chalk-white skin whose sopping hair fell to her shoulders in springy black ringlets. Her white peasant blouse and rowdy print skirt soaked with muck, clung at her tiny waist. Her lips, the color of cinnamon candy smiled chillingly.

Morgan shivered harder. Her teeth chattered her breath out in lacy puffs. "D-Diamond?"

"*Diamond?*" Lucy gasped, clearly shocked.

Morgan recognized the voice, but it sounded too young to be Lucy's. She searched the room for the little girl it belonged to.

"The gypsy necklace was mine!"

Riveted, Morgan watched the little-girl voice emerge from the withered, bloodless gash that was Lucy's mouth. Staring past Morgan, Lucy shivered, pointing. Morgan turned in the direction Lucy was pointing and gasped.

"Th-they thought I w-was sleeping." The little-girl voice said. And Morgan faced Lucy. "B-but I heard them fighting." Lucy shivered hard.

Sheathed in ice, the ceiling and walls creaked and groaned. The floor buckled. Morgan shook. She folded her numb hands under her arms and inched toward Lucy's bed.

Morgan asked, "Who are J-Jared and Elspeth Welcome?"

Lucy's vacant eyes stared. She shivered. Her child-voice whispered, "Mommy and D-Daddy."

Morgan's knees folded. Collapsing to the icy floor, she bunched the comforter in her hand and stared at Lucy.

"Why were Mommy and Daddy fighting?"

Something sparked in Lucy's eyes. "Muh-hommy said Diamond was going to have his baby. She said Daddy had to tie Diamond up and push her off Puh-hulpit Rock into the lake and bring her the pendant to prove he did it."

Her mind reeling, Morgan climbed to her feet and staggered back. She stared at Lucy with wide, horrified eyes. A dagger of cold pierced the small of her back.

"J-Jared tied up a pregnant girl and pushed her off a cliff?" Shaking violently, Morgan stared at her wrists then at Lucy, finally realizing she had been right. Diamond had been trying to communicate with her all along. Her dream had been about Diamond. Her pendant lying on the welcome mat, the rope burns on her wrists and ankles that looked black in the moonlight were Diamond's way of indicting Jared Welcome for her murder!

"I found the neh-necklace on the floor in Mommy's room and took it to Daddy." Lucy shivered uncontrollably. "He looked sad when he saw it," her lips formed a little-girl-pout, "but he said I could have it." Her mouth twisted in anger. "Mommy took it back." Lucy made a fist. "But Daddy gave it to *me!*"

Morgan's teeth chattered so hard her jaws ached. Her skin was so cold it *burned*. A tear fell and froze on her cheek. She blew into her hands and rubbed her arms hard.

"What happened to Elspeth and Jared?"

Lucy suddenly stopped shivering and stared into the distance. "Grandma Welcome told Aunt Laura and Uncle Peter that Diamond was evil and wanted revenge." Her little-girl mouth trembled. "Grandma swore Diamond killed Mommy and Daddy, and if Laura didn't take me far away she would kill me too."

Morgan reeled. Diamond killed the Welcomes?

"Far away? Like New York City?"

"Yes. Aunt Laura said Grandma was crazy, but they did it. Aunt Laura was mean. She hated the city and me, said it was my fault she had to live there. I hated her. I missed my Daddy."

Morgan wiggled her freezing toes and shifted feet. "How did you get the necklace?"

"Duh-haddy went through that door," she pointed, "and stood by the dresser. I stood in the hall and peeked out from behind him." Lucy's teeth chattered hard. "The room was so cold and foggy I couldn't see. Mommy screamed so loud it huh-hurt my ears. Daddy walked through the fog to help her. I saw my necklace on the dresser and took it. I never saw Mommy or Daddy again." Her body went rigid. "Laura said Mommy and Daddy froze to death."

Oh my God. That's why Lucy had always hated the cold.

Diamond dissolved in a roiling storm. The temperature dropped to Arctic levels. The ceiling buckled. The walls and floor heaved. Diamond hovered between Lucy and Morgan.

Terrified, Morgan rushed through the haze and grabbed Lucy's arm.

"*Get up!*" she screamed, pulling hard. "We've got to get out before Diamond—"

Every hair on Morgan's body turned white with frost. Blind with pain, she screamed, let Lucy go, and sucked in searing breaths. She coughed and doubled over. Her lungs burned. Her clothes froze to her body. Her eyes squeezed out tears. They froze speckling her cheeks. Her eyelashes glued shut. She rubbed them apart and gasped in naked fear.

Diamond stood before Lucy. Her large eyes glowed. She smiled without warmth. Her slender porcelain fingers caressed Lucy's cheek. Mesmerized, Lucy stopped shivering and reached out.

"No, Mother, don't!" Morgan cried.

Diamond wrapped herself around Lucy. Suddenly Lucy's eyes

bulged.

"Mo-Morgan, Heh-help me."

Her mouth a frozen shriek, her last breath screamed, "Morgaaaaaaaaaannnnnnnnn!!!!"

Paralyzed with unspeakable horror, Morgan watched as Lucy's mouth froze open. Her flesh turned blue. Her eyes rolled back in her head. Her brittle flesh fissured and cracked. Her arms broke off, hit the floor and shattered. Frozen blue-gray tissue and bits of blood-flecked bone littered the room. Her legs fractured and crumbled. Her spinal cord snapped. Her skull hit the floor and broke into little pieces.

Outside something flickered. Morgan stumbled toward the window. One of the two remaining broken streetlights sparked, buzzed and then blared on.

White-hot light poured through the bedroom window, blinding her and bathing the room in heat. Ice receded from ceilings and walls. Melting ice rained down her body and puddled at her feet. Warmth stung her fingers and toes. Her skin tingled and itched. Her muscles ached. She closed and opened her sore hands. Bent her stiff knees. Pressed her fingers against her cheeks. Rubbed her itching arms and legs. Exhausted, Morgan turned away from the window and gasped.

Lucy was gone. She was a monster, but no one deserved to die like that.

Morgan stumbled down the hall to the bathroom, hugged the bowl and vomited food she didn't remember eating. She closed her eyes and rubbed her temples. Through the horror of it all, she suddenly realized she was the last to see Lucy alive. If Pine Bush called, what would she say? The house had a history of freezing people to death. If she told the police how Lucy died, they'd put her in a padded cell and melt the key.

Comforted that Chuck would be home soon to help figure things out, an exhausted Morgan stumbled across the hall and fell onto her bed and into a deep sleep.

# Chapter 55

## Morgan

Bang. Bang. Bang.

Morgan stirred and opened her eyes to daylight, wondering how, after everything that happened, she'd managed to sleep.

Bang. Bang. Bang.

The front door. She dragged herself out of bed and downstairs.

"Ms. Quick?"

He was big, imposing and filled her doorway. He looked like he needed a shave and a good night's sleep.

"Yes." Parked on Midlakes Road was an old black Dodge Caravan. It looked familiar. Oddly enough, he did too.

"My family and I lived here a long time ago." He waved a large brown legal sized envelope in her face. "We need to talk."

Morgan remembered. She'd passed him on her way through town with Lucy yesterday. He was outside Placid Properties. He handed her the envelope, brushed past and walked into her house. The smell of whiskey that oozed from his pores turned her stomach.

"Hey! You—" She stopped in mid-sentence.

On the street corner, the last broken street lamp flickered briefly before going dark. Her heart racing, Morgan left the door open and followed him inside.

"Listen, you can't just walk in and—"

"Great place," he said, surveying her house like he owned it. He plopped onto the couch, pissing her off. "Mighty hot out there. Got anything to drink?"

Her glaring eyes locked with his. She frowned, puzzled. Beyond having glanced at him once, he seemed familiar.

"That's what I figured." He reached in his back pocket and pulled out a flask. He unscrewed the cap and nodded at the envelope in her hand. "It's not sealed. Open it."

Morgan opened the flap and pulled out its contents. Her eyes devoured the pages. Her shaking hand held an adoption agreement between Lucy *Elspeth* Hadley and the Thomas Connelly seniors.

Natalie's and Maggie's instincts had been right. This wasn't over.

Among other things the contract stipulated the adoptive parents were to name Lucy's son, Jared, after her father. In exchange, Lucy solemnly swore never to contact the boy. But his name was Tom. In one of their conversations, Jack Bradford had referred to Tom as Thomas J. Connelly. The J must stand for Jared. He was Tommy's father and Lucy's son, but Tom did not have her eyes.

"I know who you are, Mr. Connelly."

Morgan remembered Jack had said that Tom beat his wife. There were no other houses around. He could beat her to death, and no one would hear her scream.

"Good." He took a swig and winced. "Then you know why I'm here." His smile was thin and greedy.

"How could you want my house? Your son died here," she said, still wondering why the answer to that eluded her.

He looked distracted and annoyed. "That tall, sexy realtor, the blond, said the same thing." Tom tilted the flask and took a swig. "Must be hormonal," he said more to himself than to her. "My reasons for wanting this house are none of your business."

The reasons he wanted this house were all over him like his tacky jeans and shirt. He took another swallow, coughed and wiped his mouth on the back of his hand.

"I know you *think* you bought this house, but the truth is you got screwed, honey, because it wasn't Wainright's to sell."

He put the flask to his lips and drained it. "Lucy Hadley was my biological mother." He screwed the cap on and stuck the flask in his pocket. "I did some investigating. She never adopted you. Connect the dots."

Jack was wrong. This guy was worse than bad. He was evil. And if he knew how Lucy had died he could do major damage and then steal her house.

"By the way, I called Pine Bush and Alvarez said you took Lucy home." He craned his neck, looking around. "Where is she?"

*Oh God, no. Please.*

"Well?" His eyes were as soulless as Lucy's.

"Sleeping." Suddenly, she needed a drink more than he did.

He stood up and stretched. "I'll wait till she wakes up." He strolled to the bookcase. "These all yours?"

He ran his hands over Chaucer's *Canterbury Tales,* and Morgan felt violated. How long would it be before he knew she was lying? Kevin and Jack both said to call if she needed them. A lot of good that did her now.

Tom ran his fingers across his lips. She knew the sign. As a teacher she'd done several units on alcohol and drugs. The more strung out he got, the more dangerous he'd become.

"You know what I think, sis?" She gasped audibly. He smirked and scratched the stubble on his cheek. "I think dear old Mom would love you to wake her up so she could finally meet her real son." He ran his hands through his hair. "Matter of fact, don't trouble yourself. I'll do the honors. I know where the bedrooms are." He winked and headed for the landing.

"Don't."

He turned around and sneered. He clearly knew she was lying. He'd been playing her all along.

"Where is she?" He grabbed her shoulders. "I said where is she?"

"I don't know."

She tried to squirm free. He squeezed harder.

"You're hurting me. You'd better get out of here. My husband's due back any minute."

"You lying bitch!" He slapped her face. "I read the papers and waited in that crummy hotel for two fucking weeks while you were in the nuthouse. I know your husband's in Australia!" He shoved her across the living room onto the couch. He raised his hand." I said, *"Where is my mother!"*

"She's dead." Morgan burst into tears. He lowered his hand. He looked down at her skeptically, she thought.

"Yeah?" he smiled, "How?"

Licking her lip she tasted blood. "This house is haunted." She wiped it away and looked up at him. "A ghost killed her."

"You think I came down with yesterday's rain?" He scratched his cheeks hard. His sharp jerky movements betrayed his thirst.

"It's a long story."

And a long shot. He didn't look like he scared easily, but she had to scare him off until Chuck got back. She'd tell him the truth: If he stays in the house he's a dead man.

"This better be good." He sat opposite her and scratched his arms and thighs.

When Morgan finished, he leaned forward in his chair and said, "As a chef I can say," he raised his eyebrows like Groucho Marx, "that's the tastiest crock of crap I ever got soived."

"It's the truth."

"You know what I think?" He got to his feet and paced.

"When you brought my mom back here, she found out this house was hers and wanted you out."

*A haze formed behind Tom.*

Tom jabbed his finger in her shoulder. "So you killed her."

*Mist rose in dark angry swells.*

"I'm warning you," she said, shuddering at her last image of Lucy. "You stay here and you'll die a horrendous death, exactly like your mother and son did."

Suddenly, Tom headed for the door. Her plan had backfired.

"Where are you going?"

"To tell the police you killed my mother and now you're threatening to kill me." He opened the door.

"Okay!" she shouted. "What do you want?" She sounded terrified and exasperated and hated it.

He closed the door and walked toward her, closing the distance between them. The smell of blackmail was as strong as the stink on his breath.

"If Harlan's MO is the same, he holds your mortgage."

Jaws clenched, she stared at him silently.

"That's what I thought." He sneered. "I want you to go to Wainright's now and bring me written proof that you've started proceedings to sign this house over to me."

"Or?" This bastard was worse than his mother.

"Or fry for the murder of Lucy Welcome Quick, my mother." Tom sneered. "Do me a favor, sis?" Morgan flinched. "On your way back stop at that liquor store across from Wainright and pick up a quart of Jack Daniels."

"There's still time."

"For what?" He looked at the couch and yawned.

"To get out with your life." Her throat was sandpaper raw.

*Behind Tom the mist thickened and swirled.*

Morgan's skin tingled. "You've gotta get out now!"

"Make that two quarts. Maybe I'll snooze here until—"

*The temperature flat-lined.*

Tom shivered and frowned. "Fuck! It's cold in here."

Tom was despicable, but how could she live with herself if she just let him die? Morgan stood between Diamond and Tom.

Diamond smiled and *passed through* Morgan.

Morgan's body throbbed like an abscessed tooth. Trembling, she saw her breath. Tears crisscrossed her cheeks in frozen tracks. She blew on her hands.

Diamond slipped her arms around Tom's neck. He shivered harder. She draped herself on him. Tom screamed. His jaws froze open.

Speechless with horror, Morgan watched Diamond press her marble white cheek to Tom's face and hug him tight. Locked in her lethal embrace, his eyeballs bulged with terror. His chest heaved, forcing his breath out in rapid, frantic plumes. Holding his face in her porcelain hands, Diamond pressed her cold, dead lips to his.

Tom yowled. His flesh went from pink to blue.

The howling stopped, and Morgan stared in mute horror.

Diamond stepped back. Tom looked down. His eyes bulged at his chest cracking in two. His hips shattered. His spinal cord snapped at the neck. His head hit the floor and shattered. His torso cracked at the hips and fell on his broken arms and legs.

Sobbing, Morgan grabbed her purse and stumbled into the yard.

The wind kicked up. Twigs, leaves and dirt bit her feet. She ran hard across the lawn, fell against her car, and groped her purse for her keys.

The wind died. Clouds stalled over the setting sun. Shadows grew long and low, distorting angles and warping planes.

*Morgan's eyes twitch. She stares at the house. Her eyes are drawn to the three orange ovals in the gable. The smooth ovals erupt with human features. Three pairs of eyes open. Tommy, Lucy and Tom glare down. Locked in their cold, dead gaze, her hands go limp and her purse and keys fall to the ground.*

A mist hovered over the roof. It swallowed the tower and gable. The wind blew. Dust devils swirled, spitting sand and stone. Blinded, Morgan screamed and rubbed her eyes.

She felt the wind stop. She lowered her hands, and as she looked at the house, the clouds sailed away from the sun.

The mist was gone. The ovals were blank and smooth.

Diamond was gone. The Welcomes were gone.

Morgan's chin trembled. Her eyes welled with tears.

Sniffling, she picked up her purse and keys and walked toward the house, knowing that her incredible journey had come to an end.

Something buzzed. Morgan stopped and turned.

On the corner the last broken streetlight flickered on and continued to burn, brightly.

# Epilogue

Within days of Tom Connelly's disappearance Chuck called the police to report that someone appeared to have abandoned a Black Dodge Caravan in front of his house on Midlakes Road. While Chuck burned Lucy's adoption contract with the Connelly seniors, Morgan phoned Pine Bush Acres to inform Ms. Alvarez that Lucy would remain with her in Lake Placid, indefinitely. Morgan tendered her letter of resignation to the Greater Port St. John School District, effective immediately. Upon listing her Port St. John house for sale, Morgan was saddened to learn that Art and Mrs. Parker had passed within weeks of each other.

After Natalie enrolled at F.I.T., Kevin and she alternated between meeting in The Big Apple and Lake Placid every weekend.

On September 30th, 2008 *The North Country Tribune* ran Steve's story commemorating the twenty-fifth anniversary of Tommy Connelly's death. The moment the syndicates picked it up, Hollywood called. The moguls thought that "Bloodfire and The legend of Paradox Pond" had a nice, box-office ring to it.

After Harlan made a full recovery, Lillian moved into his house on Cobblestone Road where they became man and wife.

Following a short engagement, Maggie and Steve were married on December 24, 2009 at Queen of Angels Church in Lake Placid.

After many months of intense therapy, Morgan realized she was a very lucky woman. She had two therapists, one for each side of what she called the absurd coin of her life. On the natural side Dr. Martin Spinelli had helped Morgan face and deal with Lucy's and Chuck's betrayals as well as her own self-deception.

Having seen the photos and having felt Diamond's cold embrace, Dr. Charles Matthias, a believer, agreed with Morgan's assessment. Diamond had murdered Jared Welcome's descendants to avenge her death and the death of her unborn child. After Tommy died, Tom managed to slip away, but when he connected his own cancerous dots, greed brought him home to Midlakes Road—forever.

Dr. Matthias confirmed Morgan's suspicion that not being blood related to the Welcomes, Morgan's life had never really been in danger. Diamond had merely needed Morgan to bring Lucy home. Both Morgan and Chuck interpreted the working streetlights as a sign that Diamond's work was done.

Morgan claimed Diamond's remains. Following a small, graveside ceremony, Chuck and Morgan buried her on the hill overlooking Lake Placid.

In January of 2010 Morgan Quick and Chuck Matthias were married at the Bradford House by a Justice of the Peace. A small, very elegant reception followed.

One loose end remained.

In the spring of 2015 Morgan and Chuck stood at the edge of Pulpit Rock under a brooding, pewter sky. Chuck turned his collar up against the wind, Morgan zipped down her windbreaker. Lifting Bloodfire over her head, she held it in her hand and gazed out over Lake Placid. She pressed Bloodfire to her lips and closed her eyes.

"I keep thinking about the star-crossed love that King Phillip's Magdalena had referred to in that article, when she begged her own daughter not to wear it." Morgan opened her eyes. "Diamond wore it. I wore it." Sighing, she faced Chuck. "And look what happened to her and us the first time around."

"Are you sure you're ready to do this, love?"

Morgan nodded. "If this pendant had never belonged to Lucy, how could it be mine?" She squeezed the pendant for the last time and laughed without mirth, saying, "I won't need to do that anymore."

She dropped the pendant into Lake Placid. Eyes glistening and lips trembling, Morgan watched Bloodfire sink into the deep, dark water. "Maybe Diamond will rest in peace now."

Chuck hugged her. "I love you more now than ever."

"Back atcha." She smiled through her tears and gazed at the roiling clouds. "We'd better get home," she shivered, "According to the weather reports that hundred-year flood may be on its way."

Hand in hand, Morgan and Chuck Matthias walked toward their house on Midlakes Road.

# THANK YOU

My deepest, heartfelt thanks to Diane Czeckowicz, my dear friend, for her highly valued contributions, her enthusiasm, for her years of unwavering support and faith in me and for reading *Bloodfire* more times than I can count.

My very special thanks to my dear friend and critique partner Jan Prestopnik for her insight, innovative comments and suggestions and her expertise in the craft.

To friends and family who encouraged me to never give up.

# ABOUT THE AUTHOR

Rosemarie and her husband Joe, a retired school administrator, have been happily married for forty-eight years. They have been blessed with a beautiful family, two sons, a daughter and daughter-in-law, and two precious grandchildren.

Besides loving to write, Rosemarie loves to read and entertain family and friends.

In addition to domestic and foreign travel, the Sheperds enjoy snowshoeing in winter and cycling the magnificent Rails to Trails along the Mohawk River on the historic Erie Canal.

Lake Placid, New York is located in her backyard and in her heart. It is Lake Placid's incomparable beauty that inspired her to write *Bloodfire.*

Becoming an author has been a life-long dream. Thanks to family and friends that dream has become a reality.

If you had as much fun reading *Bloodfire* as she had writing it, she hopes you will spread the word to relatives, friends and the rest of mankind by word of mouth and by posting a review on Amazon. She welcomes any comments or questions about *Bloodfire.* If you would like to share, you may contact her at sheperd.rosemarie @yahoo.com.